The Excluded Wife

The Excluded Wife

Yuen-Fong Woon

McGill-Queen's University Press

Montreal & Kingston · London · Ithaca

© McGill-Queen's University Press 1998
ISBN 0-7735-1730-8 (cloth)
ISBN 0-7735-2015-5 (paper)

Legal deposit fourth quarter 1998
First paperback edition 1998

Bibliothèque nationale du Québec
Printed in Canada on acid-free paper

Funding has been received from
the Department of Canadian Heritage,
Multiculturalism Programs.

McGill-Queen's University Press
acknowledges the financial support of the
Government of Canada through the Book
Publishing Industry Development Program
for its activities. We also acknowledge the
support of the Canada Council for the Arts for
our publishing program.

Canadian Cataloguing in Publication Data

Woon, Yuen-Fong, 1943–
The excluded wife

Includes bibliographical references.
ISBN 0-7735-1730-8 (bnd)
ISBN 0-7735-2015-5 (pbk)

1. Women–China–Fiction.   2. Chinese–Canada–Fiction.
3. Chinese Canadians–Fiction.   I. Title.

PS8595.O665E93 1998   C813'.54   C98-900372-8
PR9199.3.W644E93 1998

Typeset in 10/12 Palatino by True to Type

Contents

HONG KONG, 1952–1955

13   People! People! People!   137

14   Disasters   155

15   Farewell My Daughter   170

PART THREE
VANCOUVER'S CHINATOWN,
1955–1987

16   Family Reunion   187

17   Isolation   197

18   Hong Kong Brides   208

19   The Roaring Sixties   221

20   Happy Now   235

21   Wheels of Fortune   243

22   A Long Way Home   262

     Glossary of Terms   285

     Bibliography   291

Preface

The earliest Chinese who came to the west coast of North America were attracted first by the Gold Rush in California in the 1850s and then by the subsequent Gold Rush in the Fraser Valley in British Columbia in the early 1860s. They were therefore known colloquially as "Gold Mountain guests" (*kam-shaan haak*). Starting in the 1880s, Canadian immigration laws had a drastic impact on the family life of the Chinese immigrants. After the Canadian Pacific Railway was completed with the critical use of Chinese labour, the Canadian government yielded to pressure from British Columbia to limit Chinese immigration. It started to collect head taxes from each Chinese coming into the country. Beginning at fifty dollars in 1885, this tax was increased to one hundred dollars in 1900 and five hundred dollars in 1903. In 1923 the Chinese Immigration Act was passed. Known more commonly as the Chinese Exclusion Act, it forbade almost all categories of Chinese from entering the country. It was not lifted until 1947.

As a result of the Exclusion Act, the predominantly male Chinese population in Canada, many of whom had already made the trip home to marry with a view to producing sons, were denied the choice of bringing their wives or children to Canada. While some Gold Mountain guests returned home, others stayed in Canada trying to make a living. To ensure the economic security and comfort of their family in the home village and to prepare for their own eventual retirement, the more successful among them sent money home to build foreign-style mansions (*yeung-lau*) and acquire farmland or shops there. The less successful never made it home. They died in Canada, but their bones were returned to their families in South China.

Between 1923 and 1947, the wife of the Gold Mountain guest had to shoulder the double burden of farm and domestic chores in the home village. Her lot was not a happy one. Married without her consent at a tender age, she single-handedly raised the children and served her husband's parents and his younger, unmarried siblings. Even though she was the one who performed the daily worship of the four generations of her absentee husband's ancestors at the domestic ancestral altar, she had very little status in her married home. Until or unless she gave birth to a son, she lived in fear of being abused by her mother-in-law or deserted by her husband in Gold Mountain. Outside her domestic confines, she was often bullied by members of her husband's lineage and had to face numerous life crises as well as natural and man-made disasters largely beyond her control. External forces might deprive her of all or part of the overseas remittances she received. She and her children also faced the prospect of being attacked or persecuted by predators or invaders who were greedy for the foreign currency and imposing foreign-style houses built with the blood and sweat of her husband in Canada. Such a woman, one who was left waiting for the return of her husband from Gold Mountain, was known colloquially as a *shaang-kwa-foo*, or a "grass widow." In this book, Wong Sau-Ping serves as our example of a "grass widow," although I refer to her as an "excluded wife" in relation to the Chinese Exclusion Act.

For twenty years after the Exclusion Act was lifted, few "excluded wives" or "excluded children" joined the Chinese community in Canada. Politics ensured that many were unable to come. For thirty years after its takeover in 1949, the Chinese Communist regime forbade emigration of its citizens, so that unless the Overseas Chinese dependents escaped to Hong Kong, they had no way of leaving the country. Canada, meanwhile, cut off diplomatic relations with the Communist regime in 1950 when the Korean War broke out. Most significantly, however, the 1947 Canada Immigration Act set an upper age limit of eighteen (extended to twenty-one in 1950) for Chinese children to be sponsored into Canada as dependents.

Since they had been denied cohabitation with their wives for the twenty-four years between 1923 and 1947, many Gold Mountain guests had no children under eighteen or twenty-one. Those with daughters of appropriate age did not want to sponsor females to Canada. As a result, there was substantial buying and selling of birth certificates in Hong Kong. A large percentage of the young male immigrants in the 1950s entered Canada as "paper sons" because they still regarded Canada as the "Gold Mountain," full of economic opportunities.

It was only with a new immigration act in 1967 that the Chinese were allowed to come to Canada as independent immigrants, without having to be sponsored by parents or spouses. This new immigration act and subsequent ones attracted a larger, more diverse, better educated, more skilled, and wealthier wave of Chinese immigrants into the country, which in turn resulted in a revival and restructuring of the Chinese-Canadian community, particularly in major cities such as Vancouver and Toronto.

Up until 1967, the Four Counties Area of Kwong-Tung (Guang-dong) Province (viz. Toi-Shaan, Hoi-Ping, San-Wooi, and Yan-Ping) was home to over seventy percent of the Chinese in Canada. In the early 1970s, I conducted in-depth interviews with seventeen Gold Mountain guests from Hoi-Ping County, who came to Canada before 1923. In 1983–84, I extended this oral history project to twelve Chinese women from the Four Counties, who came to join their husbands after the lifting of the Chinese Exclusion Act in 1947. Since then, I have conducted several rounds of large-scale household surveys in both Hoi-Ping and Toi-Shaan Counties. In sum, between 1986 and 1994, I visited this part of South China nine times, stayed in private homes and Overseas Chinese hotels, and talked to numerous lower-level cadres and peasants in Overseas Chinese villages. This book focuses on the life history of one "excluded" wife but in fact embodies the experience of many of my subjects and acquaintances. Wong Sau-Ping was among the survivors in a system to which many women had fallen victim.

One major theme running through this story is how greatly affected the Chinese families and Chinese community in Canada have been by external forces such as the international status of China and diplomatic relations between China and Canada, as well as by events and politics within both China and Canada. Readers will get a sense of how these forces influenced the identity and images of the Chinese-Canadians, the inter-generational dynamics of their families, and the socioeconomic structure, cultural life, and personal relations within their community. The book also conveys the strong impact such forces had on the relationship between the Chinese and members of Canadian mainstream society, as well as between the Chinese in Canada and their home communities in South China. Another major theme is continuity versus change in the position of Chinese women. The period covered in the book (1929–87) marked drastic social changes in all three geographical areas: Toi-Shaan County, Hong Kong, and Vancouver's China-town.

To assist the reader, I have provided definitions of a number of uncommon Chinese terms used in this volume. They are placed in the appendix. In addition to these terms, the reader might also find the naming pattern of the China-born men in this novel confusing. I will elaborate on this here.

The naming pattern I have used represents a cultural frame of reference peculiar to the rural Chinese in South China. In the pre-1949 period, lineages were dominant in counties such as Toi-Shaan. Most male peasants of the same village were related to one another along patrilineal lines. Led by the lineage chief and financed by lineage corporate property, the male peasants jointly worshipped their focal ancestors in the village ancestral hall every spring and autumn. To show their kinship solidarity, each generation of male peasants shared a common middle character, corresponding to a word in a poem passed down by the elders of the lineage. It was considered disrespectful to use the name of one's ancestor. As a result, Wong Sau-Ping's father-in-law has the middle name "Kwok." So did her husband's paternal uncle. So did the chief of the Leung lineage in Sai-Fok village and all the men of that generation. The subsequent two generations adopted the same naming practice, both in the home village and in Vancouver. For example, the generation name of Sau-Ping's husband was "Yik" and the generation name of her sons was "Kin." Such a naming practice was discontinued in Vancouver's Chinatown as the local-born generation readily adopted Christian names.

Throughout the text and in the maps, I consistently use standard Cantonese for all proper names, including China-born characters, names of places and establishments, and other Chinese terms. They are transliterated according to the Meyer-Wempe system. Their mandarin equivalents (rendered according to the pinyin system) are included in brackets either in the text itself or in the Glossary of Terms.

Acknowledgments

This book owes its origin to an oral history project undertaken in the mid-1980s. I would like to thank Wendy Jang, Trudy Lee, and Alan Jang for assisting with the interviews, transcribing the tapes, and commenting on the first draft of the manuscript. I am grateful to all the senior Chinese men and women in Vancouver and Victoria who generously shared their life experiences with us. Their touching accounts have inspired me to dig deeper into the local history of Toi-Shaan County, Hong Kong, and Vancouver's Chinatown in order to provide the context within which their full stories could be properly told. Many of my subjects, unfortunately, are not with us as this book goes to press. May this ethnography be an accurate depiction of their lives and a truthful testimony to their bravery and endurance.

In the course of researching the Toi-Shaan section, I visited many peasant homes and talked to Toi-Shaanese men and women of all ages. Here, I can only publicly thank two local historians: Mr Mei Yimin and Mr Liu Zhongmin. They willingly shared with me their private collections of local folk-songs and ditties, which were widely sung to the *muk-yue* tune. They added to my knowledge of the agricultural cycle, living habits, and local customs peculiar to Toi-Shaan County in the pre-1949 period, including the functions of maiden houses and boys' houses and details of the traditional engagement and wedding ceremonies. They also described the many crises and dilemmas faced by the villagers of Toi-Shaan from the 1930s to the 1950s. I am eternally grateful to them and all my Toi-Shaanese subjects for supplying innumerable details that cannot readily be found in written documents.

Good historical ethnography should be accurate without being overwhelming and readable without being superficial. In trying to achieve these goals, I have been helped by colleagues, friends, and relatives. Dr Mark Selden, a China scholar and an experienced editor of academic books, kindly acted as mentor to this project, patiently dispensing encouragement and feedback. Special thanks go to Dr Graham Johnson, my research partner for the South China project, who carefully examined the earlier version and generously supplied some of the photographs of rural Toi-Shaan. Drs Betsy Lominska, Edgar Wickberg, Ellen Judd, and the two anonymous reviewers offered constructive suggestions to improve the intellectual vigour and ethnographic accuracy of the book. Chinese-Canadian friends and relatives read and commented on the manuscript with the eyes of interested insiders. Some supplied me with concrete details of family life to enrich its contents. I am indebted to Lily Ho, Nora Leung, Thuong Vuong-Riddick, and my younger sister, Yuen-May Wong.

I must also thank Big Sister Dr Yuen-Ting Lai for coming up with the most suitable title, and my husband Chio for using his cartographic skills to clarify the geographical setting. My children, Sylvia and Cyril, lent their moral support and gave much assistance. They also gave me first-hand experience of the local-born generation in Canada.

The final version owes its existence to the dedication and ingenuity of two creative writers-cum-copyeditors: Larissa Lai and Deborah Homsher. They spent many hours working closely with me, with a view to widening the audience beyond scholarly and Chinese-Canadian circles. They substantially improved the book's dramatic quality, making the dialogue more natural, the characters more realistic and believable. Like foxes in Chinese mythology, they breathed life into this ethnographic account, making it more enjoyable to the general reader.

Last, but certainly not least, I must thank the editors of McGill-Queen's University Press, especially Joan Harcourt and Claire Gigantes, for their faith in this project and their unfailing support .

Needless to say, I remain solely responsible for errors or inadequacies in my description of historical events and political processes, my depiction of the scenes and characters, and the plot and layout of this book.

Yuen-fong Woon
University of Victoria
January 1997

Wong Sau-Ping's Family Tree*

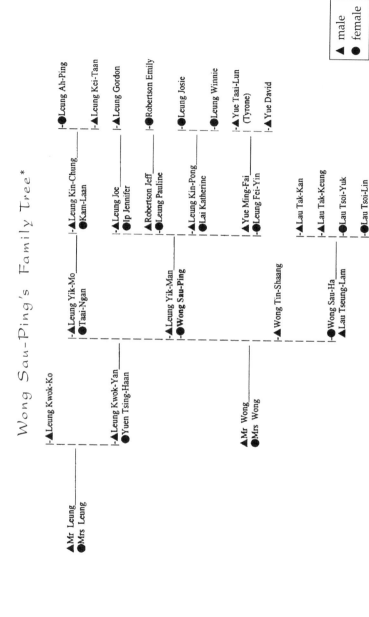

* This "family tree" is not a formal Chinese family genealogy. It is used to show Wong Sau-Ping's family and close relatives. A formal genealogy would leave out Sau-Ping's natal family, and the women would be there marginally if at all.

Characters

Leung Kwok-Yung – chief of the Leung lineage
Leung Yik-Faat – son of lineage chief Leung Kwok-Yung
Leung Sing-Fan – Yik Faat's wife
Leung Ah-Chue – Leung Yik-Faat's daughter
Leung Kin-Tsoi – Yik-Faat's son
Leung Ming – Kin-Tsoi's wife

Wong Mei-Kuen – a maiden from Sai-Fok
Chan Foo – Wong Mei-Kuen's bandit husband
Chan Lai-Sheung – Mei-Kuen and Chan Foo's daughter
Mr Kwaan – Lai-Sheung's first husband
Jack – Lai-Sheung's partner later in life

Leung Yik-Kwong – Sau-Ping's neighbour in Sai-Fok
Leung Yi-Lin – Leung Yik-Kwong's wife
Leung Chun-Fa – Leung Yik-Kwong's daughter
Leung Yik-Nang – Leung Yik-Kwong's brother in Hong Kong

Leung Siu-Hing – mother of a Gold Mountain guest in Sai-Fok
Leung (Ng) Ting-Ting – daughter-in-law of Leung Siu-Hing

Wong Wai-Fong – a maiden from Fung-Yeung married into Sai-Fok
Leung Yik-Hung – husband of Wong Wai-Fong

IN CHINA

Ah Kwai ⎤ Wong Sau-Ping's long-term labourers from Yeung-Kong
Ah Tsaan ⎦ County
Auntie Kwan – a grass widow in Fung-Yeung
Auntie Mooi – the go-between
Chai Ling – head of the Land Reform Work Team
Hoi-Laan – women activist, member of the Work Team
Leung Kin-On – a fake name for Leung Kin-Tsoi
Leung Kwok-Tung – a Gold Mountain guest in Sai-Fok
Leung Kwok-Wang – a Gold Mountain guest – victim of a bandit
    attack

---

* Excluding Wong Sau-Ping and her family.

Leung Kwok-Wing – a Gold Mountain guest in Sai-Fok
Leung Yik-Shing – the *po-cheung* of Sai-Fok
Siu Kong (Bitterface) – the bondservant (*sai-tsai*) of Sai-Fok

IN CANADA

Mr Au – Leung Kin-Pong's lawyer
Mr Chan – Leung Kin-Tsoi's lawyer
Mr Chau – Mr Cheung's lawyer
Mr Cheung – Leung Kin-Tsoi's creditor
Professor Lynden – a China specialist at the University of British
    Columbia
Mr Ma – Trustee of Leung Kwok-Ko's will
Mrs Ma – Sau-Ping's neighbour and friend in Chinatown
Mr Mak (Uncle Mak) – Gold Mountain guest retiring in Vancouver
Peter – Pauline Leung's first boyfriend
Uncle Yue (Old Yue) – a grocery store owner in Chinatown

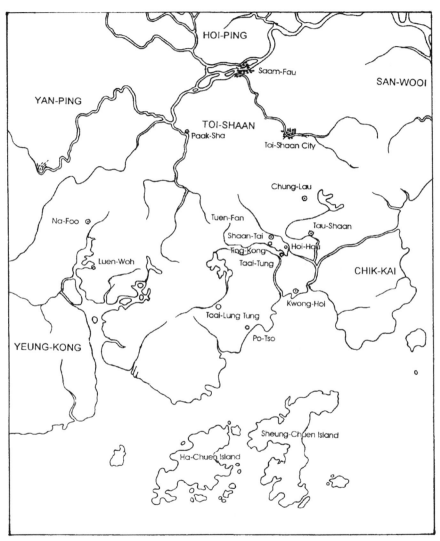

HOI-PING

SAN-WOOI

YAN-PING

Saam-Fau

TOI-SHAAN
Paak-Sha

Toi-Shaan City

Chung-Lau

Na-Foo

Tuen-Fan

Tau-Shaan

Shaan-Tai

Hoi-Hau

Luen-Woh

Ting-Kong

Taai-Tung

CHIK-KAI

Kwong-Hoi

Taai-Lung Tung

YEUNG-KONG

Po-Tso

Sheung-Chuen Island

Ha-Chuen Island

Map One: Sketch Map of Toi-Shaan County, South China

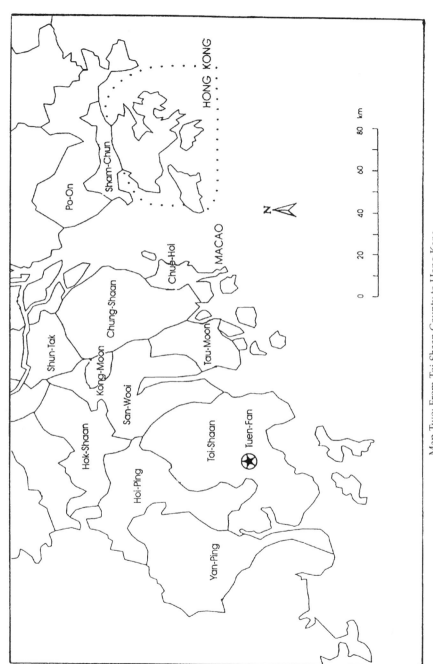

Map Two: From Toi-Shaan County to Hong Kong

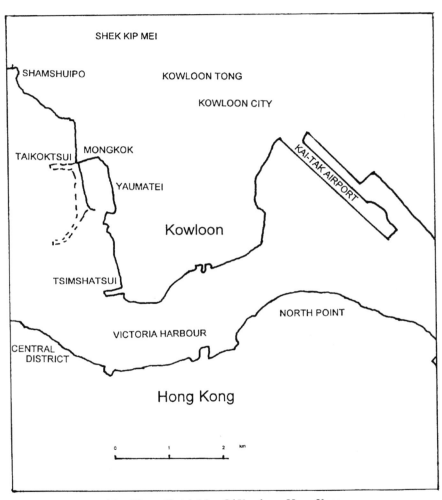

Map Three: Sketch Map Of Kowloon, Hong Kong

PART ONE

Toi-Shaan County, South China
1929–1952

CHAPTER 1
Stealing Vegetables

1929

Sau-Ping stood at the door of the maiden house in Fung-Yeung village and heard her big sister laughing inside. In a few months, when she turned thirteen, Sau-Ping herself would be allowed to step through the doorway with her possessions, choose a drawer, stow her sleeping mat, and take her place in the circle of maidens. But now she stood poised in the dark, breathing the scents of jasmine and the wooden door, still hot from the sun. She should have been fast asleep in her parents' home, five alleys away. "Big Sister," she called through the door. "Sau-Ha. Tell me another story, please?"

Her sister's voice, secure like their mother's, called out, "I'll tell you stories in the rice field. What are you doing out here?"

"Go home." "Dog barking! Crow on the roof!" "Sleep in your place." "You need your sleep, or you'll be a wet rag tomorrow in the field." Her big sister's companions called out against her, confident as boys from inside their house. Sau-Ping turned away. Many cold stars were visible that night. She was not a girl who had often felt lonely, and the sensation left her with the impression that her hands were withered and her face marked shamefully.

Seven months later, Sau-Ping crouched with her friend, Mei-Kuen, at the edge of the family field.

"Ma bought me a new face towel so the older girls won't ridicule me," Sau-Ping said excitedly, as the two girls named the personal belongings they would bring to the maiden house. "And a wooden comb, hairpins. A red hairband. All new! Ma's going to keep the mirror, though, and I'll share with Sau-Ha."

"My Ma made me some new underwear," said Mei-Kuen. "We will enter the maiden house clean, you and I. Sau-Ha will make them be fair."

"And we two are together."

"I'll keep them off!" Mei-Kuen laughed her dangerous laugh that broke at the lowest pitch and had a little thunder in it.

The day of the move to the maiden house was cool and bright. Holding her light bundle of new and old belongings along with her rolled mat, Sau-Ping stood inside the room she had entered in her imagination many times. Her sister had already carried in and placed her stool for her, and there was a clean empty drawer in the large communal dresser, ready for her clothes and hair comb. Afraid she might cry or laugh, Sau-Ping avoided looking at Mei-Kuen, who was also manoeuvring with artificial dignity, one slow step at a time, trying not to say a stupid word or make an awkward move as she placed her new underwear in her new home.

But once the two friends were moved in, the mystery of the maiden house quickly wore off, for the atmosphere of the place – alternately raucous, proud, and quiet – agreed with them. The wall of the house was made of lovely pale green bricks. There were no windows, except a small opening at the roof to let the light in. The mats were grouped together in the middle of the room on the floor. Wooden clogs were placed on the side. The maidens went in and out along a tiny strip of floor space. In the large dresser, each member had one drawer. Eight teenaged girls, as a rule, lived together in this house. It separated them from their brothers, who had their own boys' houses, and from other men, until the day of their wedding.

Sau-Ha instructed the newcomers on the maidens' code of behaviour.

"No member is allowed to touch other people's personal belongings. No one is allowed to quarrel with or bully others in this house." At the end of her list, she named one of the girls' ritual responsibilities. "Every member has to put up a fight when boys' house troublemakers come from other villages to snatch one of us for a bride. Not a pretend fight, Ping."

Sau-Ping held up her head, though her neck felt weak and shaky. She had never been a fighter. She had been trained as a modest daughter. She imagined grabbing the thick hair of some towering, unknown boy and then found herself staring at the green brick wall, trying to absorb the familiar colour and calm herself.

Sau-Ping and her companions were counting stars as they sat on the doorstep of their maiden house. Without warning, a star tumbled out of the sky, just missing their roof and falling onto the Shek Lau Fa Hills. Auntie Kwan stood in front of the maiden house, where she often paused to talk with the girls. When she heard voices cry out "There! A long tail!" she turned just in time to catch the star's strong descent and note its direction.

"So a widow is born. And widow for the rest of her life. A woman alone at her dish and alone before sleep," the older woman announced. No one spoke. Auntie Kwan's voice asked for pity, and the girls, as a group, were unwilling to grant it. Auntie Kwan turned down the alley. "Time for me, I think. Good night."

When she had turned the corner and passed the pigsty on the outer village path, young Mei-Kuen said, "If I complain that much when I am old, sew my mouth shut." She pinched her lips and made mumbling sounds.

Sau-Ping took a breath and looked in the other direction, away from the village path, as the voices of the older girls rose around her, scolding Mei-Kuen for her rudeness to an elder woman. Mei-Kuen was ruddy-cheeked, robust, a little on the chubby side, and had a sharper tongue than many people realized. Everyone in Fung-Yeung village remembered she had been a fearless child who disappeared for hours at a time and then reappeared in odd, sometimes stinking, corners: places the adults would have forbidden to her if they'd imagined any child would think of hiding there. But scoldings and punishments seemed to bounce right off Mei-Kuen. All it took was one of her defiant laughing fits to get all the other girls laughing too. Compared to her friend, Sau-Ping was thin. "Reedy" or "frail and elegant" the old aunties called her when they wanted to be nice. "Bony, bony!" or "Skinny as a chicken in winter!" the village boys yelled when she passed.

But no one laughed now. Ming-Ming, another maiden, was saying, "She's had a hard life."

"It doesn't look so hard to me," said Mei-Kuen. "She has all the time in the world to gossip. She never works."

"It's not your place to speak. You don't feel how a woman is."

"Do you think I'm the only one to speak! She spreads mean stories about all the girls and some of our parents' generation as well. Instead of sewing her mouth shut, people give her gifts in the hope that she won't make up stories about them. I say, get the thread and the needle. If she's had a hard life, she deserves it." Mei-Kuen stood up quickly and went inside.

It was only one month later that Auntie Kwan got the news from a villager that her husband's bones had arrived at the pier in Naam-Waan. Everyone in Fung-Yeung knew when she returned with the urn – villagers spoke of the blessings and the curse, the money and the absence, that rule the life of any woman married to a Gold

Mountain guest – but for days the maidens didn't see her. Then Sau-Ping glimpsed the auntie on the village path beyond the pigsty one morning. Mei-Kuen, who was dressed for work in the rice paddy, spotted her a moment later and planted herself in the path with her eyes signalling challenge, like a boy's.

The old woman stopped and surveyed them. She smiled grimly, and then her face changed: her jaw slackened with sorrow and derision, frightening Sau-Ping, who suddenly imagined that this teller of tales would predict her own future. But Auntie Kwan raised her head. "So, girls," she said. "What do you know?" Her gaze lifted to the sky, then dropped. She looked at Mei-Kuen. "You should be the one to marry a Gold Mountain guest, for you are careless. Then one day after forty-five years of solitude, like me, you will go to the pier at Naam-Waan for an urn full of bones that smell like death – the same stink here or there. My life will be lonely now. I hope you girls won't forget your Auntie Kwan now that she is really a widow. But then, what does it matter? You will all marry foolish boys from other villages and go away and forget about me. You all worry about your own mothers more than your crazy old Auntie Kwan anyway. I would have twenty children of my own to worry about me if I had-n't married a Gold Mountain guest. Gold Mountain ghost, more like, for all the good it's done me. I am drier than his bones."

"We won't forget you, Auntie Kwan," said Sau-Ping.

That was the last time they saw Auntie Kwan. There were rumours that she wandered the alleys late at night wearing rags and shouting out crazy news about men and women running through the village, visiting their lovers. She named names. One evening on the way to visit her mother's sister in the next village, Sau-Ping thought she saw Auntie Kwan carrying a round urn in her two arms, wailing nonsense into the night as she stood on the weedy bank of Saam-Hop River.

One afternoon, Sau-Ping went to the maiden house earlier than usual. She had been planting rice all day and weeding the garden that she and her mother kept to supply the family with vegetables. The evening air was so fresh and the sky so clear that she paused on the step rather than going in right away. She sat down, resting her head in her hands. Dusk was her favourite time of day, a time between work and rest, between the company of her family and the company of the girls in the maiden house. It was good to be tired like this. It was good to have family close by and still be able to have moments alone, looking out over the green fields and breathing in the smells of evening.

The sky had already turned peachy pink when the first edge of the sun disappeared below the edge of the hills. The pink deepened to a determined crimson just as the crescent moon emerged behind the sun, as though rising up from the depths of the earth to swallow the sun whole.

"Ping, get in here!" Sau-Ha came out of the house and grabbed her sister by the arm.

"You're already here!" Sau-Ping cried cheerfully. "Come and watch the sunset with me." But Sau-Ha didn't stop pulling on her arm. "Ow! Let me go! You're hurting! What's wrong with you?"

Sau-Ha clapped her hand over Sau-Ping's eyes and continued to yank on her arm. "Don't look! Come on, get into the house. This isn't a joke."

"You're mean! What's wrong with you, trying to stop a person's simple pleasure!"

"You don't even know what you're talking about," said Sau-Ha. "Staring at the sky. You know what happened to Auntie Kwan."

"The sky won't fall down and hurt her. You're hurting her," cried Mei-Kuen, who emerged from the house with her comb in her hand. "Why don't you tell us things? What is bad luck now? Why is everything bad luck for girls? I think half of it is tricks to keep us saying we're sorry and we're stupid."

"Then watch the sky! Look at it!" declared Sau-Ha angrily. "Both of you. I'm not Ma. Tell yourselves the answers!"

"What is it?" Sau-Ping had turned her eyes from the sky and fixed them on the safe wall of the maiden house.

"Ask your friend," Sau-Ha replied elegantly, sarcastically, before walking away into the shadows.

Sau-Ping couldn't stop herself. Her brow folded and her eyes filled with tears. Watching her askance, Mei-Kuen made an impatient sound and walked off, still holding her comb in her hand like a little knife.

Days later, Mei-Kuen abruptly knelt beside her friend at the edge of the vegetable field and spoke her news without introduction: "Whoever watches the moon lady biting her husband is certain to become a grass widow. That's all. Your husband goes to the Gold Mountain and you spend time with your girlfriends all day, with no husband to boss you around or beat you. That is the dreadful, awful misfortune. If you see another sunset like that, tell me. I will climb a tree to watch for it."

Sau-Ping was quiet. Over the last few days, she had overheard her sister telling tales about grass widows to the older girls in the maiden house and had come to suspect that the argument at sunset and the mysterious interdiction somehow involved these wives of distant husbands. Sau-Ha, her voice melancholy and conspiratorial, had repeated the story she herself had heard from a young man whose sister was married to a husband gone to the United States for five years. The sister had to hire a man to help her with the ploughing. Because she was alone with him often, it was easy for the villagers to accuse her of adultery. They forced her into a basket for pigs and drowned her in the Saam-Hop River.

For many days Sau-Ping had thought of this story, when she fell asleep at night and when she awakened in the morning. She could not imagine that her kinsmen could be so cruel. And yet there was a shape to adult life that she was just beginning to see. Girls and women were required to be strong in obedience. If they faltered, they were transformed into pigs and crazies and then led to the edge of the river, either by villagers, who had no mercy to spare for maimed pigs, or by the moon. Grass widows lived alone in the dark for hours and hours every night. Sau-Ping feared that darkness the way a young child does, eyes wide, unable to speak. But she was no longer a child.

The fifteenth day after New Year was the Lantern Festival. Villagers were celebrating the first full moon of the year.

In the very early morning of the festival day, Sau-Ping was awakened by the rooster. She rubbed her eyes, but it was still pitch dark. She rolled over and returned to her dreams. She was shaken gently by Sau-Ha, lying next to her. "Ping," whispered her sister, "we are going to steal vegetables tonight. You must come too!"

"Stealing vegetables?" Sau-Ping was suddenly wide awake.

"Yes. Tonight I'll take you someplace you have never been before."

"Where? Which family are we going to steal from?" Sau-Ping asked eagerly.

Sau-Ha raised a finger to her lips. "As thieves, we cannot reveal the secret location."

Sau-Ping had never seen her sister so excited. Of the three siblings in the family, Sau-Ha had always worked the hardest. The family only had six *mau* of land to farm, and the rice and sweet potatoes were never enough to feed everybody; since her childhood, Big Sister had not only farmed: she had also woven baskets and other rattan wares to sell in Shaan-Tai Market. Often she cut her fingers while splitting the bamboo, and always she cleaned and bound them herself, without asking for help or pity. As soon as her wounds were bandaged with a piece of cotton, she started weaving again. There was not much fun in her life. Stealing vegetables during the Lantern Festival was Big Sister's favourite annual pastime.

Sau-Ha had promised Sau-Ping years ago that she would be allowed to come along on the raid once she moved to the maiden house. Now the day was here!

That morning Sau-Ha and her parents went to the market. Sau-Ping was left at home to take care of her little brother, Tin-Shaang. Having spent the lucky money Ma gave them on New Year's Eve, sister and brother couldn't afford to buy firecrackers or toys – mud-chickens, tops – from the pedlar who came around, announcing his wares in a loud voice out in the alley. So Sau-Ping watched, impatiently waiting, as Tin-Shaang rode his homemade bamboo horse in the backyard.

The day seemed to last forever. Mei-Kuen had already dropped in twice, asking when they were to set off on their expedition.

At long last the sun set. Father, Mother, and Sau-Ha arrived home with food. Sau-Ping had already set the table and cooked the usual meal of rice mixed with sweet potato. She noticed Sau-Ha walk around the table swiftly, touching and counting the rice bowls and chopsticks as if to make sure that everything was exactly ready so there would be no time wasted. Then her sister swept near her and whispered, "Eat quickly so we can get going!"

Sau-Ping was startled into painful excitement and tears came into her eyes. Noticing her agitation, Sau-Ha changed her tune, ordering her sternly not to be impatient: they would still have to do the dishes and then change into their new clothing. Calming herself, Sau-Ping noticed that as her sister circled the table filling the rice bowls, she was almost laughing; Ping realized that Sau-Ha could barely contain her own singing heart. The family sat down to eat. Sweet potato rice was offered first to Pa, then to Ma. Ma gave hers to Little Brother Tin-Shaang in addition to the choicest bit of the fried fish.

Sau-Ping filled her own bowl. Her chopsticks moved like lightning and she didn't chew her food properly. She was listening to the sounds of all the teenage girls in the alley teaming up for the trip to steal vegetables.

Round as a gong, the moon rose slowly behind the ancestral hall. The few stars at its side suggested a drumstick banging noiselessly on the gong. They made their own pale light. The night air was chilly.

Mei-Kuen was already waiting by the bamboo grove. "Ping, I have never seen you this pretty. Look at your brand-new quilted jacket! It shines, and I can't even see all the flowers!"

Half listening, Sau-Ping glanced down at her jacket, which was clear white with a blue floral design. It was eye-catching in the day, when the new cloth shone, and a strong presence at night, when it glowed in the moonlight. "Sau-Ha made this by hand."

"I watched her in the house. I know. She used her basket money to buy the material. She's a good sister. We both watch over you."

"Don't forget Big Sister after you are married!" laughed Sau-Ha, who stood beside them in the darkness on the path. "Let's take this new route!"

The three maidens passed the Sai-Fok bridge. The air was getting cooler, so that Sau-Ping was again grateful for her jacket. A mountain range stood out clearly in the moonlight. It sat on the horizon like a large beast, looking down on the young women.

"This part is full of odd-shaped rocks." Sau-Ha pointed to the hilltop in the distance. "They have all sorts of strange names like Doggy Rock, Bat Rock, Chicken Leg Rock ... When you see their shapes, you can guess their names."

Sau-Ping followed the line indicated by her sister's index finger and saw a rock in the shape of a standing woman. In front of it was another round but smaller rock, balancing on top of a larger rectangular one. Sau-Ping exclaimed, "This should be called 'A Beautiful Woman.'"

"And so it is, almost. It's 'A Beautiful Woman Admiring Herself in the Mirror,'" said Sau-Ha.

Mei-Kuen laughed. "What a beautiful name for three dumb rocks!"

Sau-Ha said seriously, "There's a story."

Sau-Ping knew that she must be very quiet, because one silly word or gesture would discourage her sister from telling the story. Mei-Kuen seemed to understand and held her tongue.

Sau-Ha slowed her pace and began to speak. "A long time ago, there was a beautiful maiden. She fell in love with a scholar and they became engaged. However, his family fortune took a turn for the worse. He went across the sea and did not return. The maiden was heartbroken. She refused to marry all the other rich suitors. She stood at this hilltop day after day and year after year, waiting in vain for her fiancé to come back to comb her hair. She was transformed into a rock, forever waiting for him."

"The man must have married a white woman in Gold Mountain, one who was as pretty as a fairy," commented Mei-Kuen. "This maiden is so idiotic, still waiting for him. To me, she looks like a pile of rock."

Sau-Ping kept quiet. She did not want to argue with Mei-Kuen. To her, the rock figure looked still, modest, and majestic in the night.

The moon grew brighter and the air even chillier. The shadows and whispers of other young women were apparent along the village path. They ran into three girls from the maiden house also dressed in beautiful new clothes. Mei-Kuen called out, excited to see them, and the little group whispered together in urgent tones. Soon they were all chatting at full voice and giggling as they began to walk at a leisurely pace down the path. Sau-Ping wanted to stay with them, but her sister discouraged her. "Ping, we'll go choose the best vegetable field to steal from. You and I."

The two sisters walked quickly past their friends. They entered the backyard of a house in Sai-Fok village. Bending low, guided by the moonlight, Sau-Ha chose a bunch of green onions, two stalks of celery, and three heads of lettuce. Sau-Ping could identify the vegetables her sister took by their vague shape, but even more by their scent. Instructed to follow and imitate, Sau-Ping reached into the cool plants, sniffing for clues, but the minute she bent over to steal food from this stranger's backyard, she became so nervous she felt dizzy. She took a deep breath and forced herself to calm down. Carefully she chose the fattest green onions, two straight, crisp stalks of celery, which she tested with her hands, and three tender rounds of lettuce and slipped them into the bag her sister had made for her. She was just beginning to feel more relaxed when some dogs started barking sharply. She called out to her sister in fright. A kerosene lamp lit up the inside of the farmhouse.

"Oh dear, they're going to catch us stealing!" With pounding heart, Sau-Ping clung to her big sister.

"Don't be scared," laughed Sau-Ha merrily. "The head of the household is inviting us to go in. Keep hold of your loot. Don't let go now! Behind your back."

Sure enough, the head of the household was standing at the door, waving at the Wong sisters with a smile. Sau-Ping understood she had been dragged into yet another secret that the adults all knew but maidens had to learn. Oddly, it made her happy; she felt wild and secret and safe, all at once, standing on the edge of danger with her sister, who was behaving like a woman in daylight in the market square. "Come into the living-room. Make yourselves at home," the farmer called. Picking their way between the rows of vegetables, the girls walked towards the house.

Incense burned at the domestic altar, and there was fruit in a dish for the ancestors. Around the eight-cornered table sat two women, Leung Tsing-Haan and Auntie Mooi, the marriage broker.

"Aunties, *Kung-Hei Faat-Tsoi!*" Sau-Ha walked confidently into the living-room to greet the two women, carelessly holding the bag of stolen vegetables half-hidden behind her back.

Uncertain of the rules of this game, Sau-Ping, hands behind her back, nervously followed her sister and said gently, "Aunties, *Kung-Hei Faat-Tsoi!*"

"Hoh! Hoh! Hoh! Good, good – *Kung-Hei, Kung-Hei!*" The two women laughed jovially. Leung Tsing-Haan, hostess of the farmhouse, brought out tea and offered sweet rice pudding to the sisters. Sau-Ha plunked her stolen vegetables right onto the table and started to eat the pudding, giving Sau-Ping a mysterious smile.

Sau-Ping sensed that Auntie Mooi was studying her up and down. Abruptly the woman stood up and, her clogs clattering, moved over to Sau-Ping. "Take your hand from your back," she ordered briskly, " and show us what you have stolen."

Despite her recognition that this was all a kind of grand game Sau-Ping felt embarrassed as she revealed her booty. Leung Tsing-Haan chided Auntie Mooi. "Look, you have frightened this pretty maiden to bits."

She took the stolen vegetables gently, counted the items, and returned them to Sau-Ping one by one. "Little niece, this bunch of green onion will give you intelligence. These two stalks of celery will reward your hard work. These three heads of lettuce will ensure your health and wealth. *Faat-Tsoi! Faat-Tsoi!*"

Sau-Ping saw that she had been digging up symbols of good luck from the earth without knowing it. She felt blessed.

Auntie Mooi said, "Auntie Tsing-Haan, this maiden brought all the good luck into your homestead. *Kung-Hei! Kung-Hei!*"

Leung Tsing-Haan laughed heartily, her face creasing like a many-petalled chrysanthemum. She took a coin from her pocket and pressed it into Sau-Ping's palm. "Auntie offers you this as a souvenir."

In her fourteen years of life, Sau-Ping had never seen a coin like this. It was silver in colour. One side bore the design of a big-nosed king wearing his crown, and the other side showed the head of a buffalo-like animal with large horns. Sau-Ping showed it to her sister. "In which dynasty did people use this type of coin?"

"It looks like a foreign coin. I wonder which country it came from."

"This is a Canadian coin," Auntie Mooi explained. "Auntie Tsing-Haan's husband, Uncle Kwok-Yan, and his son, Yik-Man, are both in Canada."

"Why don't they come home for New Year?" Sau-Ping asked.

Leung Tsing-Haan's good humour vanished for a minute. She tipped her head to the side, and Sau-Ping saw a thought cross her forehead. Somehow the girl perceived that this was a heavy thought, and that it lived with the older woman as a near-constant companion.

At that moment a loud, laughing voice penetrated the house. "Auntie Mooi and Auntie Tsing-Haan, Happy New Year! So, Sau-Ha and Sau-Ping, you are both hiding here! It was tough looking for you," Mei-Kuen called into the room.

Sau-Ha, who had felt the uneasy silence from the hostess a moment ago, took the opportunity to beat a safe retreat.

"Aunties, thank you for your hospitality! We should go home now."

The three maidens left the house. The instant they had passed out of the circle of lantern light, Mei-Kuen whispered, "Auntie Mooi was looking you over, my two little pigs, and so was the Canadian coin Aunt. But not me. I'm not sweet enough. Your white jacket was a beacon, friend."

Sau-Ping understood exactly what Mei-Kuen meant. Her uneasy excitement at the thought that negotiations for her own marriage might begin was dampened not only by her friend's wit, but also by the fatigue she sensed in her sister as she moved silently along. The magic thievery and freedom of the night were finished. The "Beautiful Woman Admiring Herself in the Mirror" would soon appear ahead of them, a sightless pile of rock that had no power to move, only to wait.

CHAPTER 2

The Engagement

1932

Sau-Ping was unusually pensive on the morning of the fourth day of the New Year's Festival. She missed her big sister Sau-Ha, who had only returned for one visit since her marriage a year ago to Lau Tseung-Lam, a native of Toi-Shaan County, now living in Hong Kong.

As soon as Sau-Ping came home from the maiden house, she saw Auntie Mooi relaxing in the most comfortable chair in the living-room. Auntie Mooi herself had been married to a Gold Mountain guest, but he had died young, and so she made her living as a marriage broker. Because she was good at it, no one talked about her earlier misfortune. Sau-Ping heard her saying with great delight to her mother, "I got a blind seer to compare Sau-Ping's and Yik-Man's birthdates, and they match perfectly."

Sau-Ping pulled such a long face after Auntie Mooi left that her mother could not help but notice. She tried to console her daughter."Yik-Man may be ten years older than you, but he is a Gold Mountain guest. I negotiated this marriage for your own good. Have you not heard the saying:

If you have a daughter, don't marry her to a baker
Or she will not get half a year's sleep out of three.
If you have a daughter, don't marry her to a farmer
Or her legs will be covered in cow dung and her hair
will be full of dust.
If you have a daughter, you should marry her to a Gold
Mountain guest.
Whenever his boat turns around, she will have dollars by the hundreds.

Sau-Ping reached for her sewing box.

"Ping, you don't have to do any more embroidery today. Auntie Mooi will come tomorrow to finalize the betrothal ceremony." Mrs Wong held Sau-Ping's hand gently. "She took the pillow case with your embroidery work to show Mrs Leung. Mrs Leung was very impressed!"

Sau-Ping picked up her unthreaded needle. So this was the answer to her future: sharp and plain as the needle point. She pricked a tiny hole in the cloth where she had just begun to embroider the edge of a pink lily, thinking, "And this was how they decided. Now I am stitched in."

"Ah, you have not let me down!" Mrs Wong was saying. "I taught you to use the small needle for embroidery work the moment you turned five. You didn't pay much attention. You wanted to catch fish by the stream, so I beat you with my wooden ruler." "You told me to dry my tears," Sau-Ping said. Her eyes were dry.

Sau-Ping's mother changed the subject. "Why is it your father hasn't returned from the market with the roast pork?" She went to the kitchen to attend to the stove, talking as she moved. "You've been my good girl. Both my girls. Yesterday Tin-Shaang climbed a tree to catch birds and tore his best pair of pants at the knee, far from the seam. If Auntie Mooi sees him tomorrow!"

"Ma, where are Tin-Shaang's torn pants? I'll mend them." Sau-Ping looked into the sewing box for her coarse needle.

"You'd have to wash them and hang them out to dry, or you will be sewing rag," said Ma, holding her lower back, which she tried to ease at night by lying on the mat with a warm rock wedged under her side against her spine. "The pigs need feeding first. Pluck more sweet potato leaves and add the husk ... that bag of corn husk your father got. Don't waste feed on the old chickens that aren't laying eggs. But you know."

"Ma, couldn't Tin-Shaang help a bit?"

"No, there is no need – he is still a little boy! Of course he loves to play."

"Little Brother is already ten."

Ma didn't answer. Sau-Ping felt her body go very still for a moment; it did not want to rise and launder the boy's clothes. It did not want to depart from the house and move to the house of a stranger. She had heard in her mother's voice both pleasure – the pleasure of a lifelong teacher who sees before her a competent, handsome, successful pupil – and the slightest embarrassment. There was no need to be embarrassed. Everything was being arranged properly. Sau-Ping stood up and looked around for her brother's gashed trousers. From the kitchen came the noise of her mother chopping vegetables on the board. Heavy steam from the rice water scented both rooms. With her daughters gone, Ma would soon be lifting more buckets every day and bending to haul, pluck, and fetch without respite.

After dinner, drums were heard from the direction of the ancestral hall. Tin-Shaang had been looking forward to the lion dance performance all day, running around the house making clanging and roaring noises. Fung-Yeung was such a poor mountain village that it could only afford to sponsor this event every few years, so Tin-Shaang had been a small boy the last time he saw it. Following local custom, the lion dance team, made up of ten muscular youths, would start the procession at the open space in front of the village ancestral hall and then move to the surrounding villages, finishing up in Shaan-Tai Market.

"Let's go watch the lion dance team!" Tin-Shaang tugged his father's sleeves.

"It's already quite late. Why don't we play at home instead?" It had been a tiring day at the market and Mr Wong had no interest in joining the noisy crowd.

"I want to go, I want to go!"

"Little Shaang wants to go. Why are you throwing cold water on his fun?" Ma called from the kitchen.

"Ma, I'll take Little Brother." Sau-Ping had come out from the kitchen after doing the dishes, and she was eager to join her girlfriends in the village crowd that followed the lion dance. It would perhaps be her last chance.

Ma was silent. Then she said, "Husband, if Shaang stays home tonight, he will be leaping on the chairs and doing mischief in front of Auntie Mooi tomorrow. Do you want us to lose face?"

Mr Wong had no choice. Sau-Ping's offer could not be accepted; it was necessary to keep her sequestered from public functions from the moment of her formal engagement to the day of her wedding. Father and son left for the celebration.

Mother and daughter moved about inside the house. They continually passed near one another, but Sau-Ping kept her eyes lowered, looking for tasks she might accomplish to prepare the room for tomorrow. When she heard her mother settle unexpectedly into a chair, she did not ask whether her back was hurting. The dim sounds of gongs and shouts weighed on her spirit.

"There has been no news from Big Sister Sau-Ha for three months." Ma's voice broke the silence.

"Are Auntie Mooi's words unreliable?" Sau-Ping asked plainly, looking into the clean, empty kitchen.

"Ping, don't worry. This time, for you, Auntie Mooi has made no mistake. Every word is reliable. This Gold Mountain guest is hundreds of times better than your brother-in-law Lau Tseung-Lam. Hong Kong is far away and I cannot ..." Ma stopped for a moment. "Sau-Ha must see what's in front of her own eyes, and she must make a life with her own hands. There's nothing I can do from this house. Hong Kong is dirty. Get me Shaang's pants, Sau-Ping. They are dry enough." Ma reached over for her large, worn sewing basket.

Sau-Ping went outside to retrieve her brother's trousers, which she had hung on a dead branch to dry. She was sixteen and would be a bride soon. Glancing up, she noticed a grey dove in the smallest branches of the tree. Was this where her brother had climbed? Bird cages sold at the market were sometimes as beautiful as little palaces, lacquered and shaped so they appeared to have many rooms. Her sister Sau-Ha had been taken from the maiden house and now lived in Hong Kong. She had flown a great distance but she was still in a cage. Sau-Ping looked into tomorrow and saw clearly that she was going to be placed in a room, in a cage, far from the scented maiden house with its familiar ring of mats, and far from this house, where her mother lived.

Sau-Ping heard laughter and turned. Mei-Kuen was coming to fetch her. Mei-Kuen was a sturdy little buffalo that refused to be led by the nose. Sau-Ping went to meet her, Tin-Shaang's trousers draped over her left arm.

"Are you cloistered like a Buddhist nun?" Mei-Kuen gripped her free arm.

Ma immediately appeared on the doorstep. "Mei-Kuen, keep your sharp tongue to yourself. Come inside, both of you. What is it you want from Ping?"

As the girls followed Ma into the house, Mei-Kuen replied, "Oh, I want her to come with me to watch the lion dance performance. Auntie, why don't you come along too?"

Laying the trousers on the table, Sau-Ping said, "Why don't you have tea now with us?" Mei-Kuen glanced at her sharply, then poured herself a cup and sipped it. "What fragrant tea you have, Auntie! What dragon meat did you put in it?"

Ma laughed. "When will you give me some dragon meat?"

"Ping is your phoenix meat." Mei-Kuen circled her friend again with her arm. "Look, see how healthy and firm." She put her cup on the table. "We can dance in here. Then we can open the doors to the lion parade and let them see ..."

Sau-Ping grabbed her friend and poked just under her ribs, in the spot that made her wild. Mei-Kuen shrieked.

"Let me shorten your tongue!" Sau-Ping cried. "Let me make you dance!" The two young women chased each other around the table, giggling, grabbing, and dodging. Mei-Kuen shrieked,"Put her outside, put her outside, she'll tear down your house!"

Ma stood in the kitchen doorway, her straight mouth shut as if to hold in the maternal admonitions she would normally utter. Then she turned away and disappeared, no doubt to polish one last tile, one last dish, for tomorrow's visit. Bereft of their audience, the girls leaned against the wall, catching their breath. "Ping. Sewing and mending never cease. Leave his dirty pants and come outside," Mei-Kuen said.

"Tomorrow, Auntie Mooi will come here. It is Leung Yik-Man."

After a pause, Mei-Kuen spoke. "There are many Leung families around here. Which village do they come from?"

"It is the Leung family that live in the eastern corner of Sai-Fok village in Kat-Cheung Heung. Their menfolk are all in Canada."

"You took their green onions at the Lantern Festival three years ago! I see. Now they want them back."

Sau-Ping shook her head. "How will you fight for me if you don't tell the other girls tonight? Go out," she ordered.

"We girls at the maiden house will support you when the young men come to fetch you to Sai-Fok village."

"Yes."

Mei-Kuen stood still, thinking. Then she was gone. Sau-Ping looked around her family's room. It seemed like a little raised stage. She was alone onstage and couldn't predict what tall figure was about to leap from behind the curtain – killer or prince or beast? She thirsted for a cup of tea. Picking up the tea her friend had tasted, she drank from Mei-Kuen's cup.

Early the next morning, Sau-Ping came home from the maiden house to do household chores and feed the pigs and chickens as usual. By the time she was finished, the sun was shining brightly. Time to prepare lunch. Sau-Ping cleaned herself and bound her hair again before moving into the kitchen.

Auntie Mooi and four bondservants from Sai-Fok entered the Wong household, carrying bamboo baskets covered with a red cloth. Auntie Mooi was grinning so widely that Sau-Ping, watching silently from the kitchen doorway, could almost count her teeth.

"Auntie Mooi, you look exhausted, please come in to rest." Ma quickly offered a comfortable chair.

Sau-Ping's father greeted Auntie Mooi courteously. He would sit down beside the marriage broker and puff tobacco from his three-foot-long bamboo pipe. Tin-Shaang was wearing his mended pants. Sau-Ping could hear him jump up and down, calling "Auntie, Auntie!"

"Come, have some candies!" Auntie Mooi removed the red cloth from one of the baskets, took a bag of colourful candies from the basket, and offered it to Tin-Shaang.

Tin-Shaang took one candy, walked over to the kitchen door, and offered it to Sau-Ping, who quickly stepped back, saying firmly, "You can have it, Shaang. Go out and play. I am busy cooking." For once, Tin-Shaang did not protest or demand attention; he sensed that something was happening in those rooms.

Sau-Ping did her best to look and sound industrious, plying the meat cleaver against the board just a little more noisily than usual. Though her eyes focused on her task, her ears were tuned to the conversation in the dining-room.

"Please accept the Leung family's humble gift," said Auntie Mooi. Sau-Ping peeked swiftly as the Auntie nodded to the four men who had accompanied her. She knew that, one by one, the men would hand their baskets to Ma and Pa, then go outside to wait. Ma would place the baskets on the side table beside the two-seated chair against the wall.

Sau-Ping heard rustling and low voices, then her mother's voice, "This is very generous. Thank you." Her sincerity meant that the baskets contained perhaps a thousand rounded wedding cakes made of rice flour stuffed with yellow lotus paste, each wrapped in smooth brown paper with the delicate red mark of the baker's chop across the top. In the last basket there would be money. Sau-Ping thought she could guess when her mother offered their "return gift," nine *kan* of brown sugar, which she would place in one of Auntie Mooi's baskets.

"From now on, the Leungs and the Wongs are in-laws!" proclaimed Auntie Mooi. "When do you think would be the most auspicious time to fetch Sau-Ping?"

"I have already discussed this with Tin-Shaang's father. Since Ping will belong to the Leung household soon, Mrs Leung should be the one to decide," Ma replied without hesitation. "But everything has to follow the proper procedure so that people will not jeer at us."

"That goes without saying. I have already worked out all the details with Auntie Leung Tsing-Haan. First, she will arrange to have a letter sent to Yik-Man to call him home for the wedding. Once his return date is fixed, I will come to confirm with you the most auspicious moment to fetch the bride."

In the kitchen, Sau-Ping, meat cleaver still in hand, listened without moving. This brief exchange of words sealed her fate. The ritual conversation had passed through her body painlessly, like the sharpest needle, and stitched her to a new house.

It was now past midday. Auntie Mooi, not wanting to overstay her welcome, stood up to leave.

"Please stay for lunch," said Ma.

"I would love to, but I should be getting back."

"You must have a little more time to spare. We would love for you to stay." Pa pressed now. "Our daughter has already prepared a nice dish of steamed pork with salty egg yolk."

"You are too kind," said Auntie Mooi, and Sau-Ping knew that the go-between had returned to her seat, ready for lunch, as everyone expected.

When Sau-Ping had finished cooking, Ma took all her carefully prepared dishes into the dining area. Sau-Ping ate by herself in the kitchen, still listening attentively to the conversation between her parents and the marriage broker, who would doubtless report every detail of the afternoon back to Sau-Ping's soon-to-be mother-in-law.

"Auntie Leung Tsing-Haan must miss her son, since he lives so far away," said Ma. "Sau-Ping still has her coin from Canada. It is far."

"Not at all," replied Auntie Mooi. "She keeps herself quite busy at home with her little garden and her pigs. And she has her younger son. Of course, he is not as bright as his older brother, but he is a good boy."

"Yik-Man must be too busy to write often."

"He is busy, but he writes when he can," said Auntie Mooi. "Of course, he employs a scribe. His father's restaurant does quite well, you see, so there is no reason for him to pick up a pen himself. All he needs to do is tell the scribe what he wants Auntie Tsing-Haan to know and the scribe writes it down."

"The Leungs sound like a very prosperous family. That is reassuring to me," Ma said.

Sau-Ping was thinking that her future husband probably couldn't write. It wouldn't be surprising: few people from the village knew how to read and write; she herself did not. A song crossed her mind. She remembered Big Sister Sau-Ha singing the words, now and then, in the maiden house.

> I left my country early in life
> And did not return until age thirty.
> The marriage broker made many helpful trips.
> My parents are happy to hear her footsteps!
> They pass round candies and speak few words.

Sau-Ping imagined her sister singing the tune in a smoky Hong Kong kitchen. Then she imagined a long string of villages and cities that consisted only of smoky kitchens, each one containing a faceless woman. Chop, on the chopping blocks, the green onions fall in pieces. Are women's fates all fixed by others?

CHAPTER 3

The Wedding

1933

The auspicious day for Sau-Ping's wedding was set for the eighth day of the third lunar month, 1933.

A few days before the wedding, Sau-Ping and her mother stood knee-deep in the muddy water of the paddy-field, carefully transplanting the green rice seedlings into their new bed. They each wore two pairs of white knee-high socks to keep the leeches off their legs. An occasional faint breeze ruffled the water, and the only sound was the steady sluicing of their hands as they secured the plants in the mud. Looking at her mother, Sau-Ping noticed the marks of sorrow in her puckered brow and straight lips. They didn't say a word, as if there was nothing left to say once the gifts from the Leung family had been accepted.

The sun was about to set. A ring of mist hung around the lower foothills.

"Ma, I can finish the last bunches. Why don't you go home first? Little Brother is probably hungry."

"All right," said Ma, rinsing her hands and feet in the running stream. Her husband would be on his way back from selling basket wares. If the soup wasn't ready ...

Sau-Ping crouched to sink a limp, bright, narrow seedling in place. Ma climbed the embankment that separated one paddy-field from the next. Her back bent, she trudged homewards down the narrow path at the top of the embankment and disappeared.

It was getting dark. Sau-Ping's back was growing stiff, but she had only a few plants left in her bunch. A long shadow stretched over her, making her stumble back in the water. Rows of new rice shoots waved around her in the half-light.

The shadow's owner giggled. "I'm not a ghost." It was Mei-Kuen. "You scared me!"

"Serves you right for daydreaming. If I were a robber, you'd be dead by now. What were you thinking about?"

"Nothing."

"You must have been thinking about something. Maybe a handsome new husband!"

"It would be nice if he were handsome."

"Lift the veil and greet your future," Mei-Kuen laughed.

Sau-Ping knew instinctively that the face of a new husband would be a surprise. At times, when her companions in the maiden house grew weary of their own brothers and fathers, they acknowledged that the idea of such a surprise was strongly appealing. But Sau-Ping's own husband was doubly mysterious because he had left for Vancouver when he was ten years old and never come back. Thinking of this, she said, "I don't know anyone in Sai-Fok village who can tell me what he looks like, except as a baby."

"Ping, come out now, or you'll do damage. It's too dark. And I have a secret," Mei-Kuen added slyly. "I'll tell you if you let me have your drawer in the maiden house after you are gone."

"It makes no difference to me. Of course you can have it," replied Sau-Ping, wading slowly through the water and up onto the bank, where she peeled off her socks. She had received the top drawer in the dresser the young women shared. It was a little bigger than the others.

"Ming-Ming was in Sai-Fok yesterday."

Sau-Ping stood barefoot in the cold stream, washing her feet. Water shifted around her ankles like silk as she rubbed one foot against the other to hide her agitation. Mei-Kuen was speaking. "... passing by the ancestral hall, she met a fellow in a smart-looking western suit looking this way and that."

Sau-Ping knelt to rinse her hands.

"He said, 'Little Sister, I have come back from the Gold Mountain, and I am looking for my house. Leung Tsing-Haan is my mother. Which route should I take?' He didn't know how to make his way through the New Village to the Old Village, because he had never seen the New Village section. Ming-Ming watched him walk down the alley. She says all the *yeung-lau* in Sai-Fok block the entrances to the alleys of the Old Village, and they look like castles for white princesses! To get around them ..."

"Was it Yik-Man?"

"Ming-Ming didn't follow him, but it was. He gave her lucky money. Ask her. Another Canada coin. She said he has beautiful ears and clean hair, but he smells like ... she couldn't describe it. A different herb. Did you hear the story Ming-Ming heard about Canada? A Gold Mountain guest who came home said Canada has lots of huge fish with red meat called salmon! There are so many that if you practise, you can cross a river by stepping on their backs."

Turning, Sau-Ping began to walk home in her damp clothes. Her friend kept pace.

"People say the moon in Gold Mountain is rounder than ours ..."

Sau-Ping began running in her weighted clothes, not knowing why ...

"Ping! Ping!" Mei-Kuen was shrieking. "Stop! If I could be like you!"

Sau-Ping ran more powerfully, darkly happy in her friend's distress. She knew very well that Mei-Kuen's father had died long before and her mother was ill, incapable of managing the plans and payments necessary to engage the services of Auntie Mooi. And Mei-Kuen lacked brothers or sisters who might establish connections with Overseas Chinese families in any of the nearby villages. Now her heart was swollen with pity for her friend. It made her desperate, so that she couldn't stop running. Her feet pounded the path at a steady rate.

That night, Sau-Ping walked to the maiden house alone. This would be the last night she slept as an unmarried woman.

Even before she crossed the threshold, she could hear several young women practising their "mourning songs" to bid her farewell. They were seated on their mats, with Mei-Kuen leading the dirge. Most of the girls sang hesitantly, but Mei-Kuen's voice was strong and even frightening. Days before, Sau-Ping had listened to her friend teaching the thirteen-year-olds how to place themselves at the entrance to the village on the proper day and inform her at once if they saw strangers carrying a multicoloured sedan chair.

Standing over her companions, Sau-Ping lifted her head and howled.

"Ping, here you go again. Are those real tears of sorrow? How many handkerchiefs do you need?" Mei-Kuen teased her friend loudly, challenging her like a swordfighter.

As Sau-Ping wailed out her tune, and the words of the ritual song were truly her own. "I am missing my parents. I am worried that I might have a fierce mother-in-law." The maidens' ceremony had begun.

"Silly girl," Mei-Kuen declared, "people have to marry sooner or later. The men are all happy when they get married. So why should you cry so much?"

"Of course the grooms are happy. They bring in a wife to serve them. As for us, we marry to serve them and their parents. When do we see our Ma again? Once or twice a year."

Wai-Fong announced, "It is worse for the grass widow! We will not let you go. We will fight them!"

Sau-Ping's mood was profoundly bleak. There was something weighing on her, an alien sadness that she herself only half understood and that none of the younger girls could even begin to grasp, even though they were speaking the correct words. She wasn't sure whether they actually felt anything or were merely behaving as ritual required. Never mind, she thought; their turns would come soon enough. A young maiden poured her a cup of boiled water. She pushed it aside, spilling it onto the mat. The maiden bowed and wiped up the water. Prospective brides were expected to throw tantrums, and Sau-Ping looked wild-eyed around the familiar room, calculating what she could tear and spill.

In the corner, Wai-Fong quietly asked the youngest girl to fetch Mrs Wong because her daughter, Sau-Ping, was crazy. She spoke in a distinct voice for Sau-Ping to hear. Not long after, the slim girl arrived with a basket full of food, saying, "Mrs Wong could not come. I told her that Sau-Ping was crying her eyes out. She said, 'Don't let her forget her parting song when the sedan chair arrives to fetch her.'"

"What should we give her if she grows exhausted," Mei-Kuen asked. The discussion advanced according to custom, with clues to behavior hidden between the words.

"Some rice from this basket. It will give her stamina."

Sau-Ping didn't touch the basket. Waves of emotion gripped her and dragged at her. She hated her mother for refusing to save her. She hated everyone except her companions, the other maidens. Her wailing grew softer as her despair deepened, and she was confused when she noticed Mei-Kuen and Wai-Fong leaving the room. A girl's voice said, "They will look over the dowry for you, Ping. You cannot go yourself. They will fight for the gifts you deserve after years of obedience as a good daughter. If your mother refuses, they will stomp and scream for the village to hear. She cannot bargain down your value as if you were a rotten green onion."

Sau-Ping was breathing, resting on her mat, when the two emissaries returned to announce that they had thrown temper fits until at last Mrs Wong had agreed to their demands: new clothing, bedding, and furniture. They had argued item by item against the stingy mother until she promised to borrow money and send her husband to Shaan-Tai Market the next day for better goods.

Mei-Kuen and Wai-Fong boasted of their victory, and Sau-Ping felt tears dripping down her cheeks, for now she pitied her parents, who had been bullied by two mean girls in public. She whispered, "Go back to them. Say I want nothing more."

"Never!"

"Go back. Go back to them. Say I want nothing more. I am grateful."

"But you have to promise to eat something," Wai-Fong said. "And wash your face. And rest your voice. If you promise, we will go."

Sau-Ping rolled over and looked at Mei-Kuen and Wai-Fong, whose faces rose like heroes, because they were lifelong friends and tomorrow they planned to fight. Sau-Ping closed her eyes. It was time now for her to rest so that her eyes would be clear when the veil was lifted in Sai-Fok, her future home.

In the morning, Sau-Ping came home. She washed herself in water that had been boiled with leaves of the *taai-kwoh* tree. She then sat on a stool in the middle of the big mat that was normally used by the family for drying rice. Her companions from the maiden house arrived at the precise moment when an older woman from next door was performing the hair-combing ritual. The moment had been chosen by a blind fortune teller. Sau-Ping's hair was combed down three times and then coiled up into a bun and decorated with a cypress leaf. As her hair was being combed and combed, Sau-Ping rested. With hair bound, she knelt in front of the family altar and kowtowed three times, then turned to her parents and did the same. Her parents gave her a red packet. "This lucky money will bring you good fortune."

Sau-Ping took the packet with thanks, retired to her room, and put on her wedding clothes. She dressed herself in a high-collared red silk blouse that buttoned up from the right. She put on a pair of light blue satin pants and beautifully embroidered red satin shoes. A red flannelette flower decorated her hair. This bridal outfit had been tailored from the fabric purchased with the money Sau-Ping and her mother earned from twelve days of basket weaving. Sau-Ping had sewn the whole outfit herself, spending many laborious hours at the task.

When she emerged, her mother touched her arm gently.

Another auntie arrived and suddenly grabbed her arms. Confused, Sau-Ping struggled to keep her feet as the auntie tried to hoist her onto her back. As they scuffled, the young women began to protest. Of all the maidens, Wai-Fong wailed the loudest. She pulled the auntie's hair so hard that her bun almost came loose. The auntie yelled, "You little rascals. You shouldn't be too rough. Every one of you will be married off soon. We'll see how much you can resist!"

The girls stopped their physical protest and stood uncertainly, crowded into the Wong's front room. They cried loudly as Sau-Ping was carried on the auntie's back like a tired child. Hanging on, Sau-Ping sang in a crying voice her parting song: she had to leave before she could repay her parents for giving birth to her and nurturing her; Tin-Shaang, her younger brother, must be filial to her parents and grow stronger so he could support the family. She cried and cried until her voice went hoarse. Ma also wailed. Sau-Ha should have been at her side but was not; her husband could not spare the loss of her week's wages in Hong Kong.

The young women continued their keening until Auntie Mooi arrived. The minute she walked in the door, they gathered around her. Some pulled at her clothing, some tweaked her ears. Mei-Kuen grabbed a handful of soot from the stove to smear across her face, screaming, "We are taking revenge for Sau-Ping!"

The marriage broker, by custom, was not allowed to fight back. So Auntie Mooi cursed them. "You shameless girls. Do you want Ping to be a spinster for life?"

It was at this moment that a group of young men from Sai-Fok village came marching up the alley. Sau-Ping could see them through the window. A well-decorated sedan chair, its roof hung with strings of multicoloured beads and shells, swayed in their midst like an uncertain boat in rough water. The two sedan chair carriers were wearing smart light blue uniforms. They were both husky fellows, carrying with ease the poles that supported the empty chair. One of them had a face that was dark and wrinkled; his lips turned down at the corners as though he had never tasted mangoes or lichees or red bean pudding or anything sweet but had eaten only bitterness all his life. In spite of his soured face, Sau-Ping sensed attentiveness in this man and was not afraid of him.

When the sedan chair arrived, the villagers of Fung-Yeung all came out to watch.

Clinging onto the auntie's back, Sau-Ping looked at her mother, father, and brother, all dressed in their formal attire. They stood as if for a portrait. Sau-Ping felt someone approach her from the side. She didn't turn her head. A red veil descended over her head and face. It was long enough so that there was little danger of its slipping off during the journey. Now the whole world seemed red to Sau-Ping – the colour of celebration – and her family became shadows, distinguished only by their familiar movements, shapes, and clear voices.

Feeling a gentle tug, Sau-Ping knew Mei-Kuen was at her side, coaxing her to delay the climb into the sedan chair, which was now sitting on the ground ready to receive her. Mei-Kuen's voice demanded, "You think you can have this young woman for free?"

"We will follow your village custom. How much?" one of the young men asked. Mei-Kuen made a gesture with her hand.

"Too much," said the young man. He lifted only one hand, "How about this amount?"

"Add this." Mei-Kuen showed two fingers; Sau-Ping was glad she could see the hand through her red veil.

"Deal!" The packet was given to Mei-Kuen without further deliberation. Mei-Kuen thanked the young man and put the money into her pocket. One of the neighbours handed Mei-Kuen an umbrella – it was also red – which she promptly opened. Sau-Ping sensed the umbrella rising high over her head, sheltering her as she hung childlike on the auntie's back. She was glad of the umbrella: now that she was no longer protected by the ancestors of her own village, special precautions had to be taken to keep evil spirits away until she was safely married into the Leung household. Following local custom, the auntie who was carrying Sau-Ping knelt beside the sedan chair so that the bride could climb in without touching the ground. Mei-Kuen closed the umbrella and climbed in beside her friend. The two husky carriers lifted the chair. Behind them, other men from Sai-Fok fell into line, carrying the trunk and the items of furniture that made up Sau-Ping's dowry. The procession representing the groom's family was ready to return to Sai-Fok village with the bride.

As the party crossed the gate of the Wong residence, someone hurried up to the sedan chair and whispered, "The handkerchief." It was Auntie Mooi's voice.

Sau-Ping pulled the red handkerchief from her sleeve and flung it into the wind. For a second it hovered in the air before settling onto the wet paddy-field, where Sau-Ping pictured it sinking into the shallow water. Her heart twisted. Throwing the handkerchief signified that from then on, she was no longer a member of the Wong family.

The chair swayed beneath her. She sat close by her best friend with the warm veil covering her face. She could smell the damp cloth and the bodies of the men carrying the chair. In rhythm, her body was being carried away from her family.

The contours of Sai-Fok Bridge appeared. A man's voice said, "Madam, soon some rough village men from Sai-Fok will attack the sedan chair; you should hold on tightly to the bamboo handle from the inside. Your feet should be anchored firmly in the corner of the chair. Keep still and don't move."

Sau-Ping had heard about attacks on sedan chairs from some of the married women who returned to the maiden house to visit. One returning young woman told them that she was so shaken by the ruffians from her husband's village that she fell into the paddy-field and lost her red veil.

Sau-Ping waited and waited. All was quiet. She was beginning to feel anxious, helpless. Big Sister had told her that if no boys came to attack the sedan chair, the bride would never give birth to a boy.

Suddenly war cries could be heard from the reaches of a dim bamboo grove. Sau-Ping did not turn her head. Blurred figures swarmed around Mei-Kuen while others shoved the carriers. As her perch shook and tilted and as screams rose in the air, Sau-Ping silently held on. They wanted her to tumble out like an egg. One assailant crawled directly under the chair, shaking the bamboo legs from below. The carriers shoved him, and he wriggled out.

Then four more grabbed the bamboo handles in front and behind and lifted the sedan chair onto their shoulders. The carriers fell to the side acrobatically. Sau-Ping felt herself being lifted with Mei-Kuen on the shoulders of wild men. She hung on for dear life.

At this moment, one fellow jeered, "Oh, the bride looks so ugly. Her head is like a pumpkin and her stomach is like a winter melon!" Sau-Ping heard the sound of sand being thrown into the chair and onto her legs. The earth rolled. Then, moments later, she heard Mei-Kuen say, "They're losing." The chair shifted wildly, while around Sau-Ping victorious shouts split the air, telling her that the troupe of young men who had initially come to fetch the bride from her own village had succeeded in fighting off the toughs.

The gate of Sai-Fok village loomed above her. Through the veil, Sau-Ping recognized the old banyan tree and remembered how nervous she had been when she and her sister had stolen vegetables in this village three years before. Now, like that banyan tree, she had to put down roots in Sai-Fok.

Firecrackers! Snapping in rapid fury right in front of her chair! Sau-Ping was grateful to hear the sudden noise. Firecrackers were set to scare off the wandering ghosts that might have tried to possess her as she moved, unprotected by ancestors, from her own village to her husband's.

The procession stopped. Sau-Ping gazed at the indistinct shape of the modest house before her. Leung Yik-Man's mother lived here, while the men worked in Canada.

Mei-Kuen whispered, "They're taking your dowry into the house. Be still. Wait. Be ready."

"Kick it!" someone cried. "Kick it!"

Her groom was about to kick the door of the sedan chair. Sau-Ping tensed. Married women in her village had told her that one could tell the groom's character from the way he kicked the door of the chair.

A shadowy Yik-Man walked very fast towards the sedan chair. The kick landed. It was nothing like the upheavals they had already passed through. Couldn't he kick hard? Oh, he must be an impatient man, physically weak. He had lived too far from home for too long! Could he be an opium addict?

An auntie from Sai-Fok village took Yik-Man's place at the door of the sedan chair. Mei-Kuen popped the red umbrella open and held it over Sau-Ping's head with one hand, while helping her climb onto this auntie's back with the other. Though the woman was a stranger, her back and arms felt familiar and smelled familiar, like a real person's, not a ghost's. On the doorstep of Leung Yik-Man's house a little heap of dry grass burned vigorously; Sau-Ping caught a glimpse of the flame's true colour under her veil. There was a grunt, a shake; Sau-Ping hung on. The auntie had leaped over the little fire, ensuring that any evil spirits that might have attached themselves to the bride during her journey would be frightened away before she entered the house.

Sau-Ping was set down in the bridal room. It felt odd to be returned to the ground. The veil remained on her head. Mei-Kuen was with her in the room, saying kind things – this was a good village, the groom was handsome, certainly she would come and visit Sau-Ping, they would visit each other.

Sau-Ping was ready. With a light hand, the auntie who had carried her into the house now ushered her into the living-room, which was by now packed with guests. Officiating at the wedding ceremony was the Leung lineage chief, whom Sau-Ping could distinguish because of his long, flowing robe. This man instructed Sau-Ping and the figure beside her – Yik-Man, her still-unknown husband – to pray to the heavens. Moving in unison with her husband for the first time, Sau-Ping kowtowed in the direction of the open door. Then she and Yik-Man kowtowed to the ancestral altar of the Leung family.

Next, they knelt in front of Leung Tsing-Haan, Yik-Man's mother. Silently, Mei-Kuen poured tea and supplied a small dish of betel nuts, which Sau-Ping and Yik-Man in turn offered to Leung Tsing-Haan. In return, Sau-Ping received in her hands a lucky red packet and a piece of translucent jade on a gold chain. Then she and Yik-Man bowed to one another, slowly and without speaking. The lineage chief congratulated the Leung household on its luck.

The kowtow ceremony continued. All of Yik-Man's elder relatives in order of seniority, men and wives together in pairs, received cups of tea from the kneeling groom and bride in turn. When the last of the relatives had drunk their tea and eaten their betel nuts and all the red packets had been given to the bride, the ceremony was repeated with

Yik-Man's relatives of the same generation. For this part of the ceremony, everyone stood.

The great gathering moved outside under a huge tent that had
been erected on the ground in front of the main ancestral hall of the
Leung lineage. Tables and tables of guests were served food. The
ancestral hall would have held them all, but of course women were
not permitted inside. A musical troupe played throughout the meal
as the relatives talked and jested loudly. Sau-Ping was thankful to
have Mei-Kuen by her side, since the village crowd surrounding her
was speaking to itself. No one in the crowd could see if she was smiling or weeping. She herself couldn't see anyone clearly under her veil
and had no way to begin remembering faces and learning names.
Night fell slowly, Sau-Ping was led from the tent to the house and
back into the bridal room, a small haven.

But Yik-Man's male companions spilled through the door like a
pack of tall dogs. They teased and pestered Sau-Ping. The room filled
with the smell of the rice wine they had consumed and splashed on
one another, as they sang:

> The bride steps into your room
> We congratulate you for becoming a dragon;
> You are the dragon, she is the phoenix
> It's like the chrysanthemum and the hibiscus;
> One candle is enough for brightening the room,
> It enables her to powder her face;
> Despite her youth and innocence
> She knows how to make herself beautiful;
> The candle brightens the bridal room
> It shines on the bride and groom;
> With brotherly affection we congratulate you
> For entering a marriage of eternal harmony.

At long last, the guests began to disappear. Sau-Ping discovered
that Mei-Kuen was no longer at her side. Instead, Yik-Man, whose
shape was growing familiar, walked with her into a new room. Sau-
Ping now knew her husband's voice, but she did not yet have anything to say to him. Her mother-in-law carried a pot of sugary tea
into the room. "The two of you should drink this. Your life together
will be as sweet and smooth as the tea." Mrs Leung closed the door
behind her.

Yik-Man approached. The veil rose off Sau-Ping's face and she
saw her husband clearly for the first time. Sau-Ping liked what she
saw. Yik-Man's short hair was combed back with haircream. He was

wearing a well-tailored western suit with a burgundy tie that gave him a powerful shape; he was tall and muscular by local standards. His tie pin and cufflinks were made from agate. The three wrinkles cut into his forehead gave him a mature look. He was not old, ugly, handicapped, scarred, or crazy like some of the Gold Mountain guests who came home to marry. His ears were like those of a calf, very pleasing. His eyes were a bit small. For some reason, his complexion was dark. Was it because of the sun and the wind during the long boat trip home, or was it the smoke from the kitchen of the family restaurant in Vancouver?

While surveying her husband, she noticed that he was also gazing at her. She felt embarrassed and bowed her head.

After a while, Yik-Man found something to say. "You must be exhausted." He poured a cup of sugar tea and put it in front of her. "Here, drink this."

Sau-Ping was impressed by his gentleness. Without the veil, her head felt free. She was becoming herself again, though now she was a married woman. She put down her tea, and poured Yik-Man a cup. "Let's drink together."

After the toast, Sau-Ping quietly walked to the bed, trying to smooth the pillow. The cover was strewn with cypress leaves and popcorn, undoubtedly put there by her mother-in-law as a blessing. Evergreen leaves signified unchanging love, and popcorn signified children bouncing on the bed.

"Ping."

Her husband sounded shy. That proved he didn't have secret Canadian wives – white tall monsters – in Vancouver. With lowered head she murmured an acknowledgement.

"Are you really my wife now?" Yik-Man came close, stroking her hair. Softly she spoke her affirmative. Sau-Ping felt much more definite than she sounded. The ceremony was now complete, every preparation spent, every requirement answered. She had mourned, thrown the handkerchief, climbed into the sedan chair, held tight against a shaking, and kowtowed to heaven, to the Leung's ancestors, and to her mother-in-law. Of course she was his wife.

"Ping, you make me very happy," said Yik-Man. "Look." He bent down and opened his luggage. "You must be hungry. Here, try these crackers. Tell me if you like them." He poured her another cup of sweet tea.

By now, Sau-Ping felt really hungry. She had been roughly handled the whole day and had not had a proper meal. She munched the crackers and found them delicious.

"I ate these on the boat from Vancouver."

"There must be many such delicious things in Gold Mountain," Sau-Ping ventured.

Yik-Man laughed before he could stop himself. For an instant, he reminded her of Little Brother. "Don't believe everything you hear about Gold Mountain."

Sau-Ping raised an eyebrow.

"Every day in Gold Mountain, we work in the restaurant. We purchase groceries, put on our aprons, cook, and serve the customers. We do everything. When there are lots of customers, we run on the slippery floors between the tables, hoping we won't fall." Yik-Man shrugged. "This is the only free time for me since ... There was one day, I was thirteen, we went to the waterfront."

"It is not easy to make a living in Vancouver?"

"It is only slightly better than making a living at home."

Unlike so many other Gold Mountain guests, Yik-Man did not seem to be boastful. Sau-Ping decided that he was an honest person. "How did you make it to Vancouver?"

"When Pa was young there were too many disturbances, so he went to Canada. After a hard struggle, he and Paternal Uncle started a café in Vancouver. When I was ten, Pa borrowed five hundred Canadian dollars to pay for my head tax and my passage to Vancouver."

They sat quietly for a while, drinking their tea. It occurred to Sau-Ping that her husband was fatigued, as she was.

Out of the blue, Yik-Man said, "There is a song."

"What are the words?"

He sang the words under his breath, as if afraid the vanished guests would hear and laugh at him for his need to speak to this girl. The song was not all sweet. Here and there, growls could be heard in the tune:

> Life is tough, Motherland in trouble,
> I planned to seek work in the barbarian country.
> Pawning my treasures,
> I borrowed everywhere,
> Promising to pay exorbitant rates.
> I kowtowed to my parents and said goodbye.
> I bought my ticket directly in Hong Kong.
> I was washed in sulphur solution.
> We first passed by Shanghai.
> After Yokohama it was time to cross the Pacific.
> Clouds darkened, sea creatures howled,
> High waves shot up like a fountain,

Passengers were tossed and flipped
Like children playing on a swing.
Heads spun, vision blurred, stomach churned.
I vomited through the night.

Sau-Ping had crossed her hands over her chest. "Yik-Man," she said, "what have you seen on your trip?"

Her husband shook his head. He opened his trunk and took out a mirror with a wooden frame. "This is your present from Pa."

Sau-Ping understood very well that she and this man, who was both a village boy and a Gold Mountain guest, could not speak about everything at once. Calmly she examined the mirror. "Why didn't *Loye* [father-in-law] return for the wedding?"

"Pa wanted to save his boat fare so that we could have the money for a wedding with eighteen tables and enough for a generous bride price. This will give us face, you and I. He said to tell you that you are like a daughter to him."

"I would tell him thank-you," she whispered.

He touched her shoulder. He touched her hair.

CHAPTER 4

Bandit Attack

Sai-Fok very soon lost its mystery for Sau-Ping. In many ways it was like Fung-Yeung, her former home. Both villages were built close to their rice paddies, and both villages were surrounded by protective moats. The Sai-Fok moat flowed into a river. Inside the moat was a ring of bamboo trees. Richly layered in jade green leaves, the bamboos wound around the village like a lacy scarf.

As a new wife, Sau-Ping was not yet allowed to work in the fields and still had to wear a red gown, but she could venture outside to wash laundry in the streams, carry water home for cooking and drinking, and collect dried grass for fuel. As she moved around doing these daily chores, she noticed that the village was guarded by two fortresslike buildings, the *tiu-lau*. One stood in the midst of the paddy-fields in front of the village, the other at the back of the village. These *tiu-lau* were tall, narrow structures made of solid granite that served both as watchtowers and arsenals. From the roof, sentries could survey the land for miles and warn villagers of impending danger, whether from bandits in the mountains or armed peasants of an enemy lineage. Like those in Fung-Yeung, the few narrow openings in the wall of the *tiu-lau* served as windows, through which members of the village militia could shoot the attackers. Gazing up at the *tiu-lau* one morning, Sau-Ping wondered how it looked to her husband, Yik-Man, who had been away from this place for so long. But she had no opportunity to ask him – Yik-Man was never home. He spent every day with his male friends or visiting various uncles in the village conveying his father's or paternal uncles' regards to them.

Protected by the *tiu-lau*, the moat, and the green belt of bamboo trees was the village proper. Its two ancestral halls, like those in Sau-Ping's natal village, were elaborate and spacious buildings in the traditional style, with beautifully decorated tile roofs. The larger of the two, the main hall, housed the soul tablets of the founders of the lineage, and those of their rich or powerful male descendants and their spouses. The old banyan tree partially shaded the front of the main hall. When Sau-Ping stood for a moment under its many branches, she could look across the huge pond that had been dug right in front of the ancestral halls, in accordance with good geomancy. It was used both as a reservoir for drinking water and for raising fish. Now and again, the broad back of a carp wrinkled the surface of the water. The other ancestral hall was smaller but more elaborate; it housed the tablets of the founders of the second branch of the Leung lineage, as well as those of their illustrious male descendants and their spouses. Both ritual halls faced south, with the mountain at their backs. Behind the smaller hall was the Sai-Fok Primary School, which her little brother-in-law attended every day.

Behind the ancestral halls, also facing south, stood the houses of the villagers; Sau-Ping calculated that there must be more than a hundred dwellings. At one corner of this rural settlement was the so-called New Village, described by Ming-Ming from her maiden house just before Sau-Ping's marriage. Each of its new, pale green brick houses was two storeys tall, so that they stood out conspicuously against the sky. Some of the houses were adorned with multi-coloured ceramic tiles pasted to the brick under the eaves, showing designs of birds, flowers, and bamboo. Each house was fenced, creating a small yard at front and back. Like those in Fung-Yeung, the front gates and front doors were made of heavy iron to protect against thieves and there were iron bars across the windows. Villagers called these buildings *yeung-lau*, or foreign-style mansions, not only because they looked like castles for white princesses but, more importantly, because each had been designed and paid for through the savings of the more affluent Overseas Chinese who had earned their money in cities like Vancouver or Hong Kong.

The rest of the settlement comprised the Old Village, where Sau-Ping's family lived. It was home to the less-affluent families, including those whose menfolk overseas did not earn very much. Here, in the old section, the houses were all of one storey, like Sau-Ping's parents' house in Fung-Yeung. Some were made of baked mud, while others had brick walls and tile roofs supported by wooden beams. Since her wedding, Sau-Ping had lived in a low brick house with her mother-in-law, Leung Tsing-Haan, her husband, Yik-Man, and her husband's nine-year-old younger brother, Yik-Mo. Their house was situated in the fifth of nine alleys that criss-crossed the old section of Sai-Fok.

Sau-Ping, embarrassed by her enforced leisure, looked around for ways to make herself useful. One day, when she was alone in the house, she walked to the pond to wash vegetables and, bending over the water, noticed a colony of water beetles skimming swiftly about in the shallows. Scooping them up with her basket, she took them home to stir-fry for dinner, using her mother's recipe.

That evening, Yik-Man leaned over his bowl and scooped one of the crisp beetles into his mouth. Sau-Ping didn't move. Her husband chewed, swallowed, then smiled: not at her but at his mother. "Ma, these are good," he said. "You should try one."

"They are good," said Leung Tsing-Haan. "I tasted one. But don't waste too much oil, Sau-Ping."

For a few weeks, Sau-Ping returned every day to catch more water-beetles, preparing them for dinner with as little oil as possible. One day, kneeling by the pond, she heard somebody singing softly.

> Sour berries turn the mountain red,
> Some people are rich, some are poor;
> While some forever carry night buckets,
> Others, with stomachs full, gaze through the south window.

Sau-Ping looked over her shoulder. The singer was the man with the bitter face, one of the two carriers of her sedan chair. He was carrying two heavy buckets balanced on a bamboo pole set across his shoulders. A few days before, Sau-Ping had seen him entering the smallest mud hut in the fifth alley, their alley. She had thought at the time that the hut was likely to shatter in the next typhoon.

"Ah Kong!" Another voice. Sau-Ping lowered her eyes to the water, but not before glimpsing a villager about the same age as her husband, whom she knew to be the son of the lineage chief, Leung Kwok-Yung. The son walked like a chief himself, but he had an evil face.

"What the hell are you up to? My father is looking for you! Better go to the main ancestral hall to wash the tablets."

Sau-Ping understood now that Bitter-Face Kong must be a bond-servant, or *sai-tsai* of the Leung lineage. In Fung-Yeung there had been five *sai-tsai* families serving the Wong lineage. "As there are different kinds of flowers, so there are different types of people," Sau-Ping remembered her mother saying. Ma had cautioned her against playing with the children of a *sai-tsai*, lest the neighbours class her with them. The children of a *sai-tsai* were themselves bound to become servants. Their families farmed the land for free and lived in the shabbiest houses for free, but they had to clean the ancestral halls

of their master's lineage and do communal cooking for village celebrations. During the annual spring and autumn worship at the ancestral halls, the *sai-tsai* were responsible for roasting pigs and chopping
up the meat, which would be distributed to the male members of
their master's lineage at the end of the ceremony. They also carried
coffins during funerals and sedan chairs during weddings, thus earn-
ing red packets of lucky money to augment their income. In general,
they could be called upon to work for the members of their master's
lineage at any time.

It had always disturbed Sau-Ping to see a young member of a *sai-
tsai* family bent low under harsh words or heavy burdens, yet she
could not imagine how any village could function without *sai-tsai*:
who would do all the odd jobs that kept the village running?

That evening, to show off her cooking, Sau-Ping decided to make
her mother's special dish, rice hot-pot with sausage. She looked
over her mother-in-law's kitchen and found that all the ingredients
were there. As she pictured herself cooking this familiar dish in a
different kitchen, Sau-Ping felt womanly but also apprehensive;
probably that was why she had decided to fix the dish on an
evening when her husband would not be home – Yik-Man was dining at Shaan-Tai Market. At the same time, Sau-Ping knew very well
that she could make this dish without mistakes. As a girl she had
watched her mother make it many times. As she moved about now
in her mother-in-law's kitchen, she could hear her own mother's
voice chanting out the instructions. "You must be careful to add the
appropriate amount of water. If there is too much water, the rice
will be too soft; if too little water, the rice will be too hard and dry.
First, boil the rice for a little while, then add sliced sausages and
cover the pot. Just before serving, let the contents of the hot-pot
simmer on slow charcoal heat until you see that the colours are
right and the water is gone."

"What smells so good?" Little Brother-in-Law Yik-Mo burst into
the kitchen, looked over the stove, and then settled down, understanding that he could not taste the dish until his family had gathered
for the meal. In a short time, Mother-in-law returned to the house and
entered the kitchen, sniffing. Without expression she opened the pot
to look. "Ah."

Sau-Ping clasped her hands together.

"This is a good dish because it saves on oil," said Leung Tsing-
Haan. "We don't even have to stir-fry vegetables. This is good. We
will eat soon."

Both her mother-in-law and brother-in-law enjoyed the meal. Yik-
Mo had finished his second bowl and the hot-pot rice was half gone

when Yik-Man entered unexpectedly. Sau-Ping blushed to see him. He was a man with good habits, she had discovered, a man who did not return drunk and stinking of rice wine after outings with his friends. "Whatever you cooked smells so good I must have some!"

"I thought you had dinner," said his mother as he spooned hot rice from the pot in steaming clumps.

"But this dish ... It is –" and he said a Canadian ghost word that sounded like a sleepy man mumbling.

Later, alone with Sau-Ping in the bedroom, Yik-Man continued to praise her hot-pot. "If we put this dish on the menu of our restaurant in Vancouver, it would be popular. It could be priced quite high."

"Well," Sau-Ping said gently, "I would cook for you and help in the restaurant."

"I can't take you."

"Why not? Why can't a husband take his wife to Canada?"

"Those white devils have no hearts. They have forbidden the Chinese to enter Canada for many years – I would have needed to marry you when you were on your mother's hip. There have been no new Chinese immigrants to Vancouver for the last ten years. I was lucky to beat the ban by three years."

Sau-Ping did not move. Her eyes became blind.

She had been warned. She had been warned against marrying a Gold Mountain guest. But she had secretly imagined that all the other Gold Mountain guests were merely too selfish to share their fortunate lives in Canada with their wives. Somehow she believed that because Yik-Man was kind, he would take her with him, take her out of his mother's house into a Canada house the next time he crossed the ocean. She realized now that she had been thinking of her mother-in-law's house as a stop on the way and preparing herself, half-consciously, for the great swan's voyage across the water that would truly begin her married life. That was why she had prepared the hot-pot dish on a night when Yik-Man was not expected for the meal, because she wished to behave well and let him know of her ambitions a little at a time; if a young wife begged too hard, too early, she was certain to lose. But Canada was barricaded! It had sentries in its towers and laws written against her. She felt as if she were standing on the edge of a moat so deep and wide that no sound reached her from the opposite edge.

"I will come visit you every few years."

"Thank you."

"Ping."

"Are there men who stay and don't return to the Gold Mountain? Have you heard of such men? This is your village."

"I can't stay. I wouldn't be able to earn much here. We would all be poor, and we would all suffer."

"There are Overseas Chinese who returned for retirement, and they are doing fine," Sau-Ping pointed out. "Your lineage chief, Leung Kwok-Yung, is a returned Overseas Chinese."

"It's true that a lot of Gold Mountain guests come back to retire once they grow too old to work in North America. But Uncle Leung Kwok-Yung told me that his savings cannot stretch very far in Toi-Shaan. He wishes he could send his son and grandson to Canada, but it's against the white man's law."

"I have seen his son. He orders the *sai-tsai* to run in three directions. He looks like one who should go to a bigger place."

"Yik-Faat is a born gambler. Whenever he loses money, he throws a temper tantrum and beats his wife, Sing-Fan, and his two-year-old daughter, Ah Chue. Uncle Kwok-Yung is worried about the future of his newborn grandson. And this is the family of our lineage chief."

Sau-Ping, knowing that her fate was decided, spoke and moved like a wooden puppet thinly covered in flesh. She did not cry. After all, she had been warned. She should have guessed. She should have prepared herself for this cold hour. "Could you at least stay longer this time?"

Yik-Man looked away from his wife. "The restaurant in Vancouver is too busy to spare me for long. Even if it weren't, the longest I could stay would be two years."

"Why?"

"If I stay any longer than that, I have to pay the five-hundred-dollar head tax again to re-enter Canada. It took me ten years to repay the loan Pa got for me to enter the first time. I hope to stay long enough to hear my baby son cry, then I will go back to earn the money to raise him."

Sau-Ping hung her head and nodded. Black hair fell over her face. Yik-Man lifted it in his fingers and smoothed it behind her ears.

She lay in bed that night next to her husband thinking about her future and struggling to contain her heart, which now and then contracted with great pain because it had met injustice. It was not fair that Canada kept out the wives of Chinese men who worked so hard to serve the white ghosts in their cities. Sau-Ping thought of Mei-Kuen, who said that all men were unfair and selfish as cats – especially Gold Mountain guest husbands.

Lying very still, Sau-Ping felt angry, then suffocated, and then proud. She tried to restrain each surging emotion, only allowing herself to drift for a moment in pride. It was possible she had a secret. Her mother had told her how a married woman could watch for children. Two moons without blood. Sau-Ping had watched one full moon grow thin already. It was possible she had sleeping inside her a powerful secret. A boy!

Sau-Ping was pregnant. She spoke to her husband, who responded with joy. The next day, he marched off to consult Uncle Kwok-Yung for a suitable boy's name, which he then planned to report to the Immigration officer in Vancouver to apply for a birth certificate. In this way, he would prepare for the possibility that he might be able to sponsor his son to enter Vancouver in the future. Males of the Leung lineage who belonged to her husband's generation were named Yik. The next generation of males was named Kin. Yik-Man chose the name Kin-On for his son and then checked with the lineage chief to make sure that no other male in the Leung lineage bore that name.

Sau-Ping did not ask her husband what they would do if the baby were a girl. That would have been a bad omen. She expected that she would pick the name of a daughter, if a daughter were born.

Sau-Ping was not sleeping well. She could not stop visiting the dark place where her imagination kept portraits of her future. Soon she would be alone in the house with an aging mother-in-law, a young baby, and a little brother-in-law. There would be no one her own age in the house to talk to. Instead she would have only the long empty gaps between her husband's visits. She hoped she would get along well with her mother-in-law once Yik-Man was gone but feared greatly that she would not. Her mother-in-law was unnecessarily stingy with cooking oil. With her son gone, Leung Tsing-Haan might turn into a woman who beat her daughter-in-law for small mistakes. There were mothers-in-law who hated to see their daughters-in-law shove food into their mouths or pick up utensils in the kitchen. Sau-Ping had heard stories of such women from her sister.

But perhaps they would get along fine. Perhaps, as Mei-Kuen said, this was the perfect life for a married woman: living at ease, essentially alone, while a little stream of money kept pouring into the house from the distant husband.

Sau-Ping was lying one night with her hand on her belly, thinking about such things – her situation with her husband, her situation in the village, Canada, spoonfuls of burnt cooking oil – when she heard the terrible sound of the village gong. She sat up.

It couldn't be bandits.

Bandits kidnapped sons and imprisoned them in houses filled with excrement. They converged on the houses of Gold Mountain guests. Sau-Ping had heard so many stories. Bandits had attacked the village

where her own mother grew up. The head of the bandits was a former member of the village militia. He led the group right into the
house belonging to a Gold Mountain guest. Kidnapped the boy, Chan
Maang-Chiu, her mother had said, and made him sit, tied up, in
excrement.

Sau-Ping felt trapped inside the house of a Gold Mountain guest.

She pushed at the snoring Yik-Man until he woke. "The gong, husband." She swung her legs out of bed and hurried to the door of the
bedroom that her mother-in-law shared with her brother-in-law. Fear
gave her power as she pounded on the door. "The gong, *On-Yan*
[mother-in-law]!" Sau-Ping moved into the front room, lit the
kerosene lamp, and peered outside, into danger.

The moon was shining through the banyan tree onto the main
ancestral hall. Many houses were lit up. This was no dream and no
mistake. People were screaming and yelling. Sau-Ping could hear
doors open and close in the houses surrounding theirs. Down the
alley, she saw a brief line of men trotting towards the pond. Leung
Kwok-Yung, the lineage chief, would be in charge of organizing the
village militia.

It was not Yik-Man's place to run out and fight.

In Sai-Fok, so many adult males had gone to the Gold Mountain
that the lineage chief had used rent revenues from the ancestral land
to hire mercenaries and purchase guns. As Sau-Ping learnt from her
husband, a majority of the members of the village militia were themselves shady characters – former bandits, former police or soldiers,
landless vagrants – anybody who could shoot and kill. Standing in
the open door, she felt that all the barricades around the village had
crumbled. The village lay open and vulnerable.

Gunshots. That had to be gunshots, not firecrackers.

Behind her, Mother-in-law cried, "What's the situation now?"

Suddenly all was quiet from the direction of the *tiu-lau* in front of
the village, even the gongs. Sau-Ping stood next to her mother-in-law
in the open door. Yik-Man dived into the alley to discover news. The
only sounds they heard were whispers across the alleys. "The militia
has deserted," their neighbour called softly.

Catching a hint of movement, Sau-Ping turned to see Bitter-Face
Kong, who as *sai-tsai* should have been defending the Leungs, duck
into his squat secret mud house.

Yik-Man reappeared. "Uncle Kwok-Yung has gone to hide," he
said in a low voice.

With their hired protectors and their lineage chief in retreat, each
family was now on its own. Following the example of their neighbours, Sau-Ping and her mother-in-law extinguished their kerosene

lamp and quickly retreated into the house. Gunshots were coming from the tall houses in the New Village, A woman screamed.

Sau-Ping shivered. She moved little brother-in-law Yik-Mo to the corner where her mother-in-law was crouched and whispered to Leung Tsing-Haan, whose face was as pale as paper, "Take Yik-Mo, sneak through the back door and hide somewhere. In the hay."

"The three of you should hide. I am too old," moaned Leung Tsing-Haan. "Give me a bullet. I don't want to see."

"We are young, we can escape more quickly. Please, go now!" Sau-Ping hurried her mother-in-law and the stunned Yik-Mo out of the back door. "Get inside the haystack and don't move."

Sau-Ping ran to her bedroom, where Yik-Man, sweat dripping from his forehead, was shovelling valuables into a bag. Outside, evil footsteps accompanied the sounds of splintering wood and smashed crockery. There were screams.

"Yik-Man! No more!" Sau-Ping dragged at her husband's arm, and the two ran through the back door towards the bamboo grove. Even in desperation, Sau-Ping noticed that her husband was holding his money bag as she was holding her belly, so that they looked as awkward as a pair of unpractised, thieving children.

Yik-Man whispered to Sau-Ping that two people could not hide in the same spot without being seen. She knew that as a child, Yik-Man had often played hide-and-go-seek in this grove, and she could see that the leaves grew thickly at the top but thinly at the bottom. When Yik-Man took her to a spot among the tall bamboo stems, Sau-Ping instantly crouched there. Then he left her.

Through the stems, she stared at her house. The bandits had already entered and lit the kerosene lamp. She could hear the sounds of destruction and the bandits' excited exclamations at the discovery of some hidden treasure. Sau-Ping stared at the haystack by the back door.

The kerosene lights burnt through the night. Sau-Ping did not see when the bandits departed, but at dawn they gone. Continuous wailing could be heard from the direction of the New Village.

Sau-Ping left her hiding place and made her way home. She went directly to the haystack and found her mother-in-law on the point of suffocation in her hideout. She and little brother-in-law Yik-Mo dragged Leung Tsing-Haan out and into the house; Yik-Man returned shortly after.

The house was a shambles. In the living-room, the eight-cornered table was upturned. The domestic altar that occupied the loft of the house had been disturbed. The statues of Koon-Yam, the Goddess of Mercy, and Kwaan Kung, the God of Loyalty, were lying on the floor along with the four ancestral tablets. These supportive gods and the souls of four generations of Leung ancestors could not even protect themselves, let alone the household. The incense burner that sat in front of the ancestral tablets had been turned upside-down. In the two bedrooms, every drawer, closet, and bed had been emptied and overturned. Everything of value had been taken. From the kitchen and storeroom, dried and preserved vegetables, sweet potatoes, rice – whatever could be carried away had been taken. The bandits had urinated in the iron wok even as the Kitchen God was watching.

Yik-Man climbed the ladder to the loft and respectfully put the statues, tablets, and incense burner back in their rightful places. Sau-Ping lit the incense and poured wine in the two little cups for the ancestors. The whole family knelt in front of the domestic altar, murmuring prayers of thanks to the ancestors that no one had been hurt.

Minute by minute, news arrived at their door. Granduncle Leung Kwok-Wang, the Gold Mountain guest who had returned from the United States to visit his old wife, had been shot; his wife was badly hurt; all their money and valuables had been taken.

For the next few nights, Yik-Man was unable to sleep. He tossed and turned in his bed beside Sau-Ping. When the band played during the funeral procession for Granduncle Leung Kwok-Wang, Yik-Man bowed his head and covered his ears with his fists. Sau-Ping tried to maintain composure for the sake of the baby in her belly. But she would wake up at night unable to breathe, as if a monstrous turtle were sitting on her chest.

One week later, Yik-Man told Sau-Ping the inevitable. "The bandits stole all my savings. I have only enough money to buy a ticket back to Vancouver. I am leaving tomorrow."

CHAPTER 5

Grass Widow

1934

Yik-Man never wrote to Sau-Ping, but she didn't complain about this. Being only semi-literate, Yik-Man would have to get the Chinese Language School teacher in Vancouver's Chinatown to act as scribe. Since Sau-Ping herself could neither read nor write, she would have had to get Yik-Mo, her little brother-in-law, to read it to her. What could Yik-Man have written? Affectionate letters would be embarrassing shared with her mother-in-law and her husband's younger brother, while letters reporting on daily life were unnecessary; Sau-Ping already knew that he would be cooking, serving customers, cleaning, and washing dishes from morning to night.

Every two or three months, Sau-Ping paid particular attention to her mother-in-law's expression after she returned from the market. If the wrinkles around her eyes looked like a blooming chrysanthemum in the evening, it would mean she had collected the usual remittance from Canada at Kwong Wooi Yuen Bank in the market. It would also mean that Yik-Man, his father, and paternal uncle were alive and well in Vancouver. If she returned without a smile, it meant that only a small remittance had been received, which in turn indicated that one of the three Gold Mountain guests in their household was sick. She would ask Yik-Mo to compose a letter.

Leung Tsing-Haan never told Sau-Ping the value of the remittances they received. A daughter-in-law was like a buffalo. As long as there was enough to keep her fed, she should be content.

Six months had gone by since Yik-Man's departure. Sau-Ping learned to live with his absence. She often thought of a dog in her natal village that ran at great speed on three legs and had proven to be not only a good mother to its puppies but a tenacious guard dog as well. It was best to keep moving.

One market day, Sau-Ping was pleased to see the blooming chrysanthemum around her mother-in-law's eyes. She cleaned up very quickly after dinner.

"On-Yan, it is my father's birthday tomorrow. Will you let me visit home?" she requested politely.

"It is important to be a filial daughter." Leung Tsing-Haan nodded. She was resting in the wide chair with her head back, hands folded. She turned to look at her daughter-in-law. "Why don't you spend the night there?"

"Thank you, On-Yan!"

This was the first time since her marriage that she had been allowed to visit her parents. Sau-Ping lay awake that night for hours, unable to let go of her excitement and drift into sleep. The baby in her womb stretched and pushed, as if it could feel her blood sparking. At one point Sau-Ping felt a great hard lump rise just under her ribs. She laid her hand on it, wondering if this was the child's skull or back-side. At last the secret child moved again and settled itself, like a fish returning to the bottom of the pond. The surface of Sau-Ping's belly lay smooth under her hand. Still, her eyes couldn't close. She was going to see her home again.

Early the next morning, Sau-Ping did her usual daughter-in-law's duty. She lit the incense at the ancestral altar, paid homage to the ancestors of the Leung family, and served her mother-in-law the morning tea. Though she had slept very little, she felt invigo-rated.

"Today you don't have to do housework," Leung Tsing-Haan announced, handing Sau-Ping a gift basket covered by a piece of red cloth. "Your body is heavy, you should leave early and be careful."

"Thank you, On-Yan."

"I hope your mother knows your husband does not make money by clapping his hands on top of the Gold Mountain."

"She knows the Gold Mountain guests work into the dark for ghost customers."

Leung Tsing-Haan touched her own chin with the tips of her fin-gers; this usually meant she was thinking about the state of the household. "If they had money now, they could buy better dishes."

Sau-Ping kept quiet. She had never guessed her mother-in-law might be curious about anything. It made her feel queer to think that this woman was also a grass widow who had learned to live joined to a husband who had no smell, no voice, no hair, no flesh: a paper remittance husband. Sau-Ping did not wish to think of herself as an ally or confidant of her mother-in-law. Intimate words, disrespectful words, might sour the atmosphere in the house, and it was necessary that this first year be harmonious. Sau-Ping was relieved when Leung Tsing-Haan turned away.

On her way to Fung-Yeung, Sau-Ping peeked under the red cloth to see what Leung Tsing-Haan had sent her family. A few eggs, a bottle of common rice wine, and a red packet with only four Chinese dollars. Too stingy from the home of a Gold Mountain guest!

Sau-Ping walked forward boldly, no longer feeling herself netted in sticky sympathy for her mother-in-law. They were not girls together. They were not friends. To Sau-Ping, Leung Tsing-Haan was the woman who dreamed of cooking without oil. Half consciously, as she walked, Sau-Ping felt the familiar shapes of her village draw near. She was carrying the baby in her belly, the overnight bag on her back, and the basket on her arm. The mountains moved back into place for her. She passed through the gate and chose a roundabout path to her home so that the aunties would not keep her talking.

As Sau-Ping entered the alley of her natal home, Ma rushed out to greet her. Her strong, tanned arms grabbed her daughter's cloth overnight bag. "Come in, come in, you look tired. What does she have you do? Does she work you like a slave? I will visit her if I must! Your father will speak to her! How many months are you?" demanded Ma.

"Almost seven months, I think."

"You shouldn't have made this exhausting trip home."

"It's Pa's birthday. I wanted to come back," said Sau-Ping as she handed the gift basket to Ma, who immediately pulled back the red cloth. Sau-Ping felt an odd moment of discomfort, as if Ma had lifted her shirt to examine her naked belly.

"Is this all your mother-in-law gave you to take home? For both my daughters, lives of eating dust!" Unexpectedly strong and forlorn, Ma's voice struck Sau-Ping, who felt tears rising.

"No, Ma."

Just then Tin-Shaang came running in, yelling a song at top volume:

> Old Gold Mountain guests,
> Young Gold Mountain guests,
> Houses full of gold, silver, and silk;
> If I don't marry a Gold Mountain guest,
> How could I be so carefree?

Sau-Ping burst into tears. She put her fingers into her mouth and bit down, as she used to do when she was a little girl, but it was no use; she only coughed up more sorrow.

"My poor daughter!" Ma threw her arms around Sau-Ping. "Luckily you are pregnant. If you give birth to a boy, you'll be standing proud like the bamboo tree."

"What if it turns out to be a girl?"

"No. Your stomach is extending sharply to the front. It must be a boy! Come, dry your tears, or the neighbours might think that your mother-in-law has been ill-treating you. At least you are not Mei-Kuen. You are married. You are home. You are pregnant with a boy."

"What?"

"What. What do you ... "

"Where is she?"

Ma was staring straight into her daughter's face. Sau-Ping watched her trying to think of a lie. "I will not tell you," Ma said simply.

"Is she dead?"

"She is not dead. It would be bad for the baby. Where should I put this rice wine?" Ma asked, turning towards the kitchen with the basket under her arm. "The shelf is full of better wine. I have room next to the vinegar."

Mother and daughter spoke sparingly for the next hour. Sau-Ping put her hands to every available task. Then Pa came home from the market, and his face glowed when he found she was in the house. "Is that you, Ping? What a surprise! For dinner we will have all of us together!"

Birthday dinner for Father only meant two extra dishes – fried eggs, and pork hock stew. Silently, just before dinner, Ma displayed the gift bottle of rice wine to Pa, who opened his hands and grinned oddly. Later the wine appeared on the table, and cup by cup Pa drank half the bottle. "Very good wine," he said.

The news of Sau-Ping's visit soon spread. Right after dinner, Wai-Fong looked into the door and announced that she had arrived to take Sau-Ping to the maiden house for a visit. Ma said no, Sau-Ping was tired, she was heavy with child, no. No.

Sau-Ping said, "I am going and I will return early," and she left the house with such momentum that there was nothing her mother could do.

Sau-Ping and Wai-Fong walked the old paths together. From the outside the maiden house looked small. Stepping into its pale green interior, Sau-Ping felt her spirit try to swim out of her body and latch onto the room, hoping to stay forever. But of course there would be no place for a pregnant woman on those mats. Three of the eight maidens were newcomers. Nevertheless, everyone welcomed her warmly. Sau-Ping was given a stool. After a while she said, "And Mei-Kuen ... "

The girls launched into an account of events that had evidently been discussed many times in this room. Assuming that Sau-Ping already knew the basic story, they spoke only of the little mysteries. One of the younger girls said: "Four went out, and only three came back. Mei-Kuen was farther up the path, and the man picked her up like a chicken. Both of her shoes were by the rock. The bandits were afraid of the Fung-Yeung fighters, and that was probably why they hid near the bridge. It had to be the same band that attacked Sai-Fok village. They were like an army, with many regiments. This was not a ghost story. A band of men needed women to boil their rice.

"We waited and waited for Mei-Kuen until dawn for three nights," Wai-Fong added.

Sau-Ping had covered her face with her hands. The night before her wedding she had wailed out her sorrows in this house; now she was unable to speak or sing. She felt someone rubbing her back. It did no good. She was clenched, as if the birth had begun: clenched around her losses. Time passed. Outside crickets sang the same crisp note over and over and over again. Night was arriving.

"It was probably the bandit group from the Taai-Lung Tung Mountains," said the littlest girl, intent on keeping her place in the circle. "Headed by Chan Foo."

"They assured us that the government would catch them soon enough, but seven months have passed and we have heard nothing further. The soldiers and police only came to collect 'protection fees.' They are not going to help," said Wai-Fong.

Sau-Ping was shattered by a sense that there was a titanic empty space that had engulfed, first, her new husband, and now, her best friend. Her tongue uttered plain little facts. "Yik-Man had to leave for Vancouver because the bandits took all his savings."

"They should die by a thousand knives," declared Wai-Fong.

"Are you lonely now that your husband has left?" one of the younger maidens asked.

"Not to worry," another maiden whispered to Sau-Ping, "Wai-Fong might be keeping you company soon."

"You shouldn't tell such shameless lies!" Wai-Fong lunged to poke the quick thin girl. The maidens were ready now to drop the story of Mei-Kuen; they had told it so many times. Sau-Ping, exhausted, was ready to lie down.

"Sleep here," Wai-Fong said. "We have a mat for you."

The next day, Sau-Ping said goodbye to her parents and Little Brother Tin-Shaang. Only then did it occur to her that her mother looked older. There were a few more grey hairs in the bun, which had once been black as ink. The lines in her face had deepened. Her father too had changed since her marriage. His face seemed to have grown longer, his cheeks sallower, his wiry body leaner, almost gaunt, especially in the arms. As for Tin-Shaang, he was already taller, lankier, with distinct shoulders, no longer a little boy. She could not allow herself to dwell on these impressions. Turning her head, she walked resolutely towards her married home at Sai-Fok, not daring to waver. The shadows on the way frightened her, and at one point she glimpsed a man with burnt skin leaning forward out of the woods to watch her. It was a twisted tree.

With the villagers still out in the fields, Sai-Fok was quiet. Sau-Ping sat outdoors on the threshold of her mother-in-law's house. She must have been there an hour, not moving, when the sound of gunshot blasted from the direction of Auntie Leung Siu-Hing's house. She screamed and stumbled to her feet.

Not gunshot. Firecrackers. It was firecrackers. Another wedding. But why were there no guests, no tent, no preparations for a feast? Why was the village empty?

Through the window of the living-room, Sau-Ping saw Auntie Leung Siu-Hing sitting in a comfortable chair. Two other old women stood by her side. A bride in a formal gown, red bridal veil covering her head and face, stood in place for the wedding ritual. Beside her foot, lower than her knee, was a cock; calm for the moment, he looked as if he might fly up into the kitchen shelves at any time. The cock's red crown was decorated with a piece of red silk from which a cypress leaf stuck out. A dark green feather waved from its tail. To Sau-Ping the bird looked haughty and knowing, as if he thought his bride too large.

"First, kowtow to heaven and earth," commanded one of the two women flanking Auntie Leung Siu-Hing. The bride knelt obediently and kowtowed in the direction of the door. At the same time, the other old woman knelt down, grabbed the cock's head, and forcibly pressed the bird to kowtow as well.

"Second, kowtow to the parents." The bride turned around and kowtowed to Auntie Leung Siu-Hing. The cock, a regal puppet, was manipulated to do the same.

"Third, kowtow to one another." And they did, though the cock was beginning to struggle and threatened to peck the hand that held it.

Sau-Ping walked back to her mother-in-law's house and began preparing vegetables for dinner.

That evening she asked Leung Tsing-Haan about the wedding to the absent groom. She heard that Auntie Leung Siu-Hing's son had been in the United States for over twenty years and had neither the time nor the money to return for his wedding. As she felt herself advancing in years, Auntie Leung Siu-Hing had grown impatient. It was Auntie Mooi, the marriage broker, who put her witty tongue to work. She was able to persuade Mrs Ng from the poverty-stricken village of Mei-Leung to marry her daughter Ting-Ting to Auntie Siu-Hing's son, or rather, to the little feathered stand-in.

Sau-Ping stayed up late catching up on the housework after two days' absence. She was struggling to be fair and kind, to be a good daughter-in-law, but the impressions of the last few months weighed on her. Mei-Kuen had been stolen like a chicken ... the veiled bride stood next to a frantic bird held to the floor with two hands. Yik-Man had not bothered to find a scribe to write her a letter. Did all people with authority want girls to be their slaves? Did all absent husbands forget so easily? Sau-Ping raised her face to the window. She refused to become an evil presence in this house. She was fortunate to have been married to a good, handsome man who worked hard and sent remittances. He had given her his seed, and now she held the child inside her body. This muscular, promising unborn baby protected her from the empty darkness.

The twenty-ninth day of the eleventh lunar month in 1934 was unusually cold for Toi-Shaan. There was frost on the ground at night. The next morning, the sun was shining but the air was crisp. The village path became damp and slippery as the frost melted. Sau-Ping carried two buckets of water suspended from a bamboo pole balanced on her shoulders. She had almost made it to the door when a little boy snickered, pointing at her belly. Losing her concentration, she slipped and fell, spilling water all over the ground.

Bitter-Face Kong helped her up; she had not noticed him trudging at a respectful distance behind her.

"Are you hurt?"

"I'm fine," replied Sau-Ping, feeling embarrassed.

Bitter-Face Kong went into the house to fetch Leung Tsing-Haan. "From now on, let me help your daughter-in-law carry water."

A few days passed. Leung Tsing-Haan received a heavy gift basket from Mrs Wong containing a pair of pork legs. Sau-Ping was chopping vegetables as her mother-in-law unwrapped the basket, and she heard the silence that meant that the one woman had delivered a voiceless message to the other. Leung Tsing-Haan threw the cloth back over the great, mottled pork legs and said, "Your mother must have heard that you fell while carrying water into the house. She doesn't need to do this. You belong to our household. Your child will carry our family name. I would never overwork you during your pregnancy. Neighbours who are understanding might think your mother did this to show her concern. Those with a sharp tongue would say that I cannot afford nutritious food for my daughter-in-law."

She tucked a red packet into the gift basket next to the pork legs and then called for Bitter-Face Kong to return the gift to Fung-Yeung. "Please convey our thanks to Sau-Ping's mother," she instructed him. "Tell her that after the birth of the baby, she can send some new clothing and a new sling for her grandchild."

"When that time comes, will you say it is your baby and give it the breast?" laughed Bitter-Face Kong.

Leung Tsing-Haan retorted, "Bitter-Face Kong, if you envy me my grandchildren, why don't you get a wife yourself?"

The flash of resentment in Bitter-Face Kong's eyes passed so quickly that Sau-Ping only barely caught it. She glanced at Leung Tsing-Haan, but the older woman's expression remained impassive and proud. Bitter-Face Kong said a polite "Good afternoon" and then headed up the path leading out of the village.

Sau-Ping guessed that Leung Tsing-Haan had been stung by the perceived insult from her mother, for she decided to make a special trip to the market the next day to get a few young chickens. By the time the baby arrived, these chickens would be of good enough size to provide Sau-Ping with broth and meat during her month of confinement after the birth.

That night, Sau-Ping cooked dinner as usual. As she was scooping rice for her little brother-in-law, she felt a severe tightening across her stomach. She gasped, then closed her mouth tight.

"What?" her mother-in-law asked. "Ping ..."

Sau-Ping moved her hand across her belly.

"You should sit down," said Leung Tsing-Haan. "Let Yik-Mo fill your rice bowl."

Not wanting to reverse the proper order of things as prescribed by her Confucian upbringing, Sau-Ping refused.

"You should listen to your mother-in-law," said Leung Tsing-Haan. "You are responsible if my grandson suffers or is twisted."

Sau-Ping felt the familiar tightening and upward pull between her legs, the same cramp that presaged the arrival of blood. She looked at her mother-in-law, who nodded towards the bedroom. The cramp had receded, and Sau-Ping could walk easily towards the room. It felt good to walk a little. Once she reached the privacy of her room, she squatted, balancing herself on toes and fingers. When the muscles between her legs and up around her belly pulled again, she raised her shirt to look. This white, swollen belly was working on its own to push her child into the air.

Five hours later, Sau-Ping had lost herself. On the rack, she was embraced mercilessly by a pain that still felt familiar, but had grown so intense it terrified her. She wanted to curse her mother-in-law and her own mother. She wanted to fly over the ocean and attack Yik-Man with a cleaver. The touch of the midwife was cruel, like all the other touches she had experienced in this village. She heard the midwife say, "She is young and this is very fast." She knew that her mother-in-law kept wiping her bare legs with warm water. Brother-in-law Yik-Mo had been sent to another house.

"*On-Yan*, it hurts! It hurts!" screamed Sau-Ping when Leung Tsing-Haan rubbed her belly.

"Be patient! This is every woman's duty."

"I want to walk."

They helped her walk. They helped her settle back on her side. Then the midwife pushed her onto her back and pressed open her legs with two iron hands. "Good. You push towards me like you hate me. Good. I am down here. Push towards me."

Sau-Ping was already bent, squeezing her body to expel the weight. Time passed. She pushed repeatedly, furiously against the auntie who waited between her legs.

She felt the head stuck between her legs. She felt the head slip out, and she held herself, panting, in obedience as the auntie did something with fast, iron hands. Another push. Sau-Ping knew the body was out.

"Congratulations! It's a baby girl!"

"Ayee!" Leung Tsing-Haan wailed in disgust.

"How can it be a girl? How can it be a girl?" Sau-Ping cried.

"Boy or girl, it was decided in heaven," said the midwife as she lifted the mottled unwashed baby onto the mother's belly. The twisted, liver-coloured cord that was attached to the baby's centre slid about. Sau-Ping watched it, paralyzed – it looked like a snake. "We are not done," the midwife ordered. "She is very pretty. I tell you, this baby is one of the prettiest I have seen, and no trouble. She will marry a Gold Mountain guest. A fast birth. To the breast. This is yours." With a flick of the scissors, the midwife cut the cord.

The baby was making goat noises. Sliding the slippery child up her body, Sau-Ping suppressed her embarrassment and placed the little animal's face near her breast. The baby fought to move its head and then succeeded. Suddenly its eyes opened. Sau-Ping noticed that the eyes of her daughter were wise and deep.

When New Year rolled around, Sau-Ping was still confined at home, recuperating. Leung Tsing-Haan had regained her composure. Following the ancient recipe, she cooked chicken soup with rice wine and dried black fungus for Sau-Ping, although her face no longer showed the same kind of concern as it did just before the birth.

On the fifth day of the Chinese New Year Festival, a *tang-liu* was set up in front of the main ancestral hall of the Leung lineage. Every year, this temporary hut strung inside with lanterns was constructed to celebrate the arrival of new male members to the lineage for that particular year, be they natural sons or adopted.

On this particular day, in this particular *tang-liu*, six beautiful, multi-coloured homemade lanterns decorated with various auspicious designs dangled from the hooks on the ceiling. Some lanterns were in the shape of yellow butterflies, pink lotus flowers, a golden dragon, or a red carp. Others were decorated with images of the God of Longevity or the God of Fortune.

Sau-Ping, who was allowed out of the house for the first time, stood with a number of other women where they could watch the celebration. In the open space outside the *tang-liu* sat ten tables of male villagers. Since this was the home village of many Overseas Chinese, there were few adult males in Sai-Fok. Most of the men at this community feast were either over sixty or under fifteen years of age. Little brother-in-law Yik-Mo was there. Facing south, in the seat reserved for the host, sat Leung Kwok-Yung, the lineage chief, wearing a long quilted gown made of dark blue silk. By his side sat his son Leung Yik-Faat.

Leung Kwok-Yung raised his cup to the men at the tables. Sau-Ping heard a woman whispering to her friend, "Six new additions. It is like adding six stars to the heavens. He thanks the ancestors."

Many chopsticks dug into the steaming rice. Meat disappeared quickly from the dishes in the middle of the table. Rice wine flowed down the throats of all the male villagers. Even from a distance, Sau-Ping noticed Leung Yik-Mo scrambling energetically for the choicest meat. She turned home. Her daughter was fast asleep, bound to her back with a sling.

Later Yik-Mo arrived home to describe how delicious the feast had been. There had been ten dishes and one soup, all cooked by the *sai-tsai* of the village. The boy talked of pork with salted vegetables, stewed duck, chicken with lotus seeds, fish with black bean sauce. "It's too bad we had no lantern," he remarked.

Sau-Ping was looking at her daughter. There was no need to raise her eyes.

"Ma," Yik-Mo tugged at his mother's sleeves, "go with me to watch the open-air puppet show!"

Leung Tsing-Haan placed her hand on her son's head, bent down and patted his cheek gently without glancing at her daughter-in-law. "We'll be home soon," she said.

After they left, the house was quiet. Having nursed her baby to sleep, Sau-Ping sat at the table in the dining-room, gazing at the four ancestral tablets on the domestic altar. At the sound of footsteps, she looked up and saw the son of the lineage chief, Leung Yik-Faat, staring at her through the dining-room window. She had glimpsed him earlier at the lantern feast sitting alongside his father, but he didn't seem to be a man who enjoyed spending time with his family and kinsmen in the village. When Sau-Ping sat at night on the porch mending clothes, she had heard the gossips in the alley say that the son of the lineage chief was a compulsive gambler who spent most of his time with prostitutes. She remembered his gruff condescension with Bitter-Face Kong.

"What do you want?" she demanded.

"I've come to see if Yik-Mo wants to go with me to watch the puppet show."

"He has left with *On-Yan* already."

"Then you are here alone."

"I have my daughter."

"Can I come in?"

"I don't think ..." began Sau-Ping, but Yik-Faat disappeared from the window and emerged inside the dining-room. He looked lean and handsome in his Western clothes, like an imperfect double of her husband.

"Yik-Man has gone all the way to Canada and left you here by yourself."

"You had better leave," said Sau-Ping.

"New mothers smell like flowers," Yik-Faat laughed.

Sau-Ping's instincts registered the instant he made his move and she lunged to one side, but he grabbed her arm. "Who do you think will lose face? It won't be me," he hissed. Firecrackers exploded outside.

Sau-Ping grunted in rage and bared her teeth. Her animal reaction caught the man off guard. In that same second she heard the voice of her mother-in-law speaking to Yik-Mo about his bare feet. Sau-Ping felt the man's grip waver. Quick as a monkey, he wedged his legs through the open window and slipped after them.

Leung Tsing-Haan stood at the dining-room door. She had seen. Sau-Ping faced her.

"Tell me."

"I wish to make a report. The son of the lineage chief was trying to shame me."

"Is this the first time he's been here?"

"I wish to make an official report."

"To whom can you argue your case? Yik-Faat will accuse you of trying to seduce him. Then you'll be put into the pig basket and drowned in the river."

"Our neighbour Auntie Yuk knows who he is. The village knows what he is like. He is a great weed with black roots."

"I know what he is like," said Leung Tsing-Haan. "I know you did not tempt him. You have lived with me, and though your mother does not trust me, I have eyes. But who will argue your case?"

Sau-Ping stared at her for a long moment and then began to clear the dishes from the table.

Later that night, Leung Tsing-Haan came into Sau-Ping's bedroom to tell her a piece of good news.

"Uncle Leung Kwok-Wing has just returned from Vancouver to spend Chinese New Year with his sixty-year-old mother. He brought home a message from Yik-Man, his father, and paternal uncle."

"Yes." Sau-Ping could not make her face gentle.

"Business is getting much better in Vancouver's Chinatown. Everyone is healthy."

"Buddha has blessed us."

"Yik-Man was able to acquire a birth certificate for his newborn baby under the name Leung Kin-On."

"That is a boy's name."

"Only boys will be sponsored to Canada. He can keep the birth certificate for the future. We will give your baby girl another name. Fei-Yin? Like a swallow flying high."

"Yes. If you wish." It was a lovely name.

"Many young women keep the windows closed. The bad one you met today ..."

Sau-Ping was silent.

"I am glad I arrived when I did from the puppet show. I am not a bad mother-in-law. You are not a bad daughter-in-law. Do you like the name Fei-Yin?"

"Yes, *On-Yan*."

"Do you have enough milk for her?"

"Yes."

Leung Tsing-Haan sighed as if she were weary and left the room. Sau-Ping smoothed the quilt over her daughter.

CHAPTER 6

Better Times

1936

It was the seventh day of the seventh lunar month, 1936. Leung Tsing-Haan had been changeable and sharp since her last visit to the market, where she had received a generous remittance accompanied by a letter, which she must have taken to the market scribe for an immediate reading. Sau-Ping had noticed the letter with the familiar stamps lying on the chest in the front room of their new house, but she had refrained from asking for news. It would come.

All indications showed the family was thriving and the restaurant in Vancouver doing quite well, and for many months her mother-in-law had been cheerful, even generous. The two women, mother-in-law and daughter-in-law, had decided to host a party to celebrate the Hat-Haau Festival, the annual union of the Cowherd and the Weaver. This was their first opportunity to invite friends into their newly constructed *yeung-lau* in the New Village. Financed through the thriftiness and hard work of the three Gold Mountain guests in the family, the two-storey house was an impressive sight. Decorated outside in tiles brightly painted with scenes of fish, mountains, and willow trees swaying in the wind, it looked handsome as an embroidered panel. The inside was clean and spacious.

But a piece of worrisome news had arrived, and their preparations for the celebration were marred by Leung Tsing-Haan's preoccupation with her secret. Sau-Ping believed that the news would be divulged to her at a moment when it would be most painful – not because her mother-in-law was cruel, exactly, but because Leung Tsing-Haan had for so many years been dependent on communications from her distant husband that she had grown touchy and susceptible and required occasional release for her feelings. On those occasions, a daughter-in-law proved a handy target.

But now the earliest female guests had begun to arrive for the celebration; the weather was beautiful and the evening promising. Sau-Ping's heart lifted as she surveyed the handsome offerings and prepared to celebrate the tragic love story of the daughter from heaven and the buffalo herder from the fields who managed to meet, in the dark sky, once a year – the seventh day of the seventh month.

"What happened to that friend of yours from your home village? Didn't you invite her to celebrate Hat-Haau Festival with us?" Leung Tsing-Haan asked, pulling Sau-Ping away from the guests for a moment.

"Wai-Fong? I don't know why she isn't here. But now that I think about it, she never comes when I invite her."

Leung Tsing-Haan replied crossly, "I thought the girls from your village were better brought up than that."

Sau-Ping remembered that Wai-Fong hadn't invited her to her wedding two years earlier. But of course at that time Sau-Ping was still in her one-month confinement after giving birth and too polluting to visit anyone, let alone attend a wedding. She kept these thoughts to herself.

"Badly bred," her mother-in-law declared. "So what is her excuse this time?"

"I don't know," said Sau-Ping. "I'm sure she must have a good reason."

"Her name is Wai-Fong?"

"Yes."

"Ah. Auntie Yuk was talking about her the other day. She and her husband are not coming up with the rent for the land they farm. They gobble up all the food before putting any aside to pay their rent and debts. Please don't invite her again. She is a poor companion for my son's wife."

"Wai-Fong and I lived together in the maiden house in Fung-Yeung. We will always be friends." Sau-Ping spoke softly, but she did not mean to yield in this; she would never uproot Wai-Fong from her affections. She recalled the night Wai-Fong had crouched beside her in the maiden house when she learned that Mei-Kuen had been taken by bandits, disappearing into the air. She had known Wai-Fong since they were children. They had shared the same mat for three years in the maiden house. In fact, Sau-Ping realized, Wai-Fong had been a close companion far longer than her husband had been.

"I wonder if she is as disobedient as you are." Leung Tsing-Haan returned to the pavilion that jutted out into their front yard. The guests had congregated there, admiring the mung bean sculptures that Sau-Ping had begun preparing three days earlier, clipping at the fresh, thick mung bean shoots that had been planted in reed containers. There was a design of two dragons playing with a pearl, there was a peacock showing off its fanlike tail, and at the end of the display, Sau-Ping's elaborate favourite: a hundred birds paying homage to the phoenix.

Sau-Ping wished Wai-Fong would show up, if only to prove her mother-in-law wrong. They now lived in the same village but rarely saw one another. It was surely not the case that Wai-Fong was badly bred. But Sau-Ping knew that Wai-Fong's husband, Yik-Hung, was the son of an Overseas Chinese living in Kuala Lumpur. His father had deserted the family when Yik-Hung was about twelve, and Yik-Hung had finished only three years of schooling at the Sai-Fok School. Since then his family fortune had declined steadily. He and his mother became tenants, renting six *mau* of the corporate land belonging to the second branch of the Leung lineage in Sai-Fok. They paid half a year's rent as a deposit in order to have the right to rent the land. Then they paid fifty percent of the harvest twice a year to the corporate land manager as rent. Sau-Ping had also heard that Yik-Hung beat Wai-Fong whenever the family's cash or food supplies dwindled. He had borrowed money to finance the wedding and therefore felt justified in blaming her for his family's predicament.

According to the neighbour across the alley, Wai-Fong's family was so poor that their only source of meat was the portion of roast pork Yik-Hung received twice a year from the main ancestral hall during the spring and autumn festivals. Leung Yik-Hung had the opportunity to eat well at village feasts held at the ancestral hall or the *tang-liu*. He felt indebted to the lineage elders for letting him bid for lineage land and for providing him with occasional heavy meals. Sau-Ping wondered how long it had been since her friend had sat at the table and eaten until she was satisfied.

Of course it had occurred to Sau-Ping that Wai-Fong might be too embarrassed to visit her. Even now, Sau-Ping herself sometimes felt lonesome and pale in the large new house, like a single rice grain rattling around in a decorated bowl.

Just then, Chun-Fa and Fei-Yin came into the kitchen. Chun-Fa was a lively little girl with beautiful small hands, always full of questions; she had been born a year earlier than Fei-Yin. Fei-Yin had grown from infancy into a clear-faced, thoughtful child.

"Auntie, what is Hat-Haau Festival?" asked Chun-Fa.

"Didn't your Ma explain to you?" Sau-Ping was very fond of this little girl who lived in the *yeung-lau* next door. "All right, I will tell you the story of the Weaver and the Cowherd. Sit here." Sau-Ping allowed the children to hoist themselves onto the stools as she began telling the story.

"The seventh daughter of the Mother of Heaven was a very skilled weaver. It only took her one night to finish weaving nine rolls of silk. The designs of flowers, grass, insects, and fish that were woven into the silk all looked alive. The Mother of Heaven was very proud of her.

"One day, the Weaver saw an orphan boy working very hard taking care of the buffalo, and she fell in love with him. She came down to Earth to meet him. They were married and had a son and a daughter. They lived happily together. But in their happiness, she neglected her weaving, and he forgot about tending the buffalo." Sau-Ping's nose and eyes were prickling. She raised her head and continued, glancing outside to make sure her mother-in-law was occupied with her guests. "This upset the Mother of Heaven, who sent heavenly soldiers to drag her daughter back. The Cowherd could not stand being separated from his loving wife. He carried the two children in a big basket and flew to the sky. Seeing that he had almost caught up to the Weaver, the Mother of Heaven waved her jade magic wand. The Milky Way appeared in the Heavens, like an ocean of stars. It was so stormy that the Cowherd could not get across. However, the kind-hearted new moon took pity on the lovers. She asked the magpies to build a bridge on the seventh day of the seventh lunar month so the Weaver could meet the Cowherd once a year."

"Why are you crying, Auntie?" Chun-Fa demanded.

"For very foolish reasons." Sau-Ping quickly wiped her tears with the sleeve of her silk top. "Auntie is not feeling very brave today."

"What does 'brave' mean?"

"It means accepting what comes your way."

"Oh," said Chun-Fa. "Why is this festival called Hat-Haau?"

"Hat-Haau means to beg for skills. We women beg the Weaver to bless us with embroidery and weaving skills."

"I don't like to do that," said Chun-Fa. "I like to play in the paddy by the big stone." She gave a great yawn.

"That is well and fine for now, but you should learn or you won't find a good husband when you grow up. When I was little, my mother made me learn."

"I want to go home now," Chun-Fa said, climbing down from the stool.

As she reached out to help her own daughter get down Sau-Ping experienced a rush of love that suddenly became a decision. Quietly she asked Fei-Yin to go to their room while she took Chun-Fa home. "You can look through my drawer," she called, as Fei-Yin took off. Sau-Ping explained to her protesting mother-in-law that she was taking the tired little girl home and headed down the broad alley to the decorated front door of Chun-Fa's house. After a brief conversation with Chun-Fa's mother, Sau-Ping marched off towards the section of the village where the roofs were low and the walls plain.

Though she had never visited Wai-Fong before, she knew where her friend lived. Wai-Fong's house was small and windowless and consisted of just one room, which meant that family members sleeping on the wooden beds would breathe smoke from the stove. The outer walls were made of poor-quality brick, and there was no stone foundation above the ground. The cheap soft wood used to make the pillars and beams would easily rot. In such a house, the family could not afford kerosene and would light the room instead with a soya bean oil lamp.

Sau-Ping knocked at the door. A woman opened it a crack and peered cautiously out. When she saw who it was, she opened the door wide and stood in the narrow entranceway with an embarrassed grin on her face. "Sau-Ping! What are you doing here?"

Wai-Fong's face looked lean and drawn. Her hair was knotted into a loose bun from which long strands hung limply over her ears. Her hands were wet from washing dishes or vegetables in a little wood basin in the kitchen. Sau-Ping could see past her friend into the airless living quarters. There was a plain wooden table and beds decked with piles of crushed straw.

"It's good to see you," Sau-Ping said. "It's been a terribly long time."

"Two years," said Wai-Fong.

"All this time we've been living in the same village." "I'm married," said Wai-Fong. "Marriage changes people."

"It hasn't changed you," said Sau-Ping, lying to save her friend's face, "not even a little."

"Yes it has. Ping, what a storyteller! Look, I'm becoming an old lady before your very eyes."

"You are the same girl I shared a mat with in the maiden house in Fung-Yeung. And I will be insulted if you don't come to the party my mother-in-law and I are hosting to celebrate Hat-Haau Festival. At this moment." Sau-Ping reached out and gripped her friend's right arm. It was thinner than she'd expected.

"Surely you can understand why I've refused your invitations."

"I am lonely some days for friends," said Sau-Ping earnestly. "We have so much food, and I did mung bean sculptures. To show off for you! Remember my hundred birds?"

"One wounded buffalo on three legs," Wai-Fong said, her eyes sparking mischief. "Just give me a moment to dress. I'll come."

Sau-Ping felt an unhappy moment of relief when her friend's door closed and she could no longer see the gaunt, mean house.

Wai-Fong emerged looking much neater and nicer than her dwelling. The two young married women walked arm in arm all the way to Sau-Ping's new home. They talked about old times, good and bad.

"Have you heard anything about Mei-Kuen?"

"No, nothing. Her mother died last winter. She never recovered from the shock."

"Ping! There you are," cried Leung Tsing-Haan the moment the two arrived. "Bring the sweet cakes, the black jelly, and the fruits outside. Did Fei-Yin run away? Did you leave anyone to watch her?"

"She's in my room."

Wai-Fong had clasped her hands together and was laughing. "The phoenix! Ping! That's very good! It even has wings this time!"

Brightened by joy, Sau-Ping bustled into the kitchen. The party had begun in earnest. Playing her part as proud owner of this new residence, her mother-in-law would soon forget Wai-Fong's arrival. Wai-Fong had good manners and a kind smile when she listened to other women. A girl was expected to be loyal to her maiden house companions.

The celebration stretched into the night. Three teenagers from the nearby maiden house came to join the party, bringing their sewing boxes with them. By the pale light of the new moon, they tried to pull the multicoloured silk threads through the tiny eyes of the needles. Then it was time to pray to the Weaver. Sau-Ping took the lead in the singing.

> We beg for sewing skills
> We beg for a beautiful face
> We beg for a compassionate heart
> We beg that our parents may live for ten thousand years
> We beg that our friendship may last for ten million years

As the women sat sewing and embroidering, Leung Tsing-Haan was suddenly inspired. She swept around the circle and commanded the young women to sing another "begging" song.

> Lighted by a silver lantern and a silvery moon
> Sisters are sitting in front of the altar
> We beg to marry a good husband
> And live happily in a *yeung-lau*.

Sau-Ping, with Fei-Yin on her lap, sang this chorus more loudly than the others. Everyone laughed as they sang along, even Wai-

Fong, who was certain never to live in a *yeung-lau*. Watching her thin generous friend, Sau-Ping reminded herself that absence did not rule her life. She sang for the reunion of the Weaver and the Cowherd. The beloved scent of her daughter warmed the night.

Sau-Ping expected that she would have to pay for her hours of rebellion and enjoyment, but she did not expect her punishment to come so soon. Later that night, after the guests had dispersed, Sau-Ping sat in her bedroom straightening the odds and ends in the drawer that her daughter had toyed with earlier in the day. Fei-Yin was asleep in bed. Sau-Ping was tranquil. When the knock sounded on her door, she was mildly startled, but not afraid. Her mother-in-law had obviously been delighted with the party and the boisterous singing. She had savoured her hours of pride.

Leung Tsing-Haan entered in the shadowed room. She had a piece of paper in her hand. "Ping, we have to buy you a son."

Sau-Ping's spirit froze. "*On-Yan*. I am only nineteen."

"It will be a long time before Yik-Man comes home, I think." Leung Tsing-Haan powered forward; the decision had been made. "By my calculations, he and his father have spent most of their savings on this new house and the twenty-five *mau* of land we purchased. They have no savings left for a boat passage."

"Does it cost less to buy a new family member than to bring an old one home?"

"Where did you learn such cheek?" Leung Tsing-Haan spoke, her jaw clenched and lips quivering in rage. "There's something else I should have told you a long time ago. Why I worried about sparing your selfish feelings, I don't know. I went to see the fortune teller last year, and he said that you are fated to give birth only to girls. If only I had known this before I consented to the marriage!"

"*On-Yan*, the fortune teller must have made a mistake!"

"You must consider the future of the Leung household now. You think you are a maiden, you think you are your mother's daughter. No. You live here. We feed you. I have given birth to two sons, Yik-Man and Yik-Mo. I have done my duty by their ancestors. But Yik-Mo is only twelve. It will be a long time before he is ready for marriage. And who can tell whether the restaurant in Vancouver will make enough money ten years from now to finance a wedding for Yik-Mo? If we don't buy a son for Yik-Man, who will take care of the incense burner at the domestic altar?"

"We should discuss this with *Loye* and Yik-Man. I can hire a scribe. I can find –"

"This is not necessary. Yik-Man's father already raised it in his last letter. He has no grandson. He recommended we buy a boy from elsewhere, not adopt in Sai-Fok from the proper generation. Whomever we choose we will displease others. And there is more."

Sau-Ping did not move.

Her mother-in-law was shaking the letter with cold fury, a soldier's fury. Her voice was harsh. "Paternal Uncle was contacted by the lineage chief, Leung Kwok-Yung. He has offered his own grandson, Kin-Tsoi, to Paternal Uncle for adoption. This gives Kwok-Yung and his viper son, Yik-Faat, a place in our family fortune. If your husband has no son, it is the son of Yik-Faat the gambler who will inherit everything. Their whole family stand under the money tree with their arms open. The restaurant in Vancouver – the dishes, the table, the place – the work of all my husband's life!"

Sau-Ping felt the mammoth costly new house tipping in a way that nauseated her. She was nothing, she was worthless, she was to blame.

"So I have decided. Bitter-Face Kong will help. I will ask him to come with me. He will keep his eyes open for us in Shaan-Tai Market and help us select the healthiest-looking little boy. Without a man to handle this transaction, we could be cheated. We could get a cripple strengthened by medicine for ..."

"*On-Yan*, I am tired."

"So am I, daughter-in-law."

Leung Tsing-Haan walked over and extinguished Sau-Ping's only light. Sau-Ping sat in the dark room next to an invisible, disordered drawer.

Over the next few months, Sau-Ping heard her mother-in-law's adoption story many times at dinner. She herself had not accompanied Leung Tsing-Haan and Bitter-Face Kong to Shaan-Tai Market. She learned that on the side of the road, her mother-in-law had spotted a large jolly-looking man who had a young boy with him. It was obvious the boy had been stolen and was now being offered for sale. Leung Tsing-Haan gestured to Bitter-Face Kong, who approached the man. The bargaining started. At one point, Siu Kong asked the little boy to walk to the auntie buying pears. The boy walked to Leung Tsing-Haan, who could see that he was not crippled and that his eyes were clear. Soon the price was set: one hundred and ninety *yuan*. Bitter-Face Kong counted out the money and took the little boy by the hand.

Leung Kwok-Yan and Yik-Man were ecstatic when Yik-Mo sent a letter to Vancouver announcing the new addition to the family.

Listening to the tale over and over, Sau-Ping found herself being won over eventually, not by fatigue, but by the child. As Leung Tsing-Haan spoke, the little stranger, with his thin arms and large belly, his black round eyes, his scratched right hand and new name (Kin-Pong), stood clutching the arm of his new grandmother's chair, listening to her words. Watching the child, whom they had now washed and fed many times and dressed in spanking new clothes fit for the son of a Gold Mountain guest, Sau-Ping knew she was kin to him. They had both been adopted. This was their home by habit, and because they had no other place to go.

Under Leung Tsing-Haan and Sau-Ping's care, Kin-Pong soon grew stronger. He addressed everyone confidently as Grandma, Ma, Big Sister, Uncle. One evening, Sau-Ping discovered herself proudly contemplating the fact that next spring her family – this family – would be able to hang a shining lantern in the village *tang-liu*.

CHAPTER 7

Wartime Famine

OCTOBER 1939

Possibly because he had been stolen from his natal home at such a young age, Kin-Pong was a remarkably undemanding child. Leung Tsing-Haan doted on him, often buying him toys and candy that she would never think to purchase for her flesh-and-blood granddaughter, Fei-Yin. Sau-Ping had expected such behaviour, for of course boys were more valuable than girls, but the situation often made her feel irritated with the stranger's child and full of pity for Fei-Yin. This was not good; a mother had to know the laws of good behaviour and relay them strictly to a daughter for the daughter's own sake. Sau-Ping guarded against her natural preferences. As tradition demanded, she took the best possible care of Kin-Pong and forced a certain humility on her own daughter. But in her heart she could not say she loved the adopted boy, though she still felt kinship with him in his loneliness.

"Eagles! Look!" shouted Kin-Pong. He was sitting on the embankment between the fields where the rice had been harvested, and where now sweet potato vines covered the dry but soft earth. In his hands was a red and orange kite that Leung Tsing-Haan had bought him at the market the previous week. Sau-Ping looked where he pointed. Far away, great winged creatures soared through the sky, and she gazed at them from where she stood between the green sweet potato mounds. The eagles did not fly like birds. There were black specks dropping from their bellies.

Thunder rolled over the mountains and dark grey smoke appeared in the sky under the clouds. Sau-Ping suddenly started running towards the children, crying, "Bombs! It is bombs!" Throwing down her hoe, she grabbed Kim-Pong and Fei-Yin, half-noticing the crushed kite on the ground, brilliant as fire. Instinctively, she turned to see whether other women were running for shelter.

But most of the older women stood in the fields like stalwart buffalo, gazing at the mountains where the thunder had begun. A few bent over their hoes and continued weeding between the sweet potato plants. One auntie called to her, "It is far away. Have you trampled your plants?"

Sau-Ping bent down and picked up her tools. Her mother-in-law had left the field for a few minutes to rest; that fortuitous departure had probably saved Sau-Ping from a sour tirade. Slowly she let go of her fear as her arms returned to work. Kin-Pong was shaking out his broken kite. Fei-Yin kept her frightened eyes trained on the distant mountains. The eagles had disappeared.

"Aunties, Sisters, the Japanese have started bombing us. You should keep watch," Bitter-Face Kong cried from the top of the path.

"Ayy," the women called at him. "Go where you are needed." They continued working.

Through the course of the afternoon, however, the explosions grew louder. Some women left the fields with their children and returned to their homes, but Leung Tsing-Haan told Sau-Ping to keep working, reminding her that ceasing to work would do nothing to help the situation. They left the field at the proper time and walked home along the familiar path at a familiar pace.

By the end of the week it was hard to work in the fields. The sound of bombing from nearby villages had increased to an ugly, unnatural, mechanical roar that seemed impossible: it contained such cruel power. Black smoke rose from the hills and altered the smell of the air. But Sau-Ping and Leung Tsing-Haan both found it hard to sit at home. Sau-Ping understood they felt the same dread and shame at the thought of crouching for shelter in their *yeung-lau*, which from a certain angle looked like a perfect target for the enemy. With hands unoccupied, their worry grew all the more acute. Their sleep was continually disrupted by the relentless sounds of Japanese night raids, so that night-time became an exhausting ordeal, filled with whispers, fragments of troubled sleep, and the shivering of frightened children.

One afternoon Sau-Ping was working in the fields with her mother-in-law when she heard the thunder of warplanes so close that she thought the noise would tear the ears off her head. BOOM! The earth shook, and devil's smoke rose from the direction of Shaan-Tai Market. Another BOOM, more smoke, then the planes lifted into the sky. This time Leung Tsing-Haan and Sau-Ping ran away from the field and hurried towards home, Sau-Ping carrying Kin-Pong while

Fei-Yin struggled to keep pace. As soon as they entered the *yeung-lau*, Sau-Ping spotted her brother-in-law, Yik-Mo, crouched under the eight-cornered table. He must have rushed home from Tuen-Fan Junior High School in Shaan-Tai Market. A young man of fifteen, he was too old to wail, but his hands covered his face. Sau-Ping crawled under the table on her knees. "Your eyes! Show me your eyes! Your face!" He bared his face and looked at her. He was clean and whole.

"He is fine. Untouched. Perfect," she called to her mother-in-law, who was screaming.

"They bombed our school," Yik-Mo called to his mother. "The teachers had us hide in the basement and then we were sent home. I wasn't touched. Parts of Shaan-Tai Market were hit. The teahouse near the school is a heap of rocks and sand." To Sau-Ping he whispered, "Coming home past the market, I saw a woman without a leg. She was sitting in blood."

The full extent of the day's damage to Shaan-Tai Market remained a mystery for a few days, as Sau-Ping and Leung Tsing-Haan stayed close to the house and gathered rumours from their neighbours. They learned that some shops and teahouses in the town of Shaan-Tai had been destroyed. Eventually, they gained the courage to venture outside, but the bombing continued intermittently for two months throughout the region. Two newly established markets in the vicinity, Taai-Tung and Ting-Kong, were both destroyed. Though Sau-Ping didn't know it at the time, the bombs were slowly killing off the tap root that sustained her family in the village.

One evening Sau-Ping was telling stories to the children when Bitter-Face Kong came looking for Yik-Mo on Uncle Leung Kwok-Yung's behalf. Sau-Ping's mother-in-law stood in the doorway. "What does the lineage chief want from my youngest son?" she asked.

Bitter-Face Kong said, "He is asking only the best and the bravest young men of the village to take it on. It will be a great act of patriotism."

"Come now, Ah Kong," said Leung Tsing-Haan, "you don't need to sweeten the news for me. What is it?"

Bitter-Face Kong answered plainly, "The Toi-Shaan government has asked every village to supply fifty men to help dismantle the stretch of the San-Ning Railway and the motor roads that pass through their village. To stop the Japanese. Otherwise we will be meeting them at the gate, like the bandits."

"No. You want Yik-Mo. No. He is the only man in our house. Let the lineage chief send his own son, who is so slippery no Japanese will catch him."

Bitter-Face Kong waited. He did not try to push his way inside or to beat down this mother with words. The struggle was not between Siu Kong, the messenger, and Leung Tsing-Haan. Both knew it.

Sau-Ping's mother-in-law stood squarely, her arms wrapped across her chest. She was breathing rapidly, as if she had just climbed a mountain. "We have given much to the village. We have been respectful to those above us and gentle with those below. I would gladly send my son on this patriotic expedition, but he is only fifteen years old. And he is the only man in the house. Surely Uncle Leung Kwok-Yung would not think of leaving a household full of women and children defenceless in these times. Tell him it would be better to make this request to families with more than one son, or at least, more than one man in the household."

"Auntie, I could not agree with you more," replied Bitter-Face Kong. "If it were up to me, the slippery one you mentioned would be the first to go. He is over twenty years old, and he is strong and able-bodied. But in the end, Uncle will bully both you and I until your response is positive."

"How can I send my son to dismantle the railway and roads that have been built with money earned through the hard labour of the Gold Mountain guests from our district?"

Bitter-Face Kong said, "I won't be the one to force you to send your son, Auntie. I wish you a good night." He stepped from the lighted doorway into the dark narrow lane.

As Leung Tsing-Han turned away from the door, she noticed Yik-Mo stood directly behind her, barefoot, in his nightclothes. Mother and son were staring at one another.

"Call him back, Ma," said Yik-Mo.

"We give to everyone! We have nothing for ourselves! We –"

"Ma," said Yik-Mo, "the Gold Mountain guests don't live here. They don't know what the Japanese are like with their planes and bombs. These people are dead ghosts in flying machines. They don't even see the dead they make. I won't let them come into this village on roads we left open because we thought they were too pretty to ruin. Better to tear off our own legs and live on crutches than to die with our pretty shoes on."

"You are the man of the house now," said Leung Tsing-Haan uncertainly, trying to plead with him.

"Yes." He turned. Sau-Ping who overheard the conversations knew Yik-Mo was going to dress himself and search out Bitter-Face Kong, who would be advancing down the alley. She rose to make tea for her mother-in-law and herself.

For a number of months, Yik-Mo rose every morning at dawn to join the work crew that sledgehammered away at the carefully crafted rails of the San-Ning Railway. When the work took him too far from the village, he camped with other men beside the track; they took turns keeping watch at night for bright lights in the sky.

But this last-ditch attempt to deter the military advances of the Japanese army failed. Word had it that the Japanese had pushed through into Toi-Shaan County in the spring of 1941. While the chill of winter was still on the ground, they attacked and held Toi-Shaan City to the north and Kwong-Hoi Town to the south for eight days before they retreated.

The summer was peaceful. Like locusts, the Japanese had risen into the sky and flown elsewhere.

But at the end of the summer, the Japanese forces entered Toi-Shaan City for the second time. For seven days, there was heavy fighting at Tau-Shaan and Chung-Lau Heung in the southern part of the county before the enemy finally retreated. People said the surrounding villages suffered heavy losses. Every time the Japanese came looking for members of the underground resistance, they looted, burned, killed, and raped. They sliced women the same way they sliced their beef.

In December 1941 the Japanese took control of Hong Kong from the British and decreed that, because it was British currency, Hong Kong money was not allowed to circulate in Hong Kong or China. Sau-Ping and her mother-in-law heard of these events a month later, when their neighbour, Yik-Kwong, was forced to close down his money-changing business in Shaan-Tai Market. Listening to Yik-Kwong, Sau-Ping felt her strength evaporate.

"The Japanese have occupied Hong Kong? Goddess of Mercy, my sister and her family are in Hong Kong!"

Leung Tsing-Haan gripped her arm. "Tonight Yik-Mo will write a letter for you to your brother-in-law. "

Early the next morning, Leung Tsing-Haan left home for Shaan-Tai Market. She was going to post the letter Yik-Mo had written and collect remittances from Kwong Wooi Yuen Bank. In the late afternoon, Sau-Ping was returning with Fei-Yin from the field. She saw her mother-in-law approach under the shadow of one of the largest *yeung-lau*. Leung Tsing-Haan's face was frozen, her mouth strangely slack; she did not glance into her neighbour's windows as usual. Without a word, Sau-Ping followed her into their house, saying quietly, "*On-Yan*, you must be tired. I will make you tea." Her mother-in-law sank into a chair.

As Sau-Ping was heating the water, Leung Tsing-Haan spoke: "Kwong Wooi Yuen Bank was closed. The Japanese have Hong Kong and Southeast Asia. No remittances can reach us."

Sau-Ping approached her mother-in-law and began to massage her back. She was oddly calm. In the back of her mind, she had understood this loss was coming. The net of offices that bound their household to the Gold Mountain husbands had been torn by the Japanese bombs. "There must be some other way ..."

"Does one of us swim the ocean?" asked Leung Tsing-Haan.

It was the first joke they had ever shared.

That night at dinner, Fei-Yin was eating quickly and a grain of rice fell onto the floor. Leung Tsing-Haan's strong farmer's hand shot out and grabbed the rice-bowl from the child. "You go and eat the wind! Maggot! Our rice bucket is almost empty!"

Fei-Yin began to sob. Sau-Ping quickly picked up the grain of rice, blew on it, and put it into her daughter's mouth. She did not protest against her mother-in-law's rage, knowing it had been fed by terror. The price of rice had been increasing over the last few weeks, and now, if they were to receive no remittances ...

The next day, Sau-Ping visited Yik-Kwong's house to learn more of the network of money offices beyond Shaan-Tai Market. Sitting with her tea, she heard from his wife, Yi-Lin, all the facts that her husband had brought home from the market. Yi-Lin said that the Tin-Shing Wholesale Company in Toi-Shaan City had been hoarding rice since last year. It secretly transported rice to occupied zones in exchange for opium. As a result, the price of rice had skyrocketed. Six months before, it had cost about twenty-one *yuan* per *taam*. Now, in the middle of January, it had suddenly risen to 110 *yuan* and it might keep going up. Sau-Ping and Yi-Lin spoke quietly to one another; for both had children and both understood the impending disaster – the hunger that resulted from battles between emperors – better than they had understood the bombs.

Within days, every household in the New Village was taking jewellry from the family safe and fancy clothing from trunks, even pieces of furniture, to sell at the Shaan-Tai Market in exchange for rice. It was clear some families were trying to hoard rice themselves. Panic had taken root.

Sau-Ping and Leung Tsing-Haan soon found out that selling fancy clothing and fine furniture offered no easy way out. Practically all the richer families in rural Toi-Shaan that had relied on remittances from North America, Southeast Asia, and Hong Kong were now reduced to poverty, and they all had valuable items to sell. Where would one find buyers?

At least for the time being, Sau-Ping's family could rely on their twenty-five *mau* of land for food. Without remittances from Vancouver, the family had to fire the two farm labourers from Yeung-Kong County. Sau-Ping accompanied her mother-in-law to tell them. Anxiety marked the faces of Ah Kwai and Ah Tsaan as they moved around inside the brick house in the Old Village where Sau-Ping had lived as a new bride. The farmhands touched their belongings in despair; they would be packing that afternoon. All four understood that for Ah Kwai and Ah Tsaan, there would be no other jobs, and no other house.

Increasing hardship changed people in different ways. One neighbour, normally gentle and soft-spoken, could be heard screaming at her children for no reason. Leung Tsing-Haan vacillated between bouts of selfish rage and moments of courage. But it was Yik-Mo, Sau-Ping's brother-in-law, who altered the most radically. Work on the railroad had hardened him, and as their family fortunes took a drastic turn for the worse, he turned to face the consequences and help the family. At eighteen, he was completely shaken out of the comforts of being an "Overseas Chinese dependent," and it seemed to Sau-Ping that he stepped out of his mother's protective shell in one deliberate move and emerged wholly formed, as a young man. He took over management of the farm and showed patience with the younger children.

The spring of 1943 was exceptionally dry. Not a single cloud roamed the sky. Every day, the sun looked like it would never set, and its rays pierced the fields like hot arrows. The paddy-field cracked into a million pieces, so that the devastation in the fields reminded Sau-Ping of the devastation left by the bombs. The earth was like granite. You could cry, you could wail, you could pray, but there was just no way you could dig the soil or transplant rice.

The price of rice shot sky-high. It was the one thing in China that grew. In Shaan-Tai Market it went from 110 *yuan* per *taam* in late 1941 to 700 *yuan* the following summer, then to 1,500 *yuan* after the peanut harvest, at the beginning of 1943. Yik-Mo kept track of the prices on a calendar, so that Sau-Ping and Leung Tsing-Haan could watch to see if the price had dipped. But it never did. People took empty sacks to Shaan-Tai Market to buy rice. They returned with the same empty sacks.

"Ping, go buy some rice. Our rice bucket is almost empty," urged Leung Tsing-Haan.

"*On-Yan*, rice is now very expensive. Why don't we buy sweet potatoes?"

"Sweet potatoes are not cheap! They cost 1,100 *yuan* per *taam*. With rice, we can at least add a lot of water and dig roots to add to the pot. That would stretch our food."

"*On-Yan*, Yik-Mo told me yesterday the price of rice has jumped again. He said that there were three different prices in one day – 3,100 *yuan* per *taam* in the early morning, 3,300 *yuan* in the late morning, and in the afternoon it cost 3,500 *yuan* per *taam*!"

"Where are we living?" Leung Tsing-Haan whispered to herself. Sau-Ping noticed the older woman's eyes were blurred, and she looked away.

Every member of Sau-Ping's household knew that they were facing disaster but hoped they could outlast the war through skimping, hard labour, and invention. In mid-1943, the government allowed people to change Hong Kong dollars into Chinese *yuan* at the rate of one dollar to 4.91 *yuan*, but each person could change only $250. With five people in the household, Sau-Ping took home 6,137.50 *yuan* from the office at the market; her mother-in-law did not have the strength to go that day. At the current price, this was not enough for two taam of rice. Even if they stretched it out with wild vegetables and a lot of water, it would only last them two months.

"We have to sell the twenty-five *mau* of land. It is the only way to get money to buy more rice. We had better do this fast, before the price of rice rises again," Leung Tsing-Haan told her family. Her voice had no power behind it: no rage, no courage.

"Ma," said Yik-Mo, "if we sell all the land we have, Father, Paternal Uncle, and Big Brother will be ashamed of us for acting like pigs with our snouts in the bucket. Let's sell ten *mau* first. It may rain next year, and we can plant again."

But the heavens were not kind. Planting time in 1944 was as dry as the previous year. It hurt Sau-Ping's legs to walk on the field, as if she were walking over solid rock. Her family sold the rest of their land. They also sold their *yeung-lau* in the New Village and moved back to the old brick house that had been vacated by the two farmhands.

One morning, Sau-Ping knelt in front of the ancestral altar. She had just finished a prayer for rain when she heard the voice of her own younger brother outside. She stumbled up and ran to the front door. Tin-Shaang was talking to Yik-Mo. With great effort she kept herself from crying out. She could hardly recognize her brother. A young man of twenty-one, Tin-Shaang was reduced to skin and bone. He was naked from the waist up and wore a pair of torn pants that hung over his thighs like a great belt of rags.

"Sister!" said Tin-Shaang, his face deeply lined with despair. "Ma, Pa, and I are going to leave Fung-Yeung and look for food elsewhere."

"Merciful Koon-Yam!" Sau-Ping whispered. "Where will you be going? How will I ever see you again?"

"Sister, we don't know. We'll go wherever we can find food. We will all starve if we stay. Why aren't people in your family leaving?"

"If we leave now, the three Gold Mountain guests in Vancouver will not be able to send us remittances when they are allowed to again. We must stay here for their papers to find us." For some reason, it was this declaration rather than the terrible sight of her brother that brought the tears into Sau-Ping's eyes. She heard the foolish old hopes in her own words and felt her heart split by sadness. She let the tears fall, blinking rapidly so that she could keep sight of her brother. Tin-Shaang was too tired to wish her luck or happiness. He had already begun to walk away.

She watched as his shape became smaller and smaller. Soon it disappeared into the bamboo bushes beyond the village gate. Since the Japanese occupation, Sau-Ping had received no news of Big Sister Sau-Ha and her family in Hong Kong. She walked into the room she shared with the children, shut the door, crouched on the mat, and began to moan and cry, calling out the names of her family.

Leung Tsing-Haan exploded through the front door, beaming. "Oh, Merciful Koon-Yam! We are saved!"

"*On-Yan*! A remittance?"

"No. But news came that the Toi-Shaan government is going to sell us grain at thirty percent lower than the market price. But we have to register and pay a deposit first."

Everyone followed Leung Tsing-Haan into the room as she continued, "Uncle Leung Kwok-Yung will be responsible for collecting the deposit from the residents of Sai-Fok. He will register for all of us at the Toi-Shaan government. He promised we will receive grain ten days after the registration. We have enough. We have the deposit. We must. What do we all have?"

"What about your gold ring?" She turned to ask Sau-Ping.

"But that's the ring Yik-Man gave me as a wedding gift!"

"Have you seen your children? Their eyes are drying up like the eyes of dead fish!" Leung Tsing-Haan screamed.

Sau-Ping took her ring to Shaan-Tai Market to sell that afternoon. Very few people were there. Since 1941 the market town had lost nearly all its muscle. The teahouses, once noisy and crowded, had either been bombed or gone bankrupt or were failing rapidly. The wives of the Gold Mountain guests were thin as shadows and pale as paper as they tried to sell their household and personal effects at the pedlar stands.

Sau-Ping took her ring to Kam-Sun Jewellry Store. "Boss, please give me a good price for this."

"It's only ten carat gold," said the proprietor, without paying much attention.

"No, it is twenty-four carat! It even has a Hong Kong trade-mark."

"Everybody says the same thing." The proprietor turned the ring this way and that, pretending to look at it closely. "The most I can give you is a thousand *yuan*."

"That's not even the price of one third of a *taam* of rice!"

"You can check elsewhere. This is my firm offer."

Sau-Ping took the offer. She had already asked for an estimate at three different places in Shaan-Tai Market.

Six weeks passed. No news arrived about the low-priced grain. Yik-Mo and Sau-Ping walked together to the home of Leung Kwok-Yung.

"Here you are again!" said Leung Yik-Faat as he opened the door. "My father isn't home."

"I don't believe you." Yik-Mo pushed Yik-Faat aside. He and Sau-Ping entered the living-room.

Uncle Leung Kwok-Yung was sitting in a broad chair with his hands draped over the armrests like an old emperor's. "I have gone to Toi-Shaan City several times to hurry them up. I cannot do any more than that."

"Our rice supply is almost gone!" cried Sau-Ping. "Could you at least lend us a bit of grain?"

"Look, Auntie, I do not operate a grain shop. I don't even have enough for my own family. Please leave!" Leung Kwok-Yung got up. Yik-Faat approached, his eyes blazing, as if they had insulted his father.

Sau-Ping and Yik-Mo had to leave empty-handed. As they walked, Yik-Mo covered one of his eyes with his hand, a habit he'd got into when the terrible headaches had begun. Sau-Ping was not sure she had the strength to walk to their old brick house. She suspected that the lineage chief had cheated them and there would be no rice. Somehow, she and her brother-in-law managed to reach the house. Fei-Yin sat in a corner, sewing. The girl's hair had grown dull, and she performed her housework and farm chores far more slowly than she had a year earlier. Her legs were thin.

One week later, as Sau-Ping was sitting near the window, she heard the sound she had been expecting. The gong, struck again and again, screams and cries accompanying each new report. The gong announced that the Japanese were coming to the village. Foreign men with guns and knives were marching over the familiar fields to the very gates of Sai-Fok.

There was no need for the lineage chief to organize a retreat. The inhabitants of the one hundred and twenty-three households living in the village rushed out like swarming bees. Parents and grandparents, pack-sacks on their backs, took young children by the hand. Children cried and adults shouted as everyone trotted in a jumbled riot away from their homes, out into the wilderness.

Sau-Ping's family put their clothing and quilts into two bags. The heavier one was carried by Yik-Mo, the lighter by Leung Tsing-Haan. Sau-Ping put the pots and pans and their last ten sweet potatoes into two baskets that dangled from the ends of a bamboo pole and balanced the pole on her shoulders. Kin-Pong and Fei-Yin carried their own bundles.

As the family passed though the narrow alley leading to the village gate, Sau-Ping looked on the banyan tree to the side of the main ancestral hall. She realized it had been eleven years since Yik-Man kicked the door of her sedan chair. Here. In this village. If her husband were to come back to Sai-Fok from Vancouver's Chinatown, would he be able to find her ever again? There would be no markers, no documents, only rubble and an awful collection of doors inviting the long-awaited guest into a village of empty rooms.

CHAPTER 8

To Yeung-Kong County and Back

NOVEMBER 1944

Since 1940, motor roads and the San-Ning Railroad in Toi-Shaan County had been completely dismantled. As a result, there were no buses or trains for transporting goods or people. However, the railway station in Toi-Shaan City remained one of four pick-up points for refugees trying to flee the county. From other refugees, Sau-Ping learned that people from all parts of the county were evacuating areas under threat from the advancing Japanese forces. In small family groups, they rushed to Toi-Shaan City on foot.

After fighting their way through the crowd on a long tortuous journey, Sau-Ping's family finally reached the railway station, only to find that thousands of refugees of all ages were already there. People were trying desperately to get onto pedicabs, rickshaws, and even wheelbarrows, which they hoped would take them to connecting points for northbound buses to Shiu-Kwaan in northern Kwong-Tung (Guangdong) or to Kwong-Sai (Guangxi) Province.

Sau-Ping put down her baskets. It would be next to impossible to get everyone in her household onto the same vehicle. Yik-Mo and the children sat on the curb. Sau-Ping helped Leung Tsing-Haan unload her pack-sack and knelt to massage her mother-in-law's legs, which had once been strong as banyan roots but were now spotted with blue.

"Ping," her mother-in-law said hoarsely, "you should give the children and Yik-Mo each a grain-husk biscuit. They must be hungry."

Yik-Mo and Kin-Pong wolfed down the biscuits. Fei-Yin, her throat parched from the long dusty journey, found it hard to swallow hers. As she slowly took a third bite, a pair of dirty hands snatched the biscuit away.

"You monkey, how dare you steal my daughter's food in broad daylight!" cursed Sau-Ping as she chased the skinny girl. The thief quickly dodged into the crowd. Raging, Sau-Ping sprang onto an open crate to see if she could glimpse the girl over the shoulders of the crowd. Everywhere she saw people loaded down with so many baskets and shawls and packs that it was impossible to see their faces. One woman carried a tall boy dressed in spotless silk; terrified as a great baby, the boy clutched his mother's neck as if she were walking him into high waves and deep water. Another woman caught Sau-Ping's eye. She showed more energy than most, and her face was easy to see because she carried only a small pack on her back. For a second Sau-Ping was certain that the girl child next to her was the thief, but the face of the child was too square. The eyes ...

Sau-Ping gasped as she stared at the rough, wizened face of the mother. "Mei-Kuen?!" she shrieked. "Mei-Kuen!" She struggled off the crate, forgetting everything, and fought her way toward her friend. "Mei-Kuen! Mei-Kuen! It's Ping. Stop! Mei-Kuen!"

Sau-Ping was slapped in the face by a woman whose child she had accidentally pushed, but she fought forward, crying her friend's name. At last Mei-Kuen turned. She paused and then shrieked hoarsely, lifting both her arms above her head. "Sau-Ping! Sau-Ping! Phoenix bird! Aye yi yi yi!"

Muttering and laughing, they gripped each other around the waists, their eyes closed. It was minutes before they unlocked, and Sau-Ping took a close look at her friend.

Mei-Kuen had lost a lot of weight. Her eyes were sunken and her cheeks looked pale and purplish. She blinked frequently in a way Sau-Ping didn't remember. But some things remained the same: the inflection of her voice, her direct smart gaze.

"And this girl?" Sau-Ping pointed to the child at Mei-Kuen's side who appeared to be about nine years old.

"That's my daughter, Lai-Sheung. We have been living in the mountains, my friend. Don't ask me anything more. I am alive and it is impossible, but ..." Mei-Kuen threw back her head and laughed. "We are alive. Don't ask me any more. Chan Foo is dead."

"Come with me. Come. I have a family. I have a daughter!"

"You have lost them scuffling for me!"

"Follow me." Sau-Ping began to fight through the crowd with her friend and her friend's daughter behind her. "How long have the two of you been at this railway station?" Sau-Ping asked loudly over the noise of the crowd.

"Three days! Lai-Sheung and I have been trying and trying to get onto a pedicab, but we get pushed off every time."

They were stopped. Sau-Ping caught a glimpse of her brother-in-law and waved wildly to attract his attention.

Mei-Kuen was speaking. "I am determined to fight my way to make sure that Lai-Sheung and I get on a pedicab today."

"There is my brother-in-law, with the short hair. I have two young children and my mother-in-law. We couldn't possibly make it as a group. There must –"

"We cannot go together. You should walk to Yeung-Kong County. It is the next county to the west of Toi-Shaan, just over the mountain. I saw many Toi-Shaanese people heading in that direction."

Sau-Ping had heard about Yeung-Kong County. The two hired farmhands, Ah Tsaan and Ah Kwai, had come from Yeung-Kong. They had been experienced with such crops as sweet potatoes, yams, taro, mung beans, and red beans, all familiar foods.

"But if we ..."

Just at that moment, a pedicab arrived in the station not far from where they stood. Mei-Kuen cried, "I will see you, friend! You brought us luck!" and gripped her daughter and began battling towards it. Sau-Ping found herself buffeted by quilted bodies and baskets and cackling, barnyard voices as she tried, without thinking, to follow Mei-Kuen. Then she stopped. Not so far away, her old friend was fighting to drag herself and her daughter onto the pedicab. They were pushed off again, again, and again. Without warning, they stuck to the side; someone had opened a handhold. Mei-Kuen managed to wave at Sau-Ping. The overburdened vehicle lurched forward in slow motion, listing dangerously. Sau-Ping turned towards her family with a great effort. She could not watch this departure.

She drifted towards Yik-Mo, who scolded her when she appeared, yelling that the frightened Fei-Yin had tried to grab the hem of her jacket as she ran off. Fei-Yin had nearly been trampled before she let go, screaming that her mother was lost forever. Sau-Ping looked at her daughter, saw that the child was exhausted after her hysterical bout, and said sternly, "I would not leave you. Behave. There is no mercy here for crazy girls. Do you understand me?" Fei-Yin didn't move, but her eyes absorbed the message. Then Sau-Ping turned to Yik-Mo. "I met a person with authority who says we must walk to Yeung-Kong County. Our group is too large for a pedicab. You can see."

Yik-Mo looked around dazedly. "You tell mother," he said. "She listens to you."

Hours later, Sau-Ping and her family were walking step by mechanical step on the small road to the southwest of Toi-Shaan City. They didn't have to ask for directions: they were literally pushed along by the crowd.

Four days of walking brought them to Yeung-Kong City. It was evening. The family stopped to rest at a street corner. A few yards down the road was a building with a sign that showed it was a rooming-house. Sau-Ping spotted an advertisement on the wall and asked Yik-Mo to read it to her. "A group of young women from Toi-Shaan," it said, "have newly arrived at our rooming house. They are all lovely wives of Gold Mountain guests. For a small fee, we have been acting as job brokers for them. The price we ask is low. Those interested should talk to our manager."

Sau-Ping talked over the message with her brother-in-law. She felt that she had to act quickly because of the waves and waves of new immigrants pressing behind them, all looking for chores, food, slight chances. "Maybe someone is looking for a housemaid, or a farmhand. No matter how tough the work is, I can surely handle it."

"I should come with you."

"No. I can handle it. I want them to see I can work by myself. Look for another sign for yourself."

"Listen and watch their faces. Listen hard," said Yik-Mo. "Come speak to me first before you put your mark on anything."

"Unless there are fifty after me!"

She went into the rooming-house by herself.

In front of the registration desk stood ten or twelve women. The manager wore a long gown. He eyed each woman up and down as she approached the desk and asked her questions about her village of origin, age, and family situation.

By the time Sau-Ping had reached the front of the queue, the line of women behind her stretched to the door. She answered the questions she was asked and then took a breath and asked one of her own. "Sir, where are you taking us to work?"

"Paat-Po Town, Kwong-Sai [Guangxi] Province." The manager laughed. "Don't worry. You'll be kept very busy there."

Sau-Ping nodded, keeping her concern to herself. She didn't know where Paat-Po was, but she had never imagined leaving Toi-Shaan County. The distance would be great – not so great as the flight to Canada, but difficult to reverse.

"Not that far, not that far!" assured the manager, "There are over one thousand Toi-Shaanese workers there already. A few work as traders in the town itself, while most others work in a mine in the vicinity."

Sau-Ping was about to ask for more details when someone tugged at her sleeves. She turned to find Yik-Mo, her brother-in-law, with terror stamped on his face as if he'd slipped on a mask. "Sister-in-law, Fei-Yin is in excruciating pain. She is groaning and moaning. Come!" He gripped her arm. "At once."

Sau-Ping stumbled out the door, losing her place in line, thinking how enraged she would be if her daughter was indulging in another hysterical outburst.

There on the street stood Fei-Yin, thin and pale, calmly weaving three pieces of grass together for her little brother. Sau-Ping cried out but Yik-Mo said, "Hush. Did you want to be a slave, Sister-in-law?"

"What?"

"I spoke to a refugee who noticed that we had read the sign. According to the *Taai-Tung News*, the Toi-Shaan miners who lost their jobs in Paat-Po Town of Kwang-Sai Province have come back to act as vultures in their own county. They know the Gold Mountain money has dried up, and they try to lure the wives of Gold Mountain guests by promising them good work. Once these victims follow the swindlers to Paat-Po, they are sold to pimps who in turn would sell the women into prostitution for ten thousand *yuan* each. They are no better than the Japanese devils. Many hundreds of women have been taken to Paat-Po. That rooming-house is notorious. They should burn it."

"What are you two whispering about?" Leung Tsing-Haan demanded weakly. "Am I to take care of the children forever?"

"*On-Yan*, this town is unsafe."

"Then we will leave it," said Leung Tsing-Haan, more firmly than either Yik-Mo or Sau-Ping expected. She lifted her bundles. They hoisted theirs. The children followed, noses forward, pathetic as worn-out little dogs.

They followed mountain passes for the next two days and finally found a piece of land where they could set up a temporary shelter made of grass and branches.

With Yik-Mo as the leader, the whole family prepared the soil and planted the eyes of the last ten sweet potatoes they had brought with them. While waiting for their first harvest, the family gathered tree bark, leaves, grass roots, and wild plants for food. They dug up the edible roots of *shaan-nam*. They also consumed *pa-tsui*, the coarse, tough plant with the circle of bitter leaves, and *to-fuk-ling*, a tender root that didn't need to be ground between rocks but could simply be boiled and eaten. Both children and adults woke up some mornings with twisted, watery guts, and little Kin-Pong spent three feverish days vomiting and gagging long after his stomach was empty. It was Leung Tsing-Haan who crouched over him hour after hour. Watching her mother-in-law bent over the dry little body on the mat, Sau-Ping recognized that there was a store of loneliness in this woman, who had not seen her husband or eldest son for so many years. When at last Kin-Pong sat up, it seemed that Leung Tsing-Haan declined, as if the sadness and devotion she had used on this child had broken down her last defences and left her very weak.

One late afternoon, when Sau-Ping was still searching for something they could eat, she came across a farmhouse. The owners must be prosperous, she thought, since their field was full of food crops – sweet potatoes and melons. Sau-Ping went up to the gate to see if the farmer would be so kind as to give her family some leftovers.

Suddenly, she heard angry voices. "You damn thief, trying to steal our sweet potatoes!" Sau-Ping saw a little boy run out of the back of the house, shovelling an uncooked sweet potato into his mouth. An old farmer rushed out after him with a hoe. He caught the boy. With a few strokes, the victim fell to the ground, his skull hacked in two like a fallen melon.

Sau-Ping was stunned. Trying to get away, she slipped and fell down the slope. By the time Yik-Mo found her and carried her back to their temporary shelter she was trembling and moaning, and it hurt to open her eyes. She felt herself being dragged downwards by years of unspoken thoughts and horrible visions. Time spun away from her. When she came around, Yik-Mo told her that she had been crazy for two days. On the first day, his mother had walked several miles, trying to find the right kind of herbs for her, and Fei-Yin had sung her to sleep one night. Sau-Ping remembered nothing but the hallucinations – monsters squatting over her, squeezing dead children out from under their wings – and then the returning sensation of cold and hard ground.

Winter came and went. Bit by bit, the weather grew hotter and unbearably humid. Just as Sau-Ping began to recover, the months of hard labour and poor diet started to take their toll on Leung Tsing-Haan. She had cycles of hot flashes, when her body temperature soared, and cold flashes, when she shivered incessantly under all the coverings they could spare. These bouts came more and more frequently. Wild herbs picked from the mountain slopes did not seem to help.

One summer day, Sau-Ping panicked when she touched her mother-in-law's forehead, which was hot as a wok. Certain that Leung Tsing-

Haan had caught malaria, she sent Yik-Mo to Yeung-Kong City to fetch some quinine with money they had earned from occasional farm labour.

He did not return that night, or the next day, or the day after that. Sau-Ping could barely contain her fear. It was difficult for her to speak to the children. She bathed her mother-in-law's face, arms, and legs with water. Fei-Yin watched over her grandmother when Sau-Ping went to look for food, which was now a little more plentiful since certain farmers whose harvests had been good gave their bruised produce to the refugees they favoured. After much searching along the mountain slopes, Sau-Ping was able to find *shau-woo*. She boiled it with sweet potatoes, hoping it would provide relief for her *On-Yan*'s malaria attacks. When she hunted for food and medicine plants and roots, Sau-Ping never walked near the farm where she had seen the child murdered with a hoe.

It was on the morning of the fourth day that she saw her brother-in-law propelling himself with tired steps towards their shelter. He carried no bottles of quinine.

"The Japanese have evacuated Toi-Shaan City!" he called from a distance, waving both arms hysterically. "We can go back. Can we carry Ma? She can go back home!"

"What did you say!" Sau-Ping couldn't believe her ears.

"At Yeung-Kong City the whole market was filled with people yelling and shouting. There were firecrackers exploding everywhere. The Japanese devils have surrendered to the Allied forces! We can go home now. Tell Ma we will carry her home. I will carry her like an auntie carries the bride."

In less time than it would take to boil a pot of water, the whole family was packed. Sau-Ping carried the two baskets full of pots and pans on her bamboo pole as before. Fei-Yin and Kin-Pong, now eleven and ten years old, carried the family bedding. Yik-Mo carried his mother, Leung Tsing-Haan, on his back.

As they progressed along their path, Sau-Ping came to realize that it was the thirtieth day of the sixth lunar month – the middle of the Chinese lunar year. Every settled family in Yeung-Kong County was observing "Wai-Heung Day." Local myth had it that the King of the Earth was required to make his semi-annual report to the Jade Emperor on this day. Because the King of the Earth was gone on his trip to the Heavens, all the ghosts, demons, goblins, and monsters would emerge to create havoc on Earth. To prevent them from entering the home, every family burned incense at every corner. They tightly locked the doors and closed the windows. Secure indoors, they would grind black sesame seeds and cook them into sweet soup. The evil spirits would not dare enter for fear that they would fall into the sweet black sesame soup.

That evening, Sau-Ping's family entered a mid-sized village looking for help. Leung Tsing-Haan's body temperature was at boiling point; Yik-Mo said he could feel it through his clothing. She muttered and groaned. Sweat fell like rain from her forehead into Yik-Mo's hair and down his shoulder. Sau-Ping and the children knocked on several doors, trying to get some help, but none of the doors was opened.

"They think we are demons," said Yik-Mo. "I feel like a demon."

"This is too much for me," Sau-Ping whispered. She gave up even trying to keep her sense of direction and turned aimlessly down an alley. The family followed her.

Sau-Ping cried out, "I am a daughter-in-law who cannot find help for my *On-Yan*. Will no one give her some water? We will stay outside the door."

One door opened by a narrow slit. A pair of eyes peeked through. Sau-Ping walked towards the light as quietly as she could and said, "Please auntie, I beg you. Do this good deed for us. My *On-Yan* is sick. Could you please give her some water and a bit of dried sweet potato?"

The older woman opened the door halfway, whispering, "Poor you. I see you take care of the old and the young. I would like to help you, but the neighbours would blame me if evil spirits hung onto you as I let you through the door. I have a little shed in my garden plot out in the field. You can spend the night there." Two arms pushed out, hurriedly offering plain gifts. "Here's a pot of tea, and a few dried sweet potatoes. Buddha bless us! Please go."

The family made its way to the shed far behind the house. The next morning, Leung Tsing-Haan felt a bit better. She had slept on the hay stored in the shed. Rolling over, she whispered, "Yik-Mo, let's go!"

"But you still have a fever." Sau-Ping felt her mother-in-law's forehead and pressed her hand on her upper arm.

"Never mind. Never mind. I can make it. There could be a remittance. Maybe many remittances after these many months."

The family thanked the kind woman who emerged that morning with the rest of the villagers to resume their occupations now that the demons had gone. For the next eight days Sau-Ping and her small band walked and walked. Finally they entered familiar territory, crossing the Sai-Fok moat with its bamboo grove, passing by the old banyan tree at the side of the main ancestral hall of the Leung lineage, and at last walking down the alley to the little brick house in the old section of their own village.

Maybe there was a demon on the doorstep.

Yik-Mo caught his foot as he stepped over the wooden bar across the threshold. He fell with his mother on his back. Leung Tsing-Haan's head hit the wall, and she was knocked unconscious. She never saw the inside of her own kitchen.

Three days later, Leung Tsing-Haan was dead, and for three days after that, the kerosene lamp in Sau-Ping's house burned continuously. Following village custom, Leung Tsing-Haan's body lay at the entrance to the living-room and the rest of the household kept watch through the nights.

Over the next few months, Sau-Ping, Yik-Mo, and the children moved forward with great effort, trying to rebuild their lives in Sai-Fok. The paddy-fields had been trampled and denuded. Many of the village buildings were burnt-out carcasses.

Sau-Ping felt no great shock when she opened the door one morning to her own brother, Tin-Shaang, whom she had not seen in over a year. He looked unimaginably worn and empty. He told her that their parents were both dead; that they had been trapped between Japanese and Chinese forces while searching for food near Tau-Shaan Heung. The same explosion had killed them both, though it took their mother longer to die.

Listening to her brother, Sau-Ping tipped back her head and began to wail.

CHAPTER 9

The Post-War Years

THE FOURTEENTH DAY OF THE SEVENTH LUNAR MONTH, 1946

A new tablet had been added to the loft in Sau-Ping's brick house in the Old Village; it was Leung Tsing-Haan's. Sau-Ping lit two candles and several sticks of incense and pushed them into the bowl of sand in front of the ancestral altar. She knelt down, facing the ancestral tablets. She kowtowed three times and burned ritual money that had been folded in the form of silver and gold ingots. Amidst the fire and the smoke, Sau-Ping could call up Leung Tsing-Haan's face, a network of wrinkles and anxiety anchored by two stubborn eyes.

It was the night of the Hungry Ghost (*Yue Laan*) Festival for the dead and for wandering ghosts. Sau-Ping was not the only one who prayed in front of the domestic altar. Every villager performed the same ritual at his or her own home. There were many wandering souls in 1946, all products of the Japanese invasion. A major flood and typhoon that had battered their district two months before had also caused extensive damage, and the village as a whole felt that it was imperative, especially this year, to hold a solemn ceremony to ensure their ancestors' well-being as well as to appease the ghosts and wandering spirits.

Yik-Mo was now head of the household. Being a young fellow of twenty-two, he often consulted Sau-Ping when making major decisions. Following village tradition, he considered his sister-in-law, now twenty-nine, as his surrogate mother. The two were more like equal partners.

Sau-Ping knelt while Yik-Mo prayed before the altar. When it was her turn, she reassured Leung Tsing-Haan that her soul would be well-served by her descendants and reported to her on the family fortunes. They were no longer starving. Yik-Mo was now a shopkeeper and accountant for Lei-Kiu, a store that sold imported items in Shaan-Tai Market. Kin-Pong watched a villager's buffalo for a fee, while she and Fei-Yin wove baskets to sell and hired themselves out as labourers during busy farm seasons. Just the week before, Yik-Mo had received a draft from the family's three Gold Mountain guests in Vancouver, and they were looking into buying back their *yeung-lau* in the New Village and the farmland they had lost during the war. As she prayed, Sau-Ping assured her *On-Yan* that she would then contact Auntie Mooi to find a bride for Yik-Mo. In a separate prayer to her own parents, she promised to do the same for her brother, Tin-Shaang.

When Kin-Pong and Fei-Yin had taken their turns before the ancestral altar, Yik-Mo took Kin-Pong's hand. "Come on," he said. "Time to go to the main ancestral hall. Uncle Leung Kwok-Yung has hired a real opera troupe from the city to perform for us!"

"Oh! Yi!" Kin-Pong exclaimed in childish excitement. He turned to Sau-Ping, but she avoided his eyes. "Ma wants to come too," Kin-Pong declared, looking at her. Yik-Mo shook his head and said in the teacherly voice he had adopted since the death of his mother, "She can't. She's not a real Leung." There was no malice in his tone. It was a statement of fact, just as he might have said, "I cut my hair today."

A deep resentment welled up inside Sau-Ping. How was it that she, who in this family took the primary responsibility for seeing that the ancestral worship of the Leung household was carried out in the most respectful and thorough fashion, was not a real Leung, while this stranger's son of unknown birth, as yet a mere child, already had all the rights of a full-fledged member of the Leung lineage? Carefully hiding her feelings, she said, "A group of Daoist priests will also be there chanting prayers to the dead. We don't have the resources to make paper boats or paper *yeung-lau*, but the two of you should at least take some food, ritual money, and old clothing to burn there. You can find those yourself."

After the two men in the household were gone, Sau-Ping led Fei-Yin's to the kitchen to scoop some rice for an offering. She thought how in Yeung-Kong, not that many lunar months earlier, she and the family had been subsisting on wild plants and grass roots. The grass had caught between Leung Tsing-Haan's teeth, and she had spent hours trying to work them out with her fingers and tongue. Were ghosts hungry in the dry, empty way they had been? "Come on, Fei-Yin, we will go to the village gate to feed the hungry ghosts."

Sau-Ping and Fei-Yin set off, each carrying a basket in which they had put some old clothing and two bowls of cooked rice, which had been mixed with sweet potatoes and topped with two hard-boiled eggs.

It was a warm and peaceful summer night. The typhoon and flood had come and gone. Eager to perform the sacrificial act, women had lined the village paths all the way into the open field with clothing and bowls of rice. These were meant to help the wandering souls who had no descendants to care for their basic needs.

Sau-Ping and Fei-Yin went further out. They settled near a rock where three village paths met. Sau-Ping thought of the little boy who was killed during the war by the farmer in Yeung-Kong while trying to steal sweet potatoes. She planted three incense sticks into a bowl of sweet potato rice and placed the bowl at the foot of the rock. She also hung one set of old clothing on a tree branch close by.

She murmured a prayer. "Poor little fellow. I hope you will stop your wandering and enter the womb of some good woman to start a new life."

With Fei-Yin by her side, Sau-Ping headed home in silence. The village path looked empty and deserted at this late hour; the women had all gone home to serve their menfolk. As they trudged on, Sau-Ping still thought of the little boy and how quickly and cruelly his life had ended.

In the silence Sau-Ping became aware of a deep murmur coming from somewhere nearby. She gripped Fei-Yin's hand and put a finger to her lips, creeping closer to the sound. Near the large rock they caught the smell of incense and they could hear a man speaking. How shameful! What man would feed hungry ghosts beside the village path? And so late at night! Curious, Sau-Ping knelt by the side of the rock and listened. Her daughter crouched alongside. Sau-Ping recognized the voice of Bitter-Face Kong.

"... and my ancestors of the Siu lineage. Please accept this humble offering from me. I know this is not enough to comfort your souls, but I am still poor and oppressed. Please forgive me for being unfilial. As a *sai-tsai*, I am a bare stick, unable to acquire a wife to produce descendants to comfort your souls. By your blessing, I and two others of our lineage have survived the famine and Japanese invasion. The Leungs who demolished our ancestral halls and took over our common property four generations ago are still firmly in control. We, your descendants, are still their servants ..."

Sau-Ping did not want her daughter to hear these words. Why had she stopped to listen to Siu Kong! It was the action of a child, not a grown woman. Swiftly, she pulled Fei-Yin backwards – they would take a different path home. But a few last words reached her ear: " ... no justice in this world."

Walking quickly alongside her quiet child, Sau-Ping was shaken and frightened. The words "no justice" cut deep. Siu Kong was forced to pray at a rock, not in a proper Siu ancestral hall, because the Leungs had taken the land of his lineage, forcing the Siu ancestors to wander as hungry ghosts. In the same way, she, Sau-Ping, and her diligent daughter were both barred from entering the Leung ancestral hall. How many women in the village were bullied and excluded by the Leungs! Sau-Ping pictured the face of the thieving lineage chief, who had collected their money at the beginning of the war pretending to buy rice collectively but in return had given her family nothing but rude words. And there was Yik-Faat, the viper, whose son had now been adopted by Paternal Uncle in Vancouver. Injustice!

"Ma, slow down," Fei-Yin said calmly. "I can't see."

Sau-Ping stopped. She bent over and touched her daughter's sweet-smelling hair, asking for better thoughts. And they visited her. She tended the Leung ancestral tablets every morning because it was proper and good. She felt a kinship with the spirit of her mother-in-law after their experiences during the war. She wished for the return of her husband. She trusted her brother-in-law. She had an adopted son named Leung and would be included in the domestic altar as a Leung when she died. Sau-Ping realized she could not hate the Leungs, but many others could. Siu Kong did; the hatred in his voice was a sword hidden behind a veil of rags.

One evening that same summer, two weeks before the Mid-Autumn Festival, Sau-Ping's family was surprised by a visit from their former next-door neighbours in the New Village – Leung Yik-Kwong, his wife Yi-Lin, and their daughter Chun-Fa, now fourteen years old and living in the maiden house. Sau-Ping knew that Leung Yik-Kwong's new shop, the Wing Lung Money Changer, was located right next to the foreign goods store where Yik-Mo worked in Shaan-Tai Market. She was pleased that her brother-in-law must have behaved well in the market with his elders and earned the trust of Yik-Kwong, who was an educated man and a great help to his friends.

After the warm greetings, Yik-Kwong handed a packet of Chinese *yuan* to Yik-Mo. "Here's the money from the Canadian draft you gave me last week. My brother in Hong Kong helped to clear it."

Yik-Mo bowed his head. "Thank-you for giving us a good rate."

"Yik-Mo, I would advise you to act very quickly in accordance with the wishes of your father, uncle, and older brother in Vancouver," advised Yik-Kwong earnestly. "Use the money immediately to buy back your house and the twenty-five *mau* of land that you sold before the war. Right now, one *mau* of farmland costs about

ninety Hong Kong dollars. This is going to rise soon because a lot
of Overseas Chinese will be remitting money to buy land."

Bowing his head again, Yik-Mo replied, "I will follow your sound
advice to buy back the land. But as you know, our former *yeung-lau*
was sold three years ago to a returned Overseas Chinese from Singapore. We cannot get it back so easily."

Yi-Lin, Sau-Ping's friend, cut in. "Our next-door neighbour
returned to Singapore a year ago. They were with us in Shiu-Kwaan
during the war. When we got back, we found that our *yeung-lau* in
the New Village had been occupied and ransacked by the Japanese
devils. But our family was luckier than this family from Singapore. In
a rush to leave for Shiu-Kwaan in 1944, they forgot to take the title
deeds of their house along. So they failed to get the house back after
the war. They returned to Singapore."

"But we sold our *yeung-lau* with the title deed, so we don't have it
either," Sau-Ping said to her friend. "How can we get our property
back?"

Yik-Kwong said, "You are lucky there. The government recently
declared that they will give first priority to Overseas Chinese families
to redeem their former property before it is opened to public bidding.
This is the government's thanks to the Overseas Chinese for donating
to the resistance effort. I can bear witness to the fact that you owned
the *yeung-lau* before the war."

"You must try," Yi-Lin whispered fervently to her friend. "We
want you next to us. Our daughter Chun-Fa has seen enough. We
want her former playmate near again ..." Her brow wrinkled. She
covered her mouth with her hand and a tear fell from her eye. "Like
it was."

Yik-Kwong said, "Quickly, tomorrow. This is no dream."

The very next day Yik-Kwong went with Sau-Ping and Yik-Mo to
conduct negotiations that would allow them to repurchase the *yeung-
lau* and the twenty-five *mau* of farmland. At every step of the process,
Sau-Ping expected that the official would turn his back on her and
laugh, amazed that she had fallen for this big joke. She expected to
live in her two-storey house again? Had the war taught her nothing?
But after receiving 10,000 *yuan* tea money as a bribe from her family,
the officials were polite and efficient. With help from Yik-Kwong, the
papers were delivered, inspected, and signed. The property was registered in Yik-Mo's name. Sau-Ping stood next to him when he signed
his name.

It took three weeks to prepare the ransacked house for habitation,
but one morning the surviving members of the family crossed the
threshold together. Sau-Ping was surprised that the rooms did not

feel as large and cold as they once had, even though they now held much less furniture, it was as if she herself had grown taller and broader. Now that her family had the land and the *yeung-lau* back, Yik-Mo and Sau-Ping agreed that it would be a loss of face if the men in the household continued to do farmwork. Kin-Pong would attend the tutorial class held in Sai-Fok School to make up for his lost years of education. It was important that he should eventually attend regular classes at Tuen-Fan Junior High School in Shaan-Tai Market, which had been renovated using money donated by the Overseas Chinese. Yik-Mo would continue to work in the Lei-Kiu Store. Sau-Ping and Fei-Yin would do the farming, and long-term labourers could be hired to help.

Sau-Ping had just begun to search for good labourers when Ah Tsaan and Ah Kwai, their old farmhands from Yeung-Kong County, arrived in the village. They said they would be pleased to work for her again, and they wished to move back into her brick house, if it was empty. She told them it was.

Sau-Ping worked hard alongside the labourers. It made her uneasy to have so many things restored to their old places. She did not like feeling that the gods were lifting her up by building a pedestal under her feet; such structures always collapsed. It was for this reason that she weeded and hoed tirelessly and kept her daughter working by her side, so that she could earn and cement this good fortune before Fei-Yin entered the maiden house at the end of the year.

The money began flowing again. Now it was Yik-Mo who picked up the remittances. Sau-Ping and Yik-Mo had their *yeung-lau* in the New Village redecorated.

They had invited their neighbours, Leung Yik-Kwong, his wife Yi-Lin, and Chun-Fa, to join them in celebration of the Mid-Autumn Festival. Sau-Ping's brother, Tin-Shaang, was also coming. The house was spotlessly clean. The food was organized, fruits arranged, pudding stirred and set. Sau-Ping had been working steadily for days. There were times when she felt the presence of her mother-in-law in the house and believed that Leung Tsing-Haan was moving from room to room, a little grudging, but pleased to see these signs of bounty and good housekeeping.

Sau-Ping stood in her kitchen deftly cutting the moon cake that was to be placed on the table in the pavilion. She heard her daughter speaking to someone out in the front garden. "Fei-Yin!" she cried. "Who is here?"

Sau-Ping turned from the beautiful surface of the cake and walked through the house, still carrying her cleaver and wiping it as she moved – she really had no time.

A ragged woman and girl stood in the garden. Sau-Ping hoped they would see how busy she was, this festival day. On any other day she might have time to give them food. ... Then she saw.

It was Mei-Kuen. Mei-Kuen, who had disappeared so many times. Sau-Ping felt a shiver of joy pass through her body. Here she had a house and a feast prepared for her friend! Without knowing it, she had been preparing for the arrival of her friend!

"Aye, put down your cleaver. Do you want to eat us?" cried Mei-Kuen, smiling, though with pain in her eyes.

"Fei-Yin, Fei-Yin, take the cleaver to the kitchen." Sau-Ping was confused by her excitement. She handed the cleaver to her daughter, who was also confused. "This is Auntie Mei-Kuen, do you remember my friend at the railway station? Come in! Tea first! Fei-Yin, this is ..."

"My daughter is Lai-Sheung."

"My brother-in-law will be home soon. Come in."

An hour later, Sau-Ping was sitting quietly next to her friend. Yik-Mo had arrived home and Sau-Ping, with her daughter, should have been putting the final touches on the table under the pavilion, but instead the adults of the household were listening to Mei-Kuen. Her story of the war years was not so different from theirs, except that after the war, she had been repelled and cast out when she tried to return to her home in Fung-Yeung. It was not customary for any village to accept back a woman who had been married out, especially if she had been united with a bandit. So, like hungry ghosts, Mei-Kuen and Lai-Sheung had been begging for food ever since the war had ended.

Yik-Mo glanced at Sau-Ping as they listened. Sau-Ping opened her eyes so that he would see she intended to help her friend. Immediately, he said, "Why don't you stay with us? We have enough room in the *yeung-lau*."

Mei-Kuen kowtowed to thank them. "I hope you will at least let me earn my stay here."

"In the fields ..."

"I think Lai-Sheung and I will sell congee and buns in Sai-Fok Market every morning. We are better ..."

"Yes, that is a good idea," Sau-Ping interrupted. She realized that her friend lacked the strength to begin farmwork, and there might be plenty of customers for her treats as the village renewed itself. Money had begun to flow again. Many Overseas Chinese had even come home to retire.

So Mid-Autumn Festival in 1946 was a joyous one. Leung Yik-Kwong, Yi-Lin, and Chun-Fa arrived with contributions for the feast. Tin-Shaang showed up carrying rice wine.

Now living all by himself, Sau-Ping's brother looked older than his twenty-three years. He rarely laughed. Yet Sau-Ping could see that he was glad to visit, as if the pavilion and the shadow of the large house sheltered him from the past. Sau-Ping was relieved to hear that he was able to make a living as a part-time farmer and part-time construction worker, and that he was attending adult literacy classes in the evening. Later in the evening, their conversation naturally turned to Big Sister Sau-Ha and Brother-in-Law Lau Tseung-Lam. Tin-Shaang had sent a letter to their old address in Hong Kong but never heard a word, and Sau-Ping was pierced by worry.

Overhearing their conversation, Leung Yik-Kwong said, "I have an elder brother in Hong Kong. Give me your Big Sister's address, and I'll get my brother to look for her."

Sau-Ping smiled her gratitude gazed at this dependable man and rose on impulse to speak with his wife, Yi-Lin. "How lucky you are to be married to such a good man," she whispered. Yi-Lin's eyes sparkled. She laughed and patted Sau-Ping's arm.

Just then, Sau-Ping's other childhood friend, Wai-Fong, arrived by herself to join the party. She and Mei-Kuen greeted one another with deep amazement. Between them recognition and memory shuttled powerfully; for they had both emerged from the war as ragged women, but each remembered the other as a strong, fresh girl. Wai-Fong had lost an infant son during the war. Her husband, Leung Yik-Hung, would not allow her to bring her other two children to the party. At the same time, he allowed Wai-Fong to visit Sau-Ping because he knew that Sau-Ping would lend her friend money interest-free whenever they really needed it. He just didn't like to associate with people in the New Village in general. Sau-Ping was aware of every dirty corner in this situation. It did her heart good to see Mei-Kuen and Wai-Fong perched so near one another, sipping tea.

For it was festival time. The reunion under the moon generated its own power. Sau-Ping's family and all their guests sat out in the pavilion eating moon cakes, pomelos, star fruits, persimmons, and taro pudding. The three girls, Chun-Fa, Fei-Yin, and Lai-Sheung, sat in a circle. They put their dragon-shaped grass lanterns in the middle of the circle. Under the bright moonlight, they sang folk songs and played slap-and-clap games, laughing and giggling. Watching them, Sau-Ping was drawn back to her days in the maiden house in Fung-Yeung village with Mei-Kuen, Wai-Fong, and her big sister Sau-Ha. She remembered the green walls. She remembered her friends who, in ritual wisdom, tried to defend her from marriage and banishment.

This was the landscape now. Mother-in-law dead. House returned. Friends. Moon. Three rather thin girls in a circle. Sau-Ping watched the shadows of her two maiden-house friends. She wished she could build their futures for them. Yet she was aware, even in moments of great gladness, that she could not insure her own.

The fall and winter of 1946 had come and gone. Informed by her knowledgeable neighbours and helpful brother-in-law, Sau-Ping was increasingly aware of regional and even national news that might affect her village life. She knew when 1947 began. By this time, the motor roads that had been dismantled during the War had been completely repaired. Although the San-Ning Railway was not rebuilt, buses, boats, and ferries resumed their pre-war schedules. Over the last few months, Sau-Ping had witnessed many Overseas Chinese return to Sai-Fok to be reunited with their families. Two or three of the returned emigrants bought ten *mau* of farmland. They had learned from wartime experience how important it was to be self-sufficient in terms of food. Growing their own food would also serve as a hedge against inflation in food prices. However, the majority of the returned Overseas Chinese bought only residential plots for building new *yeung-lau*. These families preferred to use their savings to invest in small businesses in the Shaan-Tai or Sai-Fok Markets, or to buy commercial property and collect rent. Sau-Ping counted a total of thirty *yeung-lau* in the New Village section.

It was summer when Sau-Ping heard from her neighbors that Canada was finally about to allow Gold Mountain guests to sponsor their immediate family members for reunions. She saw aging parents, wives, and young children from very rich families in the New Village pack their belongings, ready to go to North America. But she herself and her children and brother-in-law received no summons. Winter came and went. It had been fourteen years since Sau-Ping had seen her husband. Yik-Man had never set eyes on his own daughter or his adopted son. What kind of man was he, that he felt no curiosity about his family after all their struggles? Was it possible he had married a woman in Canada? Sau-Ping had learned from her neighbours that some Chinese men did take new wives abroad, though they continued sending money to their families in the village. Would Yik-Man do that?

Sau-Ping tried not to think about it, but the summer of 1948 was endless. A demon had settled on her shoulder and rode with her everywhere. She could not shake off her jealousy and anger. She became convinced that her husband had another wife, and that all the Gold Mountain guests returning from Vancouver for retirement knew about it but had sworn to keep quiet. At last, she could bear it no longer. She convinced Yik-Mo that they ought to visit Uncle Leung Kwok-Wing, who had recently returned from Vancouver and built himself a large, empty *yeung-lau* in New Village. Leung Kwok-Wing had lived near the restaurant in the same Vancouver neighbourhood as Yik-Man, his father, and his uncle. He had even eaten at the restaurant; he had touched the plates and swallowed the tea. The morning of the visit, Sau-Ping stared at herself in the mirror. Her face was smooth, despite the hard years, and her eyes were unswerving.

It took only a few minutes of conversation with old Uncle Leung Kwok-Wing to dispel Sau-Ping's fear that Yik-Man had a restaurant wife. Leung Kwok-Wing was faded from his years of Canada work. He himself didn't look like a man who'd been bouncing around the ghost country with extra wives on his back. He only wanted to talk about the horrors he encountered on the boat from Hong Kong to Kong-Moon City on his return trip to Sai-Fok. He launched into his tale almost immediately, swinging his stringy, emaciated arms back and forth to imitate the rocking of the boat, the march of the pirates who had stolen all their gold, jewellry, and foreign currency – everything the Gold Mountain guests had brought for their families.

"One fellow hid some Canadian dollars under his shoe insole. The pirates did not discover that, but, unfortunately, the real Customs officer at the Pak-Kaai Pier in Kong-Moon City found the money. It was confiscated, and my poor fellow passenger was put in jail. After twenty-three years of work in the ghost city! Twenty-three years of breathing in ghost spit and ghost talk!"

Yik-Mo and Sau-Ping murmured their sympathy. During a pause, Yik-Mo asked after his father, paternal uncle, and elder brother in Vancouver.

Leung Kwok-Wing shook his head. "Your father was not in very good health when I left in May. The three of them are also low on cash. You see, they spent all their savings buying back the house and the land for you. Still, they were full of plans for the future. They want to save some money to finance your wedding and for their own retirement.

"I think they are unrealistic," he continued. "They work so hard they don't straighten up to look around." Uncle Leung Kwok-Wing pushed himself straighter in his chair, as if his muscles ached. "How can they do that when there is so much inflation here? One *mau* of land is now worth the equivalent of sixteen hundred Hong Kong dollars."

Yik-Mo said, "Yes, I know. We were lucky to buy when we did. Land now is seventeen times the amount we paid fifteen months ago."

"Yes, and the new Chinese currency that came out in May is total-ly worthless. It is like wet firewood. And the government forced everyone to exchange foreign currencies for this useless money! They give us such a ridiculous exchange rate! A Gold Mountain guest I know sent home a cheque worth twenty thousand Hong Kong dol-lars to build a house a month ago. When that money was changed into Chinese currency, it was only enough to buy some bricks. Anoth-er Gold Mountain guest sent home fifteen hundred American dollars to finance the wedding of his son. When the money was exchanged for Chinese *yuan*, it was only enough for a Western suit on the wed-ding day!"

"Then why don't my father, paternal uncle, and elder brother sponsor us to go to Vancouver instead?" asked Yik-Mo.

"You think it is that easy?" Uncle Leung Kwok-Wing shook his small head. "You are now twenty-four years old. Canadian immigra-tion law only allows Gold Mountain guests to sponsor their parents over sixty, their wives, and children under eighteen. If you tried to go to Canada as the son of Leung Kwok-Yan, you would have to pay an astronomical sum of tea money to have your date of birth changed.

"In addition, more tea money has to be paid to the Passport Office in Kwong-Chau (Canton) to get exit permits for you. There are four of you! Do you know how expensive that can be? I have not even mentioned the cost of the boat fare for everyone in your family to go to Vancouver!"

Yik-Mo sat with his chin up and his eyes veiled. Sau-Ping knew her brother-in-law well after all these years, and she could see that he was profoundly wounded. He had dreamed of joining the other men in his family. He had dreamed of taking his place in the restaurant.

They walked back together without speaking, wrapped in their own thoughts. The visit to Uncle Leung Kwok-Wing had left Sau-Ping more aware than ever that the world around her was full of pitfalls and complexities, and she resolved to learn as much about that world as she could from Yik-Mo. The family's very survival depended on it.

She began to ask him more often about news from the market. He grew accustomed to her curiosity and got into the habit of telling her stories in the evenings, after he had washed the dust of the market off his hands and face and hungrily eaten his first bowl of rice. She heard many horror stories about Gold Mountain guests and began to think of her husband as a victim of a war that was different from the one she had endured but possibly as cruel.

Most Gold Mountain guests had been abroad for too long to know their way home. As a result, some were robbed or swindled by thieves posing as porters. Others were kidnapped by bandits once they got off the bus or the boat. They were held for ransom until their families paid up. Once they were home, returned Gold Mountain guests faced more trouble. Plainclothes police from the Police Department at Shaan-Tai Market sometimes extorted money from them, charging them with possession or use of foreign currency. Not only were their foreign dollars confiscated but their family had to pay huge sums for their release. Yik-Mo knew two old men who had been treated in this manner.

Listening to Yik-Mo, Sau-Ping also learned that every level of government – the *Heung*, the District, the County, and the Province – had either police, soldiers, a self-defence corps, militia, or some other kinds of armed force. They could collect taxes, levies, or rations and vandalize villages at will. Moreover, there were numerous local military strongmen and secret societies that were semi-independent of the government in Toi-Shaan. According to Yik-Mo, some secret society members in their neighbourhood hired themselves out to landlords as thugs to collect rent from tenants. Others operated opium dens gambling outfits, and whore-houses in Shaan-Tai Market, which Leung Yik-Faat, the viper son of their lineage chief, often patronized.

It was during an evening with her neighbours that Sau-Ping first heard the word "Communists." Leung Yik-Kwong and Yik-Mo began discussing "Communists" heatedly, and even Yik-Kwong's wife, Yi-Lin, spoke her opinion. Sau-Ping gathered that many of the government forces Yik-Mo had described were growing in strength and ferocity because they had begun to fight "Communists" in the mountains. Communists were like bandits, but they claimed to be attacking for the sake of the people, not out of greed. The Nationalist government was trying to recruit more people to its side, against the Communist forces.

Sau-Ping wanted to find out more about these "Communists." She asked her bosom friend and houseguest, Mei-Kuen, whether the communists were really just bandits dressed in a new name, or whether they were the ones who had killed her bandit husband in the Taai-Lung Tung Mountains, but Mei-Kuen did not have the slightest clue.

Another evening, Yik-Mo explained to Sau-Ping about the *po-kaap* system. It had been established in Toi-Shaan County in 1932, but nobody in Sai-Fok had taken the government regulations seriously at the time. Now this old structure might begin to assert itself. The *po-cheung* for Sai-Fok was Leung Yik-Shing, who was not always on good terms with lineage chief Leung Kwok-Yung. Leung Yik-Shing's family owned and farmed about fifteen *mau* of land. Uncle Leung Kwok-Yung, on the other hand, was the proud owner of forty *mau* of

farmland. He was also the lineage chief, so it was beneath his dignity to associate with Leung Yik-Shing.

The job of their *po-cheung* was to inform villagers of government
rules and regulations. He also collected army rations and reported on
people's movements and on suspicious characters in the village. But
now his most important function was to register all men over eighteen and under sixty, and recruit a quota from this list to serve as soldiers to fight the "Communist bandits."

Sau-Ping was relieved to discover that Overseas Chinese returning
for visits for a period of less than six months were not supposed to be
conscripted, while retired Overseas Chinese or their family members
were to be conscripted last. Many in the New Village section paid tea
money to the *po-cheung*, Leung Yik-Shing, to avoid conscription. Sau-
Ping learned that both dependable Leung Yik-Kwong next door and
her own brother-in-law, Yik-Mo, had paid hefty sums just to remind
Leung Yik-Shing that they were in the special category.

Listening to her friends, Sau-Ping realized that her home was being
threatened by another war, a war pitting Chinese against Chinese.
Her brain refused to embrace the situation clearly but some part of
her spirit began to prepare. When the first recognizable incident of
this new war occurred in her village, it came not from the skies but
from the bamboo grove near the entrance to Sai-Fok. Sau-Ping,
returning from the field, heard shouts and stepped inside the grove
to hide.

A man was being chased by several other men carrying guns in
their arms. It was Leung Yik-Faat, son of the lineage chief, who ran in
fear, while regional forces led by the *po-cheung*, Leung Yik-Shing, pur-
sued him. Yik-Faat the terrified viper dodged into the village *tiu-lau*
like a grass snake into a bunch of rocks. Two or three soldiers aimed
at the tower and fired. The village militia stationed in the *tiu-lau* fired
back. Sau-Ping heard shots, but none of the soldiers dodged or threw
themselves to the ground. They must have known the village militia
would lack the discipline to take aim. Five minutes passed.

From her hiding-place in the bamboo grove Sau-Ping watched a
humiliating negotiation. The lineage chief, father of Yik-Faat, came
out from behind the *tiu-lau* and dipped into his pockets three times for
packets of money. Sau-Ping could read the gestures of the *po-
cheung* who accepted each offer of money reluctantly, each time
demanding more. He accused lineage chief Leung Kwok-Yung of har-
bouring Communists and failing to help the Nationalist army; of protecting rich Gold Mountain guest families that kept foreign currency.

Sau-Ping stayed crouched in the bamboo grove. Nationalist soldiers were well known for raping women in the villages. She saw

that the Nationalist gunmen had broken into two gangs; one turned with the *po-cheung*, Leung Yik-Shing, and jogged towards the Old Village, while the other scattered into the New Village. Yik-Faat never emerged from his hiding place. Occasional gunshots and screams sounded in the air. Sau-Ping witnessed a soldier carrying a pig under his arm and a sack of grain over his shoulder. Time passed slowly as Sau-Ping kept still, peering out through the leaves. The Nationalists marched six poor male farmers in leg-chains out of the village. Their wives and children stood in the streets wailing. Other soldiers carried pigs, chickens, and sacks of grain and sweet potatoes, their pockets bulging with money.

Sau-Ping watched the procession disappear. She could see no difference in behaviour between these soldiers and the bandits from Taai-Lung Tung Mountains who had attacked her village in 1933, or the Japanese soldiers who had invaded her village in 1944. Would the "Communist bandits" be much the same if they came to the village?

CHAPTER 10

The Tables Are Turned

OCTOBER 1949

When the People's Republic was proclaimed far away in Beijing, Sau-Ping heard the news from her brother-in-law. At first, she did not think to connect the distant event with the day's village gossip, which reported that the lineage chief was in a state because no one had seen the *sai-tsai*, Siu Kong, for months, and it was time to begin preparations for the Autumn Rites. The lineage chief had expected Siu Kong to return by this time. There was no one to clean the ancestral hall, no one to butcher and roast the pig. Village jokesters said the pig was the one who knew everything; he continued to root and roll in his pen, looking oddly proprietary, as if he and the missing *sai-tsai* had come to an agreement.

The latest gossip about Siu Kong was that he had travelled to a Communist training centre in the Taai-Lung Tung Mountains as part of an irregular band of landless farmers. It was said that the Communists taught people to read and write and ran political and military training courses. Some Sai-Fok villagers thought they were bandits, others that they were the conquerors of bandits.

Later that month the *sai-tsai* mysteriously reappeared in the village. He spoke to no one, and no one questioned him, though he spent most of his time in his shack and somehow made it clear that he was no longer going to labour without recompense for the Leungs.

Sau-Ping understood that the People's Republic had been formally proclaimed after four years of civil war between the Nationalist and Communist forces. Most of the fighting took place in the North, but bands of underground Communists had spread throughout Kwong-Tung Province, according to Leung Yik-Kwong, her neighbour. Then she heard that the southbound Red Army had successfully claimed

Kwong-Chau, the capital city of the province. The Nationalists had retreated to Taiwan and Hong Kong. In western Kwong-Tung, many troops were defecting to the Communist side. The remnants fled to the mountain hide-outs that had just been vacated by the Communist guerrillas. Hearing this news, Mei-Kuen muttered, "Cold nights, wild berries, stone pillows."

Toi-Shaan County was taken a few weeks after the Mid-Autumn Festival with hardly a shot fired. The local militia was disarmed. The surface of Shaan-Tai Market remained still, almost too still. Weeks later, Yik-Mo returned home from work and told her that his boss had come back to the store from the teahouse that morning all excited about a notice on the door of the district office. The notice declared that the People's Government of Toi-Shaan had now taken control of Shaan-Tai Market, formerly overseen by the Nationalist regime. As the *po-kaap* system, set up by the Nationalist government, was oppressive to the people, it would be abolished, but all former *heung* and district officers were to remain at their posts for the time being.

"By early afternoon, four members of the guerrilla forces at Taai-Lung Tung headquarters, accompanied by two students from Tuen-Fan Junior High School, came to our store. They said we do not have to be afraid; the new government will protect all law-abiding people. They will punish robbers and murderers, those who operate whore-houses, gambling outfits, and opium dens, and the few who attempt to sabotage the new government, but the rest will be left alone. I don't know." Yik-Mo put his head in his hands. "Possibly we will be safe. Possibly they mean to do good."

Soon the word spread, and every villager in Sai-Fok knew of the new regime at Shaan-Tai Market. Few ventured to guess what the recent changes might entail or whether the new regime was going to stay. They just hoped for a secure livelihood and stable social order after so many years of suffering and uncertainty.

After the harvest of the sweet potato crop, towards the end of 1949, the villagers finally had real dealings with the guerrilla forces now stationed at Shaan-Tai Market. It was Siu Kong who welcomed the twenty-man contingent at the village gate, leading them to the *tiu-lau* and handing over the weapons supply. News of their arrival reached Mei-Kuen and Sau-Ping in the fields where they were preparing the soil for the rice crop that would be planted after the New Year. Send-ing their daughters home, they set off quietly to see what was hap-pening. Together with a few old men and farm women, people who for one reason or another no longer bowed to fear, they watched as the head of the guerrilla forces, a young man of about twenty-five, demanded to see Uncle Leung Kwok-Yung. The lineage chief appeared in short order, his hands folded and his head bowed. The soldier told Uncle Leung loudly that from now on, there would be no self-defence corps or Nationalist soldiers bothering the villagers. All landowners were to pay thirty-five percent of their harvest to Siu Kong, who would in turn deliver the whole sum to the district office at Shaan-Tai Market.

The villagers, most of whom had hidden behind closed doors, emerged later in the day greatly relieved and surprised at the behaviour of the guerrilla forces. The Communists had not come to kill, rape, burn, or loot; nor had they carried away men as recruits. Although the thirty-five percent harvest tax seemed much higher than the rate imposed by the Nationalist regime, the villagers figured that they might in fact be better off: if the local guerrillas succeeded in a peaceful transition of power, and if they kept their promises, then the residents of Sai-Fok might be spared the numerous other payments that could previously be extracted by anybody with a gun.

The villagers also realized that the tables had now turned – their despised *sai-tsai* was the boss! With Siu Kong as the tax collector, large landlords like Uncle Leung Kwok-Yung and his son, Leung Yik-Faat, could no longer evade taxes and shift the burden onto the backs of the smaller landowners.

One early morning in the cold part of spring, 1950, Sau-Ping and Fei-Yin were leaving for the fields, when they saw Siu Kong at the door. The memory of this husky, bitter man carrying her sedan chair returned to Sau-Ping with force. She half hoped he recalled her as a timid, veiled young bride, and that the recollection would sweeten his treatment of the people in her house. She also recalled how he helped carry water when she was pregnant with Fei-Yin. Wasn't it possible he would still be kind to her? In another part of her mind, however, she realized that the *sai-tsai* had carried numerous brides for other Leung lineage members on his shoulders, and this history of hard labour did not conduce to sentimental attachments. A vision of Siu Kong praying to his ancestors for revenge at the cold rock during the dark night of the Hungry Ghost Festival just a few years ago rose in her imagination. He hated the Leungs.

"Auntie," said Siu Kong, still addressing Sau-Ping respectfully, "I am asking every family in the New Village whether they will buy Victory Bonds. Would you be interested?"

"Victory Bonds?"

"Yes, they are sold on very good terms. You hold them for five years, and you get eight percent interest. At the end of every five years, all the bond-holders will participate in a lucky draw. If you win, then you'll get back twenty percent of the capital plus the eight percent interest."

"But I am afraid by then the value of my money will decrease. Who knows what the inflation rate will be like?" Sau-Ping was hesitant, remembering the astronomical rate of inflation over the past few years.

"Auntie, we are now under the People's Government. The People's Government will not print money at will, like the Nationalist Government. The People's Government serves the people!" Siu Kong loved this slogan. "Buying Victory Bonds is your duty in building a stronger China."

That declaration actually appealed to Sau-Ping. She had heard many returned Gold Mountain guests say that if China was strong, then the Overseas Chinese in North America would not be humiliated. She agreed to purchase fifty thousand *yuan* worth of bonds but asked if she could discuss the investment with her brother-in-law. Siu Kong bowed, without expressing thanks or warnings, and departed.

That evening after dinner, Sau-Ping's next-door neighbours arrived to visit. The men spoke of new developments at Shaan-Tai Market. Yik-Kwong reported that the local communist forces stationed at the market had carried out a lightning raid on gambling houses, brothels, and opium dens. The largest gambling house was torched and the doors and windows of the nearby opium den had been broken into and the heavy smoke-stained paper screens burned in a pile outdoors. A line of captured prostitutes and opium smokers had been hustled past the door of Yik-Kwong's shop. "But not Yik-Faat? Where was he this lucky day?" asked Yik-Mo.

Yik-Kwong replied ironically, "Happy with his family."

Yi-Lin, his wife, turned to Sau-Ping. "Did the scar do well?"

"What scar? Who has a scar?" asked her husband.

"Yik-Faat's damned son Kin-Tsoi threw a rock at Kin-Pong. It nearly cut his eye. I had to sew it. That Kin-Tsoi is no good, but what can his mother do? She lives in fear of her husband," Sau-Ping said.

"And we are cousins by adoption now," Yik-Mo added bitterly. "Yik-Faat's little tiger son is my cousin by adoption. They are receiving remittances from Paternal Uncle in Vancouver."

Yi-Lin clucked, expressing her sympathy.

"And the communist government is going to control the price of grain, did you hear that?" Yik-Kwong interjected, determined to return to the topic at hand. "There is a chance they will bring order to the country. Maybe they will discipline your little tiger cousin?"

Yik-Mo laughed. "My sister-in-law's friend, Mei-Kuen, says real bandits would just pick him up and break his neck."

The women cried out, and the men laughed.

But one week later, the laughter had died. News arrived that the Communists were going to crack down on peddlers and money-lenders. Every business would be licensed and the owner required to pay a tax. What's more, the old Nationalist statute outlawing the circulation of foreign currencies was being enforced for the first time by the Communists. Sau-Ping glimpsed the stricken faces of her neighbours one evening as she stood outside in the pavilion. Yik-Kwong's money-changing business would not survive under this new regime. The foreign goods store where Yik-Mo worked was also threatened. Even Mei-Kuen's little enterprise in Sai-Fok Market might find itself choking on government regulations. Sau-Ping and her brother-in-law spoke at length about their finances. The *yeung-lau* had begun to seem cavernous and hard, as if it were preparing to expel them again. Their knowledgeable neighbour, Yik-Kwong, advised the family to change their Canadian money into *yuan* quickly; people could still change Hong Kong, American, or Canadian money into *yuan* at a good rate of exchange at the Toi-Shaan branch of the People's Bank, but it was impossible to say for how long. "As for Victory Bonds," Yik-Kwong warned, "you had better buy some, just to be on the good side of Siu Kong."

The family followed Yik-Kwong's advice.

One night in mid-June, Sau-Ping had a bad dream. She was back in Yeung-Kong County, trying to plant some sweet potatoes. Suddenly a bomb dropped from the skies. Her mother-in-law Leung Tsing-Haan was broken up into many pieces, her head split like a melon dropped on the field. In her sleep, Sau-Ping tried to scream.

Sau-Ping believed that the dream was a message from her mother-in-law's spirit. Leung Tsing-Haan was trying to tell her how brokenhearted she was that Yik-Mo, now twenty-seven, had not been married. Hoping her *On-Yan* would hear, Sau-Ping vowed that she would try to find him a bride as soon as she could. But their money was running short. The government had forbidden the use of foreign currencies; they had bought bonds that might well prove to be worthless. Sau-Ping saw that if she did not act quickly, they might not be able to afford the bride price or any kind of wedding for Yik-Mo.

The next day Sau-Ping made a special trip to Shaan-Tai Market, going directly to Siu Fung Loi Tea House where she knew Auntie

Mooi, the marriage broker, had stationed herself every market day for the last thirty years.

Auntie Mooi looked so old and wrinkled that Sau-Ping almost didn't recognize her. Sitting down, Sau-Ping got right to the point and announced the bride price her family could pay. Auntie Mooi sighed.

"Sau-Ping, I may not be able to help you for very long. This new marriage law will put all of us go-betweens out of business. Luckily I am already sixty-six and ready to retire."

"What new law, Auntie?"

"The new marriage law says that young people should have free choice of marriage partners. To get a marriage certificate at the Registration Office, they must prove that the groom is at least twenty years old and the bride at least eighteen. What's more, they have to prove that they are not forced to marry by their parents, and that the marriage has not been arranged by a marriage broker." Auntie Mooi spoke quietly, leaning towards Sau-Ping as if fearful of being overheard.

"A young man is supposed to go hunting for a girl?" Sau-Ping whispered.

"It is so shameful and improper to have young people meet one another in public before they are engaged to be married," Auntie Mooi hissed. "Like animals!"

"Can there be weddings? Do brides these days not have to cover their faces with red veils? Do they have rules about the ceremony?"

"No marriage broker. No carrying the bride. The bride walks on her two feet, like a farmer. No kowtow. Neither are the groom's parents supposed to spend money on bride price or an elaborate wedding feast. The new style of marriage is to serve tea and candy to the guests."

Sau-Ping gasped.

"With revolutionary songs," Auntie Mooi whispered, bending closer across the table. "But many of the weddings still follow the old tradition. The officer at the Registration Office at Shaan-Tai Market is easily satisfied that the modern way has been followed. You give him money."

"Is that all there is in the new marriage law?"

"Have you seen the new woman?"

"What?" Sau-Ping looked around, perplexed.

"You wish to hear the new woman speak? Go to the Tuen-Fan Junior High School, your son's school, right now. Don't talk to an old lady, you're wasting your time. The Women's League is there. You go." Auntie Mooi slapped Sau-Ping's hand encouragingly. "You were a proper bride. Go and see. What more can they do to us?"

Sau-Ping went straight to the school and, once inside, followed a noise to the large hall where a meeting seemed to be underway. Sau-Ping sat down quietly at the back. The school hall was packed with students and young women from different villages.

The speaker was a young man with a broken nose standing straight as a board on a little stool so that everyone could see him. He went on and on about "the People" reclaiming their own country. Then he bowed and stepped off the stool, and a woman of about twenty took his place. She had short straight hair pushed behind her ears, and she was dressed more plainly than a soldier. Sau-Ping guessed that she was a college student. For a long time she spoke about Chinese women. Sau-Ping grew drowsy; she was not accustomed to sitting still in a room with so many people, and the young woman spoke in a dialect that, while close to Toi-Shaanese, was sometimes difficult to comprehend. But when she heard the words "grass widow," Sau-Ping grew alert.

The close-cropped girl pointed vehemently towards the side window of the hall, as if all her enemies were crouched just outside. "My own mother tells me that her village in San-Wooi County is full of grass widows because the men have gone to Southeast Asia, Cuba, and North America. These women were married against their will. They must be granted the right to divorce if they are not satisfied. The intention of the new marriage law that our beloved Communist party has bestowed upon us is to help these grass widows. They can seek divorce from absentee husbands, freedom from abusive mothers-in-law. When the divorce is granted by the People's Court, they can even take their portion of the family property and have custody of the children. Better still, their husband has to support them and the children until they remarry. I hope you are thankful to the Communist party and will spread this piece of good news around."

Sau-Ping's face was burning. She didn't know where to look and was frightened that the entire audience would stand up and surround her, demanding, "What do you think? What do you think of the injustices against brides? Speak! Speak out!" They might place her on the stool!

Glancing quickly around her, Sau-Ping saw that the audience was listening attentively to the speaker. Relieved, she shaded her eyes and drifted into thought. She recalled the scene she had glimpsed years before when the girl Ting-Ting was married to a cock, the bird struggling under the hands of the auntie as the "couple" kowtowed. Ting-Ting still lived in Sai-Fok, and the villagers reported that her mother-in-law, Leung Siu-Hing, treated her like a slave because her husband had remarried in the United States and refused to come home.

But Sau-Ping felt that her own life had been better, and proper. Her mother-in-law had been difficult, but brave.

It was true that many grass widows in her village had a hard time – and not just grass widows. Wives and daughters-in-law were beaten by men and older women who felt baffled by the war, by the seasons, by losses at gambling or trade, by a serving of burnt rice. Leung Yik-Faat, for example, was notorious for abusing his wife Sing-Fan. Once he had thrown a bowl of steaming rice in her face.

Should a woman like Sing-Fan divorce? Sau-Ping could not imagine how a divorced woman could eat or stand or breathe in the village. She would have no property of her own: how could she get half a buffalo or a piece of farmland? Most of the farmland was corporate property held by the ancestral halls. No lineage member would agree to give or rent land to a wandering wife. Certainly the entire Leung lineage would stifle such a woman. A man's family paid so much for his wedding and the bride price that they would surely feel such a loss of face in case of divorce. And a woman could never take her sons from the family; sons were needed to continue the family and the lineage.

If she were to try to return to her village, they would shame her, as Mei-Kuen had been shamed.

And if she explored further? Even if she could make a living as a farm labourer in other places, who would worship her soul after her death? She would become yet another hungry, wandering ghost. In her mind's eye Sau-Ping looked again on Mei-Kuen and her daughter, reduced to beggars, standing outside her pavilion.

Around her people were rising. Sau-Ping stood with the crowd and walked slowly home.

The more she thought about marriage and divorce and property and banishment, the more it seemed that the speaker had been too young and idealistic to realize that conditions in a village were very different from those in a big city like Kwong-Chau.

Two weeks later Sau-Ping spotted the same young woman in the fields working with two young men from Kwong-Chau alongside Siu Kong and Leung Yik-Hung, Wai-Fong's husband. Sau-Ping was a little frightened of this young woman. But she was also curious and determined to find whatever light she could to illuminate her own future and the future of her family under this new regime, so she talked to Wai-Fong as they were washing clothes the next day at the mountain stream. Wai-Fong shook her head as she doused a pair of trousers in the cold water. "I will visit you tonight," she whispered.

That night, Mei-Kuen, Sau-Ping, and Wai-Fong sat indoors, drinking tea and talking. From Wai-Fong, Sau-Ping learned that the three young outsiders were part of the Land Reform Work Team for the Eighth District of Toi-Shaan County, stationed at Shaan-Tai Market. Last month the work team had been broken up into smaller teams of three people and the trios sent to "squat" in different villages, leaving only the core leaders of the overall team at headquarters. These core leaders were Mandarin speakers from the provinces north of Kwong-Tung. Their leader in turn was Chai Ling, a stiff, handsome man from Woo-Naam (Hunan) Province. Wai-Fong thought he was the top boss.

"Ever since their arrival last week, these three young university students have been living with us and Siu Kong. They eat with us and work with us in the fields. They talk until very late at night, asking whether we feel exploited by the rich people in the village," said Wai-Fong."At first my husband said he did not think so because the manager of the second branch of the Leung lineage allowed him to bid for land. He felt grateful for that. He also gets a share of the roast pork twice a year from the main ancestral hall during the Spring and Autumn Festivals. He would have none of these benefits if the ancestral halls for the Leungs owned no corporate land. But then the members of the Land Reform Work Team argued that our family was being exploited. The lineage land is open for bidding to all members every three years. With every bidding, the rent rises higher. So Yik-Hung has to pay ever higher rent deposits and higher rent to the lineage manager to keep the same piece of land. He then has to borrow from a moneylender at forty percent interest. As a result, we cannot afford to eat well at home. They say if we could eat decent food at home, my husband would not be so grateful for slices off the pig's hind end twice a year at the feasts."

Mei-Kuen muttered, "Let them tear down the ancestral halls. You won't find me wailing."

Sau-Ping realized that she was a woman of property while her two good friends had virtually nothing, and that she trusted many of the old traditions that her friends might be tempted to destroy. Without family traditions, each person would be a piece of gravel in the road. Life was hard; family tradition answered the requirements of life.

Wai-Fong said, "The team members explained that the Communist party will soon make both private landlords and lineage managers pay for the exploitation of landless peasants."

"I am a landlord. We hire labourers," Sau-Ping murmured.

"Oh no, but you don't have tenants. That's different." Wai-Fong glanced at her hands, which held one of Sau-Ping's teacups. Listening to her friend, Sau Ping saw that the message the Communists were preaching and the changes they had resolved to implement heralded a great reversal.

Wai-Fong said that Yik-Hung, her husband, had agreed to cooper-
ate and to enlist other poor people in the neighbourhood to support
the work team. They should pour out their bitterness against their
exploiters. But many had refused to join because they did not trust the
outsiders. Siu Kong, of course, was at the centre of this campaign; all
the *sai-tsai* families had joined. Since Wai-Fong's husband had more
schooling than Siu Kong, it was agreed he should head the Peasants'
Association, while Siu Kong, claiming his experience in fighting bandits before the war, would be the leader of the People's Militia.

Mei-Kuen snorted skeptically. Sau Ping said, "He was the first to
hide."

Wai-Fong looked at her sharply. "Hoi-Laan, the young woman of
the Land Reform Work Team, has tried and tried to persuade me to
organize study sessions for the marriage law. She says the male tenant farmers won't do it."

Mei-Kuen laughed loudly. "Yes, even the poorest married man has
a buffalo at home he wants to keep in harness. Didn't the Communists know this?"

"Did you agree to help spread the news about the marriage law?"
Sau-Ping asked Wai-Fong.

There was a pause. Then:

"Ping, you are my friend. You know my husband. He has beaten
me many times. You have seen the marks on my arm and, once, after
the festival, on my neck and ear. What if there is a marriage law? He
thinks I will go to the registry and divorce him. He can lead his Communist group, but if I try to talk of the divorce law, he will beat me
again."

By mid-1950, both the Peasants' Association and the People's Militia
of Sai-Fok Village had been formally inaugurated. They went for military and political training under the leadership of the District Bureau
of Public Security at Shaan-Tai Market. Meanwhile, the core leaders
of the two groups knocked on doors in the Old Village, trying to get
the young men and women to attend evening meetings at the Sai-Fok
School.

In the end, about seventy-five people, mostly poor tenant farmers
and landless labourers, joined the Peasants' Association. Ah Tsaan
and Ah Kwai, Sau-Ping's farmhands, also joined after some initial
hesitation, although they were not local villagers. It was Wai-Fong
who told Sau-Ping about her two employees.

Hoi-Laan, the young close-cropped woman from Kwong-Chau,
was able to find enough members to form a women's study group in

the village. The group was made up of female students and some grass widows who had been abandoned by their overseas husbands. When the women met in the hall of Sai-Fok School, it was like a meeting in an enlarged maiden house. Mei-Kuen's daughter attended one meeting and described it to her mother and Sau-Ping.

Thus, by late summer, the Old Village had become a very busy place. There were literacy classes for adults; there were small study groups and newspaper readings to discuss government directives. The villagers even organized their own theatrical group to spread the good word about the Chinese Communist Party. For the members of New Village, this was a time of nervousness and uncertainty, though Sau-Ping's neighbour, Yik-Kwong, continued his daily regimen even as his money-changing business was turning to dust and slipping through his fingers. Despite all the studies done on the new marriage law, not one single case of divorce was filed in Sai-Fok.

One morning, Sau-Ping heard a continuous brushing sound accompanied by loud cracking noises near the river. With her daughter, she went to see what was going on. Reaching the edge of the village, they watched with other villagers as members of the People's Militia of Sai-Fok chopped down the bamboo groves and filled in the moat. A neighbour whispered that the district government had ordered that the groves be chopped down to prevent bandits or members of the Nationalist underground resistance from hiding there.

Shorn of its rich protective walls, Sai-Fok looked bare. Sau-Ping had the queer feeling that dust from the dry wide world was blowing in her face, bringing further change.

CHAPTER 11

Class Struggle Meetings

Sau-Ping had a fever. It was probably just a common flu, but it left her tired and dizzy by day and unable to sleep at night. She did her best to hide it from her brother-in-law, not wanting to burden him with so insignificant a problem. Her constitution was strong. In time, the flu would go away.

But on this night, she woke from a fitful doze to the sound of knocking on a door further down the alley. She heard shouting, and then sounds of desperate pleading. The shadow of a man crossed her window, blocking out the moonlight. She told herself she was imagining things, but there was another shadow, then another. She tried to count them. Some had large humps on their backs. She thought she heard scuffling footsteps and occasional gruff laughter.

Eventually the night grew quiet again, and Sau-Ping slept. In the morning, she recalled the cries and shadows as a vivid dream.

But she had scarcely gotten out of bed when she heard someone knocking rapidly, softly, at her own outer door. Quickly winding up her hair, she moved cautiously to the front of the house. She heard her neighbour call, "Ping!"

Sau-Ping was shocked by the sight of Yi-Lin. Her hands were crossed under her neck, and her eyes were dark. "Did you see?" Yi-Lin demanded in a low voice. "Two doors down. Leung Kwok-Tung's door is broken in. You can see inside his house. Did you hear them?"

"I heard something."

"They came through the alley last night. Because he's a landlord. He's been charging his tenants half of their harvest as rent, and now there's a directive, no more than a quarter of the harvest can be taken by the landowner. And no rent deposits. The Peasants' Association broke down his door to demand back pay. Retroactive to October 1949 when the People's Republic was proclaimed. The door is in three long pieces."

"But this has been the going rate for rent and rent deposits in our village for a long time. What if the landlord doesn't have enough to pay the tenants back?"

"Then they have to borrow or sell their belongings. Or the Peasants' Association will confiscate everything."

Sau-Ping stood as if frozen. Every day, the people who had control declared a new punishment against those in the village who lived comfortably. She took a breath.

"I was told I'm not a landlord. What do you think? We have two farmhands, but no tenants. We pay them regularly and let them have our old brick house for free. Fei-Yin and I work our own land. What do they want?"

"My husband says it is simple. They want to take all the power in China."

"They talk about justice," Sau-Ping said.

"Justice this hard is no justice. It is revenge."

Sau-Ping covered her face with her hands. She did not want to see what was coming anymore.

That evening, Yik-Mo told her that in the market many landlords were selling their jewellery to earn money to refund the tenants. When she asked how many landlords there were in the village, he answered that about half the people of Sai-Fok's New Village did not own any land at all, and nearly all the others worked on their own plots, whether or not they had help. He did not believe the Communists would hurt people who were honest with their labourers and who worked the fields with their own hands. "And the members of the Peasants' Association are still frightened of Uncle Leung Kwok-Yung. He and the elders still decide who will be allowed to rent the corporate land. The Leung lineage is old. It is the backbone. If they cut it at the neck, what will they have left? A corpse." Yik-Mo dropped his voice. "Who knows? The Land Reform Work Team that issued these directives may not last very long. This may be their last directive. They may be going too far."

But Yik-Mo could not have been more wrong. The Communist regime was determined to stay. Slowly, the strength of the new organization became clear to Sau-Ping, though she still could not understand its shape or imagine who was initiating these orders. There were leaders in Beijing. The leaders in Beijing had committed troops to fight the United States forces in North Korea. But then they grew

afraid that Korea was draining too much of their force, so they directed their attention at China. Sau-Ping imagined one great eye looking
through a telescoping series of eyes, the last and smallest of which
was fixed on her own side window. The ancestors watched you as
well, but this was different: those who watched from Beijing could
not be propitiated.

When Kin-Pong graduated top of his class from Tuen-Fan Junior
High and left in the fall of 1951 to board at the beautiful Toi-Shaan
High School in Toi-Shaan City, Sau-Ping was proud. She also felt
some relief. She tried to believe her adopted son would be safe inside
the strong walls constructed with monies earned through the efforts
of Gold Mountain guests, men like his adoptive father, grandfather,
and granduncle in Canada. At about the time Kin-Pong left, Fei-Yin
returned to sleep at home. The Communists had disbanded all maid-
en houses and boys' houses in the village. The occupants were told to
attend meetings to study the marriage law and to take part in mixed-
group activities. Thus Fei-Yin and Lai-Sheung were separated from
their web of female friends and sent home.

One day Sau-Ping and Fei-Yin heard from some women gathered
near the stream that the *po-cheung*, Leung Yik-Shing, was dead. He
had taken to sleeping with a gun, and he shot himself when he heard
the People's Militia bombarding his walls and door. It all happened
at night, and by morning, there wasn't even any blood to be seen.
Sau-Ping listened without speaking and returned to the paddy.

That very evening, she opened her door to Siu Kong. He began
speaking without introduction; obviously, he had given this speech
many times. He said Leung Yik-Shing was a counterrevolutionary
who had aided the Nationalists against the people by dragging off
villagers to fight in the Nationalist army. He said Yik-Shing had collected tea money from Overseas Chinese families who required marriage or birth certificates, or who wished to escape conscription into
the army, and that he had used the money to aid the Nationalist
cause. Now Yik-Shing was dead, but many other enemies of the people remained in the village. Yik-Shing's belongings had been
reclaimed from the house and redistributed among the People's Militia. His wife and daughter were being questioned.

Here, Siu Kong took a breath; he hadn't once looked Sau-Ping in
the eye. Sau-Ping kept her face plain and alert, though Siu Kong's
mention of Yik-Shing's wife and daughter sent a chill across her skin.

"Following directives from Kwong-Chau," Siu Kong resumed,
"we have been working hard since summer to mop up bandits and

suppress counterrevolutionaries. Our campaign has now basically succeeded. There will be a public trial of all these bad elements at Shaan-Tai Market in two days. At least one member from every household must attend. This meeting has been called by Chai Ling, the leader of the Land Reform Work Team stationed at Shaan-Tai Market. It will last for two days. Everyone should congregate at the village gate on the morning of 9 September."

"Thank you," Sau-Ping said. "I will be there."

Siu Kong tipped his head and then took a great, bounding step towards Yi-Lin's house. His energy opened Sau-Ping's eyes; she realized that all the Communists in the area were bubbling with eagerness to summon other villagers to witness the spectacle they had organized.

So there she was, two days later, at the village gate. Members of the People's Militia, all wearing red arm-bands, tried to make the villagers fall into line, but the people of Sai-Fok village weren't used to lining up. A young man with an armband and a Cantonese accent bellowed, "You should see nothing but the back of a head. No faces! In line, one behind another. In line!" He yelled the same words over and over again, and people started shuffling into line. Sau-Ping felt silly looking at Mei-Kuen's rough black bun of hair and short earlobes. She felt as if she were walking inside a little cage that was being carried by an invisible giant.

Led by three Cantonese outsiders and the core leaders of the Peasants' Association, everybody marched. On their way to Shaan-Tai Market, they met up with groups of peasants from other villages. There were more than a hundred natural villages in the Eighth District. Sau-Ping had not seen so many people massed together since that day in the train station at Toi-Shaan City. She and Mei-Kuen shifted nearer her brother-in-law, Yik-Mo. The spilling crowd was directed to the yard of the Tuen-Fan Junior High School. Sau-Ping and the other villagers from Sai-Fok sat down in the area marked for them in white chalk.

People with red arm-bands started cutting through the noisy crowd, enforcing silence. People were made to sit on the ground. For a long time Sau-Ping could not see around the bodies of the men and women in front of her, but eventually the crowd settled and the public trial of pirates and bandits began. A group of men in full uniform pushed about twenty bedraggled men onto a makeshift stage fashioned from crates and boards. These "bad elements," their hands tied behind their backs, were forced to kneel.

Sau-Ping hated bandits and pirates. They had attacked Sai-Fok and stolen her family's savings, so that Yik-Man was forced to return to Canada early. They had murdered Uncle Leung Kwok-Wang's family. They had stolen Mei-Kuen off the path. Sau-Ping glanced sideways at Mei-Kuen. Her friend looked at once puzzled and focused.

Sau-Ping turned her eyes to the stage, afraid that she was not supposed to watch other people's faces. But a movement next to her elbow caught her attention. Mei-Kuen had covered her eyes with one hand. There were men on stage she recognized.

As members of the militia read out the crimes, each of the accused was made to lift up his head so that villagers could shout accusations at him.

An old man went up to the stage first. He struck one of the kneeling men with his walking stick and cried out his accusations, but Sau-Ping could only hear echoes of what he was saying. He was followed by others, until a swarm had developed. Angry peasants, made limber by rage, clambered onto the stage from all directions. The bound men were being kicked. Sau-Ping could no longer see as people stood up. A shrieking voice pierced the din.

"My daughter starved to death because of one like you! My husband wouldn't take me or her back. She is dead!" Sau-Ping was being bumped. She stood up and looked around. Mei-Kuen was already on her feet.

Up on the stage, the People's Militia could be seen in the mêlée, trying to regain control. One of them urged repeatedly, "Do not kill these criminals! The government will deal with them." But the mob was not so easily silenced; it seemed that everyone in the crowd wanted a turn at beating the bound men. In trying to protect the accused, members of the People's Militia began tossing men off the stage. For some reason, this quieted the swarm.

On a nearby platform a uniformed man was shouting something in Mandarin. The militia representatives looked towards him, and one young man with an arm-band leaped up beside him on the platform to interpret for his leader. The uniformed man had to be Chai Ling, head of the Land Reform Work Team at Shaan-Tai Market.

She heard: "The government ... the wishes of the masses ... executed. In point of fact, the government ... trial by the People's Court in Toi-Shaan City and have been found guilty."

"Guards!" the interpreter yelled out the order. "Take them away for execution!"

Sau-Ping sat down on the ground next to Mei-Kuen. As she stared at the grass, she could smell her friend's warm scent through the dust. Gunshots sounded in the air. A few people had begun eating lunch; Mei-Kuen was eating a bowl of rice. Sau-Ping was not hungry.

The afternoon session was similar, but the crimes were different in nature; now the accused were "counterrevolutionaries," *po-cheung* rounded up from villages in the Eighth District, along with some former police, soldiers, and leaders of the self-defence corps. Chai Ling once again passed sentence: some were to be shot, twenty were to be imprisoned for life, but most were sentenced to hard labour at the new mountain camps.

Next to be exposed on stage were the "local bullies" – operators of opium dens, whorehouses, and gambling outfits, smugglers, local thugs employed by large landlords to beat up peasants who were delinquent in their rent. Sau-Ping learned all this because her friend, Mei-Kuen, had discovered an informal network of people relaying announcements from the stage backwards.

Chai Ling dealt much more leniently with this group than with the others. None would be shot; nearly all would be sent to the labour camps.

Sau-Ping, Mei-Kuen, and Yik-Mo sat quietly in the house that evening. The two girls, Fei-Yin and Lai-Sheung, who were both sleeping at home now since the maiden house had been dissolved, were off in another room. The adults were expected to attend another struggle meeting the next morning.

Suddenly Yik-Mo pushed out of his chair and disappeared into the kitchen. Sau-Ping guessed that he had gone next door to hear news from Yik-Kwong. He returned sooner than she had expected and sat down in a chair that had never given him comfort.

"Tomorrow they have the lineage chiefs," he announced.

"The Communists will probably just talk to them and scold them. The punishments were lighter for the last ones today. Go to sleep," said Sau-Ping.

The crowd was gathered inside the scuffed white chalk circles in the schoolhouse yard. On the stage a militia member lunged towards an old man, then stepped back, then lunged again, barking accusations. The militia member had worked himself into a frenzy; Sau-Ping could see his red face even from a great distance. And among the powerful, rich men – ancestral hall managers, lineage chiefs – collected on stage, she could make out Uncle Leung Kwok-Yung of Sai-Fok. His clothes and his posture were familiar to her, though his arms were bound behind him. His face, narrowed by terror, looked different.

The People's representatives moved in the crowd, encouraging villagers to make accusations.

But today the audience was quiet, hesitant, and restrained. Who could strike a lineage chief? A lineage chief stood at the front of the ancestral hall and presided over the Spring and Autumn Rites. Sau-Ping's own husband, brother, father, and brother-in-law had been taught to respect the leaders of these rites. It was the lineage chief who delivered the speech at the opening of the village opera. He toasted the families at the lantern celebration, marking the births of sons who would continue the lineage. Who could kick a lineage chief? What would happen to the roast pork? What would happen to the families?

Chai Ling sensed the reluctance of the audience. Echoed by the interpreters, he exhorted the people to speak their bitterness against those who had cheated them: here they were, with their hands tied.

Some villagers did cry out. Sau-Ping guessed they had given their allegiance to the Communists and been appointed to authoritative positions as leaders of the Peasants' Associations, under orders to stir up passion against the lineage chiefs. Leung Yik-Hung, Wai-Fong's husband, shouted, "Never forget the bitterness of class exploitation! Forever remember to avenge injustice!" Whereupon, the rest of the activists, sitting in front, all raised their fists and repeated the slogan in unison.

Sau-Ping felt weak as she watched Bitter-Face Kong on the stage, slapping the face of the lineage chief, Leung Kwok-Yung. She remembered the words of hatred Siu Kong had intoned on the deserted village path during the Hungry Ghost Festival right after the war. The People's representatives had forced a path through the crowd so that residents of Sai-Fok could be brought closer to hear the accusations of their own chief. Sau-Ping, was moved forward.

The words from the stage were very clear.

"Leung Kwok-Yung, you are a wolf in sheep's clothing. You were selected to manage three hundred *mau* of corporate land belonging to the main ancestral hall of the Leung lineage. The lineage members all trusted you, and yet you betrayed them. You rented the best pieces of corporate land to your close relatives. They gained at the expense of other lineage members. You also pocketed most of the rent and the rent deposits and used the money to lend at high rates to the poor peasants in your lineage. You are a real ancestral hall termite!"

Siu Kong slapped Uncle Leung Kwok-Yung's face hard.

"You were the lineage leader for a long time, and yet you never once protected the villagers of Sai-Fok. You let bandits, secret society members, military bosses, Japanese devils, and Nationalist soldiers come into the village to kill, loot, burn, and rape. You let them carry away your kin as recruits. Many of them never returned.

"During the great famine in 1944, when villagers were eager for some rice, you swindled them. You told them that the county chief of Toi-Shaan would sell grain to them below market value in ten days' time once they put down a deposit. You in fact used that money as capital for speculation and black marketeering in the next six months. Then you gave peasants the worst kind of rice mixed with sand and pebbles.

"Where was your conscience? Do you know how many people starved to death waiting for your so-called cheap rice? Do you know how many people died from eating pebbles and sand that were mixed with the rice?"

Uncle Leung Kwok-Yung was sputtering defences: he hadn't invented the cheap rice deal, it was the corrupt county chief of Toi-Shaan.

The slap he received changed his mouth. His lip was cut.

Sau-Ping heard her brother-in-law cry, "We had nothing to eat. We ate grass when you had our rice. You had our money!" The young man's head disappeared into a bobbing storm. All around her, Sau-Ping felt muscular movement, the power of a great swarm of roused bees. She closed her eyes and was bumped hard, many times.

Even with her eyes closed, she knew when Uncle Leung Kwok-Yung was led out to be shot by the firing squad. The rest of the elders of Sai-Fok were sentenced to five years of supervised hard labour in their own village.

The struggle meeting ended after the lineage chiefs of all the one hundred and nine villages were sentenced. Sau-Ping walked home in the crowd. Few people spoke. Most were now afraid to speak out-doors where they might be overheard.

Some of the men in the crowd were walking very quickly, hoping to get back to the village and claim a portion of newly liberated lin-eage land for their own, rent-free. They were eager to open the gates to land reform. Others walked at a fast pace because they wished to slip back into their houses and bolt the doors. The great village fam-ily to which every man had once belonged was torn. Behind them all, Uncle Leung Kwok-Yung's ghost was no longer bleeding. Sau-Ping believed she could see the blood drying on his face. She walked in the current of the crowd.

A week after the struggle meetings, Siu Kong moved out of his mud hut in the Old Village section. He and the two *sai-tsai* families took over the house that had once belonged to Leung Yik-Shing, the former *po-cheung*. That was their way of sharing the fruits of victory.

CHAPTER 12

Farewell, My Village

Late one evening in autumn 1951, Siu Kong came to Sau-Ping's door and asked her family to donate money for the People's Government to buy airplanes, tanks, and cannons.

"Captain Siu Kong," said Sau-Ping, giving the former *sai-tsai* the same honorific now used for everyone in Sai-Fok, "could you kindly tell us what the donation is for?"

"To resist America and aid Korea. The United States will invade China after they overrun Korea."

"Is Canada allied with America in this war?"

"Yes, they are all part of the United Nations forces," replied Siu Kong. "They are all imperialist pigs!"

Sau-Ping and Yik-Mo nodded, saying they would certainly help China. But minutes later, after the door was closed, they spoke of their shared concern. What would Yik-Man, Father, and Paternal Uncle in Vancouver think if they knew that their hard-earned savings had been contributed to fund a war between China and Canada? Would this war affect their position in Vancouver? Would Canada define them, the Vancouver Chinese, as new enemies of the country?

Sau-Ping was reluctant to donate, but like many villagers she had come to fear Captain Siu Kong, and what's more, she knew she had no choice but to comply. Those who resisted were branded as "hidden counterrevolutionaries," and her memories of the long, deadly performance she had witnessed with the great crowd in the school-yard had not dimmed. She and Yik-Mo donated five thousand *yuan*.

"The Communist party appreciates your patriotic contribution to fight the imperialist paper tigers," declared Siu Kong. Before moving off to the next house, he added that there would be an informational meeting on land reform at the Sai-Fok Elementary School two weeks hence: "It is important that one of you be there." Yik-Mo said he would attend. Sensing the importance of the meeting, the decision seemed logical to Sau-Ping; he was a man, and he was literate.

On the day of the meeting, Sau-Ping waited at home for Yik-Mo. Lately, the impassioned discussions that she, Yik-Mo, Mei-Kuen, and her neighbours had enjoyed, discussions that helped them all understand the wider world, predict upcoming events, and attempt to form their own plans, had lost their flavour. A passive weariness had descended on the New Village. The Communists would decide the future. Directives would decide the future.

Yik-Mo returned home exhausted and took the cup of tea she offered him with a trembling hand. Slowly, he repeated what he had gleaned from the meeting. Members of the Land Reform Work Team were going to issue new directives, in accordance with which every household in Sai-Fok would be classified into different social classes, based on the economic activities of each household between 1946 and 1949. Yik-Mo rubbed his forehead, trying to remember the categories named by the speaker. "If a household relies mainly on agriculture, then it can be classified as one of six classes – landlord, rich peasant, small rentier, and three others. Labourer is one. If a household does not rely mainly on agriculture, it can be classified as worker, industrialist, or merchant." Since households in the village had so many different sources of income, there were many more subcategories; the landlord class alone was subdivided into dead landlords, feudal landlords, and others, including Overseas Chinese landlords.

"What will we be? Who is going to decide? What are these class labels used for?" Sau-Ping asked. But the Land Reform Team had said only that they would follow the principles of democratic centralism and mass line in making their decisions. Yik-Mo tried to explain.

"'Mass line,' I think, means that the officials will let us discuss government directives in public. I am not too sure what 'democratic centralism' means. Some villagers say it means that the government will listen to us and act on our desires. Others tell me that it means the government will hear what we have to say, but do it their own way anyway."

Sau-Ping listened.

"Members of the work team say that the decision-making process will be done in three rounds. In the first round, we'll discuss the issue among ourselves and give them a list. In the second round, they will check our list against records. Then they will hold closed-door discussions with the core leaders of the Peasants' Association. They will get the Peasants' Association leaders to estimate our 'standard of living' and how much of our income depends on exploiting others."

"What does 'exploiting others' mean? What does 'standard of living' mean?" To Sau-Ping the terms sounded hard as foreign coins. She remembered the odd Canadian coins she had seen long ago in Leung Tsing-Haan's palm.

"'Standard of living' means what type of house we live in, whether our clothing has patches, whether we eat rice or sweet potatoes every day, and how often we have eggs, fish or chicken."

"But how could core leaders of the Peasants' Association know for sure what we eat at each meal?"

Yik-Mo gave her a blank look.

"I'm sorry, Yik-Mo, please continue."

"As for 'exploitation,' I think they mean whether somebody lends out money at high interest, charges tenants high rents, pays farm labourers low wages or doesn't pay them at all, that sort of thing. But I could be wrong."

"Who will take part in the final round of discussion?"

"It will be the core leaders of the Land Reform Work Team at Shaan-Tai Market. These 'big brothers' from the North are the real bosses, particularly Chai Ling. You saw him. He was the one who officiated at the struggle meetings."

"Yes." Sau-Ping closed her eyes, recalling the lineage chief with a black bullet hole in his head, like a fish's empty eye socket.

Yik-Mo said that the Peasant Association would take over the corporate lands that were once controlled by the ancestral halls for eventual redistribution. Finally, property belonging to those classified as feudal landlords, landlords with commercial or industrial interests, or rich peasant families would be confiscated."

"You'll be subjected to struggle meetings by the masses if you are classified as one of those," he added.

"What of Overseas Chinese? They need our money, for Korea," she whispered. "The Nationalists gave Overseas Chinese families some privileges. Remember? Our men were to be conscripted last, and we could buy back our *yeung-lau*, remember? Yik-Mo," she gripped his cold wrist and realized that she had almost never touched the flesh of this young man, her brother-in-law. "We are in danger. We are in danger."

"Overseas Chinese landlords can keep whatever land they can farm. The rest will be confiscated for redistribution. But they can keep their personal savings, their house, their furniture, and other personal and household effects."

"For how long, brother-in-law? How did they sound? When they spoke of Overseas Chinese landlords, did they express thanks to them?"

"They sounded like always, like airplanes coming over the mountains," he said wearily, without looking at her.

Sau-Ping stood up, letting go of Yik-Mo's cold arm. "The Goddess of Mercy will bless us. We have never exploited anybody. We cannot possibly be designated as landlords, even Overseas Chinese landlords. Even if we are, they say we can still keep our *yeung-lau* and a small portion of our own land. Fei-Yin and I can still farm. We women are so used to farming anyway. You could continue to work at Lei-Kiu in the market. It would just be like the year we returned from Yeung-Kong County after the war."

Since the informational meeting in the schoolyard, Sai-Fok had been darkened by bickering. Villagers accused their neighbours and acquaintances of being rich, while claiming that they themselves were poor. Nobody collected rent or lent money. Sau-Ping and Yik-Mo had decided to let their own labourers, Ah Tsaan and Ah Kwai, keep whatever harvest they brought in from the family's land.

The discussions on class designations commenced. Sau-Ping did not attend, and Yik-Mo gave her only brief accounts of what went on. The sessions weighed on him like months of drought or months of rain. When they stopped, it was understood that the Peasants' Association and the three Cantonese members of the Land Reform Work Team had taken over and were sorting out the names of villagers on slips of paper.

A month later, the results were out. One hundred and twenty-three pieces of red oblong paper were pasted on the door of the main ancestral hall. Each paper had the name of the head of a household written on it. The papers were grouped into different social classes.

Yik-Mo walked to the fields to tell Sau-Ping and Fei-Yin that their family was listed as belonging to the small rentier class, together with thirteen other families living in the New Village section. This meant that while they lived comfortably as landlords, their main income did not come from exploiting others. "And you farm a major part of our land. You only have labourers because there are not enough ablebodied male members of the family living with us. Ah," Yik-Mo knelt at the edge of the field, "you have your feet in the dirt, and so you save my head. Let me remember that."

The women were embarrassed by his brief show of emotion. Fei-Yin glanced sideways at her mother. Sau-Ping gave her a look that meant "Be still."

But that evening, when she herself knelt alone in front of the ancestral altar, Sau-Ping felt an overwhelming relief. "Ancestors you have blessed us. We are safe. We are safe," she repeated as she kowtowed over and over again in front of the tablets. It was not until the next morning that she found the courage to ask about the fate of her fellow villagers, those she liked and those she did not.

Yik-Mo told her that Leung Yik-Faat's family were listed as feudal landlords because they relied on income from inherited land. Wai-Fong's and Siu Kong's families were both listed as poor peasants. Yik-Kwong and Yi-Lin's family was listed as belonging to the merchant class. Sau-Ping did not go to her neighbour's house to discuss their relative designations. Such a conversation would be marred by unspoken calculations, even jealousies. She did not want to sow weeds in their friendship.

Two days later the village activists knocked on every door. A struggle meeting was going to take place at the Sai-Fok Market on 5 January 1952. A representative from each family had to attend.

Yik-Mo said he would attend, but when Sau-Ping mentioned the meeting one evening, he exploded in anger. "You live in this house! You bring your friends to live! Where is my family in this house, the men who paid for it? You use me like a puppet to represent the family!"

Sau-Ping was so shocked by the outburst that when she walked to her bedroom, she found that her teeth were chattering. Early the next morning she and her brother-in-law resolved their argument with brief apologies, but she insisted firmly that she would attend this meeting and represent the household. Yik-Mo said, "Thank you. I cannot stand it."

Compared to the one officiated by Chai Ling in Shaan-Tai Market on 9 September 1951, this was a small meeting, for it only involved inhabitants of the seventeen villages under the jurisdiction of Kat-Cheung Heung. Sau-Ping stood and watched the proceedings as she knew she must.

The People's Militia had put sharp stones and coarse sand on the makeshift platform at the market. The heads of the fifty landlord households from the component villages of Kat-Cheung Heung had been kneeling since early morning, and patches of dark blood marked the sand. Sau-Ping saw Leung Yik-Faat humbled, kneeling in his blood.

Captain Siu Kong stood behind him and reeled off his accusations. "Leung Yik-Faat is as bad as his father, Leung Kwok-Yung, the former lineage chief of Sai-Fok." Siu Kong slapped Yik-Faat on the side of the head. "His family owns forty *mau* of land, and they charge very high rent. Some poor peasants have had to give up their daughters to Leung Yik-Faat until the rent was paid in full!" Siu Kong kicked Yik-Faat in the ribs, and the bound man had to scramble in the sand to right himself. "With all the rent it collects, Leung Yik-Faat's family pays no land taxes. Since the government collects taxes in a lump sum per village, Leung Yik-Faat's family collects more taxes from other families to cover its share of the taxes!" Siu Kong slapped Yik-Faat. "This bastard is rotten to the core. He uses all the exploitation money to finance his pleasures. He gambles, smokes opium, and visits whorehouses. He knows no shame! When I went to arrest him, he tried to bribe me by offering ten *mau* of first-rate land as well as his own daughter, Ah Chue.

"Should we not settle the exploitation account with him? Should we not confiscate his land and his house? Should we not seize all the grain in his storeroom and sell all his belongings?" Siu Kong lifted Yik-Faat by the collar and shook him.

"Confess! Confess!" the crowd shouted. Sau-Ping moved her mouth.

Leung Yik-Faat raised his head and cried into the air, "Captain Siu Kong, you have no right to arrest me. The final decision has not been made by the work team at Shaan-Tai Market. I will ask for a new –"

"Oh?" Captain Siu Kong paused. His arm swung back, and he slapped the face of the accused man so hard that Yik-Faat tumbled to the ground. When he righted himself, his cheek and neck were smeared with blood and dirt.

Yik-Faat cried out from his broken mouth, "My family should be considered Overseas Chinese landlords because my son, Kin-Tsoi, became the adopted son of Leung Kwok-Ko in Vancouver in 1936. We should be Overseas Chinese landlords."

At that moment Leung Yik-Hung, Wai-Fong's husband, leaped onto the platform to join Siu Kong. "You sneaky bastard! As the leader of the Peasants' Association at Sai-Fok, let me tell you this. The 'Overseas Chinese landlord' designation is given only to those who purchased land between 1946 and 1949 using overseas remittances. Your family has owned those forty *mau* of land since 1922 when your father, Leung Kwok-Yung, came home from Vancouver to retire. You cannot deny that! We will tell you what you must pay."

Yik-Faat leaned over his knees and spat out a long string of blood.

"Pig!" shouted Siu Kong.

"The Peasants' Association has decided you will pay an amount equal to twenty thousand *kan* of unhusked rice to settle your exploitation account. Your land and house will not be confiscated until the final results come down from the work team at Shaan-Tai Market," declared Yik-Hung.

Yik-Faat wiped his mouth on his shoulder. Then he went down, rolling like a caterpillar flicked onto dry ground. Siu Kong had kicked him in the spine.

Returning to Sai-Fok from the struggle meeting, Sau-Ping saw Chai Ling, the chief, accompanied by the three Cantonese members of the work team, on an inspection tour of the village. She quickened her steps.

From that day on, young activists arrived every morning and evening at those households designated as feudal landlords, commercial landlords, industrial landlords, or Overseas Chinese landlords to shout slogans, and to remind them that they had to pay their "exploitation money" to the masses or face another struggle session. Yik-Mo had heard that every time one of the landlords paid up, the Peasants' Association insisted that he or she still owed them twice as much. This tactic was designed to break the economic power of the landlords. Mei-Kuen was one of the few women who still moved about the village, speaking to people without hesitation. It was Mei-Kuen who told Sau-Ping that one grass widow in Mei-Leung was said to have committed suicide so that the Peasants' Association could no longer press her to squeeze more money out of her husband in the United States. Sau-Ping wondered if Yik-Faat had demanded that Paternal Uncle Leung Kwok-Ko send savings from the restaurant in Vancouver to help settle his "exploitation account."

One cold morning, just before Chinese New Year in 1952, Sau-Ping opened the door to her neighbour, Yi-Lin, who arrived with her daughter, Chun-Fa. "She is so lonely since the Communists closed the maiden house," Yi-Lin said, "and I have to talk to you. Chun-Fa, go. Speak with your friend."

"Fei-Yin is in the kitchen," said Sau-Ping. "You can get warm in there."

"Let's talk here," Yi-Lin looked around her distractedly. "I don't want the girls to hear."

"Is it a directive?"

"No. Death is coming in. I told my husband I wish we had wings, we could fly out of this village."

"What has happened?"

"Yik-Faat beat his wife Sing-Fan to death last night. He escaped with his tiger son Kin-Tsoi before the militia arrived. His house has been ransacked. They raped his daughter, Ah Chue."

The women sat still, listening to the voices of their daughters in the kitchen.

"The Cantonese college girl who held meetings on the marriage law told Sing-Fan to ask for a divorce."

"Let us make tea and – "

"It was after Siu Kong ordered Yik-Faat to sweep the village path to prepare for the New Year."

The two women sat in a narrow band of cold light. "Let us go to the kitchen and get warm," said Sau-Ping.

In the New Village, Chinese New Year was gloomy in 1952. None of the wealthier families dared to celebrate ostentatiously. No Overseas Chinese came home for family reunions, to distribute lucky money, or to host villagewide feasts. No Overseas Chinese donated to lion dances or traditional opera performances. At Lantern Festival on the fifteenth day of the New Year holidays, no young women teamed up to steal vegetables. Hoi-Laan, the women and youth leader, had been organizing mixed activities for young men and women in the village. Lai-Sheung and Chun-Fa tried to play, but Fei-Yin always pleaded sickness. There was a volleyball match between the youths of Sai-Fok and those of the next village. Kin-Pong had returned from school in Toi-Shaan City for the holiday. He dutifully joined the volleyball game but told his mother nothing about it.

Late one night Sau-Ping was sitting in her chair, near the empty chair of her mother-in-law. She had not lit the lamp. Hearing a whisper at the door, she opened it on her old friend, Wai-Fong.

"Sau-Ping, bad news! Bad news!" Wai-Fong sounded breathless as she stepped into the shadows of the house. "I hate to tell you this so bluntly ..." She took a deep breath. "They have decided to change your family's class label to that of an Overseas Chinese landlord!"

"Whom have we offended? On what grounds? How do you know?" Sau-Ping heard her own voice rise hysterically, and she shut her mouth with effort. It felt as if she'd swallowed a squealing piglet.

The leaders of the Peasants' Association were meeting at the main ancestral hall with the three Cantonese members of the Land Reform Work Team. Yik-Hung had ordered Wai-Fong to serve dinner and tea for the meeting, and she had overheard the discussion. Word had come down from the Land Reform Work Team that Chai Ling was not happy with the classification of the households of Sai-Fok. He did not like the passive faces of the masses in Sai-Fok at class struggle meetings. Surveying the list of names and designations in Sai-Fok prepared by the three Cantonese members, he had turned to stone, then to fire, and ripped up the list. He had seen the village for himself on his inspection tour; surely all those living in the New Village section, in their decadent tiled two-storey mansions, were landlords. He declared that those houses should be confiscated and redistributed to the People. The Cantonese members had argued that doing so would upset a lot of patriotic Overseas Chinese. Still Chai Ling had insisted that the number of landlord designations for Overseas Chinese landlords had to be raised from three to six.

"One member of the Peasants' Association suggested that your family be upgraded from small rentier class to Overseas Chinese landlord class. Yik-Hung tried to defend you. He was grateful. You have lent us money . . . I know." Wai-Fong paused. "Someone said that you must be in touch with bandits, since you harbour Mei-Kuen and Lai-Sheung."

Sau-Ping could hardly see her friend in the darkness. Everything was shadow.

"You should go before they discover you," Sau-Ping told Wai-Fong. She had swallowed the squealing pig completely, and her voice sounded plain. In fact, it reminded her of the voice of her mother-in-law.

"May Buddha help you," sighed Wai-Fong.

When Sau-Ping was alone again, another shadow, this one large and warm, entered the room.

"I'm leaving, I heard what she said."

"Mei-Kuen! No! It's their – "

Sau-Ping felt a firm hand on her shoulder. "Come into our room."

It seemed as if all the women in the house were moving like ghosts that night. In Mei-Kuen's room there was no window to expose them, and they were able to light a lamp, yet the room felt dark. Packing only took minutes. Fei-Yin and Lai-Sheung appeared, the one quiet and wide-eyed, the other tall, tense, lanky, ready again for the road. At a certain time that night, the four women – two older, two younger – embraced one another in turn. Yik-Mo never emerged from his room; Sau-Ping suspected he had drunk himself to sleep.

The four ghosts descended to the first floor of the big house. As the moon sank, Sau-Ping and Fei-Yin found they were the only two women left in the house.

Two days later, the decision on class designation for Sai-Fok was finalized by the Land Reform Work Team at Shaan-Tai Market. This time, one hundred and twenty-three slips of white oblong paper were posted on the wall of the main ancestral hall.

Sau-Ping and Yik-Mo had looked together at the fluttering strips of paper, and Yik-Mo had pointed out the one listing their name. They knew they would have to make some quick decisions about what to do when the trouble escalated, as it surely would. No one mentioned Mei-Kuen and Lai-Sheung; Yik-Mo appeared to know they had dissolved in the night. Fei-Yin had lately been suffering from nervous headaches and vomiting and they waited until she had gone to bed before discussing their fears.

"There is no question that they will eventually take away our house," said Yik-Mo.

"After all the hard work of the Gold Mountain guests. Years of work."

"I don't see what can be done."

"Nothing can be done about the house or land. Anything they want to take, we have no choice but to let them."

"But that is not what frightens me the most. I remember what you told me about what they did to Leung Yik-Faat. Kneeling ..."

"Please, Yik-Mo. We must think clearly."

"Sister-in-Law, you know I would never do or say anything to frighten you unnecessarily. But it is coming. We have seen their method."

Sau-Ping remained silent for a long moment, looking at Yik-Mo with a mixture of sorrow and affection. She knew the shape and depth of his eyes, the coldness of his wrist, even the smell of his breath. How odd, she thought, that I am married to his brother, and not to him. Certainly I know him a hundred times better than I know my own husband.

"What do you think will happen?"

"I don't know. I wish we didn't have to think about it. I am afraid they will take me away and ..." Yik-Mo tipped back his head and stared at the ceiling.

"We should flee," said Sau-Ping, surprised at her tone. Again, she sounded like her mother-in-law.

Yik-Mo looked her directly in the eye. "Listen, dear Sister-in-Law," he said, "things could get very unpleasant for all of us in a very short while. There is no telling what will happen. I want you to promise that if you are forced to make a decision, you will choose the well-being of yourself and your children over mine."

"How can you even say such a thing? How can you imagine it?"

Yik-Mo answered quietly. "We must be prepared for the worst. You must think about what I said, and do the right thing when the time comes."

The People's Militia entered the *yeung-lau* at night. Yik-Mo stood in the hallway. They took him away in handcuffs. Sau-Ping and Fei-Yin watched from the pavilion, their faces drenched in tears.

Captain Siu Kong had declared that a member from each household of the village must be present at every struggle meeting. Sau-Ping did not want to see Yik-Mo kneeling in blood on the stage. She did not want to see him being beaten and humiliated by Captain Siu

Kong or any of the young strangers who had come to the village in the last year. On the other hand, she did not know if she would ever see him again. This might be her last chance. Somewhere in her heart, she dreamed of a miracle – the instant acquisition of godlike powers with which she could save him, or perhaps a merciful intervention by the goddess Koon-Yam.

The first struggle meeting targeting Overseas Chinese landlords was held at Sai-Fok Market. Most of the "class enemies" on the stage were grass widows, women in good clothes crouching in blood. Among the handful of men was Yik-Mo, kneeling, like the others, on coarse sand and sharp stones.

Throughout the meeting the audience was sullen and unresponsive; their sympathy lay palpably with the accused. Sau-Ping raised her head as members of the Land Reform Work Team stood behind Yik-Mo, speaking both to him and to the audience. Yik-Mo would not confess his "crimes." When the team members cried out their allegations, he responded in a loud, plain voice. At every moment, Sau-Ping expected him to be struck or kicked, and she braced herself for the blow. But perhaps because the crowd was sullen, the work team allowed Yik-Mo a little time, as if this were a real trial.

When one team member accused him of exploitation, Yik-Mo replied, "Our higher standard of living and our property are not the product of exploitation. Our *yeung-lau* and our farmland were purchased with the hard-earned savings of my brother, father, and uncle in Vancouver, Canada. They were poor peasants before they emigrated to Canada. They suffer at the hands of the foreign devils while trying to make a living. Even while living a hard life in Canada, they have not forgotten their motherland. They donated to many public projects in our community. We have often donated money when requested by the People."

This was long enough. Yik-Mo was interrupted and accused of exploiting the peasants.

"No. Our family has shown sympathy to the poor. My grandmother and mother were grass widows, as my sister-in-law is now. They had a hard time doing heavy farm chores. Who has not seen my sister-in-law and her daughter in the fields?"

Sau-Ping readied herself for a blow, but instead there were more words; now Yik-Mo was called a decadent landowner. Speaking into the air, he said, "Overseas Chinese families have never been large land owners. Our labourers returned to us after the war because they trusted us. They worked alongside my sister-in-law and her daughter in the fields. We lent money to fellow villagers without charging interest. Recently we bought government bonds and donated money to help Korea. What crimes have we committed?"

"Are you accusing the Land Reform Work Team of being unjust?" a core leader of the Peasants' Association demanded.

"I am not the judge here. We own only twenty-five *mau* of land, and we have never rented any of it out. My sister-in-law and my niece do the major share of the farming. We hire two farm labourers merely to help. Who has not seen them in the field?"

Sau-Ping saw the arm lifted. Yik-Mo was slapped hard on the side of the face, a blow that felled him. He struggled up exactly like a small animal wounded by a predator. Sau-Ping watched the shape of her brother-in-law for hours. She watched as he was dragged off the platform to jail.

For the week that Yik-Mo was in confinement, Sau-Ping delivered food to the makeshift prison twice a day. On one of her visits a member of the Peasants' Association, stationed at the prison, told her that her brother-in-law was the only one among the Overseas Chinese landlords at the struggle meeting who had refused to sign a statement promising to ask the Gold Mountain guests in his family to send three hundred Canadian dollars every month to the Land Reform Work Team at Shaan-Tai Market. He asked if she thought she could convince her brother-in-law to change his mind. She replied, "I am not in a position of authority with my brother-in-law." Two days later, she learned that Yik-Mo had been sentenced to five years' hard labour in a camp on the border of Toi-Shaan and Yan-Ping counties.

In early April 1952 the People's Militia, led by Captain Siu Kong, gave Sau-Ping's family seven days' notice to move back to their little brick house in the Old Village so that the poor people of Sai-Fok could have their house. Her *yeung-lau* would be shared by four families, Captain Siu Kong informed her. Their land was to be confiscated, except for seven *mau* that Sau-Ping, Kin-Pong, and Fei-Yin could farm to raise crops for their own consumption.

That night Yik-Kwong, Yi-Lin, and Chun-Fa slipped across the divide between the two houses to express their sympathy.

"Why was Yik-Mo so stubborn?" Sau-Ping asked her friends. "Do you think he did the right thing in not signing that paper?"

"Ah, Ping, Yik-Mo did this to protect you and your children! Because of the Korean War, the Canadian and United States governments will not allow any local Chinese to send more than one hundred dollars per month to China. They are afraid that our government might use remittances from the Overseas Chinese to buy more weapons. You have three relatives in Vancouver, so the most you can get from them will be three hundred dollars a month. If Yik-Mo were to sign that agreement, all the allowances would be in the hands of the work team at Shaan-Tai Market, leaving none to your family," said Yik-Kwong.

"I don't see what to do," Sau-Ping murmured.

"Hong Kong," said her neighbour quietly. "You can establish contact with your husband from there. Overseas Chinese in North America are not sending remittances to China now, because the Chinese-language newspapers in North America say that the Communists are holding all family members of the Overseas Chinese for ransom."

"And Overseas Chinese would not retire here because their houses and farmland were confiscated." Yik-Kwong added. "Besides, those who try to come home for a visit are treated with suspicion in Canada and the United States because of the Korean War."

"You have to escape to Hong Kong for the sake of the children," urged Yi-Lin. "Our government forbids anyone to leave the country. It is not possible for you, Kin-Pong, or Fei-Yin to go to Vancouver from here."

Sau-Ping felt broken and suffocated. Her mind was fixed on the children. She murmured, "Kin-Pong is home. He was dismissed from the boarding school in Toi-Shaan City as a landlord's son. His spirit is shattered. Poor son! What future could he have here? And Fei-Yin, I fear for her. I have heard that one cannot be punished for raping a landlord's daughter."

"You must make your decision on your own," said Yik-Kwong.

"Tell her," Yi-Lin said to her husband. "It is part of the decision."

"We are trying to escape to Hong Kong." Yik-Kwong spoke in a whisper.

Yi-Lin began to speak rapidly. "The Toi-Shaan branch of the People's Bank is now monopolizing the handling of remittance cheques. My husband's money-changing business will soon be snuffed out."

"The day before yesterday," her husband took up the story, "the owners of Kwong Wooi Yuen Bank and the owners of a pawnshop in the market were tortured and imprisoned for lending money at exorbitant rates. Several owners of the grain shop were arrested, and then every shop was robbed for the "fruits of victory." Soon they will arrest me as a class enemy."

"I wish to go with you," said Sau-Ping.

"Then we need help. The border between China and Hong Kong has been closed for months. If we want to leave for Hong Kong, we need a "snakehead" to arrange the passage. After you move to the Old Village, please try your best to see if anyone knows of a snake-head. We'll do the same in the New Village. If we get to Hong Kong, my brother can help you find your Big Sister Sau-Ha's family."

Sau-Ping nodded. That night, alone in the house with the children, she dreamed of a great black snake that disintegrated into a thousand little red snakes when she attempted to follow it.

Seven days later, the People's Militia came and took over Sau-Ping's *yeung-lau*. She let it go without a word. Her furniture and other household effects were taken to the main ancestral hall to be redistributed to the poor peasants.

When Sau-Ping and the children arrived at their old brick house, Ah Tsaan and Ah Kwai were packing to leave. It appeared they had joined the Peasants' Association in the hope of getting a piece of land in Sai-Fok, but now they had been ordered to return to Yeung-Kong County.

Sau-Ping did not know what to do during her first days in the little house. She wished to hide under the bricks as if under a blanket. Then one morning she woke and understood that it was time she risked going out in the sunlight. From that hour, she took her daughter and son to the fields and spoke to certain farming women who struck her as honest in a way she could not define. All of these women knew her and her daughter. Sau-Ping told them that she was waiting for news from friends who could help her; that while she dreamed of flying over the mountains, she knew she would still be in Sai-Fok at planting time.

Most of the women nodded at her in a kind way, accepting her declarations as a broken message from a humbled landlord. But there was one dark-faced woman whose eyes sharpened as Sau-Ping spoke. Sau-Ping knew that she had been a companion of Mei-Kuen's, but now she avoided her and didn't speak to her again. She expected that Yi-Lin's husband, Yik-Kwong, with all his connections in the market, would be the one to discover the snakehead.

Then one night there was a soft knock on the door.

Ever since Wai-Fong had come at night with her terrible news, Sau-Ping's heart would pound like a drum at the sound of knocking after dark. But even if her heart had not grown braver, she had learned to act courageously. She opened the door.

It was Mei-Kuen, with tall Lai-Sheung hunched behind her.

"Sau-Ping, look at you. Let me in, quick. I am not a ghost!"

Sau-Ping gathered her old friend and her daughter into the house. Mei-Kuen was talking in a rapid whisper. "Of course I heard of Yik-Mo. Things are certainly going to get worse. And I had a message. You want to fly, I heard. Now listen. I can't stay. I am a bandit's wife. If they capture me at your home, who knows?"

Sau-Ping said, "You are welcome to stay. At any moment they could enter, whether you are here or not."

"You should know I haven't come to stay. I have come to fly. We will not be dealing with nice people, my friend. I met Leung Yik-Faat and his son hiding in the mountains. He tells me he knows a snake-head who can transport people to Hong Kong. As the asking price was high, Yik-Faat is looking for more passengers to share the cost. Is Yik-Kwong also going?"

"How did you know!" Sau-Ping asked, terrified that she had some-how betrayed her friends.

"Because he is a planner. Who always planned for you? Do your families have money?"

"Yes. I still have some foreign currency, gold, and jewellery sewed into the lining of my quilt. The militia didn't look because it was so badly stained. My daughter was sick that morning. I put the quilt under her head."

"You ... ha! You have learned. I know Yik-Faat is a swindler, but now we are surrounded by bandits. I will watch him." Mei-Kuen spoke like a commander. "He wishes to get to Hong Kong, and he needs your money to pay the snakehead. He has no reason to cheat us."

"And I am to leave my brother-in-law?" Sau-Ping asked hopelessly.

"You cannot help Yik-Mo by staying here. And I know what you will think next. Listen to me. There is no way you can get to our vil-lage to tell Little Brother Tin-Shaang that you are leaving. You must leave while you still can." Sau-Ping was silent.

"Yik-Faat suggests that it would be much safer for each family to leave on its own. We will meet at the beach just off Po-Tso village at Kwong-Hoi Heung four days from now, when there will be no moon-light. Two motorized junks will wait for us until midnight. If any group does not make it there on time, that will be their hard luck."

"Where are you?"

"Ayy, in the mud again. Don't look for me. Stay in your house for a night. Pack tomorrow."

The next night, Sau-Ping, Fei-Yin, and Kin-Pong were packed and ready to go. Side by side, they prayed in front of the ancestral altar for the last time. It made Sau-Ping dizzy to realize that she was going to leave the tablets behind. She prayed to her *On-Yan* to protect them on their journey to Hong Kong, and to help Yik-Mo out of his present suffering.

After Kin-Pong and Fei-Yin had kowtowed in front of the do-mes-tic altar, Sau-Ping slipped outdoors and filled an empty wine bottle with water from the well. "If we become ill because of the water in Hong Kong," she told the children, "we can use this water as a tonic."

There were hours left to wait. Suddenly Sau-Ping slipped outdoors again and walked on the old familiar path to the edge of what remained of her family's farmland. The scent of the earth and the cries of the frogs rose above her head, radiating into the black sky. She knelt with a handkerchief to take a handful of soil.

Returning swiftly on the path, she had just turned into the Old Village when Captain Siu Kong rose before her in the darkness. For once he was not surrounded by members of the People's Militia. Sau-Ping had no time to hide the little bundle she had been cradling in both hands.

"What are you doing, Auntie?" Siu Kong asked, using the old honorific.

Sau-Ping told her heart to be quiet and her tongue to move. No one takes soil from a field unless they are afraid the field will disappear. But wasn't it about to disappear in any case? She said quietly, "I don't know how much longer our family will own this small piece of farmland."

There were any number of criticisms Siu Kong could have levelled against this expression of bourgeois sentiment. Instead he said, "These are new and exciting times, Auntie. You must learn to grow with the change." Then he bade her goodnight and went on his way.

Sau-Ping walked on clutching the small bundle of dirt. Now that Siu Kong had seen her, should she change her plans? He might send men to wait outside her door. But what choice did she have? If she stayed, something terrible was bound to happen to her and the children; what she had said to Siu Kong would be the least of their excuses to punish her family.

And so, later that night, with a single pack-sack each, she and the children, now seventeen and eighteen years old, sneaked out of the village, not knowing when they would see it again.

They hid in the daytime and travelled silently at night. Like hungry wandering ghosts, they trekked across the mountainous paths of central Toi-Shaan to the plains of Kwong-Hoi Heung in the South. There they met up with Yik-Kwong, Mei-Kuen, and Yik-Faat and their families. Guided by a snakehead the two boats hugged the South China coast to evade the Chinese and British patrol boats, bringing the ten fugitives to an unknown future in Hong Kong.

PART TWO

Hong Kong
1952–1955

CHAPTER 13

People! People! People!

MAY 1952

Sau-Ping and Yik-Kwong stood at the crossroad between Argyle and
Shanghai streets in Kowloon. Sau-Ping was dazed. Her lower legs
were sticky with dried salt water, and she could feel grains of sand
stuck to the soles of her feet. Her skin smelled like fuel from the boat
crossing, and she had not yet recovered from the shock of that morning, when the snakehead, a burnt, brazen man with an infected red
eye, had laughed at their party on the beach and announced that he
and his friends were headed off to their own special destination.
Then he had powered the boat backwards, leaving the refugees
stranded in Hong Kong's territorial waters, for they meant no more
to him than a pile of seagrass. Yik-Faat and his son, Kin Tsoi, had
remained on the deck of the boat, and Sau-Ping had watched their sil-
houettes grow smaller until they finally disappeared into the mist
over the water. Daylight was coming in, and the stranded refugees
were in danger of being discovered. It was Yik-Kwong who had
pulled the small group together and begun to walk decisively
towards the rising sun, which was itself obscured by the structures of
an impossibly large city: Hong Kong. And now Sau-Ping stood inside
the boundaries of the city. Completely exhausted, she understood
that it was necessary to resist her fatigue.

"I have not been to Hong Kong in fifteen years," Yik-Kwong was
saying calmly, as if their passage had been easy. Sau-Ping glanced at
his wife, her friend Yi-Lin. Paralyzed with weariness and determination, her face looked hard as a mask.

"I think if you follow Shanghai Street into Mongkok District, you
should hit the boundary between Mongkok and Yaumatei. Turn left
and go down six or seven blocks. Then turn right at Pitt Street."

Sau-Ping was thankful that Yik-Kwong had an idea where her sister lived. To her it was a meaningless address on a piece of paper she couldn't even read; she would rely on Kin-Pong, her educated adopted son, to lead them through the maze of streets to "Shanghai" and "Pitt."

Yik-Kwong told Sau-Ping that his family would be staying with his brother Yik-Nang on Prince Edward Road in Kowloon Tong. "I will look you up in a few days' time to see if you need any help." Sau-Ping's thanks were heartfelt.

"For years you have helped guide my family. Without your courage and your knowledge we would not have known what to do when the snakehead disappeared this morning."

"I would bet you anything the snakehead has taken Yik-Faat and Kin-Tsoi to Kowloon City," Yik-Kwong mused, looking off down the teeming street.

"Kowloon City?"

"Yes, Kowloon City will fit Yik-Faat like water around a fish. It is a place without a government. Both the Mainland Chinese and Hong Kong governments claim to administer it, but neither can control it. So Kowloon City is a centre for gambling, prostitution, drugs. Yik-Faat and Kin-Tsoi could easily obtain heroin there."

Mei-Kuen said, "But he is a stupid bandit. He may well get caught. And I would like to be ..."

Yi-Lin interrupted. "He is gone and I don't care. May he sink into the city. Yik-Kwong, Ping has not been in touch with her Big Sister for twenty years. She is weary, and we should be moving forward while there is strength. Your own daughter is also tired. Good luck," Yi-Lin hugged Sau-Ping tightly. "Good luck, and thank you, Mei-Kuen, for telling us of the snakehead." She hugged Mei-Kuen as well. The three daughters also embraced, exchanging farewells. Chun-Fa and Fei-Yin were subdued; neither had been able to keep food in her stomach on the stinking, rolling boat.

"Write your father in Vancouver and let him know your family has arrived safely in Hong Kong," Yik-Kwong reminded Kin-Pong, handing him another slip of paper with his brother's address on it. Yik-Nang was still in the money-changing business in Tsimshatsui District, not far from where Sau-Ha lived, and could help Kin-Pong handle drafts or cheques from Vancouver.

Sau-Ping, Mei-Kuen, and their families shouldered their packs and set off into urban Kowloon. They did not look back. The traffic closed behind them with the force of water pouring around rocks. Sau-Ping felt her friends disappearing behind her, as if carried backwards by a current. She wondered if she would ever be able to find them again.

But the city did not terrify Sau-Ping. She had seen worse through the years, and she guessed that as soon as she found Sau-Ha, her Hong Kong life would radiate from that point. The section of Shanghai Street that they entered, a few blocks south of Argyle Street, was spacious and crammed with more permanent shops than she had expected. They passed jewellery stores, clothing shops, and windows filled with a hundred shoes. There were also a couple of foreign goods stores like the one Yik-Mo had worked in; Sau-Ping thought with pain of her brother-in-law, who had been trussed like an animal for slaughter and delivered to a Communist labour camp.

This had to be a new day. Sau-Ping said decisively to Mei-Kuen, "What a pleasant neighbourhood."

Mei-Kuen replied, "If your Big Sister lives on a top floor, you may be able to look at the city from her window."

Shanghai Street itself was a long and busy avenue. There were double- and single-decker buses, motorcycles, bicycles, tricycles, rickshaws, trolleys, trucks, and cars. Thousands of pedestrians hastened to and fro, oblivious of the vehicles. Sau-Ping had never seen so much movement, except at the edge of the village pond, where insects and minnows massed and darted in frantic layers.

"I would like to ride one of those huge buses one day!" cried Lai-Sheung, the adventurous daughter of Mei-Kuen. Sau-Ping glanced at her own daughter, Fei-Yin. There were tears on her face. There was nothing to be done; they had to keep walking.

It had been a stormy trip from Kwong-Hoi to Kowloon. The group had been stowed as tightly as bales of cloth, crammed along the bottom of the two stinky, motorized junks. The sound of the engines, the smell of gasoline, the heaving motion of the vessels as they sailed through rough waters, the fishy stench of the buckets of seafood, and the fear of being discovered by Chinese or British patrol boats had beaten the spirit out of the passengers in a short time. Fei-Yin had vomited repeatedly. They had sustained themselves by whispering to one another of all the new possibilities Hong Kong held, and of the hope of travelling one day to Gold Mountain. But they were reaching the point where dreams and whispers could no longer sustain them.

Sau-Ping began to notice that the city around her was changing. She didn't share her concern with her companions, but she felt that the jewellery stores and windows full of shoes were being dragged away from her by the same current that had taken hold of her friends, Yik-Kwong and Yi-Lin. As the weary refugees walked further south, the shops assumed a more practical nature. There was a rice dealer; there were tiny stalls selling bamboo ware, metalware, mirror and glassware. Kin-Pong said they were now in Mongkok District. Here, not only Shanghai Street but also the side streets and back alleys were full of people, many of whom looked poorer than farm labourers in the village. There were families squatting on the pavement with their cooking utensils, old clothing, and thin blankets all tucked into one or two cardboard boxes. Others pitched tents made of rags and mats, with bamboo poles as supports. Some lived out of wooden boxes of the kind Sau-Ping had noticed that morning piled at the end of an empty pier. These ramshackle shelters were crammed at the bottom of staircases and under verandahs. The air smelled unhealthy.

The very old, the very young, and even able-bodied men and women were covered with rags, their hair long and unkempt, their faces and bodies soiled with dust and dirt, their hands outstretched as they begged for a pittance. Sau-Ping had never seen such destitution since the day she stood in the shifting crowd of refugees who had flooded into Toi-Shaan City to escape the Japanese. She wondered what these street people in Hong Kong would do in winter or during the typhoon season, but she didn't have the strength to envision the horror.

"Here!" Kin-Pong said, with relief in his voice.

The group turned right onto Pitt Street. Though Sau-Ping was accustomed to sustained physical work, the hard surfaces of Hong Kong made her legs and hips ache. And the crowds left her breathless. They could barely squeeze between the cooked-food stalls that jammed the street. Each foodstall had a tentlike kitchen at the side where rice, hot-pots, and noodle dishes were cooked on kerosene or charcoal stoves. At the back of each stall was a wooden table on which the cook and an assistant chopped meat, gutted fish, and cut vegetables. One or two pails of water were used to wash dishes, bowls, and chopsticks, as well as vegetables. Sau-Ping wondered how city people got their water. A picture of the sparkling village paddy-fields and the nearby village stream crossed her mind.

The customers of the thousand food stalls, mostly men, squatted on benches, many of which extended into the middle of the road. These patrons were having an early lunch, obviously enjoying it, despite their congested surroundings. When Fei-Yin accidentally bumped into a squatter, he grunted and shifted sideways on his haunches like a crab; his chopsticks moved all the while, and he never raised his eyes. The road underfoot was slippery with garbage. Hovering flies occasionally landed on people's food.

Amid the crush, Sau-Ping tried to remember what her elder sister looked like. It had been over twenty years since Sau-Ha left home for Hong Kong.

"Auntie, could you please tell me how to get to – " Kin-Pong was trying to ask directions from a woman who was chopping firewood on the pavement in front of a tenement building.

"What do you want? What are you saying, you country bumpkin! You can't even talk proper Cantonese. Did you lose your front teeth? Creep away!"

Kin-Pong didn't know how to respond to these unprovoked insults. As a senior high school student in Toi-Shaan's best school, he had been respected in his home community. The group pushed along through the crowds. After a while, Sau-Ping realized that Kin-Pong was no longer asking questions of anyone; he had wrapped himself tightly in shyness and pride. She would have to help. Twice she spoke Big Sister's name in a polite voice to people on the street. Her words had no effect.

"Lau Tseung-Lam! Where does he live! Lau Tseung-Lam! Where does he live? We seek Lau Tseung-Lam! Where does he live? Our relative, Lau Tseung-Lam. Where is he?" Mei-Kuen's voice boomed straight into the crowd like a vendor's. Sau-Ping craned to see if anyone would help them. Nothing happened for some minutes, and then a middle-aged man emerged from one of the stores along the street just behind the foodstalls.

"Toi-Shaan? Where is this voice? I am from Toi-Shaan. Maybe I can help you find your relatives. Lau Tseung-Lam and Sau-Ha? They live two houses down. You are so near you could jump from here into the door. The house with a wooden clogs workshop on the ground floor." The man pointed to a worn old tenement building. Sau-Ping looked up, half-believing she might glimpse her sister staring out from a large window on the top floor. All she saw was a shabby wooden shack perched on the roof.

The tenement buildings along Pitt Street all looked the same, except that there were different kinds of workshops on the ground floor. They reminded Sau-Ping of the houses in the old section of Sai-Fok, except that these were much taller – three storeys high instead of one. Many mothers in Sau-Ping's village considered themselves lucky if they could marry a daughter to Hong Kong. Sau-Ping perceived that these "fortunate daughters" really lived as poorly as some of the poorest villagers at home.

As the group of five approached the wooden clogs workshop, they saw a middle-aged woman resting on the bottom stair, holding two bunches of vegetables. She was talking to another woman who was energetically scrubbing laundry on a wooden board immersed in a wooden tub of water. The woman with the groceries looked old. She was thin, her cheeks sagged, and the skin around her eyes was creased with worry. Her hair, done up in an untidy bun, had already turned half white. But there was something in the shape of her eyes and the way she moved her hands that Sau-Ping instantly recognized; after so many years of separation, here was Big Sister, near enough to touch.

"Sau-Ha?" whispered Sau-Ping. She tried again, louder this time. "Sau-Ha!"

The woman turned her head and squinted violently. "Hmm. Toi-Shaan?" she said. "Yes, what ..." Then a change came over her face, a moment of light. "Ping?" Big Sister scrambled to her feet. "Sau-Ping! Is that you? Aiya!"

"We are alive," said Sau-Ping. "My daughter, my son, here, here they are." She gripped Big Sister's hands.

"You're so thin! What sneaky devil has been eating up all your food? And this is Kin-Pong! Already so big! Is this Fei-Yin? Aiya!"

Mei-Kuen laughed her thundering laugh.

"Mei-Kuen!"

"Do you have the comb you took from me in the maiden house?"

Sau-Ha shrieked, laughing. "You threw that comb at the fish! You said it was no use trying to comb out your hair, it was buffalo hair." She turned. "Look at Fei-Yin! Look at you! Oh you are beautiful. But you are so pale."

Fei-Yin bowed her head.

"She is tired," her mother said. "The boat ride made her very sick."

"Aiya! Today you came on the boat! You must be tired. Come upstairs. You can take a short nap in the triple-decker in my cubicle. I have to return to Reclamation Street to get more groceries for lunch. Come. No talking. We will talk later. Poor Fei-Yin."

Up they went, climbing three flights of grimy stairs. It was so dark that they could barely see the ground. Piles of raw wood blocks and finished wooden clogs, yarn and bundled cloth, were stored at the foot of the stairs, on the landings, and even on the stairs themselves. They had to be very careful not to trip. Weary beyond measure, Sau-Ping could not quite comprehend that here, after so many years, she had reunited with Big Sister. Instead, her attention was claimed by the slippery steps and the big mounds of sharp wooden blocks that could tear open her ankle if she stumbled.

They reached the third floor and walked along the hallway. On one side was the common kitchen, with a built-in concrete bench and a tap. Seven wood stoves were placed on the bench. On top of each stove and hanging from the ceiling were seven kitchen cupboards for leftovers. On the other side of the hallway was a common bathroom with a big night-soil bucket and several chamber pots. Beside these pots was a small area with a tap for bathing. There were buckets filled with water, one for each tenant. The area was partitioned off by a piece of plastic cloth to provide minimum privacy.

Sau-Ha opened a door and led her visitors through. The room inside was lit by one glass bulb shaped like a small gourd that dangled from the ceiling; Sau-Ping knew the little bulb had electricity burning inside it, not kerosene. It produced a feeble light, just enough to reveal that the walls were patched and raw, the cracks plastered over in big white stains. The room itself had been divided with particle board into a number of cubicles – five? seven? – each with a door. At the moment, all the doors were open. The particle board did not reach all the way to the ceiling, so chicken wire was used to close off the top to deter thieves. Sau-Ping noticed a cock-loft built halfway across the ceiling that could be reached by means of a ladder. It comforted her; the families must climb the ladder to pray before their ancestral tablets. She wondered how so many tablets would be arranged.

The cubicle furthest away from the door, the only one with a wooden window and a balcony outside enclosed by chicken wire, was the largest. Sau-Ha explained that the family of the tenant-in-chief lived in this relatively bright and spacious cubicle. From the tenant-in-chief, Sau-Ha's family sublet the second cubicle from the door. The small band of refugees crowded in the dark and stuffy little space. Shut off on both sides, neither daylight nor fresh air could reach the compartment. The three-tier bunkbed took up most of what little room there was. Three layers of wooden planks, each with a mat on top, formed the sleeping area for the whole family of seven. Sau-Ha said that she and Lau Tseung-Lam slept on the bottom tier with their six-year-old son. The four older children, two girls and two boys, occupied the two upper tiers. Their clothing was tightly stacked at the side of the beds together with their bedding. Under the bunkbed, miscellaneous household effects, including extra blankets and quilts for winter, extra water basins, cookware, preserved vegetables, salted eggs and fish, firewood, dusters, a broom, and a sewing box, were stowed in a manner that reminded Sau-Ping of the ship's hold in which she and her family had been packed like eels just the night before. A small chest of drawers stood beside the bed. Sau-Ha said that the family usually sat on the bed when they ate, using the top of the chest of drawers as a dining table. The drawers also served as a desk for Sau-Ha's six-year-old son, the only child they had in school.

The other five cubicles in the room were similarly furnished. The members of one family were outworkers, Big Sister said; they made drinking straws for a beverage factory. The members of another family threaded beads and did embroidery work for a living. Sau-Ping glanced up at the electric bulb and concluded that she would not have been able to thread a needle, or even find a needle, in this faint light. Two single but unrelated men shared a bedspace in the cock-loft on a shift system, Sau-Ha said. One worked the days, the other nights. They had no cooking privileges.

Sau-Ping felt her heart sink. In Hong Kong, then, the cock-loft was used as bedspace for humans instead of sacred space for worship. Did people here have space for ancestral tablets at all?

She was more dismayed than she would ever admit by this, her first glimpse of Sau-Ha's meagre living conditions. At home in Sai-Fok, she had seldom had news of her sister. She knew Sau-Ha worked long hours and took few holidays, but still, she had some-how imagined that life in Hong Kong was more comfortable than life in the village, perhaps even brilliant, with electric lights and women sparkling at night and the riches of the world mixing on the streets. She hadn't expected a castle – but these cramped, forbidding quar-ters? Sau-Ping was reluctant to breathe in this space. "I'll come help you do groceries," she said, ready to descend into the relatively open air of the street.

"No need. You must be exhausted after such a long and dangerous journey. Why don't you take a nap with the others? There's lots of room."

Sau-Ping was tired in body and spirit. This dark space depressed her, though she knew it was a haven after the terrors she had so recently witnessed in her own village. She couldn't help but think of her open, spacious, clean *yeung-lau* in Sai-Fok. She reminded herself that her property had been confiscated by the People's Militia.

"Please Big Sister, I am not tired. I'll come with you." Sau-Ping spoke from her heart, as she felt her Big Sister examining her face in the dim light. Both women knew these living quarters were dreary, and both recognized the obvious: that all five refugees could not fit in this cubicle. But each was glad to be looking on the face of the other.

"I would enjoy your company very much," said Sau-Ha with sim-ple dignity.

Mei-Kuen and the three teenaged children stayed in the cubicle to rest, and the reunited sisters trooped back down the dark stairs.

Reclamation Street was jammed with mobile pedlars and the fixed stalls of hawkers. Some pedlars had portable trolleys or carts, others simply displayed their goods in a basket or spread them on a blanket on the ground. The mass of hawkers blocked the entrances to the line of minuscule stores on either side of the street. These stores carried various dried, preserved, and salted vegetables, eggs, seafood, Chinese tea, herbal medicine, kitchenware, charcoal, firewood, brooms, and feather dusters.

At this time of the day, business was at its height. Some hawkers chanted their distinctive calling songs. Others clicked two pieces of wood or beat a gong to attract attention. Thousands of customers bargained with them to get a lower price, extra portions, or fresher produce. Still others bought drinks, steamed cakes, deep-fried pastry, or other foods that had either been precooked at home or were made on the spot. There was hardly any space for pedestrians, let alone vehicles.

"This market is ten times more crowded than Shaan-Tai Market," thought Sau-Ping, excited in spite of her exhaustion and her disappointment with Sau-Ha's place in this city. The festive atmosphere was infectious. Out of one eye she watched Sau-Ha getting three eggs and two squares of tofu from a hawker whom she patronized regularly. Glancing away from Big Sister, she surveyed the cakes and fruits in the other hawkers' stalls.

"We need to line up at the government-run rice store next," said Sau-Ha. "I have brought the family's ration cards with me. My family members are each entitled to six *kan* of low-price rice every ten days."

"That is generous! The government gives you rice?"

"Yes, it started after the Japanese devils left Hong Kong. With ration cards, we've been able to get food cheaply. Peanut oil, sugar. Rice of course. On several occasions, the government even gave out free quilts and blankets. A few cold winters there has been firewood."

"Do you think we could get ration cards?"

"I doubt it. The cards are reserved for people who've been here, residents of Hong Kong since before the middle of 1948. It is possible ration cards will be given out without restrictions sometime next year. There are rumours. The government made no promises."

"I would prefer a government that makes no promises to the government we have seen." As she spoke, Sau-Ping discovered that even so far from the village, her tongue remained stiff from fear, and she worried someone would overhear and report her to one of the People's representatives.

The sisters regarded one another directly. "What do you have left?" Sau-Ha asked.

"No property in China. After nearly twenty years."

"The world was not easy for our parents. I think it is even harder for us."

"Yes, but we are – " Sau-Ping had intended to say that she was grateful to be out of the village, over the water, with her feet on dry ground, but a pedlar, his cart piled high with rice bowls and bamboo baskets, rumbled straight for her, and as she dodged to make room for him, she nearly fell on the slippery street.

Sau-Ha caught her arm. "I should get you off the street. What would Ma say to me? Be careful for Little Sister!"

"Yes." Sau-Ping's eyes prickled. She found herself battling head-on through the crowd with tears slipping down her cheeks. It was not often she allowed herself to think of her mother, a stern but gentle figure who had been absent from her life for so many years. She wiped her face. "When will I meet my nieces and nephews?" she asked her sister.

Sau-Ha replied, "My older children are all at work today for nine or ten hours. They only have a very brief lunch break. So they are not coming home for lunch."

"What do they do?"

"My two eldest sons are casual construction workers. Tak-Kan is nineteen, Tak-Keung seventeen. They each earn about three dollars a day when they are employed. They'll eat at the construction site today. My daughters, Tsoi-Yuk and Tsoi-Lin, are fifteen and thirteen years old. Tsoi-Yuk has just changed her job. She now works in a factory making electric torches and flashlights in Sai Yeung Choi Street. Paid by piece-rate. She earns about two dollars a day, but lunch is not provided, so she buys lunch at the foodstall. Tsoi-Lin is working in the small weaving factory on our second floor. She is also paid by piece-rate. She gets less than her sister, but her lunch is free. She usually eats with her co-workers and the boss's family."

They had returned to the tenement house. They paused to catch their breath in the shadows on the first floor, next to a great, fat pile of fabric tied with rough strings.

"So at lunch you'll meet only my youngest son, Tak-Wa, when he gets home from school," Sau-Ha continued. "So far, he is the luckiest of my children. With all the others working, we thought we could afford two dollars and fifty cents a month to send him to a primary school."

"My son Kin-Pong was able to go to school," Sau-Ping said. "He was in Toi-Shaan High School, in Toi-Shaan City."

"I don't know how long we can keep supporting Tak-Wa's education."

"Why?" asked Sau-Ping.

Sau-Ha spoke plainly. "My husband was laid off from his job as a night watchman at a warehouse. It used to be a steady job paying twenty-five cents an hour. His employer liked him because he was very reliable, but there is no business because of the Korean War. He is now asking around for any type of employment. He should be back for lunch soon. When there are wars, some of the stronger countries like the United States close the gates to Hong Kong and Chinese goods. When the gates close, my husband has no work. Many warehouse workmen in our neighbourhood are out of work."

"The wars came to us in the village as well," said Sau-Ping. "The remittances would arrive. Then they would stop. You are right, the gates open and close far away. A thousand little people cannot swing them an inch."

"Tsoi-Yuk, my fifteen-year-old daughter, used to work in a factory gumming rubber shoes. But she was laid off because rubber was a strategic material, a war material. So that gate was shut. No more rubber to be imported into Hong Kong because it might go to China. Luckily, she found this job in the flashlight factory six months later. We are also lucky that there is lots of construction in Hong Kong, rebuilding houses that were damaged in the war. So my sons have jobs. I usually sew at home. I make a little."

Sau-Ping nodded. She understood work.

When the sisters returned to the cubicle, Kin-Pong was already awake and writing letters. Sau-Ping discovered she had not an ounce of energy left in her body, so she joined the rest and lay down on the bunkbed.

She awoke not long after, feeling itchy. Sitting up in the dim light, she found, by running her hands along her skin and peering closely, little red bites already swollen fat with blood here and there on her legs, arms, and back.

Sau-Ha noticed what she was doing. "Bed bugs," she said. "I just aired the planks last week and poked all the bugs out of them. I don't know how they got back so fast. They must come from the other tenants' beds." She gave Sau-Ping some ointment to put on the bites.

Lunch was ready and set out on the makeshift table when Tak-Wa, Sau-Ha's youngest son, squeezed into the cubicle. Sau-Ping stared at him as he offered greetings, directed by his mother. He resembled her brother, Tin-Shaang: the cheekbones, the bright dark eyes. He even displayed the same air of privileged discontent she remembered in her little brother in Fung-Yeung village; years ago it had irritated her but now it gladdened her heart, because she knew that her own brother, Tin-Shaang, had been crushed and wizened by catastrophes just as he was about to become a man. The same was true of her brother-in-law, Yik-Mo. And now, Sau-Ha's young boy did not look very happy, but he was young, energetic, and still shining from years of familial attention. He leaned against the little chest of drawers and sighed loudly.

"What is the matter, Tak-Wa?" his mother asked.

"The nurses came to our school again."

"With the needles?"

"We had to line up for our second diphtheria injection. Just last week, we had our second typhoid. Before that the smallpox pricks. Next week, the teacher said, all school children are going to have vaccinations against tuberculosis."

"You are the rag for the young girl who practises her embroidery!" laughed Mei-Kuen, who had awakened earlier.

The boy's mother said quietly, "The brother that was five years older than you died of typhoid, Tak-Wa. You are not the only one having all these shots. Adults also. Haven't you heard the loud hailers touring Pitt Street in their vehicles?"

"My friends say the United States puts poison in some of the medicines. It is secret how much. Your arms swell."

"No. That is talk."

"But that is not all! It is not only me who receives the foreign gifts. Ha!" and the boy laughed.

"What?"

"This." Tak-Wa picked up his heavy schoolbag and fished out a package neatly wrapped and stamped. "The teacher told us that this comes from the Church World Service. It is milk powder and a packet of cheese. Smell it. You can smell it through the wrapping."

"*Chue-shi*? Sounds like pig shit. Could I take a look?" asked Sau-Ping, reaching forward. She put her nose to the paper. "Ugh! It smells like pig shit all right."

Mei-Kuen put out her hands and took the package. She sniffed it and said, "Poison pig shit," then handed the whole thing to Sau-Ha.

Sau-Ha lifted the wrapped, odorous solid. "Like soap for washing dishes. We don't have enough water as it is. Who wants to try the foreign devils' soap?"

"Can you sell it?" asked Mei-Kuen.

"Yes, on the black market."

"Out it goes!"

Sau-Ha then held up the white powder. "What is this for?"

"It's made from cow's milk. The teacher said we should mix it with water and drink it. It is good for our bones."

Sau-Ha made a sound under her breath. "Milk from between the legs of a foreign devil's buffalo. They use them to farm, and then they drink the milk from between their legs. That is why they grow so big, the foreign ghosts.

By this time, everyone was awake. The girls commented on the odd smell in the cubicle. Then footsteps sounded down the hall, and

Sau-Ping raised her eyes to see her brother-in-law, Lau Tseung-Lam, swing into the room. With heart pounding, she stood up. "Hello, Brother-in-Law."

Stunned by the pack of guests in his home, Lau Tseung-Lam stood very still. His hair was grey, his eyes perpetually half-shut, but he had muscles like a farm labourer. Sau-Ping introduced everyone in her group to him.

"There are many refugees this year. I am glad you escaped," he said after the introductions had been completed. "Did you have a hard time finding us?"

"We were lucky that Leung Yik-Kwong, our former neighbour, guided us here. He is joining his brother at Prince Edward Road. I gave him your address, and he said he'll look us up in a few days."

"Hmm." Lau Tseung-Lam nodded once. "They live in Prince Edward Road? His brother must be well off. I don't think they'll be so keen to help poor fellow villagers for very long. But Sau-Ha and I are glad you are here. Yes. I am glad."

Sau-Ping noticed Big Sister and her husband exchange glances as everyone squeezed in and applied themselves to their bowls of rice. It was a joyous meal, despite the lack of space and the uncertain future.

It was the schoolboy who raised the question Sau-Ping had been asking herself now for hours. "Where are Auntie Sau-Ping and Auntie Mei-Kuen going to sleep tonight, Ma?" Tak-Wa asked.

There was silence. Mei-Kuen sat up straight and took in a long breath, apparently readying herself for another long walk. Sau-Ping said quickly, "We will be advised, Big Sister."

"The problem is that the tenant-in-chief would kick us out for bringing relatives in. He already did that to the family who used to occupy the next cubicle."

"That is true," added Brother-in-Law, Tseung-Lam. "We would all be out in the streets with our bedding."

"There are few affordable places. Hong Kong is not like Toi-Shaan where villagers own their houses. To live in this place, we have to put down a year's rent as key money. Right now, we pay nineteen dollars per month ..." Sau-Ha faltered. "My sister comes from across the water with my nephew and niece, and I talk money with her," she murmured.

"This building has government-imposed rent control. If we lose it, we are unlikely to find anything else we can afford," her husband finished.

Sau-Ping spoke firmly. "We could see your bunkbed would never fit another five people. Big Sister, we will be advised by you."

"We will find a place," said Sau-Ha. Though she tried to speak with confidence, she sounded unconvinced.

Tseung-Lam raised his hand. "I can take you to the warehouse at Yaumatei. Even though I don't work there anymore, my old boss still likes me. I think he will give me permission to have family sleep there for a couple of days. It is almost summer. You will not be too cold there."

"That would be a great relief!" declared Mei-Kuen.

"But Uncle Tseung-Lam, where are we going to sleep after that?" asked Fei-Yin, raising her tired face.

"I'll ask my two elder sons Tak-Kan and Tak-Keung. They have been construction workers for so long, maybe they can think of a way."

"Big Sister, listen to me." Sau-Ping reached across the dresser and gripped her sister's thin, cold hand. "I am so grateful that we have arrived safely. My children are alive. We are grateful for your help."

Sau-Ha bent her head.

"I would like to go to a temple to thank the gods for their blessings," said Sau-Ping. "My children are alive, with their feet on dry land. We are not drowned in the salt water. We are not kneeling on the stage for the Communists. Where is there a temple, Big Sister?"

Sau-Ha said quietly, "Tin-Hau Temple," and her lively son, Tak-Wa, added, "Just a few blocks down Shanghai Street towards Yaumatei. Fishermen everywhere. Smells like fish. But there are lots of different gods in that temple – one for every problem ..."

"It is at the public square on Temple Street. Very close to the warehouse I mentioned," added Tseung-Lam in a steady voice. Sau-Ping guessed that her brother-in-law was embarrassed to be found without work, unable to offer his wife's family better accommodations, but he recognized that apologies and shame would profit nobody. He and all the members of his family scrambled to survive in Hong Kong. The newcomers must do the same.

Little Tak-Wa was begging, "Can't we go to the Temple Street market with the shrimp and vegetables? Ma?"

"I have an idea," Sau-Ping announced. "Why don't we visit the temple, and then eat at the cooked-food stall. Let me pay for dinner. Then the five of us can follow Brother-in-Law to the warehouse."

"Ping, you have been here only half a day, and you are already so organized! But we cannot let you pay for dinner. Tseung-Lam and I should pay. We are the local residents!"

"Big Sister, you have already paid for the groceries for our lunch. Look at all of us at your table! I still have a bit of money left," Sau-Ping patted the side of her trousers.

"A Gold Mountain husband, yes. Now that you are in Hong Kong, the gate may open. You will be moving to posh Prince Edward Road, and we will wash before we dare to visit you."

"He'll probably send you money soon or pay your way to Vancouver," announced Brother-in-Law.

It stung Sau-Ping to hear these comments by Big Sister and Brother-in-Law, comments that implied she and her family had lived a life in Sai-Fok cushioned by perpetual luck and luxury. They discounted her losses and her own hard work. What of children? What of companionship? The generous size of Big Sister's family had not escaped Sau-Ping's notice; at least Big Sister had been able to live with her husband. Three sons! But Sau-Ping kept her thoughts to herself and said merely, "Yik-Man does not even know that we are in Hong Kong. Is there anywhere Kin-Pong can mail the letter to his father in Vancouver?"

"And," said Kin-Pong, touching a pocket of his own trousers, "we also need to mail this letter to Uncle Tin-Shaang."

"Kin-Pong! You have already written our younger brother in Fung-Yeung!" exclaimed Sau-Ha.

"I was going to write one to Uncle Yik-Mo too, but I don't know the address for the labour camp in Toi-Shaan." Kin-Pong closed his eyes. His face suddenly crumpled and he hid behind his hands. Tak-Wa watched, amazed at the sorrow of his new relative.

Sau-Ha declared with energy, "I will take you to the post office at Yaumatei now, and then to the temple complex. Tak-Wa can do his homework here while Tseung-Lam takes a nap. When my other children finish work, they can all come to Temple Street to look for us."

"Can we steal vegetables on the way? Will you lead us into new troubles, the way you did when we were young?" asked Mei-Kuen mischievously.

"You we will sell as a slave at the first stall!" Sau-Ha declared, fighting to raise the spirits of the little group.

"I will take the cheese to scare them off! I will throw it in their faces! Give me the pig shit!"

Under cover of the shrieks and laughter, Kin-Pong recovered his composure, and Sau-Ping looked for their pack-sacks, which they hoisted back onto their shoulders. Like a sword sharpened by years of careful grinding, an old, old question passed through her heart when she looked at the packs: Will I ever be allowed to settle in one place alongside my husband?

It was so much better to be outdoors than to be crowded in the cubicle on Pitt Street on this warm and sultry day. Sau-Ping, Mei-Kuen, and their children followed Sau-Ha, who knew the city. At last, Kin-Pong looked up and asked, "Temple Street?"

"Yes, and this is the square," said his aunt.

Temple Street was a self-contained avenue that led directly into the public square. Besides the numerous open-air restaurants and cooked-food stalls, there were hawkers' and pedlars' stalls pitched at the edge of the square and along Temple Street itself. There were specialized corners catering to the needs of men; there vendors sold men's shoes, clothing, and belts. There were also women's corners, where a great variety of garments and accessories had been hung out for display. There were hawkers' stalls selling miscellaneous items, including metal goods and other hardware, curios, flowers, and even goldfish. Then there was the service corner, featuring barbers, hairdressers, shoe-repair pedlars, tinsmiths, tailors, palm-readers, fortune-tellers, and mobile Chinese herbal doctors. Sau-Ha walked her visitors from one corner to another so that they could look over the riches of the Square. Then they turned to the quiet temple.

The temple complex was made up of four temples covered by a long line of green-tiled roofs. Together, the complex was called Tin-Hau, although only the Main Temple was dedicated to the Queen of Heaven. To the right of the Main Temple was the Sheng-Wong Temple, dedicated to the City God. Next door was the Fuk-Tak Temple dedicated to To-Tei, the Earth God. To the left of the Main Temple was She-Tan, a temple dedicated to the District God of the Yaumatei community.

Sau-Ping was interested only in the Main Temple, so that was where she headed. Her family remained outside as she entered the space full of smoke and incense and picked her way through the throng of worshippers. The scents lifted her spirits and gave her hope. She raised her face to look on the Queen of Heaven.

The imposing figure of Tin-Hau stood framed against a central wall made of scarlet wood. She was dressed in a heavy embroidered red robe. Standing before her were four clay figures, each seven feet tall. The first was Tin-Hau's bookkeeper, who held a huge pencil with which he recorded people's virtues and failings. The second was the keeper of Tin-Hau's gold seal. The third and fourth fearsome-looking clay figures were the goddess' guards, called Thousand-Li Eye and Favourable-Wind Ear.

Sau-Ping put oil money in a box placed at the side of the entrance. She purchased joss-sticks and paper offerings from the temple keeper. The Main Temple drum sounded and the ceremonial brass bell was rung when Sau-Ping burned the offerings.

From Tin-Hau's altar, she took two pieces of wood, each about four inches long. Both pieces of wood had a flat side and a rounded side. As every temple had a slightly different set of rituals, Sau-Ping asked the temple keeper for instructions. He explained that she could seek Tin-Hau's advice or help by tossing the two pieces of wood onto the stone floor while kneeling in front of the goddess' statue. If one piece of wood landed with the flat side up and the other with the flat side down, this signified approval or a "yes" in answer to a direct question. But if both pieces landed with the flat sides up, it meant disapproval or a "no". When both pieces landed flat side down, they were to be thrown again.

Sau-Ping threw the two wooden pieces many times. She had many questions in mind, and she murmured them soundlessly as her hand threw the sticks in the shadow of the goddess. Would she, Kin-Pong, and Fei-Yin ever go to Vancouver to be with Yik-Man? How long would they have to wait? A year? Two or three years? Ten or twenty?

The sticks did not seem to fall in any pattern. Sau-Ping remained puzzled, so at last she gave up the sticks in her hand and turned to face the wall to the left of Tin-Hau. There she prayed at the altar of Koon-Yam, the Goddess of Mercy, who was dressed in white. Sau-Ping had always prayed to Koon-Yam when she was in Toi-Shaan, and Koon-Yam had always answered.

Next she turned to the altar placed on the wall to the right of Tin-Hau, and prayed to the statue of the Green Horse God. This god, according to the temple keeper, was a symbol of steadiness and reliability. He often heard and sympathized with the heartfelt prayers of wives who had been deserted by unreliable husbands.

Having prayed, Sau-Ping tied a pair of red chopsticks to the horse's left foreleg, as instructed by the temple keeper, hoping that the Green Horse God would send a reminder to Yik-Man that a husband without a wife was no more use than one chopstick without the other.

Sau-Ping emerged from the Main Temple into the bustle of the square. Her family and friends still stood where she had left them, but the little crowd had been increased by six: Brother-in-Law and Sau-Ha's five children. Greetings were exchanged all around. It was time for the evening meal at the open-air foodstall.

Each person selected a meal, and then the family settled on a bench near Fuk-Tak Temple. The conversation soon turned to the subject of where Sau-Ping and Mei-Kuen's families were going to live. As the city dwellers thought long and hard about rental spaces that might be affordable, Tak-Kan, Sau-Ha's eldest son, raised his chopsticks and gave his opinion. "Tomorrow there will be no construction work for me and Tak-Keung. We can help Auntie Sau-Ping and Auntie Mei-Kuen build a hut up at Shek Kip Mei in Shamshuipo District. I figure there are around fifty thousand people living up at Shek Kip Mei.

There must be some Toi-Shaanese amongst them. It is only about an hour's walk from our home. We can get materials."

"Husband? What do you think?" Sau-Ha asked, turning to Tseung-Lam. He was thinking, looking at the ground and nodding his head.

"Hmm?" his eldest son demanded. "Pa?"

"Yes," he said. "I believe it is safe. We will look for a good place."

Sau-Ping and Mei-Kuen exchanged a look. "Yes," said Mei-Kuen. "That suits me. One prayer answered."

Sau-Ping smiled and bent to her rice bowl; suddenly the shrimp and rice and greens had become fragrant and delicious.

As night came, the public square was lit up by lanterns and light-bulbs. The place was jammed with people. In the middle of the square were performers and Cantonese opera singers. It was like a free nightclub for the poor. Sau-Ping, Mei-Kuen, and their children felt welcome and excited, though Brother-in-Law cautioned them about the crowds at the back of the temple complex, where open-air gambling casinos and portable mahjongg huts were set up. Many men were hot at it. Sau-Ping kept a close eye on her children. She noticed how Kin-Pong examined the men reclining in a corner with a lamp, inhaling smoke through a short bamboo pipe. They were all skin and bones, just like the addicts in Toi-Shaan before the Communist takeover. "The use of heroin is common in this neighbourhood," Lau Tseung-Lam murmured to his sister-in-law. "My sons do not come here."

Kin-Pong had been approached by an older woman whom Sau-Ping took to be a begger, but there was something odd about her. She spoke with a narrow, false smile on her face, and she was dressed too cleanly. Sau-Ping heard only the words "... our girls are just ..." before she saw her sister's husband and eldest son deftly separate the woman from Kin-Pong.

Soon after, Lau Tseung-Lam took the five refugees to the warehouse for the night. First thing in the morning, he, Tak-Kan, and Tak-Keung planned to gather discarded wood from the construction site the two boys worked at; that would do for the frame and floor of the hut. By going through the dump at the seaside in Taikoktsui, they hoped to collect enough material for the roof and the walls. Then they could start building a house for Sau-Ping, Mei-Kuen, and their children on the hills of Shek Kip Mei.

CHAPTER 14

Disasters

Shek Kip Mei reminded Sau-Ping and Mei-Kuen of Fung-Yeung, the village where they were born in southern Toi-Shaan. Both were located up on the higher slopes of a bare mountain. There was no electricity. People either went to bed when it got dark or relied on moonlight or a small oil or kerosene lamp to do their chores. Since most people had nothing worth stealing, and since the weather at that time of the year was warm and sultry, doors were kept open in the daytime to let in fresh air and sunlight. Children, some clothed, some naked, ran in and out of their neighbours' huts.

But there the resemblance ended.

Shek Kip Mei was enormous. Brother-in-Law said he had heard there were ten thousand squatter huts – one hundred times as many as in Fung-Yeung. Terrace after terrace of huts climbed up the slope like gargantuan stair steps, in a tightly packed, ramshackle progression that reached halfway up the hill. In Fung-Yeung the houses all faced south. In Shek Kip Mei, they faced in all directions. Some huts jutted out on platforms supported by wooden stilts. They could only be reached by ladders. Other huts hung precariously on the edges of cliffs. Unlike the houses in Fung-Yeung, which were made of brick or mud and built to last, these squatter huts were framed and floored haphazardly in wood posts and planks and then draped in a variety of materials to make the walls and roofs – wood, bamboo poles, packaging paper, zinc board, corrugated iron, sheet metal, tar paper, box-tops, wire netting, rope, canvas, rags – whatever could be salvaged from rubbish heaps in the back alleys, narrow streets, or at the pier of Hong Kong. Many of these shelters were so poorly constructed that an onlooker could see through into their interiors. Typhoons and harsh winters would devastate the occupants of these flimsy creations.

What's more, while Fung-Yeung was a single-surname village, Shek Kip Mei's inhabitants were total strangers to one another when they moved in. They spoke different dialects and had come from different parts of South China or Hong Kong. In Shek Kip Mei, there were no ancestral halls, *tang-liu*, *tiu-lau*, maiden houses, boys' houses, or other public buildings that defined "village" for Sau-Ping and Mei-Kuen. However, the women found that they met with cooperation and assistance from their new neighbours, who did hold one thing in common with them: poverty. Sau-Ping and Mei-Kuen soon learned that inhabitants of this huge village, which was not really a "village," had been sufficiently united and organized to form the Shek Kip Mei Kaifong Association, located down the hill on the main street of Shek Kip Mei.

But the main difference between this place and their home village, the most worrisome day after day, was that this place had so little fresh water. Not that Sau-Ping, Fei-Yin, Mei-Kuen, and Lai-Sheung would have minded carrying buckets of water on a bamboo pole; in Toi-Shaan, they had carried water from mountain streams or fish ponds to their village home several times a day for as long as they could remember. But that was child's play compared to the efforts required of people who needed water in Shek Kip Mei.

It wasn't long before the women learned from their neighbours that Hong Kong had no big rivers. For its fresh water supply the mammoth city had to rely on rain, which fell mainly during the summer. To treat and store this rain water, the government had constructed reservoirs; imagining a "reservoir," Sau-Ping pictured a row of a hundred buckets, each as large as a house and filled to the brim with stagnant grey water. However, water shortages persisted. After typhoons, the hard rains too often ran down Hong Kong's steep hills towards the sea faster than the reservoirs could catch them. The water resisted capture.

Sau-Ping's neighbours understood that many Hong Kong residents resented the swarms of homeless refugees who had fled Mainland China in the last few years above all because they were all dipping their buckets into the general water supply. Each year the Hong Kong government imposed severe water restrictions, like the one that was in force when Sau-Ping and Mei-Kuen arrived. Water could only be collected in buckets during a five-hour period each day.

Thus, Sau-Ping found herself, along with a mass of other Shek Kip Mei refugees, standing in a seemingly infinite queue in the heat, hours before the main tap was turned on. Their household had barely enough water for drinking, cooking, and laundry, let alone rinsing their mouths and wiping their faces and bodies. Only about once a month could they afford the luxury of a bucket bath.

Sau-Ping had always been able to bathe. For years after her field-work, she had rinsed her limbs in the running stream without a second thought. This torment – the absence of water – weighed on her, and she was not the only one who found refugee life bitter. She often heard her son weeping at night. Kin-Pong had been a top student in the Toi-Shaan Senior High School, the magnificent school built in the 1920s largely from money donated by the Chinese in Canada. He had been looking forward to a bright future in Toi-Shaan. And now, what could he do? Recite poetry in his head as he squeezed out dirty rags to wipe his hands and face?

Sau-Ping and Mei-Kuen kept track of their children, but in the end there was only so much they could do to ease their passage into this new situation. For the women had quickly found themselves confronted by a terrible problem: they needed to find work to earn the money to feed themselves. Both hoped that Yik-Man would send money soon, but they could no more make a remittance appear than they could fill their buckets with water by staring into the sky. Sau-Ping heard herself speaking angrily of Yik-Man. She had very few savings left. She imagined her husband, once again, sleeping alongside a Vancouver wife. She envisioned them pouring great buckets of hot water down one another's backs.

Mei-Kuen did her best to ease her friend's growing depression. She reminded Sau-Ping that the children were alive, that they weren't sleeping in the streets of Hong Kong, and that they had better air to breathe than those who rented musty cubicles with bunkbeds. "We don't have to listen to any tenants-in-chief. We don't have to pay rent and we have ventilation, sunlight, and privacy. Besides," Mei-Kuen continued aggressively, "all our children have grown up. I don't think we'll ever starve to death. All we need is to figure out a way to make a living."

Sau-Ping felt comforted by her old friend's optimism. It was good that the children were grown, for the struggles of women with young children were terrible to watch. She still remembered seeing a pregnant woman the other day wailing beside the road after she had slipped and fallen down the slope, spilling her buckets of water. Nobody let her jump the queue for a second chance at the tap. Sau-Ping had watched the woman's hands paddling desperately in a little mud puddle, trying to retrieve the spilt water.

"We will ask the neighbours. We will talk to the neighbours, the way you did when you wanted to leave Sai-Fok," said Mei-Kuen.

The next day, as Sau-Ping stood overlooking the crowded, sloping, difficult terrain that had so suddenly become her home, she heard a familiar voice call out, "Hey Sau-Ping, guess who's come to

see you?" There was Brother-in-Law, leading a wonderful steady figure – Leung Yik-Kwong – up the steep path towards their hut.
Behind Yik-Kwong was another man, well dressed and dignified,
who gave the impression of being perfectly content climbing up the
dirt path in his good shoes. Sau-Ping clasped her hands together and
beamed. She called to the children, who emerged from the shack –
Mei-Kuen was off queuing for water. Introductions were made. It
turned out that Yik-Kwong had brought his older Hong Kong brother, Yik-Nang, to visit.

"So you are Sau-Ping," said Yik-Nang. "I am delighted to meet
you. Your husband Yik-Man and I were playmates in Sai-Fok. Of
course, I haven't seen him for years. He left for Canada when he was
ten, and I left for Hong Kong shortly after that. It's a coincidence that
you lived next door to Yik-Kwong when he was in Sai-Fok. And here
we come together. So often this is how it happens. I am sorry we were
not able to visit you earlier."

Yik-Kwong spoke up. "I have started working for my brother in
Hong Kong. My wife sends her greetings to you."

Sau-Ping responded happily. She was deeply pleased to hear that
Yik-Man had a childhood friend in Hong Kong, and that her old ally,
Yik-Kwong, had once again landed on his feet.

"It took me a long time to find your sister at Pitt Street," Yik-
Kwong explained. "Since we had never met before, I had no idea
what she looked like. I'm sure I would have had an equally difficult
time trying to find your hut, but luckily your brother-in-law was free
to take me."

"We had to jump from rock to rock," laughed the Hong Kong
brother.

"We sometimes had to walk right through someone's hut because
there were so many together with no path in between!"

"Have you any news about Sai-Fok?" asked Sau-Ping eagerly.

"No, not really," said Yik-Kwong, "except that I saw Kin-Tsoi in
Tsimshatsui yesterday, just across from our money-changing store.
He passed like a jackal."

"Has he found work?" Kin-Pong spoke up, anxious to hear of anything that might lead to employment.

"Well, yes, if you call pushing dope a job," said Yik-Nang. "I'm
sure that at night he's busy handing out white packets to big-nose
sailors, American sailors."

Sau-Ping made a noise inside her mouth that signified disap-
proval. Brother-in-Law added that there were drugs all over
Tsimshatsui to satisfy the American soldiers resting from the war in
Korea.

"We work near the neighbourhood they have chosen as their playground," said Yik-Nang. "For us, it is necessary. In this money-changing business, we rely on the foreign currency of the soldiers. But I would advise you and your daughters not to frequent Tsimshatsui."

"Fei-Yin hears you, I am certain," said Sau-Ping. "Thank you."

The conversation stalled for a minute. Yik-Kwong and Yik-Nang were surveying the waves of shanties that stretched down the mountainside. Sau-Ping remembered what Mei-Kuen had said to her about asking questions. She gathered her courage and said, "We are now all looking for work. Do you have any suggestions?"

The brothers regarded one another.

"My friend Mei-Kuen used to sell congee and buns at the Sai-Fok Market in Toi-Shaan. Do you think we could operate a cooked-food stall? She spoke about that. We have seen so many of them in Kowloon."

"That's not a bad idea further down the road," said Yik-Nang, "but I think you should start with something easier to handle. May be you could sell fruits and vegetables."

"Why is that easier than a cooked-food stall?"

"You need a lot of money to set up a food stall. You must buy all the cooking utensils. The fuel."

"Benches, tables," added Yik-Kwong. "License, rent. And the government issues only a limited number of food hawkers' licences per year, and the applicants must have a Hong Kong identity card."

"And the officials and the policemen will still give you a hard time," said Yik-Nang. "You can be evicted when the streets are widened. You can be fined for dumping. You can be fined for blocking traffic or selling unclean food, especially when there is typhoid about."

"Then it's impossible," Sau-Ping said quietly, her muscles relaxing in despair.

"Yes," confirmed Brother-in-Law Lau Tseung-Lam, eager to speak his mind in front of the elegant Hong Kong money changer. "I've seen many foodstall operators on my street paying off inspectors, officers, and policemen, one after another. Money. More money."

"But selling fruits and vegetables, you can carry your baskets of produce and run like hell when these police, officers, or inspectors come!" declared the well-dressed Hong Kong brother, Yik-Nang, laughing.

Even Kin-Pong laughed.

"What happens if we get caught?"

Brother-in-Law spoke. "I heard from unlicensed pedlars on my street that their goods are confiscated and they are fined. If you cannot afford the fine, you might go to jail for three weeks or so."

"Even if we could run fast and avoid jail," Sau-Ping said, half to herself, "we don't have the money to start selling vegetables and fruits."

"Well," Yik-Nang raised his hand, "I will lend you some money as starting capital. You can pay me back when you receive Yik-Man's cheque. That will come soon."

"Oh, how kind of you! We would pay you interest."

"No. Never. I come from Sai-Fok too, and Yik-Man was my friend. Listen," Yik-Nang said, squinting up the hill as he made his plans for Sau-Ping, "I have a regular client in Shamshuipo who operates a wholesale market. Just tell him that you are my relative, and he'll sell you vegetables on a credit basis. He might even give you the better-quality stuff at a lower price. Here's his address." He handed a slip of paper to Sau-Ping, who handed it behind her to Kin-Pong. "I am sure Tseung-Lam can show you how to get there. Yes?"

Brother-in-Law nodded smartly.

"But I must give you another piece of advice," said Yik-Nang, who more and more resembled his brother in Sau-Ping's eyes. "Some of you should find other employment. During rainy days, in the typhoon seasons, or if there are floods and droughts in the New Territories or South China, you'll have a hard time getting supplies. Your baskets will be empty."

"Or the vegetables won't be fit to eat," Tseung-Lam concluded. "I've seen plenty of those."

The two brothers, Yik-Nang and Yik-Kwong, stood on the slope with their forearms crossed over their lower ribs, posed identically, though they had not seen one another for years. The picture made Sau-Ping smile. She began to hope once more that her prayers would be answered and her own family one day reunited.

Later that day she explained everything to Mei-Kuen, who was very pleased by the idea. They agreed to try selling vegetables. But even with Yik-Nang's connections and interest-free loan, the family discovered that getting started in the hawking business was difficult. On the first day, though they had received detailed directions from Uncle Tseung-Lam, Kin-Pong and Fei-Yin got lost looking for the wholesaler. By the time they found his stall, he had gone home for the day. His son, a boy of about fourteen who had only recently taken on his own unsupervised shift, was nervously wary of swindlers and refused to believe the two siblings were actually relatives of Leung Yik-Nang. They had to buy already-wilting vegetables at full price. By the time Sau-Ping's group set up their stall, all the good spots were gone and the morning rush was well over. They made no profit that day.

On the second day, Yik-Nang's friend the wholesaler was in and he sold them vegetables at a small discount. They set up early in the market. But at around half past eight in the morning another vegetable pedlar came to their spot, insisting that it was his turn in that space. He threatened to pummel Kin-Pong if the group did not move.

Eventually, after days of small successes and mishaps, Sau-Ping's group settled into a routine. Twice a day, in the early morning and early afternoon, Kin-Pong would push his wooden cart to the vegetable wholesaler to buy fresh produce. The group would set up their stand on Yu Chau Street in the vicinity of Shamshuipo Market. By around two in the afternoon, when business had grown slack, Kin-Pong, Lai-Sheung, and Fei-Yin would take turns lining up at the public tap for their daily supply of water. Then by evening, the rest of the group would push their pedlar's cart up the steep hills of Shek Kip Mei, carrying the remaining vegetables in their baskets. They used the leftover greens, which would have been given to the pigs in Toi-Shaan, for dinner and shared the rest with their neighbours. They stored the hardier vegetables, such as ginger and sweet potatoes, outside their hut to try to sell again the next day.

To increase their chances of finding customers, Sau-Ping's group worked out a division of labour. The two women managed the pedlar's stand, staying put with the bulk of their supplies. Their three teenaged children moved around, each with a small basketful of vegetables and fruits to sell in the vicinity.

Like other pedlars and hawkers on their street, Sau-Ping's group paid a fee to the "black society" for protection. They took part in a system of rotation whereby every owner of a hawker's stand got a chance to be at one of the two entrances of the street. Those so favourably situated on a particular day were duty-bound to act as sentries. Whenever the sentries spied a policeman or a government official at the street entrance, they would cry, "Run, ghost! Run, ghost!" At this signal the hawkers, like a great flock of gulls taking wing, darted off with their produce to hide until the official or policeman had departed.

Late one morning when business was at its height in Yu Chau Street, Sau-Ping and Mei-Kuen heard the cry "Run, ghost!" They ran so fast that their cart collided with another pedlar's cart and their vegetables and fruits tumbled off into the ditch. The women stared helplessly at the damp green ruin around their feet and the upturned cart, which Fei-Yin later told her mother reminded her of a house that had fallen off a mountainside.

This unfortunate, but perhaps inevitable, incident forcefully reminded Sau-Ping of Yik-Nang's warning: it was clear that the little band of refugees could not depend on vegetable sales to support them year-round, so the members of their group started looking for additional work. Mei-Kuen had found out from the neighbours that there were quite a number of unlicenced handicraft workshops and small cottage industries in the Shek Kip Mei settlement. They might have employment prospects there.

After much searching they found a subcontractor for a plastics factory in Kowloon who happened to be a native of Toi-Shaan. He promised Sau-Ping and Fei-Yin that he would give them work whenever he received a large order for the assembly of toothbrushes or plastic flowers. A few days later he knocked on their door, and that same day Sau-Ping and Fei-Yin found themselves crouched in a long shack outfitted as an illegal factory, where crowds of women assembled stiff flowers from buckets of lurid, bright red plastic petals that resembled rose petals but were much too thick and evil smelling to be attractive.

Between hawking and plasticware assembly work, Sau-Ping and Mei-Kuen's families worked odd jobs in Hong Kong to survive. As was true for so many inhabitants in Kowloon, their income fluctuated widely. A day of hawking could be ruined by bad local weather; a day of industry work could be ruined by storms in the world market.

Four months later, Sau-Ping, who had just returned from her factory work, stood on the hill looking down at the landscape below her, a landscape that was not beautiful but had become familiar. Beside her stood Big Sister, Sau-Ha. They were watching Kin-Pong climb the slope with two buckets of water balanced on his shoulders. Sau-Ping didn't dare to call out, because she was afraid he might be startled and spill the water. In her hand was a letter that Sau-Ha had delivered, a letter from Vancouver! When Kin-Pong raised his head, she raised the letter in the air. His face lit up as if he had turned it into the sunlight. But mother, son, and aunt decided they ought to wait to read the letter until the rest of the group had arrived home. An hour later, they saw their small band with the familiar cart trudging up the hill. Sau-Ping made no sound, though her heart was thumping vigorously. Kin-Pong called for his sister to hurry. When they were all assembled, he read the letter aloud.

Kin-Pong, My Son:

I am so glad that you are safe in Hong Kong. We in Vancouver are extremely upset that the "communist bandits" took our land and our house, which were the harvest earned by so many years of our blood and sweat.

Your grandfather died three months ago after a long illness. He was heart-broken when he learned that your uncle Yik-Mo had been sentenced by the "communist bandits" to five years of hard labour.

Your grandfather's last wish was to have his bones transported back to Toi-Shaan for permanent burial. However, the elders in The Toi-Shaan Association here did not want us to have dealings with the "communist bandits." So your granduncle Kwok-Ko and I arranged for a very elaborate funeral for your grandfather. We bought a grave plot at the Overseas Chinese Cemetery in Vancouver.

Between medical expenses and funeral expenses for your grandfather, I have no savings at all. Luckily, Uncle Yue in the general store next to our restaurant was kind enough to lend me some money. He is also from Toi-Shaan, and he sympathizes with our family situation.

Attached is the bank draft. You should use part of this money to purchase a third-class one-way ticket at the shipping company. I need you to come to Vancouver. With your grandfather gone, and granduncle's health deteriorating, the restaurant is short of hands.

One piece of good news. Since 1950 the Canadian government has modified its immigration regulations. They now allow us to sponsor our children under twenty-one (instead of under eighteen) to Canada. But you should come as soon as you can because no one can tell how long this new regulation will last.

The boat takes eighteen days from Hong Kong to Vancouver. It only runs once a month. You should come in the next few months. Winter is cold here compared to Toi-Shaan or Hong Kong. We can find you clothes I think.

The Canadian Commissioner's Office is at the Union Building on Peddar Street, Central District, on Hong Kong Island. That is where you should apply for your visa.

Let me know the date of your arrival.

From Father.

p.s. Send my regards to your mother and sister.

Sau-Ping's emotions changed dramatically with every sentence of the letter. She was sad that her *Loye* had passed away, and that he could not even be buried with his ancestors in Sai-Fok. She thought about her parents-in-law's marriage. They had died more than a thousand miles apart from one another, after years and years of separation. Each had laboured dutifully for years in honour of the other but had received no comforting words or praise from their partners in all those days, all those years. And now her own life ...

"Regards to your mother and sister." Such a brief line.

She was grateful that Yik-Man remembered her and remembered to send money. He had not discarded her memory and her years of lonely familial devotion.

"Regards to your mother and sister." A brief line.

Kin-Pong would be leaving soon, and then there would be no one but females in the shack on the dry mountainside. Of course, this was the fate of all the Toi-Shaan mothers who had husbands in North America. Their sons left as soon as they received word that even a thin opportunity had opened for them. That was the way it had been for the last hundred years.

But what of the daughters? Sau-Ping could not bear to look at Fei-Yin's face. Her daughter had lived through years of hard work, startling disasters, terrors, and now, bad dreams and beggerly conditions. And what did she earn for it? A slight mention at the conclusion of a long letter. Fei-Yin was Yik-Man's natural daughter. She was also the eldest child. Kin-Pong was an adopted son. Why should Kin-Pong and not Fei-Yin get sponsored to Vancouver? It was true that Fei-Yin was only a girl, and in the past girls were usually not sponsored overseas, but now times were different, and the Exclusion Act had been repealed, which meant Yik-Man could now sponsor everybody in his family. Surely Fei-Yin and Sau-Ping could be as helpful in the restaurant kitchen as Kin-Pong! But the men only looked to men and to boys. Sau-Ping felt her spirit move angrily, pushing against her throat and choking her. She could not help but ask, "Did your father mention anything about getting me and Fei-Yin to Vancouver eventually?"

"I am afraid not," said Kin-Pong, whose face was red as if he had been standing above a steaming rice pot. He understood the full implications of his mother's question.

Sau-Ping glanced at her sister. Sau-Ha's head was bowed, shielding her face. Then she looked to Mei-Kuen and saw a gathering storm. Without warning, Mei-Kuen walked out the door.

Kin-Pong raised his eyes and looked straight at his mother. "Ma, I can't go to Vancouver and leave you here. You'd be all women. Who's going to help you carry water, or go to the wholesalers to get vegetables? Or read the letters? What about typhoons?"

Like a prowling tiger, Mei-Kuen slipped back inside the hut. Her face was intent, her eyes burning. In a dangerous voice she spoke to Kin-Pong, "I know you are a good son and brother. Look at me. Don't worry about us. We women are tough! We have been through many typhoons, floods, and landslides in Toi-Shaan. Long before you were born, your mother and I carried water, weeded, transplanted, harvested, and did the heavy farm chores. You are a schoolboy and your father ... I remember how he kicked the sedan chair. He is a kite in the wind. He is a man without muscle!"

"Friend," called Sau-Ping, rising to stop the storm that had suddenly entered their flimsy house. "For years my husband –"

"I lived in mountain caves for ten long years with bandits! I will take care of your mother and sister!"

"Auntie, I didn't ..." Kin-Pong had risen to his feet.

"Mei-Kuen be quiet," Sau-Ha ordered. "Don't make trouble!"

Fei-Yin cried out, "We will go eventually, Auntie Mei-Kuen."

"A kite in the wind!" Mei-Kuen made a grab for the letter that Kin-Pong held loosely in his hand. She got it and waved it fiercely over her head. "Off the side of the mountain! A paper husband!"

"Stop!" Sau-Ping cried sharply. "Stop!"

Mei-Kuen threw the letter on the floor of the shack and exploded out the door.

"Fei-Yin, your father and Kin-Pong will work hard in Vancouver. They will earn enough money to bring us there eventually." Sau-Ping spoke rapidly, trying to outrace an hysterical sadness. "I am sure ... Kin-Pong you must go."

"Ma, I'll tell Father to send for you. As soon as I get there. And Big Sister Fei-Yin. Before she reaches the age limit of twenty-one."

Sau-Ping struggled to speak. "Cash the draft. We can pay off our loan. Yik-Nang is so kind. People are so kind."

Kin-Pong met her broken declarations with frantic reassurances. "Ma, tomorrow I will visit the money-changing shop. I'll pay them."

"Yik-Kwong can help you get the ticket. Ask how to take the ferry to the commissioner. I must go outside!" Sau-Ping announced abruptly. "Please don't follow me!"

Fei-Yin rose, her face bloodless. Kin-Pong stood like a statue, frozen by the sight of his mother overcome with disappointment and anger. Sau-Ping looked at them for a second before she ran out into the heat, down a path, around a set of children playing with stones, to a great ledge that overlooked the side of the mountain. She stood there, staring into the sky.

Sau-Ping felt a presence at her back and turned to face her sister, Sau-Ha.

"I am fine," Sau-Ping said.

"He is a good husband."

"You must go home soon. It is growing dark."

"I wanted to see you first."

"I am fine." Sau-Ping took a breath and spoke boldly, straight into the dome of the sky. "There is something that could happen. I didn't want to talk about it in front of the children. If Kin-Pong goes to

Vancouver, we have no one here except women. Will Yik-Man think of us? Or will he forget us?"

"I don't know," her sister whispered, looking off the side of the mountain.

"I cannot be selfish and keep him here. My mother-in-law Leung Tsing-Haan let Yik-Man join his father in Vancouver at age ten. I have kept Kin-Pong by my side for so many years already. I should now let him go to Vancouver. He will be a great comfort to Yik-Man who has just lost his own father. He's an educated young man, like your youngest son, Tak-Wa. I don't want him to be selling lettuce in the dirty streets of Shamshuipo all his life."

"He must go if there is a chance and money."

"Besides," added Sau-Ping, "the restaurant in Vancouver is a family business. It would help me and Fei-Yin in Hong Kong if the restaurant prospers."

The two women stood side by side at the edge of the mountain.

The first year without Kin-Pong, 1953, seemed long and monotonous to Sau-Ping. The only interesting event in Hong Kong was the festivities to celebrate the coronation of Queen Elizabeth II. In the months before the coronation, British flags and multicoloured ceremonial archways appeared in all the major streets, decorated with traditional symbols fit for royalty. Sau-Ping did not join the crowds to watch the lion dance and parades, but from the higher slopes of Shek Kip Mei, she could see the illuminated ships and the fireworks over the harbour at night. She wondered what it would be like to be the big-nose queen of the powerful nation that controlled Hong Kong.

Some months later a typhoon hit the city. Cold wind pierced through the cracks of Sau-Ping's hut, followed by torrents of water that ran down the walls and soaked the floor boards. The four women in the shack were plagued by typhoons that year. They joined with their neighbours in seeking ways to keep their shelters dry and waterproof.

Sau-Ping didn't worry much when she started coughing. A little cold is inevitable in damp weather. Another typhoon came – she learned from a neighbour that it was called "Susan" – shortly after Mid-Autumn Festival. It blew like a monster out of the belly of the ocean and levelled many of the weaker huts at Shek Kip Mei. Afterwards, Sau-Ping's coughing grew worse. She coughed so hard and so painfully some evenings that she had trouble breathing and couldn't sleep. Perspiration soaked the clothes on her back. She often found herself walking the paths outside with a high fever. Her arms and face lost flesh.

"Ma, you should go see a doctor."

"Don't worry, Fei-Yin. I just have a cold. With some herbal medicine, I'll recover."

"Then you should at least take a break, Auntie Sau-Ping," said Lai-Sheung. "Ma and I can handle the hawking business and line up for water, and Fei-Yin can do the plastic flowers."

"I'll be fine. Really."

Another month passed. When Sau-Ping tried to push herself up in bed after a coughing fit, her arms shook. She found spots of blood in her palm when she spit. Mei-Kuen pleaded with her and later cajoled her into seeking medical help. Exhausted and emptied of spirit, Sau-Ping went to the herbal doctor who operated out of his squatter hut at Shek Kip Mei. A few days later, the blood she coughed into her palm was thicker. She sought out the Western doctor who kept up a small private practice in Shamshuipo.

And then, for no reason, her spirit returned and Sau-Ping grew stubborn. If it was time to die, she would die; she had worked, wandered, and prayed long enough. Doctors were an unnecessary expense.

She continued to take the Chinese herbal medicine together with the Western drugs, but as soon as the coughing eased and her spit cleared, she stopped buying the medicines. She insisted on doing her usual share of the work. She felt armoured in numb habit and pride. If it was time to die, then it was time to die.

One day she was so weak that she fainted while climbing up the hill after working at the factory. Mei-Kuen discovered the unconscious Sau-Ping in the mud and dragged her to the chest clinic at the Shek Kip Mei Kaifong Association. There Sau-Ping looked into the clean face of a doctor who told her she had chronic tuberculosis.

The doctor told Mei-Kuen that the family should get anti-tuberculosis drugs from the dispensaries at the clinic and make sure that Sau-Ping took the drugs regularly. She was to have a check-up every month, and the rest of the group were to be inoculated against TB at the medical station operated by the St John's Ambulance Brigade. They were also advised to eat separately from Sau-Ping to avoid becoming infected.

Sau-Ping walked home with her friend. The air drifting out of the great empty space at the edge of the mountain cooled her face. She decided she did not have tuberculosis. Her body was merely tired of working, wandering, and praying.

Suddenly, panting hard, staring up at the path she had to climb to reach her home and her bed, Sau-Ping had a moment of vertiginous fear. No — it was tuberculosis. She knew about the disease from Toi-Shaan. The survival rate was not high.

That evening she spoke from her bed, where she lay panting heavily. "Mei-Kuen, Lai-Sheung, Fei-Yin, I am so sorry. I caught this deadly disease ..." She coughed. "I don't want to heap shame on you." Speaking made her cough more. "For your own sakes, keep my illness a secret from everybody, including my sister Sau-Ha, Yik-Kwong, and Yik-Nang. Don't let other pedlars or customers know. They will flee from you. Make sure our co-workers and the contractor at the plasticware workshop don't find out. Just tell everyone I have pneumonia, and that I am taking it easy for a few days."

"Your husband?" Mei-Kuen asked succinctly.

"Please don't let Yik-Man or Kin-Pong know."

Mei-Kuen raised her chin and said nothing.

Prompted by her daughter, Sau-Ping visited the clinic regularly for the next few weeks. She got a bit better, then she got a bit worse. As the Christmas season arrived she was wrapped in low spirits. One afternoon she listened to Lai-Sheung report on the wild doings of the Europeans in Hong Kong, stories Lai-Sheung had heard from a literate member of the Shek Kip Mei Association who received a news magazine. There were drinks made with eggs beaten to clouds and triangular pine trees made of green plastic, like giant plastic flowers, and giant chickens to eat, some weighing more than a newborn baby. Sau-Ping closed her eyes, thinking about the many worlds the world contained. The next day she rose from her bed again and walked to the medical dispensary, where she waited three hours for her drugs.

On Christmas night, 1953, Sau-Ping was drowsy from the effects of the medication. Lying in bed, she suddenly found herself staring into a blue space. There, in the very centre of the air, was her mother-in-law, Leung Tsing-Haan. Her face looked thin and worried. "Sau-Ping, you have forgotten to burn incense for me."

"*On-Yan*, please forgive me," Sau-Ping whispered hoarsely, struggling out of her quilt. She lit the incense pot at once and burned a generous amount of ritual money, breathing in the smoke, half-thinking it might combat the tuberculosis. "I am sick with an incurable disease. I should jump off the mountain. Or take a knife. I am a burden now."

"Don't die, Sau-Ping. Don't be like me. Be with your husband and your son. They are just over the water, and that stream is no wider than your hand. You can jump it."

"*On-Yan! On-Yan!*" Sau-Ping murmured.

"Ma! Ma!" Screams.

Still in her dream, Sau-Ping smelled the incense smoke and wondered why it had turned rancid. She tried to open her eyes. She was being dragged.

Slap! Someone had slapped her face. Splash! Water on her face, water scurrying down her neck and into her shirt. Sau-Ping felt herself fall. She was crawling on the floorboards, half-awake, and there were hands on her back.

Fei-Yin was dragging her to the door and screaming. She could see her daughter's feet. "... whole mountainside is burning!"

"What, Fei-Yin? Tell me. Speak."

"Run, run with me. Get up. Run with me!"

"On my back!" cried a thundering female voice. "Put her on my back!"

Bounce and bounce and bounce. The heat and the smoke choked Sau-Ping. She knew she was riding on Mei-Kuen's broad strong back, and that they were running full tilt down the mountainside. The whole squatter area was a sea of fire, beating inside unmarked shores in red-hot waves, scorching and melting the earth and engulfing its creatures. The place smelled of acrid burning plastic, metal, wood, cardboard, and tarpaper – the terrible incense of this place, thought Sau-Ping clearly. The screaming of the old and the young, men and women, filled the air. The wind that followed in the wake of the flames howled. Dogs barked as if they were being beaten with sticks. Houses crumbled into ash, like little tents of ritual money eaten by the fire. Sau-Ping's eyes were wide open as she clung to the strong neck of her friend. Had her own incense fire done this? "Fei-Yin, run with us!" she screamed and heard her daughter's voice, "I'm behind you." Just to the side of her face, Sau-Ping saw and felt a can of kerosene explode. Mei-Kuen jumped. A woman was running down the hill carrying two small children, one of whom gripped her hair. There was a man with his arms full of pots and pans.

Sau-Ping opened her eyes to the blackness that waits under a complete roof of fire. A long time later she was watching a sky full of boats. Then she was speaking to Yik-Man under the banyan tree. And then she was stirring a few grains of rice in a huge pot of boiling water alongside her mother.

CHAPTER 15

Farewell, My Daughter

Sau-Ping wavered in and out of consciousness that night, delirious with fever and confusion. She heard the word "camp" and "fire." Mei-Kuen, Fei-Yin, and Lai-Sheung often stood near her, and brought little sips of water. Sau-Ping clearly heard her own daughter say, "We came all the way from Sai-Fok to end up like this! Why is heaven so unfair?" Sau-Ping did not hear her friend's answer, but somehow understood that now they were all riding on Mei-Kuen's strong back.

By the next day she could make herself concentrate, and she understood that her small group was housed in a makeshift camp. There had been a fire in Shek Kip Mei, caused by an illegal factory in the heart of the squatter area. Acres of the still-smouldering mountainside had been burnt. The government had set up relief camps, and members of the relief committee, with the help of the police and the army, were gathered at tables in each camp, registering the fire victims. Fei-Yin told her mother the government promised to help. She said many people from the mountain with serious burns had been transported to hospitals, and there were official people wearing bright red crosses on their sleeves who had arrived with trucks full of quilts and jackets. The Shek Kip Mei Kaifong Association was organizing kitchens to distribute free meals.

Hearing this news, Sau-Ping closed her eyes and rested.

But then a moment came when she felt a stranger holding her arm. When she opened her eyes, she was looking at the top of the tent. Near her stood a doctor who spoke about "quarantine." Sau-Ping instantly comprehended that her illness had been discovered. She would be separated from Mei-Kuen, Fei-Yin, and Lai-Sheung. Wearily she waved her hand in the air to signal to her daughter and friends that arguments would be of no use. She felt herself being lifted.

In the camp for tuberculosis patients, the clothing and sheets were very cool. They had an odd scent. Fei-Yin was the only one allowed to visit Sau-Ping in this camp. Seeing her daughter for the first time the next day, Sau-Ping asked anxiously about her situation.

"Oh Ma, you don't have to worry about us. We're out of the relief camp. Uncle Yik-Kwong and Auntie Sau-Ha's families heard about the fire over the radio and came to take us to their homes. Even from where they live, they could see the red sky. Mei-Kuen and Lai-Sheung sleep on two folding cots at Uncle Yik-Kwong and Uncle Yik-Nang's flat on Prince Edward Road. By special permission from the tenant-in-chief, I am staying in Auntie Sau-Ha's cubicle on Pitt Street. I share the middle bunk with Tsoi-Yuk and Tsoi-Lin."

"But what are you doing for a living?"

"The plastics assembly workshop in Shek Kip Mei burned down in the fire, so we lost that, but Uncle Yik-Nang offered to lend us some money to start the hawker business again."

Sau-Ping closed her eyes and sighed with relief. The weight on her heart, even the tight pain in her chest, eased. She thanked Koon-Yam, the Goddess of Mercy, for her caring relatives and friends. At the same time, it distressed her to be lying idly in bed while Mei-Kuen and the daughters worked in the streets, and she felt shamed now that the secret of her illness was known to everyone. "So they all know that I am sick."

"Yes, and they were upset that you hid it from them for so long. They also blamed me for not writing to tell Father and Kin-Pong."

"Fei-Yin, I don't want your father and younger brother to worry about me. They must be having a hard time in Vancouver. Particularly when your granduncle Kwok-Ko is ill."

Fei-Yin bit her lip. There was a long pause. Then she said, "Ma, I have already asked Uncle Yik-Kwong to help me write a letter to Father and Kin-Pong, letting them know about the fire and your illness."

"Why!"

"Because we need somehow to give you medical treatment, good medical treatment, and nourishing food, and tonics from ginseng and *tong-kwai*. Your health will never improve if you continue to eat nothing but leftover vegetables, rotten rice, and salt fish. You treat yourself like a *sai-tsai*. It goes too far," she said, her voice dropping. "All our money and personal belongings are gone. Auntie Mei-Kuen, Lai-Sheung, and I are desperate. We need money to repay the loan from Uncle Yik-Nang. We also need money to move to another place to live. Right now, I am an added burden for Auntie Sau-Ha's cubicle and her household budget. Lai-Sheung and Auntie Mei-Kuen are crowding Uncle Yik-Nang and Uncle Yik-Kwong's flat. Father must send us money. It is the proper time to ask."

Sau-Ping could argue no more.

For the next six weeks, Sau-Ping was given free medical treatment while staying in the tuberculosis camp for fire victims. Her health improved slightly, although she still coughed incessantly and there were traces of blood in her spit. One day, Fei-Yin came to see her with a piece of good news. "Ma, we can move back to Shek Kip Mei!"

"How did that happen?"

"The government sent bulldozers there to remove all the debris. They are giving fire victims permission to rebuild huts on the upper slopes. They will even supply the posts for the four corners of the hut, and building material for the roof!"

Sau-Ping looked into the pale face of her daughter, wondering at the girl's hidden reserves of strength. "I'm surprised they are taking such an interest in our well-being."

"If only we could afford it, they are offering an even better deal, but it costs ten dollars a month, which we simply don't have."

"What is it?"

"They levelled the land at the lower slopes, and built many rows of two-storey brick cottages with fireproof roofs. These cottages are administered by the government, and former squatters at Shek Kip Mei who can afford to pay the ten dollars per month in rent can now move into them. But applicants must have Hong Kong identity cards."

"But if we build our own, we don't have to pay rent at all?"

"Exactly. It's still not a *yeung-lau*, but it's better than living off our fellow villagers and relatives. Uncle Tseung-Lam and my cousins Tak-Kan and Tak-Keung have already helped us build the new hut at Shek Kip Mei in more or less the same spot as before."

"We are so lucky to have them."

"Oh, Ma, I'm looking forward to moving out of Pitt Street. Poor Auntie Sau-Ha. She has to listen to all the grumbling from the tenant-in-chief. And the two servants from Shun-Tak at Uncle Yik-Nang's flat are getting rude to Auntie Mei-Kuen and Lai-Sheung."

"Will we be safe from disaster on the mountain this time?"

"It should be better. The government terraced the upper slopes and built retaining walls to prevent landslides. They have also made sure that the huts are properly spaced, and between the rows of huts they've built fire-lanes and paved them with cement. So even if there is another fire, it won't spread to the whole area."

Sau-Ping pushed herself up in bed. "I expect to be out of here soon. Then I can help."

Her daughter smiled without argument, but sorrow remained a part of her face. Sau-Ping realized she would never be able to set out a feast of perfect happiness for this daughter who had seen so much and felt herself so often discounted by her father's relations. Partnership with the boisterous Lai-Sheung had been good for her, but Fei-Yin's soul had not changed; it was slow to excitement, quiet, hopeful, and accustomed to disappointment.

Sau-Ping, released from the tuberculosis camp a few days later, was taken by Mei-Kuen to their new squatter hut in Shek Kip Mei. There in the hut she had a small ground-level ancestral altar set up, with one tablet for all the souls of the Leung ancestors and a separate one for Leung Tsing-Haan, her mother-in-law. She also put a statue of Koon-Yam there. Every day, just before pushing the pedlar's cart to Yu Chau Street, Sau-Ping and Fei-Yin prayed at the altar.

But prayers did not help Sau-Ping's health, and her illness took a turn for the worse a week after she returned to Shek Kip Mei. Over her friend's protests, Mei-Kuen applied to the Medical Social Services for help. Soon a volunteer doctor from the mobile clinic run by the Catholic Welfare Committee paid Sau-Ping a free home visit. On his recommendation she was sent, after a long wait for a bed, to the Kwong Wah Hospital.

Fei-Yin, Lai-Sheung, Mei-Kuen, and Sau-Ha took turns bringing her such nourishing food as liver, pork hock, lean meat, chicken soup, eggs boiled in Chinese wine. But no one in Sau-Ha's family ever visited the hospital. Neither did her friends from the New Village, Yi-Lin and Yik-Kwong, much less Yik-Kwong's brother Yik-Nang. They merely sent their warm regards. Sau-Ping did not blame them; she understood that she was a "TB ghost" whom everyone wanted to avoid. She would do the same if she were in their shoes. Even the nurses in the hospital kept their distance from her.

She was worried, however, about the expense of her medical treatment and the nourishing food prepared on her behalf. She suspected that staying in the hospital, even at a subsidized rate, would cost an enormous amount. There were charges for X-rays, specialist consultations, tests, daily maintenance, and bedspace, among others. More than once she tried to find out from her visitors how much they actually had to pay, and where the money came from, but she received no satisfactory answer. They had apparently agreed not to tell her.

Sau-Ping was finally discharged from the hospital in the early summer of 1954. As soon as she got back to the hut, she insisted on knowing the truth. Fei-Yin answered simply. "Ma, I really don't know. Father and Kin-Pong directly sent a cheque of eighteen hundred Canadian dollars to Uncle Yik-Nang's money-changer shop to be converted into Hong Kong dollars. We used some of that to pay back the loan to Uncle Yik-Nang for our hawker's business. We also used it to cover your hospital expenses and food costs."

Sau-Ping's heart started to pound, making it difficult for her to breathe. "Eighteen hundred Canadian dollars! How on earth could they have raised so much money so quickly? I thought Yik-Man still owed money for Kin-Pong's passage."

"I don't know. I don't know."

"Have they borrowed against the restaurant or sold ... they have nothing to sell."

"Ma, I don't know. They haven't told us."

Sau-Ping's emotions and thoughts were confused bcause of her prolonged illness. One moment she felt worthless and soiled and imagined jumping off the side of the mountain to save her family these exorbitant expenses. The next moment she felt feverishly resentful. Her husband had no right to keep secrets from her! He was engaged in some trickery. Why did he never write to her? Did he think she had no face, no heart, no voice?

A few days later, when they heard that Sau-Ping had been given a clean bill of health from the hospital, Yik-Kwong and Yik-Nang arrived for a visit and told their side of the story.

"What Fei-Yin said is correct," said Yik-Kwong. "Even before receiving Fei-Yin's letter, Yik-Man and Kin-Pong knew about the fire from the local Chinese newspapers. In fact many Chinese in Vancouver donated money for fire relief in Shek Kip Mei. Your husband and son sent us a cheque directly after receiving the letter I wrote on Fei-Yin's behalf. They sent the cheque to us because they were not sure where you and Fei-Yin would be after the fire."

Sau-Ping was calm now. She said, "My husband does not forget us."

"Your filial son Kin-Pong begged Yik-Man to raise passage money for you to go to Vancouver as soon as you were better," said Yik-Kwong, who then spoke about the crowded, unsanitary conditions on the mountain.

Sau-Ping was holding herself very still. She felt feeble and bright as a single blade on a rice plant surrounded by acres of water. Vancouver. After so many long years, her husband had sent money to bring her to Vancouver. She was no longer a young bride. She was ... Sau-Ping lowered her eyes and gazed at the backs of her hands.

"Ping," said Yik-Kwong, and he touched her knee to claim her attention. His brother, Yik-Nang, was speaking about the passage money. "Your passage money is being kept at our money-changing shop. I thought it might be unsafe at Shek Kip Mei."

"Ma, are you listening?" whispered Fei-Yin.

"I had a conversation with an Overseas Chinese from North America who came to my shop yesterday. He said that the Canadian Commissioner's Office is very strict about admitting immigrants who have had tuberculosis. They usually won't grant a visa until their medical staff are satisfied that the scars on the applicant's lungs show no active growth."

"Yes," said Sau-Ping.

"They insist on waiting at least one year after you've had your first clear X-ray. So, if you trust me, I will continue to bank your passage money and pay you interest for it, until you get your visa from the Canadian commissioner in Hong Kong."

The two men were gone. Sau-Ping had thanked them and seen them off before following her daughter back into their squatter's hut. Her eyes passed over the bag of government rice and the pale cabbage in their pedlar's basket, the little black cooking stove and the thickly hemmed government cotton quilt. She was grateful to her friends, to Kin-Pong for his devotion, to Yik-Man. In her former life, she thought, she must have done something good.

Her eyes rested on a worn pair of cheap shoes Fei-Yin had purchased at a stall near Sau-Ha's tenement house. The girl had walked miles and miles in those frayed shoes, hauling vegetables, until her feet had come to resemble her bruised and lumpy wares. Poor daughter, poor child who was no longer a child. Fei-Yin had been happier working in the paddy.

Fei-Yin. Why was there no mention of Fei-Yin's passage? And how had Yik-Man secured so much money?

That evening Sau-Ping exerted every effort to cook her daughter a fine meal. She sent Lai-Sheung to borrow or beg all the ingredients necessary to make rice hot-pot with sausage. The sausage wasn't as good as in the country, but the fragrance of the dish sweetened the air like incense. Fei-Yin ate a big helping, and Sau-Ping was comforted.

Two weeks later Sau-Ping was standing alone outside the hut – her companions had gone off to sell vegetables but she had been too tired to accompany them. As she carefully rinsed the girls' clothes in a small amount of water, a pair of black trousers came into view. Raising her head, she saw Leung Yik-Faat, a sardonic smile on his face. Behind him stood his drug-dealing son Kin-Tsoi, who had grown very fat in the hips and arms.

"Sau-Ping." Yik-Faat laughed and bowed dramatically, like an actor. "We have not seen you since our boat trip. We have come to ... greet family," and he laughed again.

Sau-Ping said nothing. She disliked being reminded that Paternal Uncle had adopted the worthless Kin-Tsoi. And she was almost sickened by her knowledge that this grinning man, Yik-Faat, had beaten his wife to death – witnesses had said the corpse was black as if it had been burnt. But Yik-Faat had made it possible for her and her party to cross into Hong Kong. If she had tolerated him for a while to profit herself it was not proper to be rude now, when she, her daughter, and her friends were living in relative safety.

"What do you want, Yik-Faat?"

"I came all the way from Kowloon City to visit you. Why are you so cold to me? We are fellow villagers and close relatives!"

"We are relatives because Paternal Uncle adopted Kin-Tsoi, but we are not close relatives."

"Hasn't Yik-Man told you?"

It was coming, the explanation for one of Yik-Man's secrets. Sau-Ping stood up. "What?"

"Ping, my old neighbour, you are now the proud mother of my son Kin-Tsoi! His new name is Leung Kin-On – your son Leung Kin-On!"

"What?"

"Yik-Man has not told you then. I thought not. He sold your daughter's birth certificate to Uncle Leung Kwok-Ko."

Sau-Ping kept her feet and did not change the expression on her face. The frozen sensation of calm that entered her body was akin to hysteria. Deep in her spirit, she felt that there was now nothing more the men of the Leung lineage could do to her. The moment her daughter was stripped of the document that marked her birth, she herself, the mother, was also stripped bare. Without an identity, Fei-Yin would never be allowed to enter Canada.

"You don't like it! But it was for you. Uncle Kwok-Ko has been ill for quite some time, and he wanted Kin-Tsoi, his adopted son, to be at his deathbed. So he offered to buy Fei-Yin's birth certificate for eighteen hundred Canadian dollars. This is an enormous sum of money. It represents ten years of his savings," said Yik-Faat.

Sau-Ping did not speak.

"You are lucky Yik-Man still wants you, a TB ghost, as his wife."

Sau-Ping stared him in the eye.

"Be reasonable. Fei-Yin can't use the certificate to go to Vancouver anyway. She is a girl. The birth certificate clearly states that Leung Kin-On is a male. Besides, I understand your daughter is twenty years old already. Only one more year, and then the certificate would be worthless anyway. But Kin-Tsoi is the right age, and with the business I'm doing, I can pay for his passage."

Sau-Ping knew full well that the term "business" was a euphemism for dope pushing. As she gazed on the two men, Kin-Tsoi turned and wandered off uphill. He was bored.

"Good-bye," she said.

"No, no. Not good-bye." Leung Yik-Faat smiled and shook his head, his beaming eyes lit by appetite for power of all kinds. "Kin-Tsoi is going to have an interview with the Canadian commissioner soon. I need you to tell us details about your family situation in Sai-Fok, in Hong Kong, and in Vancouver. We must sit down now and talk. That is why we are here. Kin-Tsoi!" he turned and yelled. "Dolt! Come down here to listen to your ..."

"No," said Sau-Ping. "I won't do it."

"No?" Yik-Faat raised his hands, feigning helpless disappointment. "Your husband has sold a false birth certificate. If the Canadian government finds out ... Well, I'm not certain but there could be trouble."

Sau-Ping felt cold. She looked at the damp clothes in her hands and slowly began to wring them out. When she was done and the clothes were hung up to dry, she and this devil and his son would enter her shack, and there she would tell them about her life as a young bride, about her mother-in-law and her brother-in-law, about the birth of Fei-Yin and the purchase of Kin-Pong, about the wartime famine, the brief years of prosperity, and the encroachment of the Communists, who always arrived at the door shining with a sense of their own righteousness.

Yik-Faat stood smiling. Kin-Tsoi had returned. They watched Sau-Ping working over her daughter's shirt. Spreading it out on a string fixed between two shacks, she was afraid that this poor empty garment might slip into the dust. With trembling hands she tried to balance it carefully. It hung there. When Sau-Ping nodded, the two men followed her into the hut.

Mei-Kuen came home before Sau-Ping had finished answering Yik-Faat's questions, and moments later the girls returned from their hours of vegetable hawking. Mei-Kuen, instantly sensing her friend's distress, signalled to the girls to be quiet.

Sau-Ping felt her daughter settle behind her. She continued to answer each of Yik-Faat's questions with care, though she felt she was draining both herself and Fei-Yin in the process. Kin-Tsoi never said a word and, it seemed, paid little attention, but his father leaned forward like a thief planning a raid, which in fact he was. Sau-Ping had the frightening impression that at any moment he might stretch out and lick her with his snake's tongue, so hungry was he for details.

After she had told the pair all that was necessary, Sau-Ping was in utter despair.

Yik-Faat stood up. He had drunk her blood, and he looked fit, even young, and consummately evil. He slapped his son on the shoulder. "Now you are Leung Kin-On. Leung Kin-On. Kin-On. We will practise so that you reply to your name. Kin-On." Kin-Tsoi shrugged off his father's hand.

From the corner, a low voice from the corner asked, "Who is Leung Kin-On?"

It was Fei-Yin who had spoken. Sau-Ping twisted herself around to face her daughter. "You are!"

Once again Yik-Faat laughed. "I think we had better go before the explanations. I did want to say, since we are newly bound by stronger family ties, that I have a friend who runs an entertainment business in Kowloon City. He has just opened a new dance hall called the Golden Princess in Tsimshatsui. He expects very good business. In addition to the big-nose soldiers and sailors, Tsimshatsui is now flooded with big-nose tourists! I'll put a good word in for Fei-Yin. And for Lai-Sheung, too. Since they must both stay in Hong Kong."

"Go see the devil, pig-shit!" Mei-Kuen, who had been quiet all this while, rose like a lion.

Kin-Tsoi had already disappeared, having pocketed his new identity. Yik-Faat leaned towards Sau-Ping. "I knew we would someday have a son together," he whispered. "You were such a beautiful girl before the troubles ..." He moved to pat her shoulder, but she leaped up to scratch his face. "Oh oh!" he cried, and walked calmly out the door.

"What has your husband done now!" Mei-Kuen bellowed. "I can smell it. What has he done to your daughter? How has he betrayed you now?"

Speaking very clearly, Sau-Ping said, "Before Fei-Yin was born, Yik-Man reported to the birth registry that we had a boy. Leung Kin-On. He received a birth certificate in that name. When I had a daughter, Fei-Yin, Grandma gave you your name. But the birth certificate your father kept still bears the name Leung Kin-On.

"Your father sold your birth certificate to Uncle Leung Kwok-Ko, who wishes to have his adopted son Kin-Tsoi with him in his illness. He used the money for my hospital, and my ..." Sau-Ping's voice dissolved.

"Then I have no identity for travel."

Sau-Ping put out her arms. Somehow understanding the gesture, Fei-Yin came over and settled on her mother's lap, where she had not been cuddled for many years. Fei-Yin was tall but light-boned. Her warm scent comforted her mother. Mei-Kuen left the house and returned with the clean clothes that had been drying outside. Fei-Yin's shirt was among them. Watching Mei-Kuen fold the clothes, Sau-Ping began to sob. In her arms Fei-Yin cried silently. Sau-Ping had her right hand on her daughter's face; the girl's tears slid between her fingers.

Mei-Kuen and Lai-Sheung made dinner. At last, the bereaved mother and daughter separated from each other and drank the tea made by their subdued friends. "Yik-Man should have consulted me," Sau-Ping whispered.

Standing abruptly, Mei-Kuen raised her leg and stomped hard, once, on the floor. Sau-Ping realized her friend could not utter the words that swarmed in her mouth – they were curses on her absent husband.

Neither Sau-Ping nor Fei-Yin could sleep that night. In the longest hours, before daybreak, Fei-Yin rolled over and whispered to her mother. The two women put on their jackets and walked outside to a large rock near the cliff where they often stood. Sau-Ping struggled against an urge to fly off the rock and put an end to her life. The moon was nearly full. That it had not been marred by this day brought some peace to the mother and daughter.

The next morning, instead of hawking vegetables at Yu Chau Street, all four women went to share their sadness and indignation with Sau-Ha and Lau Tseung-Lam. Shocked at the news, Sau-Ha was at a loss to find comforting words.

"But daughters have never been consulted when their parents made plans for them," she said at last, heaving a long sigh. Sau-Ping was certain that her sister was thinking about maidens they had known in Fung-Yeung who were married off blindly and dropped into the unknown. She and Sau-Ha had been two of those maidens.

Brother-in-Law Lau Tseung-Lam waited until the women calmed down. Then he said plainly, "There is really nothing anyone can do at this stage. Fei-Yin might as well make alternate plans and look for a permanent job in Hong Kong. I do know that more cotton-spinning and garment factories have been built recently in Kowloon operated by the local Shanghainese. And nylon-knitting too, those are some of the best. With free accommodation in dormitories and subsidized food. But the priority for these jobs goes to those with Hong Kong identity cards."

"Well, we will just have to adopt her legally so she can apply for one," said Sau-Ha without fuss.

Sau-Ping glanced swiftly at her daughter, uncertain how she would react to this bartering over her future and references to another adoption. But Fei-Yin's face was bright. Looking at her, Sau-Ping felt both gratitude and pain; for she recognized that her faithful daughter must have been imagining horrors through these last dark hours: lonely nights in Hong Kong, destitution, fire, hunger, prostitution. The girl looked fragile, but years of labour and loss had toughened her. Sau-Ping said softly, "Thank-you, Big Sister! Thank-you. But I don't want my daughter to be a burden on your family."

"Don't be silly. We are sisters! Besides, Fei-Yin is already twenty years old. She doesn't need anyone to take care of her. Who knows, she might take care of me and Tseung-Lam when we grow old!"

Mei-Kuen spoke up. "Let us for once ask the girl what she thinks of these plans."

Fei-Yin announced that she was happy to accept Sau-Ha's offer. "At least I will be part of a family. I will be someone." Besides, she liked her aunt and uncle and got along with their five children, particularly Tsoi-Yuk.

Sau-Ping sat in her sister's cramped, stuffy, lightless apartment, greatly relieved. But then another painful thought visited her. She turned to her loyal friend, Mei-Kuen. "What will you and Lai-Sheung do after I have gone to Vancouver, if Fei-Yin moves into a factory dormitory?"

Mei-Kuen put on a look of wild amazement. "Me! The one who has eaten meat she couldn't recognize in the mountains and asked no questions? Don't worry. We'll manage. We won't be lost, bless us, we know our way around. We might be able to sublet half a room in the six-storey resettlement blocks at Shek Kip Mei. They may be crowded, but the price is low and the government will keep them in good repair. And eventually," Mei-Kuen gained energy as she spoke, "I'd like to become a clothing hawker instead of selling fruits and vegetables. There are already quite a few of those along Sai Yeung Choi Street in Mongkok District. It's good to sell ready-made clothing. You never have to worry about bad weather affecting your supply, and clothing is easier to store. And a clothing cart is so much lighter than a vegetable cart. We can escape more easily when the police come to check our license."

Sau-Ping was crying again, even as she listened smiling to Mei-Kuen. She feared being separated from these beloved people by an entire unimaginable ocean and the changeable barriers erected by the foreign new world – Canada.

Hong Kong experienced particularly bad weather in 1954–55. It was as if the heavens were out of joint. The damaging typhoons in summer did not improve Hong Kong's water supply and the winter was cruelly cold and arid. It was Hong Kong's driest year on record. Throughout the city, the water supply was restricted to only two and a half hours per day.

Even while struggling for a living on the higher slopes of Shek Kip Mei, Sau-Ping considered more than once the question whether or not she should go to Vancouver to join Yik-Man and Kin-Pong and leave Fei-Yin in Hong Kong by herself. She remembered her mother telling her about the "three obediences." A woman should obey her father when she was young, obey her husband after her marriage, and obey her son when she grew old. But what kind of man was Yik-Man anyway? She had even forgotten what he looked like. They had been together for a couple of months when she was sixteen, then they were separated for twenty-two years. What kind of man had Yik-Man become as he matured in Vancouver? Was he still the loving man she had been happy to speak with and touch when they were first married? Or had he changed after all these years of restaurant work in the foreign devils' country, altering in colour and taste, like an egg kept in vinegar?

Over more than twenty-two years Yik-Man had given her no sign of affection. He had left Sai-Fok after the bandit attack in 1933. He had not consulted her about his decision to leave. From then on, he had never addressed her in his letters or sent her money directly. Any acknowledgment or money had always come through Leung Tsing-Haan, her mother-in-law, or through Yik-Mo, her brother-in-law – and all while she was working so hard to take care of his family and his ancestral tablets in Sai-Fok.

In Hong Kong it was the same. His correspondence was always addressed to Kin-Pong, sometimes even to Yik-Kwong or Yik-Nang who were not even close relatives. And then he had sold Fei-Yin's birthright. This final act she could not swallow and digest. She had tried, but when she thought of Kin-Tsoi travelling to Canada as her son, the image nearly choked her nor could she forgive Yik-Man for selling his own daughter's birth certificate. And if she could not forgive him, how could she live with him? Why had he left her, his wife of so many years, to learn of what he had done from a thief and a villain?

Should she refuse to go to Vancouver?

Sau-Ping tried to imagine herself severing all ties to her husband and his family. In the end this was impossible. If she refused to go to Vancouver, certainly all remittances would stop, but Sau-Ping's fear of losing the money was less acute than her fear of losing a twenty-two year commitment to loyalty. Mei-Kuen had called Yik-Man a paper husband, but Sau-Ping understood that this paper man, sweating over the stove in a restaurant somewhere far away, was flesh and blood. He had kept his word to her for the most part and provided her with money that had allowed her to live, for a few years at least, in the beautiful *yeung-lau*. And what if she did stay in Hong Kong with her daughter? Fei-Yin had a good chance of landing a job in a factory now that she had become the adopted daughter of a Hong Kong citizen. Fei-Yin was now twenty-one years old. She would probably get married soon and have her own children. Then Sau-Ping would be a burden to her. And Kin-Pong? If she cut her ties with Yik-Man, she would lose all contact with Kin-Pong, her filial son.

It seemed that no matter what she did, she would be a burden. She must merely decide in which direction to throw the tired, confused weight that was herself. In the end, Sau-Ping decided to follow the dictates of fate:

> When you are married to a chicken
> You follow the chicken;
> When you are married to a dog,
> You follow the dog;
> When you are married to a monkey,
> You'll run around in the hills!

In late April 1955 Sau-Ping passed the medical examination mandated by the Canadian Commissioner's Office. Yik-Kwong helped her buy her ticket to Vancouver.

One afternoon she boarded a great steady ship with hot clear smoke pouring out of a stack. She had said her goodbyes on the dock, and behind her Fei-Yin, Mei-Kuen, Lai-Sheung, Sau-Ha and Yik-Kwong's families were shrinking into small figures. Sau-Ping had worked for many years, and she could make her legs carry her into the ship. They had paid a small sum to have her heavy luggage stowed on board, but she carried what she would need for the voyage on her back. She imagined how fine it would be if she could change her daughter into a little caged bird and steal her onto the deck. "What is that?" people would say. "Just a little swallow," she would answer.

Sau-Ping turned to look over the side of the ship, as everyone else was doing. She raised her arm.

Once the boat had left the Hong Kong harbour and she could no longer see even the shapes of those who had come to bid her farewell, Sau-Ping found a place on deck where she could avoid looking at the water. She was thinking about the evening when she had prayed at

the Main Temple in the public square in Hong Kong. Now she understood why she could not get a definite answer from Tin Hau when
she had thrown the sticks: she asked the wrong question. She had
asked how long Fei-Yin, Kin-Pong, and she herself would have to
wait before leaving for Canada. The fact was that none of them
would go at the same time. Kin-Pong had left more than two years
ago. She was leaving now. And Fei-Yin would be left behind forever.
Like the banyan tree in Sai-Fok, or like the happy circle of friends in
the maiden house, Fei-Yin had been dragged into the past.

PART THREE

Vancouver's Chinatown
1955–1987

CHAPTER 16

Family Reunion

The ship was huge. Easily twenty times the size of the fishing junk that had carried Sau-Ping and her family to Hong Kong in 1952, it seemed more like a big floating island than a ship. This particular vessel combined cargo with passengers and was so crowded that Sau-Ping was virtually confined to the bottom bunk for the entire eighteen day journey. Every now and then, seeking fresh air, she climbed to the deck and watched the sea, the skies, and the stars. But most of the time she stayed below in her bunk. All she could hear was the sound of the engines, like the continuous noise of downtown Kowloon, or the noise of people shouting slogans during struggle meetings in Toi-shaan. Sometimes the waves were subdued, like the groans of her mother-in-law just before she died, or the weeping of her brother when he brought her the news that her parents had been killed by stray bullets, or Fei-Yin's sobbing at the pier when they parted. Sometimes they were so forceful that she thought she heard Mei-Kuen screaming as she was being raped by the bandits. At other times the sound of wind and sea reminded her of the fire that had engulfed Shek Kip Mei, or the strong gusts that blew through her hut during typhoon season. Along with many of her fellow passengers, Sau-Ping threw up again and again. The place reeked of vomit. Sau-Ping prayed to Koon-Yam for mercy.

For the first few days, she ached for Fei-Yin, Sau-Ha, Mei-Kuen, and Lai-Sheung. But gradually her mind turned towards the present and the future. She wondered whether this was the same terrible boat that had taken Kin-Pong to Vancouver more than two years ago. In Yik-Man's day, she thought, the voyage to the Gold Mountain must have been even more crowded and reeking.

What did Vancouver look like? She guessed that the streets were

not paved with real gold but might be plated with gold in certain
neighbourhoods, or built from a foreign stone coloured like the sun.
Gold Mountain Canada was proclaimed the great source of wealth and
good fortune, but lying in the bottom bunk, Sau-Ping recalled that
many Gold Mountain guests of her parents' generation had returned
to the village poor, wounded, or handicapped. Others had died young
or disappeared. Thinking back over her own experience of war and
famine, then glancing around her at the packed bodies in the belly of
the ship, she wondered how many dead Toi-Shaanese travellers had
been tossed over the side through the years, into the deep black sea.

There was a shore on the other side, she knew, and in the land
bounded by that shore people ate food at restaurants and spoke to
one another and dressed in clothes and breathed air and used coins to
pay for goods. What did the Canadian foreign devils look like? Were
they all drunk and obnoxious, like the ones in Tsimshatsui? How
could she cope? What if she caught one of their foreign diseases?

Sau-Ping rolled over and stared at the wall. One question repeated
itself more insistently and painfully than the rest: did Yik-Man really
want her there?

"I am old and a TB ghost who has just recovered. I am no longer the
young bride he once knew. I wonder if he has concubines or lovers?
I wonder how many prostitutes he has visited during our separation?
What will I do if he keeps his lady friends after my arrival?"

She mustn't think about these things; she remembered other grass
widows in the village telling her that jealousy on the part of the wife
was grounds for divorce. Men could not hold themselves in place the
way women could. How could she expect Yik-Man to do otherwise?
How many men were really faithful to their wives? Yik-Man had
been sending remittances home, and that should be proof enough
that he had no intention of abandoning his family or deserting her,
and that he had not wasted all his money on gambling or prostitutes
like many Gold Mountain guests she had heard about.

On the other hand, it was unforgivable that he had sold Fei-Yin's
birth certificate. She could not perfectly subdue the anger this act had
ignited in her. Yet in a matter of a few shorts days – she was going to
face this man, her husband.

She resolved not to complain. She did not want to become a nagging wife, a weed in her husband's life. She was prepared to start a
new life, to build a new family on the ashes of her shattered family in
China and Hong Kong.

Sau-Ping bunked near a young woman whose brother spent his time
with a talkative group of young men who kept careful track of their

progress across the ocean, so she knew that this day was 23 May 1955, and that the ship was approaching Burrard Inlet, Canada. People around her began packing and stowing their belongings to carry off the boat, and she began to roll up her bedding with trembling hands, listening to the noise of the great engines cutting back, backing up, levering the hulk of the vessel into the dock. Sau-Ping did not want to climb to the upper deck until the ropes were set and the ship was firmly bound to land. For this reason, she was one of the last voyagers to mount the stairs into the sunlight. A young man she had paid to drag her heavy trunk waited just behind her.

She stood on the deck of the ship, looking out at Canada. The bustle around the docks seemed familiar after Hong Kong, but the land in the distance stopped her cold. Against the blue sky she saw snow-capped mountains and forests full of evergreen trees. After noisy Hong Kong, after the deafening roar of the ship's engines, the place seemed frightfully quiet. She made herself one of the crowd and walked down the tilted path, off the ship, into Canada, carrying her bundles. She had known many men in Sai-Fok who had walked this path, but relatively few women. Her heart beat hard as she lined up at the Immigration counter. The hired man had disappeared, leaving the trunk beside her. As she moved forward, she shoved and dragged it with feet and hands.

The queue was as long as the queue for water at Shek Kip Mei. It took hours to get to the front, but finally there was only a young man in front of her. The Chinese officer in uniform, who stood as an assistant alongside a foreign ghost who was seated in a high chair behind the counter, called the fidgety young immigrant forward. The foreign ghost growled something, and then the Chinese man – the interpreter – spoke. She heard them discuss the traveller's papers in low tense tones. The three-way conversation grew louder, until the foreign ghost seated at the table clapped his hands hard and slapped the table. He picked up the traveller's papers and snapped at them with two fingers, then began to shout. Coolly, the translator said, "We believe these are forged papers. Follow the officers there. Next!"

Sau-Ping wanted to run and hide, but of course there was no place to hide and no place on this alien shore where she could manage for more than a few hours without help. The translator called her forward and asked for her papers. As she raised them to the desk she felt her papers – her precious, detailed papers – grabbed out of her hand by the foreign ghost official. He looked at the documents with a rocky face, licking his thumb to flip the pages. The interpreter's face was also expressionless.

"What is your husband's name? What sort of business is he in?

Who are his partners? Do you have any other relatives here? Show me your health report."

Sau-Ping shivered in her padded cotton jacket. It seemed so cold for late May, even though the big-nose ghosts and their assistants were all wearing thin clothing. She was travel-worn and shaken to find herself actually standing on this foreign floor after so many years of imagining Canada. The interpreter was speaking Toi-Shaanese, but she still could not understand clearly. She mumbled and stumbled.

Miraculously, the hand of the foreign ghost moved over to the stamp pad. He stamped a chop on her passport. This tiny movement was more powerful than the great ship's engines, more powerful than the ocean waves, more powerful than fear. It meant she had stepped through an invisible door and entered Canada.

"Ma! Ma! Over here. Ma! You're here!"

Sau-Ping turned to the crowd on the other side of the barrier ropes and saw her adopted son breaking forward, like a man wading through a river that reached just under his arms. Feeling frozen and weightless, she walked towards him. His arms came out and she was buried against his chest. Kin-Pong had grown taller and much more muscular. His body smelled of garlic, soya sauce, vinegar, and grease.

"Ma, you lost so much weight. You must be tired." Kin-Pong's face was wet with tears as he picked up the luggage. "How's Big Sister? I miss her so much."

Sau-Ping sighed. She would not speak to Kin-Pong about the sale of Fei-Yin's birth certificate. "Where is your father?" she asked, and looked her son in the eye. He was her filial son – she could not imagine him agreeing to the sale of his sister's identity.

"Oh, he is busy at the restaurant. Father said I am stronger and better at handling heavy luggage. Uncle Fong will give us a ride home. He drives a fruit and vegetable delivery truck. Father said he'll manage lunch today, but I should be at work around four o'clock to prepare for the dinner shift."

Sau-Ping nodded, instantly comprehending her husband's message. She resolved to act according to the arrangements he had made until she faced Yik-Man himself, looked into his eyes, and saw the spirit of the man she had married so many years ago.

Uncle Fong was a Gold Mountain guest from the Tong-Hau district of Hoi-Ping County. He smiled broadly at Sau-Ping when she and Kin-Pong emerged from the crowd. His front tooth was missing.

"You're lucky to have gotten through so easily. Sometimes newcomers are detained for months before they are allowed to get this

far. When I came, they put me in a dark cell for almost four months,"
Uncle Fong reported as they moved towards his truck. "They would-
n't let us wash and then they called us dirty. And the food was terrible! Vegetables that stank like old clothes!"

Kin-Pong hopped into the truck. Sau-Ping climbed in slowly. She
was weary, and this was her first real ride in a motor-driven land
vehicle – she couldn't remember anything of the transport ride to the
camp for tuberculosis patients.

But she knew about cities from her time in Hong Kong. She quickly recognized that the streets of Vancouver were black and grey, not
golden, but the city itself seemed pretty. When Uncle Fong
announced that they were driving through the centre of Vancouver,
she was startled to find it clean and spacious. Her eyes devoured the
sights as they tumbled backwards, away from her, at dizzying speed.
The truck passed a long building with shiny glass windows. Inside
were life-sized figures of lanky ghost women dressed in beautiful
clothes. "That's Woodwards," said Uncle Fong. "It's a department
store." Sau-Ping had no idea what a department store was, so she just
nodded politely.

The streets looked deserted compared to urban Kowloon. There
were no refugees lying around under staircases, no crowded avenues
lined with pedlars belting out their calling songs. Certainly there
were people, stepping off the trollies or walking down the sidewalk
in modest groups, past the quiet little shops and boxes filled with foreign flowers – red ones that looked like lilies, but with the petals
gathered upwards, and bright yellow ones that looked like the butt
ends of exploded firecrackers. Looking out the window of the delivery truck, Sau-Ping saw the occasional Gold Mountain uncle plod-
ding down the street by himself, this one with a cigarette hanging out
of his mouth, that one still wearing a greasy bloodstained apron. A
truck marked with strange ghost letters shaped like a broken dish
and a little flag – "CP" – turned out of a sidestreet in front of them. It
reminded her of the big delivery trucks she saw sometimes outside
the vegetable wholesalers' place in Hong Kong.

She was even more impressed with Vancouver when Kin-Pong
told her that there were no typhoons or water shortages here; water
poured out of the mountains, he said. But in winter there were many
dark and rainy days in this city, and it was colder than Hong Kong.
She agreed, wrapping her arms around herself. If she had to wear a
quilted cotton jacket in May, how could she keep warm in winter?

"Here's Chinatown," Kin-Pong said.

Sau-Ping, staring hungrily out the window of the truck, felt herself
trembling with happiness. The buildings reminded her of Shaan-Tai

Market in Toi-Shaan before the Communists. There were narrow streets crowded with Chinese customers. Fruit, vegetable, and dried-seafood stands covered by canvas canopies extended into the streets. There were signs bearing Chinese symbols and pictures for restaurants, herbal stores, pawnshops, association halls, and grocery stores. Kin-Pong read the words out to her, and even the names sounded like those at home.

They got off the truck and thanked Uncle Fong warmly for his help.

"Anytime," said Uncle Fong. "All you need to do is ask. Us Chinese have to help each other out – can't rely on the foreign devils!" With that, he roared off.

Kin-Pong said, "Here, Ma. The one with the four windows. The name is Peach Garden Restaurant."

He led Sau-Ping towards the four windows under a sign with blossoming branches painted on it. She tried not to stare inside, afraid she would see her husband frozen and glaring from his domain. In partnership with Leung Kwok-Ko, three generations of their family had operated this restaurant. Sau-Ping discovered that she was literally hungry to enter it.

But Kin-Pong directed her to the side of the main door and up a flight of narrow stairs to the floor above the restaurant where the family had its living quarters. Sau-Ping wondered whether she was walking over the head of her husband. Even with its low ceilings and rough partitioning, the accommodations seemed far more spacious than the cubicles in Sau-Ha's residence on Pitt Street in Kowloon. Several bunkbeds stood near the entrance. These, according to Kin-Pong, were temporary accommodations for fellow Toi-Shaanese who were out of work or else had just come to Vancouver from other parts of Canada, looking for work.

"Where do the three of us sleep?"

"At the very back. Come, Ma," said Kin-Pong. Taking out a bundle of keys, he unlocked the door leading to the back section of the building.

Sau-Ping entered the room where her husband had been sleeping for years. A small ancestral altar stood on a shelf against the back wall. Incense and small wine cups were placed in front of the tablet of her father-in-law, Leung Kwok-Yan. So he had prayed too? Sau-Ping eyed the rest of the room. It was so small that there was almost no room between the few pieces of basic furniture.

"Once he knew for sure that you were coming, Father purchased this double bed and a dresser. He also partitioned off the room. So now I have a bed next door to you," said Kin-Pong, as he led Sau-

Ping through the small side-door to his own cramped quarters. "There is another floor just above us. Granduncle Kwok-Ko and his adopted son Kin-Tsoi live there."

Hearing Kin-Tsoi's name sickened Sau-Ping; the gorge rose in her throat, and she literally had to swallow the bitterness. Kin-Pong noticed his mother's mood but said nothing. He poured tea for her and sneaked a sideways glance at the clock on the wall.

"Ma, I've got to work in the restaurant. You take a rest now, and I'll bring you food from the restaurant kitchen once it is ready. Father will be eating downstairs with me and Kin-Tsoi in between serving customers."

"When will I see him?" Sau-Ping asked quietly.

"As soon as he can get free." She nodded.

Once on her own, Sau-Ping grew restless. Looking around for something to do, she found a piece of rag and wiped the mirror, the dresser, and the bed poles until they shone. She made the bed and swept the floor. She opened the closet and gathered the scattered clothes inside. She folded the ones that were relatively clean. Finding the bathroom, she washed the soiled ones and hung them on the bamboo poles that stuck out of the small window at the back.

On top of the dresser she saw a pile of old letters. She couldn't read, but from the stamps she could tell that they came from China and Hong Kong. "What treasures from a typical Gold Mountain guest!" she sighed. Tears stood in her eyes. She straightened the letters and wiped the surface underneath.

Finally exhausted, Sau-Ping lay down on the bed and dozed off. She didn't hear Kin-Pong return and place a take-out dinner box on the table next to the bed. It must have been midnight when Sau-Ping woke to a heavy footfall on the stairs. She sat up. A man entered the room.

His forehead was carved with the wrinkles of time. His eyelashes were much thinner than she remembered. His hair was turning grey. He looked shorter and more crooked than before. He was not the groom she had once known. Their eyes met.

"You are back, Yik-Man. I am ..."

"I am glad you have arrived."

"Thank you for my passage money."

"Did you want your food?"

She looked at the food in the box. It had come from the restaurant. She was about to taste prepared food from the restaurant where her husband had worked since he was a boy. She drew it towards her and picked up the chopsticks. The first bite was delicious, though saltier than she expected. Yik-Man propped himself against the dresser. Her adopted son Kin-Pong entered the room. Though Sau-Ping was hungry, she ate only three more bites before saying, "I would like to make you tea. Would you like tea?" She rose.

Sau-Ping tried to help, but it was really her son who made the tea. Tasting it, watching Yik-Man raise the cup to his lips, she remembered their wedding night. As on that night, the familiar tea comforted the man and woman who were strangers to one another and made it possible to speak. The three sat around the table and talked. Everything they said was somehow both obvious and mysterious.

"Ping, we have not been together for more than twenty-two years."

"In those twenty-two years, you must have worked from early morning to late into the night in the restaurant. You have had a hard life."

"And you, you took care of my mother and my younger brother. You ... I still do not understand how you brought the children to Hong Kong. Kin-Pong told me about Hong Kong."

Sau-Ping nodded. She could not open her eyes without seeing her daughter, Fei-Yin, who was doomed to live apart from her forever, in Hong Kong.

Glancing up, hearing her silence, Yik-Man grimaced. His face was already concentrated and furrowed by years of work, but now his eyes were nearly shut. Sau-Ping realized that he had questioned his decision to sell his daughter's birth certificate but found no other answer to their troubles. He said firmly, "Now you are here. And Uncle Kwok-Ko has an adopted son to burn his incense."

"How is Uncle Kwok-Ko? Now that we are together, I should go upstairs and pay my respects to him."

"He is asleep. Tomorrow very early we will visit. He wakes at four coughing." She nodded.

Kin-Pong retired to his room. Sau-Ping and Yik-Man undressed themselves in the dark. She lay under the blankets, which smelled mildly like the mops on the ship, and felt the bed move when her husband curled in behind her. Their backs touched because the bed was small. She had been nearly this close to the strangers on the ship. Bone-tired, she soon fell asleep.

Sau-Ping saw Uncle Kwok-Ko for the first time the next morning when, after a long struggle, he managed to pry open the door for her, her husband, and her son. Leung Kwok-Ko coughed incessantly in a way that reminded Sau-Ping of her own illness – that sort of cough was a torment. Uncle Kwok-Ko was running a high fever, and he walked bent over like a tree with more than half its roots pulled out of the ground. Kin-Tsoi was nowhere to be found.

In accordance with Toi-Shaanese customs, Sau-Ping knelt and poured tea for Uncle Kwok-Ko.

"Sau-Ping," said the old man between coughing fits, "you are a good woman. I am sure that you can help Yik-Man with the restaurant business, now that I am no longer of much use."

"Uncle," replied Sau-Ping politely, "you praise me too much. I am an illiterate village woman fresh off the boat. I need you to instruct me how to be of service. I would also like to thank you for giving firm guidance to Yik-Man and Kin-Pong in building up this family business, especially after *Loye* passed away."

"Ping", said Leung Kwok-Ko as he took the cup from her in his trembling hands, always wary of the next cough, "I wish to express my gratitude to you for letting me have a chance to bring my adopted son here. I am sorry that my grandniece, Fei-Yin, was left behind as a result."

Still kneeling, Sau-Ping said, "Fei-Yin is with my sister's family. She'll be fine."

"And for what purpose?" Leung Kwok-Ko became agitated. "This Kin-Tsoi turns out to be an unfilial son. He seldom takes care of me. He is very lazy at work in the restaurant, and as soon as the restaurant closes, he heads off to gamble or visit prostitutes. I am afraid one of these days he will owe so much money that he will pawn the restaurant to pay his debt. It could be our ruin!"

Sau-Ping was at a loss for words.

Yik-Man quickly changed the subject. "Uncle, you look tired. We had better not stay."

Back in their own quarters, Yik-Man said to Sau-Ping and Kin-Pong, "Let's not worry about Kin-Tsoi too much. He is still young, he'll mend his ways as he matures."

Sau-Ping stood watching her husband and son. She fully understood they had made a bad bargain in Kin-Tsoi: they had purchased trash. But this was not the time to correct her husband. He was no fool. She suspected that he perceived the full implications of his decision and the worthlessness of the young man he had arranged to bring to Canada. What could she do? She could pray that none of them would suffer for his decision.

"Yik-Man, where is *Loye* buried?" Sau-Ping asked. "I would like to pay my respects to his soul."

"Father was buried in the Overseas Chinese Cemetery. We'll go there for Ching-Ming [*Qingming*] Festival. Right now, we can pray for his soul here. I have kept his incense pot in our bedroom, as you can see."

Sau-Ping opened her trunk and one by one took out a Koon-Yam statue, a tablet representing all the souls of the Leung household, and the special tablet for her mother-in-law, Leung Tsing-Haan. "Yik-Man, I have brought *On-Yan's* tablet here. We should place it at the domestic altar beside *Loye*'s tablet. Let us burn some incense and kowtow to our parents before we work this morning. It is a family reunion for them as much as it is for us."

Kneeling beside her stranger husband, Sau-Ping stared at her mother-in-law's wooden tablet where it now stood next to her father-in-law's. For one dizzying moment, the wooden boards looked deathly cold and meaningless. Then they took on body and strength. Here was the reunion.

CHAPTER 17

Isolation

Sau-Ping was set to work that very morning, the morning after her arrival. Yik-Man told her matter-of-factly, "I am the chief cook, and Kin-Pong and Kin-On do the rest. Now that you are here, you can help by washing dishes and cleaning up. Kin-Pong and Kin-On can take turns being cashier and waiter." Everyone in the family knew never to call Kin-Tsoi by his real name in public.

For a brief moment, Sau-Ping was taken aback by her husband's lack of ceremony. But then surely she did not expect him to handle her as if she were a maiden. She remembered what a practical-minded young man he had been when they married. "Don't worry," she said. "I'll be the fastest dish washer you ever had."

Peach Garden was a chop-suey restaurant on West Pender Street; in time Sau-Ping learned that there were many others like it in Vancouver's Chinatown. The cashier's counter was to the left of the entrance. Behind the counter, in the corner, a little shrine for the Door God sat on the floor. Further up the wall, just behind the cash register, was a shelf supporting a little statue of Kwaan-Kung, the god of loyalty. Both the Door God shrine and the Kwaan-Kung statue protected the restaurant from evil spirits that might try to sneak in and cause damage. On both sides of Kwaan-Kung's statue were red couplets that proclaimed "May Business be Prosperous" and "Ten Thousand Returns for Investment Capital."

The once-white walls of the eating area were beginning to grey. The menu, taped to the walls, offered almond chicken, sweet-and-sour pork, deep-fried prawns, honey-garlic spareribs, chow-mein, fried rice, combination three-course meals, and combination four-course meals with fortune cookies. The square floor tiles, mopped clean every now and then, were a bit worn and unevenly aligned after years of heavy traffic.

There were twelve tables of various sizes. The tablecloths were clean but old. On top of each table was a small stand for salt, pepper, vinegar, soya sauce, and hot sauce. The openings to these seasoning jars were made very small so as to prevent waste.

The kitchen was stuffy. By the time Sau-Ping stepped into the kitchen that first morning, the two large garbage cans in the corner were already mouldy and smelly. Against a greasy wall on the far side were two huge stoves on which sat two gigantic woks, one for cooking rice, the other for frying. On the other side of the kitchen was a rectangular reservoir made of brick and cement. It was used to rinse dishes and cutlery. The tap had rusted and could not be turned off properly. Rust stains bloomed beneath the leaking faucet.

The restaurant staff were already in the kitchen preparing food at 8:00 A.M. The restaurant opened its doors at 11:00 A.M. Sau-Ping put on an old torn greasy apron and rolled up her sleeves. Work made her feel at home. Soon she heard the sound of customers speaking in *sz-yap* and *saam-yap* dialects. She heard ghost words too.

Clean dishes, forks, knives, and chopsticks that were piled beside the sink were taken out to the dining-room. Dirty dishes, forks, knives, and chopsticks kept coming back. Sau-Ping was told to wipe off any excess grease, leftover food, and sweet-and-sour-sauce with a piece of rag, then scrub the dishes with a rough, abrasive soap powder, rinse them briefly under the cold-water tap, immerse the dishes and cutlery in the sink for a brief soaking, and then wipe the dishes dry. The dishes and cutlery were so greasy that they were slippery even after being soaked, but Yik-Man refused to let Sau-Ping rinse with hot water. "We have to save fuel," he said.

Sau-Ping's speed soon picked up. She was pleased to be able to supply all the clean dishes and cutlery on time for the next order. She was scrubbing vigorously at a particularly greasy plate when all of a sudden she felt a sharp pain and saw the cold tap water dripping red with blood from her fingers. She must have cut herself on a chipped plate. Instantly the pain from the cut was heightened by the cleaning powder, but she kept quiet so as not to disturb Yik-Man, who was sweating copiously over the stoves, his face glowing red from the fire. Periodically he stopped to take a swig from a large jug of cold water that he kept at his side.

Soon Sau-Ping's hands, working like machines in an assembly line, were completely numb. Kin-Pong came in frequently. "Ma, are you tired?" he asked. Before Sau-Ping could reply, he had taken the clean dishes from her, gone to Yik-Man's stove to fetch the chop-suey order for a patron, and left pieces of paper in front of Yik-Man with more orders.

"I am not tired. My fingers do not hurt," she said to herself. "I have been waiting for twenty-two years to work beside Yik-Man. How could I be anything but happy?"

But she could not bear glimpsing, speaking with, or breathing the air near Yik-Faat's son, Kin-Tsoi, now called "Kin-On." He was supposed to be sharing the cashier's and waiter's duties with Kin-Pong, yet clearly he was not doing his share. Whenever he came in he dumped the dirty dishes beside Sau-Ping and then, instead of fetching the order for a customer, stood idle for a few minutes, watching Yik-Man cook.

"Kin-On," said Yik-Man, "you'd better hurry out, the patrons are waiting for their food!"

"Kin-Pong can serve them. I want to be the cook."

"Okay, okay, you watch me ... To do the chop-suey, you stir the vegetables and meat around in the wok, about ten or twelve times, like this. You have to know how much sauce to add, not too much, not too little. Try not to waste. You also have to watch the stove. The temperature of the wok cannot be too high or too low." Yik-Man bent down to stoke the charcoal stove with iron tongs.

"Let me do it!"

Though she refused to look, Sau-Ping was certain Yik-Man had stepped back from the stove and handed over his cooking utensils, despite the multitude of paper orders fluttering above the wok. It took Kin-Tsoi quite a while to get a single dish ready. Then: "Oh, it's so hot in here! I am becoming honey-garlic spare ribs!"

"Then go out to serve the customers."

"Coming ... coming!" Kin-Pong cried out to an impatient diner as he burst into the kitchen with a pile of dirty dishes. He left two scraps of paper in front of Yik-Man, calling, "Deep-fried prawns and chicken fried rice." He then picked up two dishes of chop-suey and several bottles of beer between his fingers.

"Kin-On, hurry up!" urged Kin-Pong. "Lots of customers are waiting for their dishes! And there are many tables to be cleared."

By midnight Kin-Tsoi had already disappeared into the city streets. Kin-Pong muttered to his mother, "He's off to the gambling casino. Not so good here as in Hong Kong, he says." Sau-Ping made a noise in the back of her throat. As she removed her apron, she found it hard to lift her arms above her head. Yik-Man handed her a mop. She, Kin-Pong, and Yik-Man swabbed the kitchen and dining areas, locked up the restaurant, and went upstairs to sleep.

Soon Kin-Pong was snoring; Sau-Ping could hear him through the flimsy partition.

Late one night, Sau-Ping could no longer hold her tongue.

"Yik-Man, I would like to speak to you about Kin-Tsoi." She began softly, so as not to disturb her exhausted son.

Her husband shrugged and did not look at her.

"Not only is he not sharing the waitering with Kin-Pong, he is also keeping you from your work! The two of you have to cover for him constantly. It isn't fair!"

"You think I don't know?" said Yik-Man, sounding impatient. "But this restaurant is based on a partnership between Father and Uncle Kwok-Ko. Kin-Tsoi is Uncle Kwok-Ko's adopted son and will become an equal partner with me when Uncle Kwok-Ko passes away. Technically speaking, he and I are of the same generation, though I am his father in the eyes of Canadian Immigration. I can't tell him what to do. The only one who can tell him what to do is Uncle Kwok-Ko."

"Is it possible to talk to Uncle Kwok-Ko, then?"

"Couldn't you tell that Uncle Kwok-Ko has no control over Kin-Tsoi at all?"

"All this hard work to be shared with a robber bird," she whispered.

Her husband's face soured, and she could not be certain whether he was angry at her for speaking her mind or angry at Kin-Tsoi for his lazy, arrogant behaviour. The room went dark. With her back to Yik-Man, she instantly fell asleep.

It was very dark when Sau-Ping awakened. Her husband's hand was gliding from her left shoulder down to her right shoulder. Then it drifted down her spine. He rolled closely against her. "Ping, do you remember when we hid from the bandits?" Yik-Man whispered.

"Yes." She rolled to face him.

The restaurant was closed on the eve of the Lunar New Year in 1957. It would not reopen until the second day of the New Year.

Sau-Ping woke up around eight in the morning, trying to figure out what groceries to get for the New Year's Eve dinner with Uncle Kwok-Ko's family. Both today and tomorrow Yik-Man would be playing mahjongg all day at the Toi-Shaan Association Hall, though he was still curled in bed, taking advantage of this two-day vacation. Kin-Pong was all geared up to help with the kungfu demonstrations on the streets of Chinatown organized by the Dartcoon Club. All the cooking would be left to her.

Sau-Ping stood up. Then she felt dizzy and queer in the back of her throat. Struggling to get to the chamber pot, she threw up on the floor. She sat down on the bed shivering. A question had been nagging at her for the last few weeks, and this was the answer.

Yik-Man sat up. "Are you sick, Ping?"

"No, Yik-Man. I think I'm pregnant."

"You can't be serious!"

"I can't think what else it could be. I can't often see the moon, but you have a calendar for the weeks. It has been seven weeks."

"I'm going to be a father at the age of fifty-one!" Yik-Man's voice was full of excitement. Limber as a young man, he jumped out of bed, ran into the adjoining room, and shook Kin-Pong awake. "You're going to have a little brother!"

Sau-Ping had already risen to fetch rags to clean up the mess on the floor. She was pleased by Yik-Man's reaction and strongly believed that this time she would give birth to a boy. The restaurant in Vancouver was a man's place. Her instincts told her that sleeping above the kitchen and working over the dishes had prepared her to conceive a boy.

She continued to wash dishes in the restaurant until labour began and Yik-Man took her to Grace Hospital in September 1957: she took note of the date on the calendar near the cash register.

Sau-Ping sat in the waiting-room for expectant mothers. The hospital reeked of alcohol and reminded her uncomfortably of the tuberculosis ward at Kwong Wah Hospital in Kowloon, where she had stayed some three years ago. The birth pangs had increased in speed and frequency; they came in long, slow waves that united the lower part of her spine and trunk in a stern, tight pain. But this was a time of great joy compared to the weeks in Kwong Wah Hospital. She hoped that the infant settling to be born might be a boy. Still, she was frightened. She had never imagined herself giving birth at the age of forty-one.

Yik-Man had accompanied her into the hospital to help with the admission procedures. He was not allowed to witness the actual birth, and he was not in the waiting-room now. The receptionist at the admission desk had queried Yik-Man about Sau-Ping's medical history. Now and then, Yik-Man turned to his wife and asked her a question in Toi-Shaanese. When a slow wave of pain approached and began to swell, she bowed her head and closed her eyes, breathing fast. She heard Yik-Man mumbling his replies to the receptionist in hesitant English. Raising her head, she glimpsed the puzzled face of the woman behind the desk.

When this procedure was finished, Yik-Man had walked Sau-Ping into the waiting-room and sat down beside her for a moment, just long enough to say, "They won't let me stay with you any longer. You have to just wait here and do what they tell you."

"How can I when I haven't got a clue what they're saying?"

"I tried to tell them you don't understand English, but they said it doesn't matter."

"It might not matter to them, but it matters to me! What if something goes wrong? "

"Nothing will go wrong," said Yik-Man a bit crossly.

Sau-Ping caught herself. She didn't want her husband to think she was dissatisfied with him in any way. "Never mind," she said. "You go home. When I come back I will come back with our first natural-born son."

Yik-Man touched her hand and departed.

She was taken to a small room with two beds where the drapes, wall, ceiling, and bedsheets were all white, the colour of death and mourning. She shared the room with another expectant mother, who let out a piercing shriek every now and then, whenever labour pains or leg cramps struck her. Sau-Ping tried to be more dignified and subdued, but when her labour intensified shortly after midnight, she could not swallow the groans in her throat.

There was no mother, no mother-in-law, and no village midwife. She was not giving birth at home but at a hospital where nobody understood her. She prayed and prayed to Koon-Yam for mercy. Some nurses came and wheeled her into a large room with blinding yellow lights.

After twelve hours of labour, the baby's head still had not come out. The doctor disappeared, leaving Sau-Ping in the hands of the nurses and a young man in a long white coat. When the doctor came back he said something to the nurses. Then the foreign ghosts set up a white screen so that Sau-Ping could not see what they were doing to her belly. One of the women wheeled a tray glittering with equipment to the other side of the screen so that Sau-Ping couldn't see. Then the nurse with the biggest nose turned her head, looked into Sau-Ping's eyes, reached down, and held her arm warmly. There was a terrible sting and a forceful prick around her belly button. Sau-Ping cried out and tried to kick, but her feet were bound. Then her body began to turn very cold. The foreign ghosts covered her with many blankets. Under partial anaesthetic, she was frozen with terror, staring at the death-white screen, but somehow the warm hand of the foreign woman convinced her to be still. She did not believe this woman would let the foreign doctor steal or kill her baby. There was nothing else to do but live and be still.

Sau-Ping closed her eyes tightly. She realized that she was not giving birth properly. The nurse had given her a piece of towelling to chew on, and her teeth ground into the cloth, powered more by terror than pain. Then a weight was slipped out of her. She heard a nurse speaking some ghost words. In front of Sau-Ping's eyes dangled a plump baby girl smeared in blood, with the cord still attached to her belly. A big gloved hand slapped the baby, who began to wail, and then she was taken behind the screen. Sau-Ping felt them doing something more to her. Now and then there was a needle-sharp pain on her belly, and her body under the blankets jumped. Each time that happened, the doctor and the nurses muttered words that must have been apologies, but most of them never looked at her, only at her middle on the other side of the white cloth wall. Sau-Ping closed her eyes. She could not speak. The infant was another girl. She waited to be wheeled into a bed.

When she awoke, she was in a ward for new mothers and there was a needle taped to her wrist that connected her arm to a bottle with a tube leading from it. She saw a bedpan on a shelf near her feet. Her belly hurt badly when she moved at all, but she did not reach down and touch herself because she had come to realize that the foreign ghosts had cut her open to take out the baby and then stitched the cut with thread. She had heard of this being done in Hong Kong hospitals. Sau-Ping decided she would look at the thread and her own sliced abdomen later, when she had more strength.

She shared the ward with five other women – all Canada ghost women. They chatted amongst themselves, often making sounds like old men spitting. Sau-Ping looked at the needle in her arm. She examined the blanket stretched over her flat body.

The door opened. A middle-aged Caucasian nurse came in wearing a white uniform, cap, and shoes. She stood over Sau-Ping's bed and talked gibberish, but she smiled pleasantly. Yik-Man walked in behind her looking nervous. He clasped his empty hands together in front of his body as though he had just received them and had absolutely no idea what they were for. The nurse poked a glass tube into Sau-Ping's mouth and took her pulse. Yik-Man sat down beside the bed and began translating what the nurse told him.

Sau-Ping was to lie in bed for two more days. They had cut the baby out because it would not be born – it was backwards, with its bottom, not its head, facing down. The nurses would feed and bathe the baby. On the third day when Sau-Ping was no longer receiving sugars from the water that came through the needle in her arm, they would still wash the baby. However, except for the 2:00 A.M. feeding, Sau-Ping could nurse the baby herself every four hours.

While he was translating, Yik-Man kept a stern impersonal expression on his face. Sau-Ping knew he was disappointed that the new baby was not a boy. She felt guilty at having let him down. Had Leung Tsing-Haan, her mother-in-law, been right when she predicted years ago that Sau-Ping was fated never to give birth to sons?

Kin-Pong came to see her in the early afternoon. His face beamed and he spoke to her happily. He had consulted some of the restaurant patrons, he said, and they suggested that his baby sister should be given the name Po-Yin, or Precious Swallow in Chinese, "Po-yeen," Pauline, in English.

The seven days of recuperation in Grace Hospital were not a happy time for Sau-Ping. She was unaccustomed to the food. The meat was tasteless and dry as leather. The vegetables were either completely raw or cooked until they were mushy and yellow. She was dying to have some ginger water to get rid of the wind in her abdomen, and some red date water or rice wine with chicken and black fungus to restore her blood loss. Neither Kin-Pong nor Yik-Man had the time or the knowledge to prepare those tonics and bring them to the hospital. To make things worse, the place where she had been cut and stitched back together hurt when she tried to shift in bed or sit up.

On the third day Sau-Ping was told to get up and walk around and to wash her hair and body. The nurse made her commands clear by means of hand-signals, and by holding out the soap and washcloth, and though Sau-Ping wanted to resist, resistance proved impossible in the end. These were all activities that a woman ought to shun for a month after childbirth. Didn't these nurses know anything about the female body? She would suffer from rheumatism when she grew old if she touched water too soon after giving birth. Exhausted by her ordeals, Sau-Ping settled back in bed and towelled her hair. Tears dripped down her face. She wiped them off with her sleeve.

Kin-Pong came to take her home from the hospital on the seventh day. He mentioned that he was thankful his father had the foresight to take out medical insurance beforehand. They rode in Uncle Fong's truck, Sau-Ping holding Pauline in her arms. Kin-Pong told her that Yik-Man had agreed to his request that she be let off dishwashing for three more weeks so that she wouldn't get rheumatism in years to come.

It was understood that she would work, however. Sau-Ping carried the baby in a sling on her back, and in between feedings she helped peel onions and chop vegetables and meat, acting as assistant cook to Yik-Man.

She and her husband rarely spoke while they worked, and they had had no intimate talks since Pauline was born. Pauline's wailing just before the 2:00 A.M. and 6:00 A.M. feedings woke both Yik-Man and Kin-Pong every night. The family atmosphere grew tense. One night a foreign customer complained that there was a bug in his chop-suey and stood up demanding that he and his four friends, two of them women, ought to have dinner for free. Kin-Pong had tried to placate him, but at last the man threw a water glass at the wall and stormed out, dragging his friends in his wake, leaving behind a table loaded with half-eaten dishes – food that had not been paid for. Hours later, when the last dish was cleaned and the last bag of trash carried outside, Yik-Man had just settled into bed when Pauline began her wailing. Sau-Ping carried her back and forth. Pauline would quiet down briefly, then begin again. At about three in the morning, Sau-Ping heard her husband stir. She turned to see Yik-Man in the half-dark with a beer bottle upraised in his hand. He brought it down hard on Pauline's head! In that instant, Sau-Ping screamed, tried to twist out of his way, and the sound of the baby's cries changed and became wild. Kin-Pong was out of bed and in his parents' room in a flash. "What happened? Was there an accident?"

Yik-Man still clutched the beer bottle and held it half-raised as though in preparation for another strike.

Kin-Pong knew immediately what had happened. "How dare you hit my baby sister!" he cried. "Put it down!"

"I'll do whatever I want with her. She is nothing but goods on which a man loses money!" yelled Yik-Man.

"Is it her fault that she was born a girl? Why are you so concerned with having a son? Look what happened to Uncle Kwok-Ko when he bought a son. Who is the goods?"

Yik-Man bellowed, "To continue the family line I must have a son!"

"You have me. I am a filial son."

"I want my own flesh and blood!"

Kin-Pong was speechless. His anger suddenly drained right out of him. He turned around and disappeared back to his little cramped space.

Sau-Ping was stung by Yik-Man's cruelty. Her heart raged and her tongue loosened. "How could you say this to Kin-Pong! He has been *our* son for more than twenty years. He suffered with me in Toi-Shaan and Hong Kong. He gave his sweat and blood to the family restaurant. He works so hard that he has no recreation, no chance to learn English and better himself. How could you say such unkind things to him?"

Yik-Man got up and strode out of the room, slamming the door. Sau-Ping heard his footsteps as he rushed down the stairs. "The two of you can go back to Hong Kong with that squealing pig! I'll kill her next time!" Yik-Man shouted so loudly that Sau-Ping was sure everyone in the building could hear. "I am going to visit a woman who knows me!" He slammed the door behind him.

Sau-Ping began to wail. She cried into the frozen Vancouver darkness, she cried against the hard electric lights. This land had cut her belly apart as if she were a melon! This land had transformed her husband into a machine who was all speed at work: a machine without a heart.

When the first desperation had passed out of her, Sau-Ping heard her daughter wailing. She quieted herself; it was necessary to tend to the child. But as she nursed the hurt infant, who had a great lump forming on her head, she thought about her own situation. Never had she been so lonely in the world! Except for Kin-Pong, she had no support, nobody to share her pain. In her years at Sai-Fok she and her mother-in-law, Leung Tsing-Haan, had struggled against one another, but at least they shared a common fate as grass widows. They had often prayed together. And she'd had friends in Sai-Fok, Yi-Lin, Mei-Kuen, Wai-Fong, and Brother-in-law Yik-Mo. Even in Kowloon, working as a vegetable pedlar in Yu Chau Street or fashioning plastic flowers in Shek Kip Mei, she had companions – gentle Fei-Yin, reasonable Sau-Ha, courageous Mei-Kuen, boisterous Lai-Sheung. Leung Yik-Kwong and his brother Yik-Nang on Prince Edward Road in Hong Kong were more concerned about her welfare than her own husband.

Her companions and relatives had thought that she would find happiness joining her husband in Gold Mountain. What kind of companionship could she find with Yik-Man? Having lived in Canada since the age of ten, he could understand some English. He was at home in Chinatown and had long-term friends. He socialized and played mahjongg with them at the Toi-Shaan Association Hall or the Chinese Benevolent Association whenever he had some time off from the restaurant. He never took her anywhere. He must be ashamed of her because she was a village bumpkin.

At that moment, she wanted to leave. But where could she go? She did not have the money to go back to Hong Kong. Besides, she had no Hong Kong identity card. With an infant, how could she earn enough to lead an independent life? She would hate to be a burden on her sister Sau-Ha or her eldest daughter, Fei-Yin. She could not consider returning to Toi-Shaan either. She had no house and no land there any more. If she could find her way back to that distant home, she would be arrested as a former landlord and class enemy.

Little Pauline was growing quieter. Sau-Ping found herself singing an old song to the baby as her feet crossed to the stairs and she descended into the dark restaurant. It was so quiet! Light from the streetlamps and electric signs came in through the curtains that covered the front windows. The cash register was silent as a rock. The ticking of a clock only intensified the silence. Alone among the twelve tables, Sau-Ping sat down in a customer's chair and nursed her child. She would have liked to comfort Kin-Pong, but it was necessary to quiet the baby first.

An hour later, she heard the sidedoor open. Yik-Man's heavy footsteps mounted to their bedroom. They stopped. Yik-Man had discovered that she and the baby were not in the room. Sau-Ping did not feel like climbing the stairs to tell Yik-Man of her whereabouts. She sat in the restaurant chair at the empty table with her sleeping child in her lap. Her eyes fixed on the shining vinegar bottle.

The big shadow of Yik-Man entered the room. Powered by dread and decision, Sau-Ping's heart beat faster. Her right hand covered the bump on the infant's head. "Yik-Man," she said plainly to the shadow in the restaurant, "I have been a good wife to you for many years. But I will not tolerate the person I met tonight."

"I will be better," he said. "When I saw the bed was empty, I feared you were gone."

"Where would I go?" she demanded. "Where else do you want me to travel, husband? Haven't I gone far enough for you and your family? You wish to send me on another journey?"

"How is the child?"

"She has a great bump on her head from the beer bottle, but I do not think it necessary to take her to the doctor. You didn't strike with all your force."

"I am going up to sleep. Would you come upstairs, Ping?"

"I will be up soon."

Yik-Man left the room. A while later Sau-Ping climbed to their bedroom with the sleeping child, who settled into her small bed without a murmur. For a few hours, Sau-Ping lay with her back to her husband's. She did not fall asleep. When it was time to work, she rose and began dressing.

But that day was better. Yik-Man worked calmly in the kitchen. Once, when the lunch orders were coming thick and fast, he complimented Kin-Pong for his efficiency. Then, as Sau-Ping stood chopping bok choy, she felt her husband come up behind her, within reach of Pauline in the sling. He rubbed his palm across the infant's skull to feel the bump. Then he returned to the stove. Sau-Ping leaned over quickly and wiped her face with a rag. There was hope.

CHAPTER 18

Hong Kong Brides

1958

Sau-Ping got pregnant again the following year. This time the delivery was much simpler. She didn't even go through labour. Instead, the doctor requested that she come to the hospital four weeks before the baby was due. She experienced the same operation as before, but this time the surgeons used a mask to make her sleep through the entire procedure.

It was a boy! When the nurse brought him to her wrapped in a blue blanket the morning after the operation, Sau-Ping could not express the extent of her joy. She stayed in the hospital for five restful days and prayed to her mother-in-law's tablet the minute she got home.

Yik-Man was excited beyond words. He consulted Uncle Kwok-Ko on naming the baby. Uncle Kwok-Ko suggested "Kin-Tso," meaning "glorifying the ancestral line."

"The closest thing in English is Joe," said Yik-Man. And so Joe Leung got his ghost name.

The family restaurant was closed for one day in honour of baby Joe's one-month birthday. The Leung family gave a banquet to celebrate its first Canadian-born son in three generations.

With two young children, Pauline and Joe, added to the family, some domestic rearrangements had to be made. Kin-Pong took over the space that had been used to accommodate unemployed Toi-Shaanese. The tiny room adjoining Sau-Ping and Yik-Man's bedroom was now used as a nursery for his two young siblings.

Likewise, new arrangements had to be made about work. At the age of one, Pauline was crawling around and learning to walk. It would be dangerous for her to scramble through the kitchen while Sau-Ping washed dishes. Besides, Yik-Man wanted to make sure that his natural-born son Joe had the best home-care. So Sau-Ping was relieved of her job as a dishwasher for the time being.

According to Yik-Man, it was easy these days to employ a teenage boy at a low wage to wash dishes. Many youngsters had entered the country as "paper sons," just like Kin-Tsoi. Since they could not speak English and were not welcomed by the mainstream Vancouver society, many were stuck in Chinatown and willing to do any job at all.

Sau-Ping was free at last from her double burden. She took great pleasure each day in walking around Chinatown with her two young children. She often passed a curio shop that sold, among other things, colourful kites that fascinated Pauline and Joe. Sau-Ping loitered there and made friends with the four senior men who sat on the bench in front of the shop sunning themselves whenever the weather was nice. After a few days' acquaintance, she found out that they were all surnamed Mak and all came from Chung-Lau Heung in Toi-Shaan County.

Sau-Ping felt sorry for these Gold Mountain guests. They had been subjected to severe hardship and ill treatment by the foreign ghosts in British Columbia when they were young, and now, severed from all ties in China, they had been forgotten by the government of Vancouver. The first Uncle Mak had lost his whole family in Toi-Shaan during the Japanese invasion. The second didn't know the whereabouts of his wife or children. The third and fourth had family left in Toi-Shaan, but for a variety of reasons they could neither go home nor sponsor their families to Vancouver. They kept up a correspondence with their families and sent them remittances through relatives in Hong Kong. These four Uncle Maks and eight other fellow villagers now rented a two-storey house on Dunlevy Street. There they created a kind of family for one another; at the very least, they kept one another company.

One day in 1959, the uncles gave Sau-Ping news of Communist China. One of them had come across an article in the *Chinese Times* about the sufferings brought about by the Great Leap Forward, which had started the year before. Another said that he had read an official release by the government in Taiwan published in the same local newspaper, with terrible news about Toi-shaan: "It said that during the Great Leap Forward, the Commune cadres insisted that everything be shared as a group. Now the wives of the Gold Mountain guests are shared by all the men in the commune."

"I hope this is just a rumour."

"Sharing a wife is the least of the problems. There is a terrible famine in Toi-Shaan. People are eating coarse husks unfit even for pigs. Others are so hungry that their stomachs have swollen like pigs' bladders full of air. Some people's arms are so swollen that they are

the same size as their thighs. Still, people are forced by the Communists to march up the mountains and use their bare hands to con-
struct the Taai-Lung Tung dam. People are dying."

Sau-Ping knew a little about Taai-Lung Tung because the band of
outlaws Mei-Kuen had been forced to join had camped in those
mountains. It was a merciless terrain. She didn't wonder that hungry
workers were dying if they were forced to labour in such a place. She
wondered whether Yik-Mo or Tin-Shaang had to work on the dam.

That night Sau-Ping asked Yik-Man and Kin-Pong whether they
had heard anything about the Great Leap Forward and the recent
famine in China. Kin-Pong said he had received a letter from Uncle
Lau Tseung-Lam in Hong Kong that very day but had not had time
to read it. He did so now and found that his uncle, too, could speak
of nothing but the natural disasters and famine. Sau-Ping remembered chewing on leaves and feeding the children dry husk biscuits
during the wartime famine in Toi-Shaan. She was deeply concerned
for her brother-in-law Yik-Mo, her confidant and friend for so many
years, who had ended up a prisoner in China. She knew he had been
released and that he had married, but life had not become easy.

"Yik-Man," she urged as they rested late that night, "we have to
mail some care parcels to your younger brother Yik-Mo in Sai-Fok.
Yik-Mo was designated as a landlord. His wife is also considered one
of the five bad types because her father was executed for his association with the Kuomintang. Their family must be suffering in this
famine much more than other peasants in the village."

"My poor brother! I wish I could sponsor him to join us here." Yik-
Man looked towards the door. "The problem is I don't know how
much to send. And it is so difficult to mail parcels to Mainland China
from Vancouver. The Canadian post office does not have direct mail-
ing services to China."

"We must seek advice from other families."

"I have spoken to some others." Yik-Man turned silent.

"Yes?"

"There is a problem." Yik-Man lowered his voice. "My friends at
the Toi-Shaan Association Hall spoke of it months ago. If we send
packages to China, the Canadian government here may decide we
are Communists and deport us."

"That's ridiculous," Sau-Ping cried. "The Communists nearly
killed your brother! We lost everything to the Communists!" But on
second thought, she was not surprised.

"I suppose any government can label you as it chooses." She was
thinking hard, and it occurred to her that they would have to rely on
intermediaries.

"What of this? We can send a draft to my sister Sau-Ha and brother-in-law Lau Tseung-Lam in Hong Kong and ask them to purchase essential items and send them off through the Hong Kong post office. I am sure my sister will be sending things to my brother Tin-Shaang's family in Fung-Yeung, if the situation is as bad as the news reports."

Kin-Pong took his cue from Sau-Ping. He knew that she was reluctant to ask Yik-Man to spend money on her side of the family.

He said, "Father, if we ask Auntie Sau-Ha and Uncle Tseung-Lam to send things to Uncle Yik-Mo, we should also ask them to send care parcels to Uncle Tin-Shaang's family as well, funded by us. I am sure both sides of the family need these relief parcels badly." Yik-Man nodded half-heartedly.

Done!

Sau-Ping thought about this moment all the next day and into the night. She remembered how at first, many years ago, she had resented the arrival of her adopted son, Kin-Pong, who was purchased by her mother-in-law off a market street from a thief. With the years he had become a gentle filial son. She knew that Kin-Pong often thought of his family in Mainland China, perhaps because his own life in Vancouver was so monotonous. Kin-Pong had become quite moody since the move from his former room. His only contact with other young people came through the Dartcoon Club. He had been part of the coordinating committee for the four-day "Chinese Festival" during Chinese New Year in 1959, but even then he remained so bound by his work that he couldn't participate fully. Moreover, he had obviously felt squeezed out of the close family circle by his two young siblings, especially Joe, the natural-born son. This little brother seemed to have usurped his place in the hearts and minds of their parents. Sau-Ping discussed her concerns with Yik-Man that night.

"Yik-Man, I think we should find Kin-Pong a wife. He is already twenty-four years old. In his loneliness I am afraid he might go with Kin-Tsoi to visit prostitutes or gamble."

"This has also crossed my mind," said Yik-Man deliberately. "Besides, our restaurant could use an extra pair of hands now that you are busy raising the children. We should find ourselves a hard-working daughter-in-law."

"I do not know how to begin in Canada," said Sau-Ping.

"Hmm. I suppose you've noticed that there are still many more young men than young women in Chinatown."

"Yes. Most people sponsor boys rather than girls from Hong Kong to Canada," Sau-Ping said carefully, trying not to think of her grown daughter in Hong Kong. "But if everyone continues this way, the boys will never be able to find wives and the next generation will have no sons. In your generation, you came back to Toi-Shaan to marry me. Why can't we send Kin-Pong to look for a bride in Hong Kong?"

"I had thought of that. But I've heard so many horror stories in Chinatown recently. The current immigration law allows Canadian citizens to bring over whomever they are engaged to, provided that they're married within one month of arrival. One young woman from Hong Kong came as fiancée to a poor Overseas Chinese. As soon as she arrived, she broke her contract and married a richer Chinese man instead. We have to be careful."

"Husband, I would like to consult Kin-Pong tomorrow night after work. He can write a letter to ask Auntie Sau-Ha to help come up with a reliable match," said Sau-Ping. "My sister and her husband understand how to manage this in Hong Kong. And they have sons themselves."

"Yes, yes," Yik-Man responded, nodding strongly this time. "That's a good idea."

Kin-Pong was exhausted when he came in from work the following evening. It was a Friday night, and the restaurant had been particularly busy. Kin-Tsoi had disappeared before the second supper rush, leaving Kin-Pong to run the place alone. The young man's white waiter's jacket was splashed with sauces and grease stains that bore witness to the long day's work. His hair clung limply to his head and his eyes drooped with tiredness. He went straight to the bathroom to wash up.

"Kin-Pong, I'd like to have a word with you," called Sau-Ping above the sound of water gushing from the tap.

"Coming, Ma," Kin-Pong answered, controlling his voice so that it sounded willing and polite, though Sau-Ping knew that all he really wanted was to collapse on his squeaky, narrow bed, pull the sheets over his head, and go to sleep.

"It won't take long," she said.

Kin-Pong came into her room dressed in a clean pair of pyjama pants and an undershirt.

"Kin-Pong, I think it's time you thought of getting married," she told him.

Kin-Pong raised an eyebrow. He had been so busy with work, marriage was probably the farthest thing from his mind. "I don't know anyone who would want to marry me, Ma," he said. "There are so few Chinese girls in Chinatown. Surely you don't want me to marry a *kwai-mooi*?"

"Of course not. Your father and I would like you to choose a bride from among the women of Hong Kong. I would like you to write to your Auntie Sau-Ha and ask her to engage a matchmaker."

Kin-Pong smiled. "You want me to get married the old-fashioned way. I was afraid you were going to get all modern on me when you started having Canadian-born children." His eyes sparkled and he chuckled.

"You thought we had forgotten you," she said gently. "You thought that we only wanted to keep you as a slave. Your father is in agreement with the idea of getting you a bride."

He touched her arm, smiling. "Thank you."

In a month's time, a small parcel arrived from Hong Kong. Alone with her two toddlers, Sau-Ping opened the packet to find a letter and forty photographs of young women! Unable to read, she went upstairs to consult Uncle Leung Kwok-Ko. Uncle Kwok-Ko took out his glasses and read the letter from Lau Tseung-Lam, written on behalf of Sau-Ping's sister, Sau-Ha.

Sau-Ha explained that she had gone to several Kaifong Associations in urban Kowloon and talked to the go-betweens stationed at each one. They were eager to help and would only charge if the match succeeded. They all said they knew the girls' family backgrounds and would provide more details on request.

Uncle Kwok-Ko explained that the words written on the backs of the photographs gave each young woman's age, the date and hour of her birth by the lunar calendar, and the location of her ancestral village. Sau-Ping asked Uncle Kwok-Ko to help her pick out those of Toi-Shaanese origin. He was happy to oblige.

"I agree with you that it is important for a daughter-in-law to speak the same dialect as the rest of the family. Besides, women in Toi-Shaan are usually very adaptable. They are hard workers, faithful wives, and caring mothers."

There were ten photos of women from Toi-Shaan.

"Do you want me to help you match the birthdates of these young women with that of Kin-Pong?"

"I am afraid I don't know Kin-Pong's exact birth date. You see, On-Yan bought him in Shaan-Tai Market when he was two years old. I guess I'll let Kin-Pong choose his own favourite from among the ten photos here."

Kin-Pong was uncharacteristically bashful when he took the photos from his mother. "Is there one you prefer?" he asked her. Sau-Ping smiled, pleased at having raised such a filial son.

"I've already narrowed it down to include only Toi-Shaanese girls. I will leave the rest up to you."

Kin-Pong went to his room, closed the door, and did not come out for the rest of the night. Sau-Ping rose noiselessly from her bed now and again to glance down the hallway at the crack under his closed door; it glowed until early morning. Kin-Pong appeared in the restaurant bleary-eyed and a little scruffy. He worked quickly but more clumsily than usual all day. As soon as the restaurant was closed, he returned to his room and stayed inside with the photos again until the small hours of the morning. Again Sau-Ping found herself awakening every few hours. Noiselessly she checked on her two young children, and on her grown son. The next night well after midnight, she rose to see that the light in his room was extinguished and guessed that he had made a choice. She and Yik-Man waited in their room the following morning. Kin-Pong knocked and appeared in the doorway. He produced a single photograph. It belonged to a young woman by the name of Lai Ka-Lin; Christian name: Katherine.

Sau-Ping liked her son's choice. She passed the photo to her husband, who took a quick look and said, "It's okay with me provided that Kin-Pong likes her."

"Are you sure you don't want to pick another one, Kin-Pong?" asked Sau-Ping.

"No, she's the one. I'm sure."

"Well, I think we should check out her family background and her temperament very carefully. We don't want to make any mistakes. Kin-Pong, why don't you write Auntie Sau-Ha and Uncle Tseung-Lam to get more information from the go-between? We should also get your sister Fei-Yin to make friends with this Katherine Lai just to sound her out."

"Yes, Ma."

Another three weeks passed. A second letter from Sau-Ha arrived. Yik-Man, Sau-Ping, and Kin-Pong gathered at midnight at Uncle Kwok-Ko's apartment. Kin-Tsoi was not there as usual. Uncle read the letter aloud:

Katherine Lai is the youngest daughter from a family of five siblings from Tuen-Fan District in Toi-Shaan County. During the Japanese invasion, her parents wrapped her up in a red cloth, wrote her name, her village of origin, and her date of birth on it, and abandoned her by the roadside.

A kind woman snatched her from certain death and took her to Hong Kong. She could not afford to raise Katherine either. So Katherine was admitted by the Fanling Orphans Home in the New Territories, which is run by Catholic missionaries. At seventeen, she left the orphanage and became a waitress in a dim-sum restaurant. The kind woman worried about her future, so she took Katherine's photo to the go-between in Mongkok Kaifong Association, hoping that Katherine would be able to marry a good family in Gold Mountain.

"An orphan?" Sau-Ping said to Kin-Pong. "She won't bring any dowry with her if you marry her."

"A dowry would be of great help to us at this time," confirmed Yik-Man. "When I married your mother, my mother received furniture and bedding from her family."

Sau-Ping was pleased that Yik-Man still remembered the contents of her dowry. At the same time, she knew how many long, silent, shy, passionate hours her filial son Kin-Pong had spent staring at the ten photographs before he chose this Katherine.

"And wasn't I a good bargain?" she said. "Think twice, Kin-Pong, before you decide. It is your decision."

No one spoke. Sau-Ping looked directly at her son and motioned with one hand.

"If it's all the same to you, Ma," said Kin-Pong, taking a deep breath, "I'd be happy to marry her with no dowry at all. If she's an orphan then we have something in common." He turned and looked his father directly in the eye. Yik-Man didn't dare say another word.

"It's fine with me if it's fine with your father," said Sau-Ping. Yik-Man nodded his head but still didn't speak.

"Is that a yes, Pa?" asked Sau-Ping. Yik-Man nodded again.

"All right, then," said Sau-Ping, "we'll wait for Fei-Yin's report, and if she likes this girl we'll send you to Hong Kong for three months to see how you two get along."

From that point events moved quickly. Kin-Pong left Vancouver by plane on 4 April 1960 for his three-month courtship in Hong Kong. Yik-Man hired another young man to wait at tables in his absence, as Kin-Tsoi refused to cover for Kin-Pong. To cut costs, Kin-Pong would stay at Sau-Ha's cubicle on Pitt Street. Sau-Ha's two daughters, Tsoi-Yuk and Tsoi-Lin, were now living in factory dormitories, so there was an extra bedspace for Kin-Pong.

Sau-Ping lived with the contented feeling that she had at last been able to help arrange a happy prospect for one of her children. Her world was turning in the proper direction. For this reason, the ugly surprise that visited the family one month later struck her painfully. At one in the morning there was a loud knock on the street-level door. Yik-Man, who was not yet fully asleep, rolled out of bed to answer. Sau-Ping followed him silently and listened in the dark near the top of the stairs. Yik-Man opened the door to two uniformed men, one a white ghost, the other a Chinese policeman.

The white officer spoke quickly in English. Sau-Ping heard the words "Kin-On Leung." Her husband answered in his imperfect English. She understood the meaning of one of Yik-Man's phrases – he sometimes used it in the restaurant when a customer complained about a dish. It was a phrase of apology. Yik-Man was shaking his head and saying "no."

"If it's all the same to you, we'd like to come in and take a look," said the Chinese officer, politely enough, in words that Sau-Ping could understand. But then the two of them pushed past Yik-Man in a manner that was not polite at all.

Sau-Ping fled in the dark to her bedroom. Within moments the two policemen were standing beside her. They looked through everything, turned the light on briefly in the children's room, and then marched upstairs, where Sau-Ping heard them rouse old Uncle Leung Kwok-Ko from his bed. Trying to move in accordance with their commands, Uncle Kwok-Ko began to cough violently. Sau-Ping understood that these men were looking for Kin-Tsoi and that they had not found him. Sau-Ping stood in the hall as Yik-Man led the frightening officials back to the lower doorway. They muttered polite thanks and pushed past him again before he could even step aside.

Sau-Ping was shivering. These policemen came in and out as they pleased. It reminded her of house searches and arbitrary arrests in Sai-Fok under the Chinese Communist regime.

Kin-Tsoi did not appear at all that night. At first, Sau-Ping and Yik-Man thought that he must have gone to gamble and visit prostitutes as usual. Yik-Man wondered aloud whether Kin-Tsoi knew the police were after him and had already gone into hiding.

"It is possible we won't see him again for a very long time," he said sourly.

Yik-Man went to the Chinese Benevolent Association the next morning and found that the RCMP had already been there. Apparently, they had taken the list of association members as well as other documents and correspondence. Later that afternoon, Yik-Man told Sau-Ping that, from what he had gathered at the association, it appeared that the police raid on their house was part of a sudden crackdown on illegal immigration among Chinese communities throughout Canada.

A week later Sau-Ping went upstairs in the morning as usual to check on Uncle Kwok-Ko. He lay flat on his back in bed, staring up at the ceiling.

"Good morning, Uncle," said Sau-Ping.

The old man's eyes didn't move. He appeared to be staring at something on the ceiling. But there was nothing there.

"I brought you some tea." Sau-Ping leaned down to place the cup on the bedside table. Only then did she notice something strange about those eyes. She touched Uncle Kwok-Ko's cheek. It was as cold as a restaurant plate.

Shocked, she clattered downstairs to the bathroom where her husband was brushing his teeth. "Yik-Man! Uncle Kwok-Ko is dead! He must have died sometime in the night."

Throwing down his toothbrush, not even bothering to spit, Yik-Man ran upstairs. He touched his uncle's face and cried out. Great pity, sharpened by anger, passed through Sau-Ping. Poor Uncle Kwok-Ko! He had left this world with no one at his deathbed, nothing to fix his eyes on but a rough ceiling. Ten years' savings spent to buy a worthless "paper son," and he died utterly alone.

Uncle Kwok-Ko was buried at the Overseas Chinese Cemetery beside Leung Kwok-Yan, Yik-Man's own father. Yik-Man and Sau-Ping gave him an elaborate funeral, financing the service with Uncle Kwok-Ko's share of the restaurant profit supplemented by their own family savings. Since Kin-Tsoi was not in Vancouver, it was Yik-Man and Sau-Ping who had the tablet made for the soul of Uncle Kwok-Ko, and they placed it on the ancestral altar in their bedroom. This enabled Sau-Ping to pray for his soul while paying daily homage to her own parents-in-law.

Since Kin-Tsoi was nowhere to be found and nobody knew whether Uncle Kwok-Ko had left a will of any kind, Yik-Man locked up the living quarters shared by Uncle Kwok-Ko and Kin-Tsoi on the top floor of the restaurant and deposited half of the restaurant's profits into a separate account for the time being.

On 4 July Kin-Pong arrived home from Hong Kong. The minute she glimpsed his face, Sau-Ping knew that her son was successfully, joyfully engaged to Katherine Lai. Kin-Pong was a good-hearted young man and news of his granduncle's death had saddened him; he appreciated the years of hard labour and companionship that Uncle Kwok-Ko had shared with his own brother, Kwok-Yan, and with Yik-Man, his nephew, as they all tried to keep the restaurant in business. But Kin-Pong could not suppress his own joy. He had chosen a partner. A new phase of his life was opening. The family sat down to talk in the restaurant kitchen late that night, after the day's work was done.

"What is Katherine like?" Sau-Ping asked.

"She's lovely. You'll like her, Ma and Pa. She is very genuine and she has a good temperament. Very frugal and hard working too. We got to know one another well."

"Did you tell her that we are not a rich family?"

"Yes, I told her many times. I said life is very hard in Vancouver, and our restaurant requires a lot of hard work from every member of the family. She understands that. She was trained to work hard in the orphanage. Now she works in a teahouse in Hong Kong, and she knows how hectic running a restaurant can be. Ma, I think she will be an asset to the family because she learned to speak very good English from the Catholic nuns who brought her up." Kin-Pong could not stop praising Katherine.

Sau-Ping felt a bit nostalgic. "How is Hong Kong?" she asked.

"Very good. There are many factories now and a lot of job openings. Lots of highrises, new construction. Big Sister Fei-Yin and Auntie Sau-Ha's daughters, Cousins Tsoi-Yuk and Tsoi-Lin, are all skilled workers in a garment factory where the food, according to the girls, is better than in other factories." Then he shook his head and his eyes darkened.

"But, Ma, the New Territories were a mess when I was there. They were packed with starving refugees from South China. Worse off than we used to be when we first arrived in Hong Kong."

Sau-Ping remembered those days very well. Why did such tragedies hit China so frequently? she wondered, recalling the rubble pits left by the bombs and her brother-in-law, Yik-Mo, bleeding on his knees, as his Communist accusers danced around him. And now the Great Leap Forward and the Great Famine. It was a good thing so many of her family had escaped to Hong Kong and to Vancouver.

"How are Auntie Sau-Ha and Uncle Tseung-Lam?"

"Well, Uncle Tseung-Lam has stopped working. So they both stay at home. They are concerned about their children. Their three sons are all doing very well. Cousins Tak-Kan and Tak-Keung were construction workers before, you remember. Now they are building contractors. Auntie Sau-Ha's youngest son, Cousin Tak-Wa, is doing well in high school. He studies all the time under dim light in the cubicle so he has become very shortsighted. But Auntie Sau-Ha is worried about her two daughters, even with the good food in the canteen," Kin-Pong continued. "Cousin Tsoi-Yuk is dating the son of her factory boss. She seldom brings her boyfriend home. Auntie Sau-Ha senses that Tsoi-Yuk must feel ashamed of their cubicle on Pitt Street. And Cousin Tsoi-Lin is withdrawn and sulky. She has resolved never to get married. Big Sister Fei-Yin told me that Tsoi-Lin was raped by the male factory supervisor. She tried to kill herself once."

"Merciful Koon-Yam!" cried Sau-Ping, thinking of the time Mei-Kuen was raped by bandits long ago. Her thoughts surged around a vision of her own lost daughter, left behind in the great city. "Is Big Sister Fei-Yin happy these days?"

"Ma, I think Big Sister really wants to be in Vancouver with us. She said that she is pleased to know that you have given her a little sister

Pauline and a little brother Joe. But she hopes that you have not forgotten to love her as well. She said one day she would save enough to take a trip to Canada. She particularly wants to see Pa, whom she has never met."

Yik-Man didn't utter a word.

"Kin-Pong," said Sau-Ping, "I am concerned with Fei-Yin's future happiness. Did Auntie Sau-Ha contact a go-between for her?"

"Ma, you are so old-fashioned! Many young people in Hong Kong now choose their own marriage partners. Big Sister Fei-Yin is seeing a machinist she met in her garment factory when he came to service the machines. His name is Yue Ming-Fai, and he lives and works out of what they call the 'engineering complex' in Shanghai Street in Yaumatei. A very honest, easygoing man. I like him. When I went out with Katherine, he and Big Sister sometimes came along. We had double outings."

Sau-Ping could not imagine a "double outing" with four unmarried people, two men, two women. The walls erected by families to protect a modest young woman were crumbling even in China, not to mention Hong Kong! Yet she asked no questions about these outings (did the girls speak? did hands touch? did they watch one another eat?) because it was much more important to learn about the young man: Yue Ming-Fai.

"Where does Yue Ming-Fai's family come from?"

"From Toi-Shaan City. He escaped from China and is now by himself in Hong Kong."

Good, thought Sau-Ping, at least he is Toi-Shaanese. "What do Auntie Sau-Ha and Uncle Tseung-Lam think of him?"

"At first they didn't like him. They thought that he was too poor, but now they have changed their minds. They reasoned that marrying rich may not be an advantage in every case. Cousin Tsoi-Yuk's boyfriend is very rich, but he is cocky and sneaky as a rat. At least Yue Ming-Fai is genuine and honest. He also has good technical skills. He even knows how to fix cars and trucks. Given a chance, it would not be difficult for him to land an excellent job."

"Why does Fei-Yin never talk about him in her letters?"

"She said she will definitely consult you and Pa when the time comes. But from my observation, I think they are both very serious. They are saving desperately for their wedding."

Sau-Ping nodded, hiding her emotions. She was concerned for her distant daughter. Free-choice marriages did not please her. Young people were so immature. Could they be relied upon to make hard, rational judgements? She wished she could be in Hong Kong to help Fei-Yin evaluate her suitor. As it was, she could only trust Sau-Ha's judgement.

"Did you drop into the money-changing shop in Tsimshatsui to see Uncle Yik-Kwong and his brother Yik-Nang?"

"No, Ma, they are no longer there. Auntie Sau-Ha doesn't keep in touch with them any more. They have become such rich bankers that Auntie Sau-Ha felt out of place trying to contact them."

"What about Auntie Mei-Kuen and her daughter Lai-Sheung? I haven't heard from them for a long time."

"*Ayi*, yes. I forgot to tell you! Auntie Mei-Kuen is now a clothing pedlar in Sai Yeung Choi Street in Mongkok. She sells women's clothing, most of which she obtains from factory outlets at a low price. She is doing very well. But she is not very happy because Lai-Sheung has left. You'll never guess where she is!"

Yik-Man interrupted dryly. "Will this dull news go on forever?"

"No, Pa. Ma, Lai-Sheung is no longer in Hong Kong. You won't believe this," Kin-Pong continued. "Lai-Sheung is now in Canada, in Nanaimo! She married a Mr Kwaan from there. Thirty years older, this man. Almost Pa's age. This Mr. Kwaan was a widower, and he came to Hong Kong looking for a second wife. Lai-Sheung didn't consult Auntie Mei-Kuen. She wanted to go to Canada to get rich so she could sponsor her mother here. It was too late when Auntie Mei-Kuen found out. She gave me Lai-Sheung's address and asked us to help if her daughter gets into trouble in Canada."

My poor friend, she must be lonesome, Sau-Ping thought. Why did these young women never learn that the streets of Gold Mountain were not paved with gold but were slippery with dishwater and perpetual work? Poor Mei-Kuen! Poor Lai-Sheung!

CHAPTER 19

The Roaring Sixties

1960

Sau-Ping leaned carefully back into the leather seat of the rented Mercedes, which was festively decked out in multicoloured pom-poms. She did not wish to wrinkle her beautiful embroidered shirt. The red, gold, and silver threads caught the afternoon light, reminding her of light flashing on the surface of the pond in Sai-Fok. She had rented the traditional outfit so that she could attend Kin-Pong and Katherine's wedding in proper style. Beside her sat Yik-Man, slightly uncomfortable in a stiff Western suit, rented from the same Keefer Street establishment. The Mercedes was one of two that had been hired from a Chinese taxi company one block over on West Pender.

Since Katherine was Catholic, the ceremony was to take place in a church. They had selected one at the south end of Main Street, where the Caucasian Catholic pastor had a particularly good reputation in the Chinese community. The Mercedes pulled right up in front of the double wooden doors in a powerful, subdued, dignified way that satisfied the mother of the groom.

Sau-Ping had entered a church for the first time in her life the previous day, when she arrived for the wedding rehearsal. She was impressed with the heavy solemnity of the place, the high ceilings and multicoloured windows through which strangely patterned light radiated. Compared to the temple of Tin Hau near her sister's home on Pitt Street in Hong Kong, the church seemed stern and foreign. She wondered how the interior of this church compared with the interior of Sai-Fok's main ancestral hall, a place that she, like other village women, had been forbidden to enter.

Today the church was filled with guests, all dressed in their holiday best. The regular clients at Peach Garden Restaurant all sat together in neatly pressed shirts and their best pants. Each had slicked his hair back with copious handfuls of pomade. The four Uncle Maks were there, perched shyly at the back. Kin-Pong's friends from the Dartcoon Club sat over to one side, joking quietly among themselves beneath the strange coloured windows. There were many people whom Sau-Ping didn't recognize. She thought they must have been friends Yik-Man had acquired during the long years of her absence, when he was still a young man. Although there were some women in the group, they were far outnumbered by the men. Sau-Ping wondered how long it would be before the balance between men and women in the Chinatown community was righted.

Sau-Ping and Yik-Man settled in the front pew with Pauline and Joe between them, squirming in their uncomfortable new clothes. The foreign ghost lady at the organ pounded out a sombre, foreign tune. Sau-Ping began to feel uneasy when she saw a white figure move up the centre aisle. It was Katherine, covered in diaphanous white fabric from top to toe. "Such an unlucky colour," thought Sau-Ping, shivering at this deliberate conjuring of bad spirits at a time when one ought to be careful to choose auspicious colours and symbols. She had wanted to help Katherine choose her wedding dress and help her plan the party, but Kin-Pong had insisted that Sau-Ping allow Katherine to handle these arrangements on her own, with help from no one except the sister of one of Kin-Pong's friends from the Dartcoon Club. He must have known Katherine would do this strange, unlucky thing, thought Sau-Ping crossly, and yet he insisted that she, his own mother, keep out of it. Possibly for the first time in her life, Sau-Ping was upset with Kin-Pong. She was even more upset when, after a barking exchange of ghost words, Kin-Pong lifted Katherine's white veil and kissed her. So shameful to do such a thing in public! Sau-Ping stiffened with shame. Her face grew hot.

She felt much more at ease after the Christian ceremony was over and Katherine had changed into a red Chinese-style bridal gown. Kin-Pong remained in his rented tuxedo, but Sau-Ping had no real objection to that.

But because of the church ceremony, the logic of the traditional Toi-Shaanese wedding had been disturbed. Instead of coming from her home village to Kin-Pong's village, Katherine and Kin-Pong climbed into one of the decorated cars together. Honking loudly all the way, it wound towards the Peach Garden Restaurant for the Chinese part of the ceremony. No rowdy boys attacked its cool metal surface the way they had attacked Sau-Ping's sedan chair so many years ago. Nor did Kin-Pong, who was already inside the vehicle pressed close to his bride, try to kick its door in, giving the bride a chance to guess at his character.

However, Sau-Ping had made sure that certain elements of the traditional ritual were observed. Firecrackers blasted away like gunshot as soon as Katherine and Kin-Pong arrived at the restaurant. The bride and groom kowtowed to the sky at the entrance. They kow-towed to the Earth God shrine at the cashier's counter. Kin-Pong then carried Katherine up the stairs to the mezzanine floor. They knelt in front of the domestic shrine and kowtowed to the ancestral tablets for Grandparents Leung Kwok-Yan and Leung Tsing-Haan, and Granduncle Leung Kwok-Ko. Then they kowtowed to Sau-Ping and Yik-Man who sat facing the domestic shrine. Lastly, they bowed to one another.

Sipping the cup of tea sweetened with sugar and lotus seeds served to her by Katherine, Sau-Ping finally became a mother-in-law.

The fourteen-course banquet that followed the ceremony in Peach Garden Restaurant was the best meal that Sau-Ping had eaten since the one-month birthday celebration of her youngest son, Joe. The caterers were proper, efficient, and generous – no chop-suey for the guests! The great banquet concluded with sweet *tong-yuen* soup, and Sau-Ping looked around at the crowd of contented guests scooping up the last drops and laughing in company with one another. Then, following Toi-shanese tradition, Katherine was teased by some of the envious bachelors, Kin-Pong's friends from the Dartcoon Club, for the rest of the evening.

Watching Katherine and Kin-Pong toasting one another, Sau-Ping thought how lucky Katherine was. To live with her husband! A true gift. She felt joy for her filial son, not envy of his bride, and she was glad that Canadian immigration policy would at last allow these two young people to live a normal family life. Perhaps one day she might be allowed to bring her own daughter to Canada. The thought of joy and sorrow were never far apart.

The newlyweds were to live in Kin-Pong's quarters over the restaurant. Sau-Ping had arranged to have popcorn and cypress leaves scattered over the new double bed on their wedding night, in accordance with Toi-Shaanese tradition. Besides the new bed, a dress-er had been purchased for the newlyweds and the old bunkbeds removed. There was no longer room to provide shelter for unem-ployed or transient fellow villagers.

Four days after the wedding, the newlyweds started work in the restaurant. Katherine, who spoke English, waited at tables and served as cashier. Yik-Man proposed to keep the hired dishwasher until Pauline and Joe were old enough to go to school; then Sau-Ping could resume her duties in the kitchen. Sau-Ping was worried that her daughter-in-law might not want to start work so soon after her wedding, but Katherine said simply, "I don't mind working. You and *Loye* have been working so hard. I should share the burden."

From then on Katherine stood in place at the front of the restaurant, and in a short time business had improved dramatically: Katherine's smile attracted customers where Kin-Tsoi's scowls and ill manners had turned them away.

A month after the wedding, two letters arrived. Kin-Pong read them aloud as the family crowded around the table in Sau-Ping and Yik-Man's bedroom at midnight.

One letter came from Sau-Ping's sister and brother-in-law in Hong Kong. The other was written by Yue Ming-Fai. Both letters talked about the same thing – Yue Ming-Fai had proposed to marry Fei-Yin.

Sau-Ping had been expecting this to happen. Fei-Yin was already twenty-four! She would be an old maid if she did not marry soon. However, Sau-Ping still worried that Yue Ming-Fai might not be reliable. Could he and Fei-Yin manage financially?

"Yik-Man, I think we should give Fei-Yin a decent dowry. At least send a bank draft so that she can obtain some household items to start her married life."

Her husband replied sternly, "I can only afford a hundred dollars. We have spent a lot on Kin-Pong's trip to Hong Kong. We have spent an even greater amount on the wedding banquet and household furniture for Kin-Pong and Katherine. We have also been sending money to Sau-Ha and Tseung-Lam to purchase basic necessities for Yik-Mo and Tin-Shaang's households in Toi-Shaan. If I am the money tree, my arms have been stretched in a hundred directions, like the banyan.

"We ourselves need to save money for future use," Yik-Man continued. "Our living quarters are getting very crowded, and we must find new accommodation soon. Pauline and Joe are growing up really fast. Besides, who knows when a grandson is coming?"

Sau-Ping found it hard to argue, for Yik-Man was speaking the truth. But a hundred dollars! That was too little. Yik-Man received eighteen hundred dollars from Uncle Leung Kwok-Ko when he sold Fei-Yin's birth certificate. Now she was getting married. Was a hundred dollars all she would receive from her natural parents who owned a restaurant in Gold Mountain?

Yik-Man finally settled on two hundred dollars. Needless to say, Sau-Ping did not receive travel money to return to Hong Kong for her daughter's wedding. The family had "no extra money" for the trip, and besides, who would take care of Pauline and Joe in her absence if she sailed away on a pleasure trip?

One fine day in December 1960, Sau-Ping strolled to the curio shop with Pauline and Joe. She saw only three Uncle Maks sitting on the bench in front: Old Mak had passed away recently after learning that his wife in Toi-Shaan had died of starvation. The news had brought on a stroke, and three days later his companions had found him dead. They had pooled their money to bury him at the Chinese cemetery, but they told Sau-Ping that they wanted his bones to be taken home some day, so that his soul could be reunited with his wife's.

"Maybe it is good he chose the time he did," said one of the three Uncle Maks. "Something very bad will be coming our way soon. The government paid our landlord six thousand dollars to purchase our rented house. It is to be demolished to make way for MacLean Park Public Housing. So will all the other houses on the block. We have to move out some time next January whether we like it or not."

The thinnest Uncle Mak spoke up. "Where shall we live? Eleven of us can't crowd into one tiny apartment in Maclean Park. We don't want to be separated from one another. We have been sharing our lives for the last forty years! We can't rent a bigger place outside Chinatown. We can't afford the high cost." Sau-Ping was struck by the open desperation on his wrinkled face.

"Even if we could," added the third Uncle Mak, "the white people may not let us move into their neighbourhood. They might send their children to throw stones at us or beat us up or vandalize our place. We can't speak the foreign devil's language. How could we live there with any peace of mind?"

Sau-Ping understood their predicament. Yik-Man had told her two months ago that the City of Vancouver had decided to demolish the houses in the Strathcona area. All the merchants on West Pender Street opposed to "slum clearance." They were afraid that if the Chinese residents in the Strathcona area were scattered and dispersed, the businesses in Chinatown would lose them as customers. Yik-Man had signed a petition sent by the Chinese Benevolent Association to City Hall to protest the decision. In the end, however, the neighbourhood's opposition to the project had no influence on the Vancouver municipal government, which began stage one of the "slum clearance" project in January 1961.

It wasn't certain whether Sau-Ping and her family would have to move from their home above the restaurant – the only home Sau-Ping had known in Canada. But by 1962 Pauline and Joe needed more space. Now five and four years old, they could no longer sleep comfortably in their baby cribs beside Sau-Ping and Yik-Man's bed. And Katherine was pregnant. Though neither said so outright, both Sau-Ping and Yik-Man hoped that Kin-Tsoi would stay away from the restaurant. If he disappeared for good, maybe Kin-Pong's new family could live upstairs.

But one morning, as the family were having their congee before starting work, a loud knock sounded at the door, and in came Leung Kin-Tsoi with a woman – his new wife.

Sau-Ping and Kin-Pong were shocked by the young woman Kin-Tsoi had brought home, for she had no spirit; her eyes were yellowed and deeply weary. Kin-Tsoi called her Ming. He told them that he had gone to Prince Rupert to escape the police who were searching for illegal immigrants. There was plenty of gambling in Prince Rupert, and one night at a casino he met an old man whose second wife, the woman Ming, had just arrived from Hong Kong. The old man proceeded to lose all his savings at fantan. In an effort to reclaim some of his money, he put his wife up as a gambling asset and promptly lost her to Kin-Tsoi! For a while Ming and Kin-Tsoi lived in a single room above an automobile repair shop. Then Kin-Tsoi had heard that a general amnesty had been granted to illegal immigrants.

"So, I'm back!" Sau-Ping turned away as Kin-Tsoi laughed. She did not like his sour tiger's breath tainted with alcohol. She watched as he mounted the stairs to the rooms she had hoped Kin-Pong and Katherine might have. His wife walked behind him, bent under the weight of their belongings, keeping one hand on the wall as she climbed. Sau-Ping had the unhappy impression that this young woman had been partially blinded by her hard life.

That night Sau-Ping could not sleep. Kin-Tsoi's story made her think of Lai-Sheung, Mei-Kuen's daughter, who had also married an old man for his money and come to Canada with him. Where was Lai-Sheung now? Sau-Ping resolved to get Kin-Pong to write Mei-Kuen to ask about her daughter and send the message that if ever Lai-Sheung found herself in trouble, she must come straight to the Peach Garden Restaurant in Vancouver's Chinatown. Yik-Man protested against her plan, but she held her ground until he agreed to let Kin-Pong write the letter; no doubt he believed nothing would come of it.

Being an honest man, Yik-Man had immediately given Kin-Tsoi half of the profits the restaurant had accumulated over the last two years, and in no time at all Kin-Tsoi had resumed his old way of life, gambling and visiting prostitutes after the day's work was done. Whenever he lost at the casino, he beat Ming the way his Pa beat his Ma in Toi-shaan when he was young. Many times Sau-Ping saw bruises on the young woman as she bent over the rust-stained sink in the restaurant kitchen. She rarely spoke and never laughed. But somehow Ming survived, working hard in the kitchen, scrubbing with energy at the dirty dishes as if she could clean her own life.

One night Kin-Tsoi beat Ming so badly that she began to bleed; only then did Sau-Ping learn that she was pregnant. Kin-Pong and Katherine took Ming to the emergency ward, where she miscarried. Sau-Ping nursed her back to health with Chinese herbs and tonics. Sau-Ping did not enjoy entering the top floor where Ming lived with Kin-Tsoi – it was filthy and hopeless and it had a rank smell, as if Kin-Tsoi urinated on the walls when he was too drunk to find the pot – but she could not let Ming suffer alone. One evening, Ming sat up in bed and said, "I'm going to leave him. I'm going to San Francisco someday. I have uncles there."

Sau-Ping tried to dissuade her. Unlike a lot of Toi-Shaanese women, she saw nothing wrong with an abused wife trying to get a divorce. But she remembered that Kin-Tsoi's father, Yik-Faat, had beaten his wife to death in Sai-Fok for daring to ask for a divorce. She mentioned this to Ming, who said, "I don't plan to tell him."

But for a long time, nothing happened. Sau-Ping understood: how could any woman sever all ties with the men who were familiar to her and swim out into the dark world alone?

There were now enough people working in the family restaurant to allow Yik-Man and Sau-Ping to shop around for a house in between shifts. They wanted to move before their first grandchild was born. The price of houses in the Strathcona area had plummeted since, as everyone knew, the area was slated for the next round of "slum clearances." Yik-Man knew that it was risky to buy property there, but he was desperate to find a house close to work. Besides, it was difficult for a Chinese family to buy outside of Chinatown because of the resistance of homeowners in white neighbourhoods. In the end they bought a small house on Keefer Street at Hawks, three blocks away from Lord Strathcona Public School. The whole family moved in in September 1962, in time for Pauline to enter kindergarten.

In December Katherine had her baby, a little girl with soft downy hair all over her head. Kin-Pong and Katherine were delighted with their first-born, even though she was a girl. Kin-Pong gave her the name Josie, in honour of his own four-year-old brother, Joe. Yik-Man and Sau-Ping hid their disappointment. After all, Kin-Pong and Katherine were young; they lived together; they would eventually bear a son. Sau-Ping looked after the new baby while Katherine worked in the restaurant. At age forty-seven, she was the mother of two young children and the grandmother of an infant.

Sau-Ping was happy in the house on Keefer Street. It was not as big as her *yeung-lau* in Sai-Fok, but she now had a decent kitchen in which to cook her favourite dishes – no more bowls of restaurant chop-suey! Even better, there was land she could work both in front and back – it had been eleven years since she'd had a chance to grow crops. When spring arrived in 1963, Sau-Ping bought a hoe, a spade, and a trowel and started gardening. Sometimes she brought the little ones into the dirt with her. At harvest time, her Chinese neighbours came to admire her gigantic bok-choy and spinach.

Sau-Ping and Yik-Man firmly believed that their Canadian-born descendants should have both Chinese and English educations. If their children and grandchildren did well in school they could make a name for themselves in mainstream society and bring glory to the ancestors of the Leung lineage. But it was equally important that the children should maintain their Toi-Shaanese dialect and not forget their cultural origins. Sau-Ping taught the young children Toi-Shaanese songs. She told them stories and myths from their ancestral homeland. She insisted that they kowtow before the domestic altar every morning, practise good Chinese table manners, and address their seniors in the correct kinship terms. She took extra care to prepare typical Toi-Shaanese dishes at home, particularly during major festivals.

Sau-Ping also made sure that Pauline and Joe studied hard. Every morning, with Kin-Pong's baby Josie strapped to her back, she walked her own young children to Lord Strathcona School. When they returned she sat with them to make sure that they did their public school homework. After an early dinner, she strapped Josie on her back again and walked Pauline and Joe to Mon-Keung, a Chinese-language school on West Pender Street operated by the Wong Association. She picked them up in the evening and supervised their Chinese homework.

Late one night Sau-Ping remarked to Kin-Pong, "Josie is growing very quickly."

"Is that so?" he replied politely.

"Yes," said Sau-Ping, "she's quite heavy now."

"She doesn't look so heavy," said Kin-Pong. "She's still a little small for her age, I think."

"Ah, she's pretty heavy," said Sau-Ping. "I should know because I carry her to and from the English school and the Chinese school every day when I take Pauline and Joe."

Kin-Pong raised an eyebrow. "Is it a lot of trouble, Ma?"

"No," said Sau-Ping. "It's no trouble. Not really. Unless she throws a tantrum, but she only does that once or twice a day. Sometimes three times. But I'm used to it."

Kin-Pong fully understood the message behind his mother's words, but offered no solution. Instead, he defended his wife.

"Ma, I know if we were in China, your daughter-in-law would take care of you in addition to her own children. But this is Gold Mountain. Katherine is being filial in her own way. Her work in the restaurant benefits the whole family, including you. Since she has been there, we've done much better. I'm sorry if Josie is a lot of trouble, but we must think in terms of efficiency."

Sau-Ping nodded. "Efficiency" was one of her husband's favourite words. Only later, when she was sitting alone, did she allow herself a long sigh of frustration. How her son had changed since their days as squatters in Shek Kip Mei! First he'd had a Western-style wedding, allowing his bride to dress as an unlucky ghost and then kissing her in public. Now he was telling his mother that she had no right to be served by her daughter-in-law! How long, she wondered, before he began to look like a foreign devil? But she would keep her mouth shut. A woman must listen to her father when she was young, her husband after marriage, and her son when she was old. And she was indeed nearly an old woman – a grandmother after all. She must listen to her son, no matter what crazy things he said.

Yik-Man joined the Strathcona Property Owners and Tenants Association to discuss ways of opposing stage two of the "slum clearance" project ordered by the municipal government. The meetings came to nothing, however, and between 1964 and 1966 many more houses in Sau-Ping's neighbourhood were claimed by the City with little compensation. Bulldozers displaced hundreds of Chinese residents in the Strathcona area. Chairs, kitchen cabinets, tables, and broken window awnings appeared on the sidewalks. People they knew became desperate, frustrated, and angry. Sau-Ping was reminded of the days in Sai-Fok when the communists appropriated the *yeung-lau* of the Overseas Chinese dependents, including their own. Even while reminding herself that the residents of Strathcona did not have to go through struggle meetings or serve in labour camps, she felt the neighbourhood darkened by the shadow of a distant government that was ultimately determined to enforce its will on the people whose laments it refused to hear.

By some strange coincidence, whenever Sau-Ping had bad dreams about the political persecution she experienced in the early 1950s, bad news arrived from China. One day in late 1966 Kin-Pong received a letter from Uncle Lau Tseung-Lam and Auntie Sau-Ha in Hong Kong. The letter began with the usual greetings and family news. They had just moved out of Pitt Street to a new apartment in North Point, which had been purchased by their eldest son Tak-Kan and his wife. Their second son, Tak-Keung, and his wife had lived elsewhere since their marriage four years before but they left their baby daughter with her grandparents during the day, with the result that Tseung-Lam and Sau-Ha were now looking after three grandchildren – Tak-Kan's two boys and the new baby girl. Tak-Wa, their youngest son, had entered the University of Hong Kong that October to study economics. He lived in a university residence, Ricci Hall, but came home for holidays. As for their daughters, Tsoi-Lin, now twenty-seven, still refused to consider marriage, while Tsoi-Yuk's rich husband took one mistress after another. She wanted to sue for divorce, but she needed his money to live as she was now accustomed to living. Sau-Ping felt sorry for her nieces. Then:

I am returning the draft you sent for Tin-Shaang and Yik-Mo. I don't wish to frighten you, but the situation in China seems to have taken a turn for the worse. People with overseas connections, especially those who have already been designated as class enemies, may be in more serious danger than before. The newspapers are talking about a new movement in China called the Cultural Revolution. We hear that Chairman Mao has managed to mobilize high school students to carry out a new plan to wipe out all of our traditions in the name of destroying feudalism. The students, calling themselves Red Guards, act like vandals, destroying ancestral halls, gravesites, and temples. It's so shameful, so much against the proper order of things.

There have also been tales of the Red Guards harassing Hong Kong Chinese when they return to visit their home villages. The Red Guards think these folk too bourgeois and corrupted by Western influences. Nowadays anybody with Overseas Chinese connections is considered a foreign spy. Such people can be arrested, dragged to struggle meetings, beaten up or tortured, and then thrown in jail.

So we had better not write or send any parcels to Tin-Shaang or Yik-Mo in Toi-Shaan yet because we might be endangering them. As for the draft I am returning, you can send another one if and when the Cultural Revolution ends.

P.S. A recent visitor said that students from The Toi-Shaan Senior High School were particularly destructive and vicious. They beat up and imprisoned teachers. The school principal had to wear a plaque. He was paraded up and down the streets of Toi-Shaan City twice a day!

After reading the final sentences out loud, Kin-Pong sighed. "Toi-Shaan Senior High School is my Alma Mater. The world is really turning upside down. How can anyone have the heart to beat up a respected teacher?"

Sau-Ping and Yik-Man both shook their heads in dismay, and Yik-Man murmured, "For once I am thankful that Father and Paternal Uncle are buried in Vancouver's Chinese cemetery."

Sau-Ping shuddered, for an ugly thought had come to her. Had *On-Yan's* bones in the Sai-Fok village graveyard been dug up? What about the graves of her own parents in Fung-Yeung? Had the bones of their ancestors been exposed, scattered in the fields?

For the rest of the day, Sau-Ping brooded over the news of Mao's Cultural Revolution. She thought about the three Uncle Maks on the bench outside the curio shop. First their house had been demolished by the City, and now they could not even contact their families back home. Would their people starve in their native village if they were no longer able to send money or packages? And what of her own brother, Tin-Shaang? What of her courageous brother-in-law, Yik-Mo? Would he be persecuted again, he whose family had already been labelled part of the landlord class?

That night she dreamed of skeletons running together and butting their terrible white skulls against one another, like mountain goats. When the skulls hit, they made thunder, and when the thunder touched the paddy-field, the rice began to wilt until all the strong shoots lay black, rippling on the surface of the water.

August 1967 brought news about Hong Kong that caused the family concern. According to the *Chinese Times*, the Cultural Revolution had spilled over into Hong Kong. There were stories of strikes, curfews, and riots. The newspapers also reported Red Guard threats to "liberate Hong Kong from the British imperialists." There were even a few border clashes between the Red Guards and the People's Militia on one side, and the Hong Kong Police and Gurkha soldiers on the other. Kin-Pong read the news and relayed it to his mother and Katherine. Yik-Man also brought home news from his friends at the Toi-Shaan Association Hall. At Sau-Ping's urging, Kin-Pong wrote a letter to Fei-Yin and her husband, Yue Ming-Fai, asking them about their situation and their plans.

A reply soon arrived from Yue Ming-Fai.

Dear Father-in-Law and Mother-in-Law, Kin-Pong and Katherine:

Thank you for your concern, but you need not worry because we are okay. It is true that for four months in summer, Fei-Yin was unemployed. The garment factory closed down as a result of the riot. Luckily, she received relief pay from her union. I was also out of work the whole summer because many factories were not in operation and I had no machines to service. But the situation is easing now, and we have already resumed work.

Still Fei-Yin and I are scared to live in Hong Kong. We fear that the Red Guards will arrive someday to liberate Hong Kong. This would be terrible for us and our two-year-old son, Taai-Lun. It is like civil war in China now. This summer, for example, factional fights were so severe that hundreds of dead bodies floated down the Pearl River into Hong Kong's territorial waters. Most were the bodies of young people, probably killed as a result of gang fights or execution by the People's Liberation Army. Their hands were tied at the back and their heads chopped off. They were put into sacks and dumped into the river. There were so many of these corpses floating around that Hong Kong's beaches have become infested with sharks.

We heard that as of July this year, Canada is opening its doors to independent immigrants from Asia for the first time. We heard that Canada accepts applications from those who are either rich, educated, or else have a special skill that Canada needs. Is this true?

Right now, there are lots of Hong Kong people applying to leave the colony. Every day there are long queues in front of both the Canadian Trade Commissioner's Office and the American Consulate. We have to stand in line for hours just to get an application form.

We don't know how long we will have to wait, or whether our technical skills are needed by Canada. But if we are successful, would it be possible to live with you and work in the restaurant until we find jobs in Vancouver?

May you all be in good health and the restaurant be prosperous.

Yours humbly, Yue Ming-Fai

Sau-Ping was excited to learn that Fei-Yin and Yue Ming-Fai might have a chance to join the family in Canada. She vividly recalled the trauma of fleeing to Hong Kong with Fei-Yin and Kin-Pong to escape the communist persecution in the early 1950s and fervently wished for the daughter to escape Hong Kong if it appeared that the Communists were now preparing to cross the water and take that city. And how good it would be to see her lost daughter again, the daughter she hadn't talked with for twelve years; Fei-Yin, whom Yik-Man had never met at all. How good it would be to meet their son-in-law and to cuddle their grandson, Taai-Lun.

"Surely we can put them up when they come?"

"Ma, of course we should help Big Sister's family," Kin-Pong said immediately.

A few days later, Sau-Ping decided to visit the restaurant after sending the children off to Chinese school. On entering, she noticed her husband and son huddled in a dour conference at an empty booth at the back near the kitchen. She sat down.

"What is it now?" she asked. Kin-Pong explained that he'd just heard the City of Vancouver had approved a plan to build a new eight-lane freeway system that would cut through their neighbour-hood. According to the plan, eight huge pillars would be built at Car-rall Street to support the giant road in a place where it would sail high above the ground. The freeway was mapped to pass over the roofs of businesses on West Pender Street, including the Peach Gar-den Restaurant. If all the traffic followed the giant elevated road, it would bypass the businesses that lay in its shadow. The restaurant could go bankrupt.

"But we will fight this proposal!" Yik-Man suddenly bellowed. "We will fight!"

For the next six months, Yik-Man attended more and more meet-ings held by the Chinese Benevolent Association. He was a member of the committee that hired a lawyer to draft a petition to the City on behalf of the Chinese merchants. Their petitions were supported by many organizations and individuals: Yik-Man told his wife that he was surprised to learn there were so many sympathetic white people in Vancouver.

Over the next few months, Yik-Man went through dramatic mood shifts. Sometimes he was hopeful, at other times he was depressed. Sau-Ping often heard him swearing under his breath. At sixty-two, he had had enough of the Canadian government. One evening, after returning home from a long day's work, Kin-Pong happened to men-tion that one of his friends had tried to calculate how many hours of labour were necessary to earn enough money to pay the Canadian property taxes. Yik-Man, who was standing near the door, suddenly shouted, "I have suffered enough from those crazy ghosts! When I was young, I had to pay a five-hundred-dollar head tax to come here. My father and I starved during the Depression. During the war we donated our savings and many Chinese fought alongside the Canadi-ans. After the war, we fought to change the laws so we could bring our families over. We work so hard we become dry husks. Now they play this dirty trick on us, trying to destroy our neighbourhoods and our businesses. What have we done to deserve such lousy treatment?"

In January 1968 City representatives announced that the new free-way would not pass over Carrall Street. But the crisis was not yet over: in Strathcona, the third stage of the "slum clearance" project might begin at any time. The neighbourhood had to keep on fighting.

Six months later Yik-Man was more hopeful. He told Sau-Ping that a good prime minister had been voted into office. His name was Pierre Trudeau, and he favoured a policy that allowed many cultures to exist alongside one another in Canada. He would respect Chinese culture and put a stop to the demolition of the Chinese community in Strathcona.

Over the next few months, Yik-Man and the other members of the Strathcona Property Owners and Tenants Association worked harder to draw up an alternate plan for neighbourhood self-improvement. The group forwarded the plan to Canada's minister of Transport when he came to Vancouver in December 1968. Yik-Man came home elated on the day of the minister's visit. He was sure that their home would be saved from demolition.

But years of stress had taken a toll on Yik-Man's health. Though Sau-Ping didn't know it at the time, her husband was slowing dying of cancer.

CHAPTER 20

Happy Now

Pauline sat in front of the hallway mirror in the Leung house on Keefer Street smearing blue eye shadow over her eyelids. She wiped her blue-stained fingers on a piece of paper towel and then, with a red lipstick, carefully drew in big bright red lips. "You look like one of those weird Chinese opera guys," said Joe, laughing.

"I do not!" cried Pauline indignantly. "Mom! Joe said I look weird. I don't look weird, do I?"

Before Sau-Ping could answer, Joe, gazing into the mirror, stuffed a pair of plastic fangs into his mouth and grabbed the red lipstick from Pauline.

"Joe! I wasn't finished! Give it back."

"You already have a bloody mouth. Now it's my turn," said Joe, smearing red make-up all over the lower part of his face.

"It's not blood! It's lipstick," said Pauline.

"Looks like blood to me," said Joe, turning his face this way and that in the mirror to ensure that the effect of his work was every bit as gory as he intended.

"You're not going out like that, are you, Joe?" said Sau-Ping. "*Aiya!* So horrible."

"That's the idea, Mom. I'm king of the blood suckers. It's the holiday for ugly demons."

"The holiday for ugly demons. I will never understand," sighed his mother. "You're going to take Josie with you, aren't you?"

"Do we have to, Mom?" asked Pauline. "Josie is such a pain."

"What does that mean, a pain? She's your little niece. It's your duty to take good care of her."

"She's so slow, Mom," said Joe. "And she always does stupid

things. She can't even say ..." Joe quickly spoke a bundle of ghost words "properly."

Josie, who had come up behind him, pushed him out of the way so she could see her fairy costume in the mirror. "Can too," she said.

"Say it, then," said Joe.

The little girl's tongue produced a bunch of ghost words that sounded exactly the same to Sau-Ping.

"See, I told you," said Joe.

"Sounds fine to me," said Sau-Ping.

"You weren't listening, Mom. You don't really hear English," said Pauline.

"Say it again, Josie," said Joe.

The noises were produced again.

"See?" said Pauline, turning triumphantly to her mother.

"Like I said, sounds fine to me," replied Sau-Ping evenly. "Now you had better get going before it grows too dark."

Sau-Ping was tired. She and Yik-Man had had a long argument about whether to close the restaurant on this day when young Canadians walked the streets dressed like ugly demons. Ever since they had added fried wonton, roast pork, barbecued duck, and soy sauce chicken to the menu, the number of customers had increased dramatically and Yik-Man couldn't imagine sacrificing a full day's profits. "Of course it must stay open," he insisted. "When my father and uncle ran the restaurant, it was open three hundred and sixty-three days a year, rain or shine. We only close for two days during Chinese New Year."

"But Yik-Man, last year there was so much vandalism. To open the restaurant is just to invite it. There was paint – you had to scrape it off – and broken eggs on the window ledges. Some of it is still there. I see the yellow yolk when I come in the door."

"Nonsense!" said Yik-Man. "If I were well ..." He shut his mouth hard and was silent. Yik-Man had lost weight in recent months, and there were times when he stopped in the middle of his work, as if he were listening to a distant voice. Sau-Ping, who was often able to help out in the restaurant since all three children now attended school, realized that in those moments her husband's body was being twisted with excruciating pain. He had continued to get up at seven o'clock every morning and walk to the restaurant with Kin-Pong and Katherine to do some of the preparatory work for the day, chopping up green onions, mincing meat, mixing up the sauce for chop-suey, but earlier and earlier his energy gave out and he would come home at around three for a nap. Then one day he arrived home at one o'clock; a few weeks later it was eleven, just a few short hours after his departure. Sau-Ping had suggested that he stay home and rest until the sickness passed, but he wouldn't hear of it. "I'm not that sick. The pain will go away on its own." But soon he was so thin that the change became obvious even to himself. When that happened, he stopped mentioning his pains at all.

"Kin-Pong thinks it might not be a bad idea to close the restaurant too," said Sau-Ping gently.

"It's one thing for that good-for-nothing Kin-Tsoi to be so lazy!" cried Yik-Man. "But my own son?"

And so it was settled. The restaurant would keep its doors open for the Canadian demon's holiday.

After the children had left in their costumes, Yik-Man decided to go to the restaurant to work the evening shift. Fearful of his condition, Sau-Ping had no choice but to follow him. She helped Ming with the dishes while Yik-Man chopped all the meat for the evening's chop-suey and fried rice dishes. Now that Kin-Tsoi beat her less and ignored her more, Ming had become a reliable, stolid presence in the kitchen. As the two women chatted quietly, Sau-Ping noticed out of the corner of her eye that her husband had put down the cleaver and covered his eyes, gripping the edge of the counter. Sau-Ping reached for him, "Yik-Man, now you must get off your feet!" She helped him upstairs to where they had once lived. Yik-Man lay down on one of the cots kept there for resting between the lunch and dinner shifts.

Returning to the restaurant downstairs, Sau-Ping sat in one of the booths wrapping seasoned ground pork and shrimp in flour wrappers to make won-ton. In the kitchen, Kin-Pong was cooking and Ming was leaning over the sink, scrubbing dishes. Everyone was busy except Kin-Tsoi, who had disappeared again.

Katherine, six months pregnant with her second baby, was the only one out front. She was serving customers when the trouble started. Three men walked in wearing tight black suits with skeletons painted down the fronts and nylon stockings pulled over their heads. Sau-Ping stood up.

They were gibbering ghost words at Katherine, who looked frightened but managed to reply to them in their own language. Then the white men linked hands and surrounded her, dancing in a slow circle. Sau-Ping walked forward.

"Get out, get out, we will call the police!" She knew her words meant no more to them than the cackling of a frantic hen. One of the skeletons said something rough. Katherine responded energetically and he leaned forward and growled in her face. Sau-Ping instantly thought of the cleaver lying unused on the kitchen counter, but she did not want to leave Katherine, whose voice was cracking in fear. The three demons suddenly unlinked their hands and moved to the front window, where the roast ducks, soy sauce chickens, and lengths of roast pork hung under the bright heater lights. One of them began to unhook the cooked meats and hand them to his pals, and with their spoils slung over their backs they walked out of the restaurant. Katherine stood immobile, unable to do a thing. Sau-Ping yelled and ran out behind them, grabbing at a fine duck, but one of them turned and shoved her hard. She fell to the sidewalk, scraping her arm. The thieves began to run, and at that moment Kin-Pong dashed out the door, alerted by Katherine. It was too late. He ran wildly down the block but they had gone.

Katherine, sitting dazed on the stool near the cash register, was being comforted by Ming and one of their regular customers, Old Chan. The ghost men had told her they wanted to eat for free because the Chinese had taken jobs from white folks in the city. She had told them her family was not rich, that everyone worked hard, but the ugly one had growled at her, "We know you've got secret organizations. We're taking a little something for our trouble." As Katherine was speaking, a police car passed by. Old Chan ran outside to flag it down and returned a few minutes later with two white police officers in tow. Kin-Pong, Kin-Tsoi, Ming, and Sau-Ping all gathered at the front counter to face them.

The questions and answers began politely, but within moments Sau-Ping could see that something was going wrong. The officers looked impatient, as if they were talking to a gang of rough kids. Katherine and Kin-Pong raised their voices. The larger officer shrugged. Kin-Pong threw up his arms and made an angry declaration. The two officers turned and left the restaurant, walking calmly, as if they'd just eaten dinner. Sau-Ping could see they had no intention of pursuing the thieves.

"Ayia!" Kin-Pong cried. "They won't go after the thieves because they had masks on! We can't identify them so they are free to steal. Where's Pa? What will Pa say?"

"He's upstairs on the cot. He doesn't feel well."

Katherine was crying. "They had stockings over their faces. I couldn't see their faces. What will Loye say?"

"These things happen!" Kin-Pong exploded. "That is what the police say to us: these things happen. No, not to white restaurants, they don't; only to Chinese!"

"Yes," said Old Chan. "Always the way. Do not awaken Yik-Man. Let him sleep. It is just more of the same."

Someone at the restaurant door claimed Katherine's attention. "Joe! What happened to you? Where is Josie?"

The circle of agitated adults turned to see a young boy with real blood streaming from his nose, pouring down over his lips. The child's eyes were wide. Katherine grabbed Joe and began wiping him frantically with a napkin from one of the tables. Smeared with real and fake blood, the eleven-year-old adventurer looked more horrible than he'd hoped.

"What happened?" cried Sau-Ping.

"Got beaten up," said Joe, trying to sound nonchalant.

"I will need soap," said Katherine, who was calmer now that she had something to do. "Come with me, Joe, we'll fix you up so you don't terrify your poor mother. But you have to tell me where Josie is, child." She took his hand and led him towards the restroom. A moment later Pauline stumbled through the front door dragging Josie behind her.

"What happened?" Sau-Ping asked, trying to quell an irrational anger born of fear: Pauline was not to blame. Still Sau-Ping shouted at her, "How could you let such a terrible thing happen to your little brother?"

"We were stopped in Shanghai Alley by a bunch of kids dressed like the king of blood suckers only more real than Joe's costume, and like ghosts and pirates. They all had masks on, so we couldn't tell who they were. Two of the big ones grabbed me and Josie, and Joe tried to fight them. But he got beat up instead. They're all over the neighbourhood!"

"How come you didn't help him? You're his big sister after all."

"Mom, it was impossible! They were holding me back. And there were so many of them."

"Hmmph," said Sau-Ping. "Do you know them?"

"I ripped off some of the masks," said Pauline. "Some of them were people from my class."

"Why did they attack you and Joe?"

"I don't know. Sometimes they call me 'Chinese pig' and pull my braids in class. I don't know. They probably didn't know it was me in my costume." Pauline was near tears.

"How come you never told us about this? Did you tell your teacher?"

"I'm no tattle-tale!" the girl said shakily. "But I sure wish I wasn't Chinese."

Sau-Ping said, "So this is the meaning of the demon's holiday. Behind masks, they show what they are." She regretted their decision to keep the restaurant open and wished that the whole family had hidden behind closed doors at home instead, just like Yeung-Kong peasants did during Wai-Heung Day in Old China. She noticed that Katherine had emerged from the restroom with a cleaner Joe, who pressed a wet towel to his nose and kept his head tipped back to stop the nosebleed. Sau-Ping, Pauline, and Josie followed them into the kitchen, while Ming quietly took over the cash register.

Hearing groans from upstairs, Sau-Ping quickly ladled out a bowl of Chinese herbal medicine, which had been brewing for hours, and carried it upstairs to Yik-Man. Settling herself next to her husband, she handed him the bowl with care. Wearily he propped himself up against the wall and sipped the medicine.

"What was it that I heard downstairs?" he said.

"I'll tell you tomorrow." Yik-Man nodded and slid back under the worn blanket. Sau-Ping was astounded by this reaction from a man whose entire life had been devoted to his restaurant. Her husband was truly ill.

It wasn't until two days later that she judged her husband to be strong enough to hear the news. She told him a mild version of what had happened, and again he surprised her, speaking less about the stolen meat than about the children, Joe, Pauline, and Josie, and their school. Sau-Ping suggested that Katherine, whose English was good, should complain to the school principal about the racial taunting the children were subjected to; she had an appointment with her doctor the next day and she could drop by the school on her way home.

"Forget it, Ping. It's useless. The children were beaten up outside school. The principal won't have anything to do with it. What you have seen is part of Canada. Even Pierre Trudeau can't stop it. They want Chinese votes and taxes but they think we are rats off the ship. Ahhh." Yik-Man slid down on the couch and covered his face with his hands. "I am tired."

"Yik-Man, I will get you medicine."

Uncovering his face, he gazed at his wife. The deep creases on his eyes revealed his intense pain. "Ping," he whispered, "I don't think I'll live to see Kin-Pong and Katherine's second child ..."

"I will get you medicine," she repeated, turning her back so that Yik-Man would not see her crying.

"... and I don't think I'll live to see my daughter Fei-Yin, my son-in-law Yue Ming-Fai, or our grandson Taai-Lun. If Fei-Yin lands in Vancouver after my death, please tell her I'm sorry I sold her birth certificate."

"Husband –"

"And Ping," Yik-Man continued, "if the Cultural Revolution should end, please return to Sai-Fok to see my younger brother Yik-Mo. Try to retrieve our *yeung-lau*. Take Father's, Uncle's, and my bones back home for reburial. If my mother's grave has been disturbed by the Red Guards, please bury her again. I know you have been loyal to her memory. The ancestors of the Leung family will be so grateful to you!"

"Yes, I will do these things," she replied simply. "Put your legs up."

As she bustled in the kitchen to brew more of her husband's medicine, Sau-Ping's thoughts travelled back to Fung-Yeung. She saw Auntie Kwan embracing an urn full of dry bones and wailing by the river, now and again stumbling and drenching her clothes. Sau-Ping looked out into the yard, where most of her vines had been blackened by the recent frosts. She had already turned over the earth to prepare for next spring. The doctor had said Yik-Man probably wouldn't make it to Christmas.

Late that night Sau-Ping dictated a telegram to her daughter and son-in-law, informing them of Yik-Man's condition. She also had Kin-Pong take down messages to her sister, Sau-Ha, and to Mei-Kuen. This done, she sat in her Vancouver kitchen until the small hours of the morning. The children were asleep. Yik-Man also slept, assisted by pills from the Canadian doctor and by her own herbal medicines. Alone, she drank tea and let her thoughts drift aimlessly. Yik-Man wanted to save the *yeung-lau* in Sai-Fok, but he had never set eyes on that grand house ... He asked that his bones be returned to his home village, yet he had visited the place only once since he was ten years old ... She had lived many years without her husband, and now the grass widow was about to embark on another kind of widowhood. How did attachment survive so many years of absence? Would her Canadian-born children ever understand such an attachment, or had their blood been thinned and their spirits weakened by this cold, frantic nation in which they were destined to live?

Snow came unusually early that year, at the beginning of November. Sau-Ping had received a telegram from Fei-Yin saying that she and her husband had saved roughly half the funds necessary for their passage, and that they had managed to secure both application forms and the coveted visas, thanks to the mechanical skills of Yue Ming-Fai. When Sau-Ping told Yik-Man the news, he said, "Send them whatever money they need. Tell Kin-Pong to help."

A week later Yik-Man was dying in the hospital. The restaurant was closed. The family took turns staying with him until it became evident that death was near. Then they all gathered around his bed and remained there day in, day out. And so it was, one evening in late November. As they sat without speaking amid the white curtains and chrome, there was a knock at the door.

Katherine called out in English while a weary Sau-Ping said "Come in," in her own language. Both women rose, expecting another nurse with a bedpan or a needle or a fresh gown. A tall, thin

Chinese woman entered the room. After a long pause, Sau-Ping whispered, "Fei-Yin?"

"Ma," said Fei-Yin. A husky Chinese man looking uncomfortable in a tight, Western suit had stepped quietly in behind her, holding the hand of a three-year-old boy. But Sau-Ping hardly saw them. She was gazing into the kind eyes of her beloved daughter.

"Fei-Yin, how did you find us?" Sau-Ping whispered, so as not to wake Yik-Man. "Why didn't you write us?"

"We weren't certain we could book passage on such short notice. We had the address of the restaurant from the telegram, and we took a taxi there and saw the message saying the restaurant was closed. It was the wife of Kin-Tsoi who told us that you had taken Pa to this hospital. All of our belongings we left on the second floor of the restaurant."

Sau-Ping touched her daughter's hair, her hands, her arms. Smiling gently, Fei-Yin quietly introduced her family and then stood by the bed as Yik-Man, suddenly awake, struggled to sit up.

"Pa," whispered Fei-Yin.

"Yes," said Sau-Ping. "He's been waiting for you."

"Pa." Fei-Yin leaned over the bed. Katherine stood back to give her more room, lightly touching Fei-Yin's elbow to signal her greetings.

Yik-Man, his eyes shut, spoke in a dry whisper. "Fei-Yin ... your birth certificate ... I was wrong ..." He fell silent for a while, and his chest heaved with effort. Then he spoke again. "Thirty-five years ... a long time ... happy now..." He opened his eyes for one long moment and gazed at her.

Yik-Man remained alive for two more days, but he did not speak again. On the morning of 20 November, at the age of sixty-three, he died in his sleep.

Peach Garden Restaurant was closed for a ten-day period of mourning. It reopened on 1 December in anticipation of the Christmas festivities.

CHAPTER 21

Wheels of Fortune

DECEMBER 1969

Early in December Sau-Ping and Fei-Yin were in the kitchen at home talking together about life in Hong Kong and conditions in Mainland China. Yue Ming-Fai was out looking for work. Joe, Pauline, and Josie had all gone to school. Little Taai-Lun, Fei-Yin's son, was playing by himself with a bowl of shiny stones and buttons. It was nearly lunchtime.

Someone came in the front door of the house. Sau-Ping, signalling Fei-Yin to be quiet, rose to see what was going on. Kin-Pong and Katherine faced her in the hallway.

Fei-Yin had followed her mother. "Hey! Why are the two of you home so early? Aren't you supposed to be working at the restaurant?" she asked.

Kin-Pong looked at Katherine.

"Well ..." said Katherine, returning his glance.

"We were locked out of the restaurant this morning," said Kin-Pong, his eyes still pinned on his wife as if he could only believe what had happened because she had witnessed it too.

"A large padlock," Katherine said, nodding at her husband.

Kin-Pong sighed. At eight that morning when he and Katherine had arrived at the restaurant to open shop, they had found a big padlock on the front door and, taped to the glass, a letter from a lawyer named Chau addressed to "the incumbent proprietors." According to the letter, Peach Garden Restaurant had changed hands. The lawyer's client, a Mr Cheung, would assume ownership of the restaurant on 1 January 1970. "The present owner" was expected to move out by 15 December at the latest, so that Mr Cheung could renovate.

Kin-Pong and Katherine had gone in the side door and up to the top floor to speak with Kin-Tsoi and find out what was happening. Kin-Tsoi was not there. Ming was not there. The apartment looked as if a tiger had ripped it apart. They had found an overturned bottle of cheap rice wine, a broken mirror; they had seen blood on a blanket.

Sau-Ping had led everyone towards the kitchen as Kin-Pong spoke. Now he was seated at the table. "I don't know where Ming is," said Kin-Pong. "The apartment was ransacked. It usually looks bad, but –"

"We hope she's not hurt," said Katherine in a low voice so that little Taai-Lun wouldn't hear.

"I don't know what to do," muttered Kin-Pong. "I wish Pa were here. We walked to the club but no one had any news. I even looked through the windows of the casino. It was empty. I won't be able to talk to those people."

"Who is this Lawyer Chau?" asked Sau-Ping.

"I've never heard of him."

"We have a telephone."

Kin-Pong went into the other room. The women waited, listening to the rustle of the phone book and then to Kin-Pong's voice. They heard him say distinctly, "I'll come to your office at once!" before the receiver rattled into place.

Kin-Pong returned to the kitchen, his face inflamed. "That bastard Kin-Tsoi! Three nights ago at the casino, he lost at dominoes and signed our restaurant over to Mr Cheung to pay his debt. The creditor believed that Kin-Tsoi was the sole owner because he and Ming were the only ones living in the building. Lawyer Chau said if I want to contest this, I have to produce proof of ownership. What more are they doing to us?" Kin-Pong raised his fists and was about to strike the top of the oven when Katherine rose to her feet. Controlling himself, he said "Ma, do you know whether there was any signed contract between Granduncle Kwok-Ko and Grandfather when they started the restaurant? Did Pa say anything about this before he died? Do you know whether Granduncle Kwok-Ko, Grandfather, or Pa left a will?"

"No. He never told me. He never showed me!"

Katherine said firmly, "We will fight it step by step, Kin-Pong. Don't terrify your mother. Don't terrify the child." Kin-Pong growled, "I'm going out. I'll be back in an hour."

The front door slammed behind him. The three women sat stonily while Fei-Yin's son played with his buttons and polished stones, tumbling them over his small hands with pleasure, as if they were golden coins. Watching her grandson, Sau-Ping wondered whether she herself would wind up like this child, reaching for gold but finding gravel instead. After decades of ceaseless labour, would all their savings be lost because long ago the men of the family had made a bargain with Yik-Faat and his tiger son?

Kin-Pong worked feverishly to save the restaurant. He turned first to the leaders at the Chinese Benevolent Association for advice. They said there was no such thing as a written contract amongst the older generation of Chinese in Vancouver. Partnerships were mostly based on verbal agreements between brothers or second cousins. In the late nineteenth and early twentieth century, every male worker who entered Canada had claimed that he was a partner in a business because the merchant class was exempt from head taxes. Lawyers were never involved in these partnerships since most people could neither read nor write, and since they trusted one another's word. In any case, before the war there were no Chinese lawyers in this ghost country. Only those on the voters' list could practise law, and the Chinese had not been allowed to vote until 1947.

Because the family's livelihood was at stake, Kin-Pong had no choice but to sue Kin-Tsoi for signing away the restaurant without his, Kin-Pong's, permission. Acting on recommendations from the leaders of the Chinese Benevolent Association, Kin-Pong hired Lawyer Au, a new immigrant from Hong Kong, to file suit against Kin-Tsoi. Lawyer Au at once contacted Lawyer Chau to have Mr. Cheung, his client, agree to delay his takeover of the restaurant until the matter of ownership had been cleared up. The trial was set for 15 January 1970.

Sau-Ping had never been in a civil court before. She hoped the hearing would not be like the "struggle meetings" in Toi-Shaan during the early 1950s, in which guilty and innocent alike suffered physical violence. When she walked through the great doors accompanied by Katherine and Fei-Yin, she was surprised to discover that the courtroom resembled a huge pawnshop. The judge was seated in a chair behind a high podium that looked like a pawnshop counter. Below the podium sat two people – the court interpreter and court stenographer, as she soon learned – whose job it was to record the words of the participants. The lawyers representing Kin-Pong and Kin-Tsoi sat at the tables in front of the judge. The witnesses sat at the back, waiting to be called to testify. There were very few onlookers.

Kin-Tsoi had taken shelter with a gambling pal since the end of November. When he was notified about the lawsuit, he wisely used his official name, Leung Kin-On. He was represented by Lawyer Chan, a Canadian-born lawyer of Toi-Shaanese ancestry. As the hearing opened, Lawyer Au and Lawyer Chan outlined their clients' cases before the court while Katherine explained to her mother-in-law what was going on.

The first witness was seventy-two-year-old Uncle Yue, who operated the grocery store next to the Peach Garden Restaurant. A court official walked across to the witness box and jabbered in English. These ghost words were translated then by the court interpreter into Toi-Shaanese: "Please place your left hand on the Christian book and raise your right hand. Do you swear that you will tell the truth, the whole truth, and nothing but the truth?"

"I do," Old Yue answered in Toi-Shaanese.

Lawyer Au asked the witness whether he knew the owners and staff of the Peach Garden Restaurant. Old Yue answered clearly and with dignity.

"Yes, your honour. My grocery store was opened the same year as Peach Garden Restaurant in 1915. It was then known as Peach Garden Café. I was about sixteen years old, helping my father with our family business. As far as I know, Peach Garden was then operated under partnership between two brothers from the village of Sai-Fok in Toi-Shaan County. The partners were Leung Kwok-Yan and his younger brother Leung Kwok-Ko. Five years later, in 1920, Leung Kwok-Yan sponsored his son, Leung Yik-Man, to come to Vancouver to help with the restaurant. Yik-Man was then a boy of nine or ten.

"Leung Kin-Pong," the old man continued, pointing at Kin-Pong, "was the son of Leung Yik-Man and the grandson of Leung Kwok-Yan. He was sponsored by Leung Yik-Man and came to Vancouver in the fall of 1952. I even lent Leung Yik-Man money so he could pay for Kin-Pong's boat ticket. The defendant, Leung Kin-On," Old Yue recalled, "did not arrive in Vancouver until sometime in 1954."

"But do you know how my client, Leung Kin-On, was related to the rest of the Leung family?" asked Lawyer Chan.

"No ... I don't know," replied Old Yue. "He doesn't act like the rest of the men in the family."

Sau-Ping saw the enemy lawyer approach the judge and heard him chatter. Katherine whispered, "He says they must see written documents and not listen to the memories of old men."

The judge nodded. He turned to Lawyer Au and asked a question. Sau-Ping guessed he was demanding written documents.

The good lawyer nodded vigorously and spoke, moving towards the pawnshop judge with papers in his hand.

"It's the old restaurant license," Katherine translated for her mother-in-law. "Dated 1915. Between Leung Kwok-Yan and Leung Kwok-Ko." She paused. There was more going on. "And Leung Kwok-Yan had a will made in 1950 bequeathing his share of the restaurant to his son Leung Yik-Man."

The judge took a look at the documents. He nodded.

Sau-Ping suddenly heard her own name. "He's explaining that Kin-Pong is the surviving son and you're the widow, *On-Yan*," whispered Katherine. Sau-Ping sat up straight and held her face steady.

The enemy lawyer was shouting and flapping one of his arms in protest. Sau-Ping guessed that he was calling them all liars. The judge said something. The lawyers returned to their tables and straightened their papers. The few people in the courtroom began to stir. "He's calling a break, *On-Yan*," whispered Katherine. "Do you have any written proof here in Vancouver that you were married to *Loye* and that Kin-Pong is your son?"

Sau-Ping simply shook her head. When she and Yik-Man were married in Toi-Shaan in 1933, they had not registered their marriage. To the villagers, a bride was a legal first wife from the moment she appeared at the groom's front door in a red sedan chair. The couple's marriage was considered legitimate once the bride and groom had kowtowed to the heavens, to the ancestors' tablets at the domestic altar, to the members of the groom's senior generation, and finally to one another. But were such marriage customs and rituals considered legal proof in the eyes of Canadian pawnshop judges?

As for Kin-Pong, he had been kidnapped from Yeung-Kong County at the age of two and then purchased by Sau-Ping's mother-in-law from Shaan-Tai Market. There were no adoption papers. Luckily Yik-Man had obtained a birth certificate for Kin-Pong in Vancouver. Lawyer Au should have no problem getting a copy of it from the Immigration office.

Katherine complained, "We are the plaintiffs. How come the whole trial sounds like we did something wrong? No wonder the Chinese say, 'When you're alive, don't get involved with the magistrate's court, and when you're dead, don't get involved with the underground king's jail!'"

After the recess, the enemy lawyer approached the judge. He started yelling and flapping his arms again. Katherine muttered to Sau-Ping and Fei-Yin, "He's saying Kin-Pong is the *purchased* son of Leung Yik-Man, but Kin-On is the *natural* son. He will give the judge a birth certificate and immigration records to prove his client's identity. *Ayii*, he says Chinese law only recognizes the natural son!" Katherine was suddenly on her feet, crying out something in English. The guard moved towards her, ready to eject her from the courtroom. Sau-Ping dragged her daughter-in-law back onto the wooden bench.

But then Fei-Yin rose to her feet and cried out in Toi-Shaanese, "That man who gambled the restaurant away is not Leung Kin-On. His real name is Leung Kin-Tsoi. He is not Leung Yik-Man's natural-born son. I am Leung Kin-On! I am Leung Kin-On!"

The judge hammered on his pawnshop counter, and the guard, turning to face them, again started to move in their direction. Sau-Ping rose to her feet to protect her daughter. The rapping of the hammer grew sharper, and the judge called out something to the guard. The good lawyer was gesturing and calling to Fei-Yin in Toi-Shaanese, "Please sit down, I will try to have you admitted as a witness, but not unless you sit down. He will throw you out if you speak when it is not your turn. Sit down. I will do my best." Fei-Yin settled back, her face flushed, her hands trembling.

Sau-Ping entertained no hope that her daughter would be called to testify before the pawnshop judge. But within ten minutes, after numerous conferences near the judge's counter, Fei-Yin was summoned by the translator and Sau-Ping watched her daughter walk calmly to the witness box. Mildly surprised by her daughter's composure, it then occurred to Sau-Ping that Fei-Yin had been through worse than this.

After saying her oath, Fei-Yin related how her father, Leung Yik-Man, had wrongly declared her to be a boy when he visited the Immigration officer in Vancouver upon her birth in 1934, and he thereby obtained a birth certificate under the name "Leung Kin-On" in Canada. She described how, subsequently, her father had sold her birth certificate to her granduncle Leung Kwok-Ko in 1954, so that the latter could sponsor his adopted son Leung Kin-Tsoi for immigration to Vancouver. The translator repeated these details at great speed in English and then reeled off the arguments of the good lawyer, who explained that Leung Kin-Tsoi was only a paper son, and that no one had produced documents establishing his relationship to Leung Kwok-Ko. Fei-Yin returned to her seat.

Sau-Ping could see that these Chinese family relationships totally confused the judge, who looked puzzled and bemused, as if someone had challenged him to read the day's news in a bowl of chop-suey. The hammer rose and when it struck the wood, the report sounded through the room. The judge spoke. Katherine whispered to her mother-in-law, "The case is postponed for six months."

Sau-Ping barely heard her. In the last few minutes, a terrible thought had formed in her mind. She realized that one of the family's guilty secrets had been openly declared in court. When the courtroom began to empty, she held Katherine's arm and whispered, "Please ask the good lawyer, if they know Yik-Man sold the birth certificate, will we go to jail? Will we be deported?"

Katherine nodded and immediately approached the good lawyer. They spoke for a while and then shook hands firmly, as if Katherine were a man. Returning, she said to her mother-in-law, "A general amnesty was declared for all illegal immigrants about eight years ago. The family will not be punished."

The good lawyer himself, carrying his case full of papers under his arm, now came up the aisle to Sau-Ping. "Mrs Leung," he said in Toi-Shaanese, "you will not be prosecuted by Canada. But to support your case I suggest we engage the services of a China specialist at the university to explain Chinese traditional customs surrounding marriage, adoption, and inheritance to this judge, if he is our judge the next time. Strange though it may seem, many judges are more inclined to believe a university China specialist than to believe a Chinese. We may also need an affidavit from you. My secretary will get in touch with you."

During the six months between the first hearing and the second, scheduled for June, the Leungs passed through difficult times financially. The restaurant had to remain closed until the ownership disputes were resolved. Worse, unless Kin-Pong's family won the case, the restaurant would legally belong to Mr Cheung, Kin-Tsoi's creditor.

Katherine gave birth to a baby girl in February. In her eagerness for the family to win the case, she named the newborn Winnie. Suddenly freed from restaurant work and burdened with weeks of free time, Kin-Pong and Katherine often walked the streets of Chinatown when they were not at home taking care of the baby. They told Sau-Ping how different West Pender Street looked when viewed from a perspective other than the inside of the restaurant. They were both pleasantly surprised at how cosmopolitan Chinatown had become. To Kin-Pong in particular, Chinatown by night had gained a kind of splendour. In the early 1950s, he remembered, the only non-Chinese on the streets were drunks, gamblers, dope pushers, and prostitutes. Now many tourists visited the Chinese stores to buy groceries, dry goods, novelties, gifts, souvenirs, and curios. Some were Caucasian visitors from the States, others were Chinese from smaller towns in British Columbia. And there were lots of new immigrants from Hong Kong, Taiwan, Southeast Asia, and even Peru. On the weekends, the new immigrants enjoyed fancy Chinese dinners and watched Chinese movies afterwards. To cater to this affluent clientele, the older commercial establishments were renovating their businesses, and many enterprising new immigrants had rented or bought shop spaces to start their own concerns. Katherine and Kin-Pong described the sights they had seen with great enthusiasm at dinner. It was never very long, however, before their spirits fell again; no one in the family could escape for long their worries about the fate of the Peach Garden Restaurant.

Fully realizing the difficulties faced by their family, Fei-Yin and Yue Ming-Fai had been desperately looking for work since their arrival. Luckily, there was a labour shortage in Vancouver, and they had both landed jobs in a relatively short time. Yue Ming-Fai entered a partnership with some Hong Kong friends to run a garage; educated by recent events, the partners hired a lawyer to draw up a formal written contract. Fei-Yin was hired by a Chinese-owned factory, not far from Chinatown, that manufactured men's shirts for sale all over Canada.

Since Sau-Ping's house on Keefer Street had become too crowded, particularly with Winnie's arrival, Fei-Yin, Yue Ming-Fai, and their son Taai-Lun moved into a rented basement apartment on Cambie Street. Not long after, to the family's great surprise, Ming reappeared. When Kin-Tsoi came home on the night he had gambled away his share of the restaurant, he had nearly strangled Ming. She had fled, she explained, but now had no place to live. It was Katherine who contacted Lawyer Au, who in turn contacted Lawyer Chan and Lawyer Chau and convinced them to agree to an out-of-court settlement that would grant Ming temporary refuge in her old quarters on the second floor of the restaurant. The entire family knew that Kin-Tsoi had already lost his right to the restaurant at the gambling table. This was the one place Ming might be safe from him. Uprooted, confused, oddly resilient, Ming was able to manage for herself, but she was unsuccessful in finding a new job. For the time being she would live on social assistance.

The trial resumed in mid-June 1970. Again Sau-Ping sat between her daughter and daughter-in-law, and again Katherine translated at a frantic rate.

This time, Lawyer Au brought in one Professor Lynden, a Caucasian specialist from the University of British Columbia, as a consultant. According to the professor, the Kuomintang government in China passed a Family Law in 1931 that made marriage registration compulsory. However, the law was only publicized in the major coastal cities; it was practically unknown to people in the countryside. Professor Lynden also described the customs and rituals that made up a legally constituted marriage for the villagers in Toi-Shaan. His description tallied with the information Sau-Ping had sworn in her affidavit.

The judge accepted Professor Lynden's testimony and Sau-Ping was accepted as the legal wife of Leung Yik-Man. When Katherine translated this finding, Sau-Ping raised her chin and gazed at the judge.

The professor had gone on to explain that according to village tradition in Toi-Shaan, all sons, whether natural, adopted, or purchased, had equal rights of inheritance. This testimony convinced the judge to rule in favour of Kin-Pong's right of inheritance.

But the most damning evidence against Kin-Tsoi's claims to Peach Garden Restaurant came when Lawyer Au approached the bench with a new document. It was Leung Kwok-Ko's will, dated 12 April 1960. It said: "My adopted son Leung Kin-Tsoi, who came as a paper son of Leung Yik-Man using the name Leung Kin-On, is an unfilial son. I therefore disinherit him. I now bequeath my share of Peach Garden Restaurant to my nephew Leung Yik-Man. And if he should pass away, then my share will be given to his purchased son, Leung Kin-Pong."

Laughing, clapping her hands, Katherine announced to her mother-in-law that Granduncle Kwok-Ko had a will after all, and that he had disinherited Kin-Tsoi.

"*Ayii!*" Fei-Yin rose, her hands clasped to her chest.

Exhausted, confused, and deeply grateful, Sau-Ping found herself looking at Kin-Tsoi, who was gripping the back of the bench in front of him. Once at midnight Sau-Ping had seen a large rat frozen by the light from an open door behind the restaurant. Now Kin-Tsoi's face reminded her of the rat – sharp, immobile, and infinitely calculating. In a moment he would disappear, creeping back into the darkness to scavenge in a different alley.

It was Leung Kwok-Ko's public denunciation of this rat's behaviour that swung the judge's decision conclusively in favour of Kin-Pong and Sau-Ping. Before the trial their fondest hope had been that they could retain half the title to the restaurant. Now, it seemed, Peach Garden would be exclusively theirs.

But no one understood how the lawyer had found the will of Leung Kwok-Ko. Was it authentic? Who had been the trustee?

The day after the trial, Kin-Pong went to Lawyer Au's office. Only then did he find out that his lawyer had got hold of his granduncle's will through Lawyer Ma, one of his associates at the law firm. It so happened that Ma had been privately approached by Ming, who wanted to sue for divorce from Kin-Tsoi. When Ming described her grievances against her husband, she also mentioned Kin-Tsoi's current dispute with Kin-Pong over the ownership of Peach Garden Restaurant.

The name of the restaurant rang a bell, and Lawyer Ma had quickly checked his files after Ming had gone. He was the trustee for Leung Kwok-Ko's will, which had been written and filed some ten years before, when Kin-Tsoi had been hiding in Prince Rupert. Leung Kwok-Ko was disgusted with his unfilial paper son and touched by the respect and care he had received from Sau-Ping, Yik-Man, and

Kin-Pong. He had anticipated that one day Kin-Tsoi might toss his portion of Peach Garden Restaurant onto the gambling table: he clearly felt no allegiance to the business or to the men who had worked in it for so very long. So Leung Kwok-Ko had approached Lawyer Ma to make his will. At the time, the RCMP investigation of "paper sons" was at its height. Leung Kwok-Ko therefore instructed his lawyer not to divulge the contents of the will prematurely, for fear it would get Yik-Man in trouble with the law. He stipulated that Lawyer Ma should produce the will only if ownership of the restaurant was contested.

Thank Koon-Yam for Leung Kwok-Ko's foresight! Thank Koon-Yam for poor, weary Ming who had had the courage to approach a lawyer to file for divorce. And she had approached the right lawyer!

Kin-Pong reported that he had found out more about Kin-Tsoi's present predicament. Lawyer Au had informed him that Kin-Tsoi would soon be facing another lawsuit; for Mr Cheung, his creditor, was now after him to pay his gambling debt. Since Kin-Tsoi no longer held any rights over Peach Garden Restaurant, he would either have to pay his debt with cash or spend time in jail.

That afternoon Sau-Ping's entire family visited the Chinese cemetery to offer prayers of thanks at Leung Kwok-Ko's grave. Then they all went to the second floor of Peach Garden Restaurant to express their heartfelt gratitude to Ming. She stood humble and stolid amongst her only furnishings, a cot and two trunks.

"Ming," said Kin-Pong, "you don't have to worry from now on. Your divorce will go through with no problem. We would like you to continue working at the restaurant for a salary."

"No, Kin-Pong," Ming answered. "I am going to San Francisco. I have three uncles in San Francisco. Thank you. I will write to you. I have always wanted to live in San Francisco."

"You must let us help you," Sau-Ping said, looking around the bare room that reminded her of the different bare, sad rooms that had been part of her own history in Hong Kong. "You must. Yik-Man would agree."

Ming could not be persuaded for days, but at last she accepted a substantial gift of cash from them, along with a new trunk and a pretty dressing case. Weeks later, she was gone. When Sau-Ping visited her husband's grave the next day, she found a brilliant red cloth flower in a porcelain bowl sitting there on the ground. A blue painted dragon curled around the bowl. It had to be from Ming.

In the meantime, the family was beginning to plan for the restaurant that was now entirely theirs. Katherine suggested that they should take out a bank loan to renovate Peach Garden into a "Hong

Kong-style" restaurant in order to compete with other restaurants in Chinatown. She had worked in a Hong Kong restaurant and had apparently given this a lot of thought. She suggested they open the mezzanine and second floors to expand the restaurant's capacity. They would improve the service by employing Hong Kong students as part-time waiters and waitresses and dressing them in nice uniforms. They would improve the menu by varying their dishes and applying for a liquor license. For lunches, they might hire a chef from Hong Kong to serve dim-sum in addition to roast pork, barbecued duck, and soya sauce chicken. For dinner, they would have two kinds of menus, the chop-suey menu in English for foreign devils, and a Chinese-language menu listing authentic Cantonese dishes for Chinese customers.

Evening after evening, the family discussed their plans over dinner. Sau-Ping, Fei-Yin, and Katherine spent hours considering how they might decorate the new improved restaurant. One evening, the three women were gathered on the sidewalk, staring at the worn sign with the peach blossoms painted on it.

"I will feel sad to take it down," said Sau-Ping, who was carrying Winnie to give Katherine a break. "It was one of the first things I saw when I arrived in Vancouver."

"It was the first thing I saw too."

Bewildered, Sau-Ping turned her head.

A dark, young, rather rough Chinese woman was grinning at her devilishly. She was wearing a nice striped silken dress and a warm coat for this rather chilly summer evening, but the huge suitcase at her side was scratched, broken, and taped. A lit cigarette dangled between her fingers. "My mother said you might have work for me."

"Lai-Sheung!" screamed Fei-Yin. "You're here!"

"My unjust, selfish husband is dead." Lei-Sheung made an easy movement with her right hand, and the smoke from her cigarette circled into the air.

Sau-Ping's heart turned over. She felt the rebellious, comic spirit of her oldest friend, Mei-Kuen, draw near her. Sau-Ping reached up to pat the cheek of Mei-Kuen's half-wild daughter. "You are like your mother," she said, smiling.

Lai-Sheung replied quietly, "I hope to work to bring my mother here."

Sau-Ping nodded, smiling to herself. She yearned for the day when Mei-Kuen could come to Vancouver. They would see one another again every day, just as they had in the maiden house in Fung-Yeung village. When the paths of their two lives finally joined again, a great circle would be closed and healed. Thinking of her friend, Sau-Ping felt peaceful, as if she were breathing the atmosphere of the maiden house. She vividly recalled the beautiful pale green walls, the ring of sleeping mats, and the neat top drawer containing her own belongings. Mei-Kuen's daring laugh rang in her memory.

But it would be years before Lai-Sheung could save enough money for passage. Sau-Ping seriously doubted whether one woman could manage to bring another woman across the ocean. She resigned herself to wait a long time for this reunion.

And time passed. Pauline and Joe grew into teenagers, and Sau-Ping found herself confounded by their Canadian manners and clothes. Pauline, her daughter, was the most difficult to handle, for this hybrid girl had no patience with Chinese customs that commanded women to obey and serve their fathers, husbands, brothers, and sons. She scolded her sister-in-law, Katherine, for being subservient to Kin-Pong and once even accused Sau-Ping of abandoning Big Sister Fei-Yin – her own first-born daughter – in Hong Kong without a fight! Pauline thought it horrible that a woman like Katherine would allow herself to be married to a man who had chosen her from a batch of photographs, and she declared herself to be uninterested in Chinese boys because they were too "short and wimpy." She wanted someone who looked like a hockey player!

Sometimes Joe related Pauline's complaints to Sau-Ping, and in this way the mother learned that Pauline wished she could live a life that was free of curfews, glittering with brand-name clothes, punctuated by swift automobile rides, and unburdened by housework, the sort of life she insisted all her Caucasian classmates enjoyed. She hated wearing old-fashioned homemade outfits and being forced to help out in the restaurant for free whenever a waitress happened to be ill. "She says she hates the way the restaurant smells, it gives her a headache," Joe reported.

Sau-Ping, thinking of her own history, found herself growing deeply angry at her daughter as she listened to these complaints. She herself had begun to do field chores, carry water, cook, sew and embroider and take care of her younger brother Tin-Shaang by the time she turned six. Fei-Yin had been raised in the same way, and Fei-Yin had grown into a strong, uncomplaining, honest woman. "In those days, I was happy just to have an occasional candy from my parents for being a good girl," Sau-Ping muttered to herself. But alas, she was helpless to remake her younger daughter.

The struggle with Pauline reached its peak during the girl's last year of senior high school, in 1975. On the night of Chinese New Year, there was a terrible argument at the dinner table that ended when Kin-Pong stood up and shouted that Pauline was just a rat, eating at the table and giving nothing in return. Pauline ran to her room in a fury, screaming and wailing at the top of her lungs. She slammed the door and turned on loud music. Not much later, Kin-Pong and Katherine drifted off to bed. No one had the energy to speak of this problem again. Sau-Ping found herself sitting alone in the front room, looking out at the streetlights and thinking of her girlhood days. What would have happened if she, Sau-Ping, had ever screamed at an elder? She would have been beaten hard with a stick.

Early the next morning, Sau-Ping knocked on Pauline's door. There was no answer, no sound. She called for her sons, and Kin-Pong forced open the door. Splinters of wood broke loose. Looking in, Sau-Ping saw the bed was made and empty hangers dangled in the open closet. The window was open, and the room was very cold. In the following week, Joe learned from his friends that Pauline had moved into a basement apartment on Charles Street in the poorer part of town with a Caucasian boy named Peter, who had also left his parents' house.

Months passed. Then one evening Kin-Pong, hearing a knock on the front door, moved down the hall to answer it when the door swung in towards him, pushed by an invisible arm. Impelled by an instinct she couldn't name, Sau-Ping followed her son. There in the doorway was her Chinese-Canadian daughter, Pauline. She looked skinny. Her hair was tied back and covered with a dirty bandanna, and her shoes and the hems of her jeans were soaked. Pauline knelt on the doorstep. "Big Brother, I was wrong to disobey you. Please take me back," she said.

"Come in then," Kin-Pong said simply, though months before he had vowed never to allow Pauline back in the house, for her actions had humiliated the Leung family.

After being offered a cup of tea, Pauline told her story. She and Peter had tried to survive on odd jobs. Then that afternoon he had disappeared for hours and failed to show up for supper. It turned out that he had visited his parents and agreed to leave his Chinese girlfriend. When at last he returned to their dark apartment, Pauline was sitting on the floor, eating a box of take-out chop-suey. It was delicious, hot, and smelled like home. When Peter began his fumbling explanation, she felt such rage she threw the chop-suey at him, ran out into the rain, and found herself walking home, hungry to rejoin her family.

This experience with her daughter taught Sau-Ping that a new challenge had appeared on her horizon. All her life she had struggled to keep her family together in the face of threats and danger. Often she had succeeded. Often she had failed. Now the forces that threatened to shatter her family were not, on the face of it, terrifying so much as appealing and tempting. Brand-name Clothes! Avon cosmetics! Fancy cars! Pop music! White guys! Only a few months later, she learned that Mei-Kuen's daughter, Lai-Sheung, had moved in with a Caucasian man named Jack. Sau-Ping met Jack a few times and had to admit that he had friendly eyes and a human smile, but she did not think her friend, Mei-Kuen, would approve of her daughter's new alliance with a foreign devil. But she was caught off guard when she discovered that Jack was helping Lai-Sheung save up money to bring Mei-Kuen to Vancouver. This was a true filial gesture. Still, even with Jack's help, it would take time to save up passage money.

It did take time. But then the day arrived – 14 September 1980 – and when Sau-Ping walked into her garden that morning, she laughed to see the sun alight in the eastern sky, as always, as if this were a normal, unexceptional day. Hours later she stood in the airport. None of her surroundings appeared real to her; she did not quite believe that the long, sleek hallways and travel posters could ever produce her earthy, unpredictable friend Mei-Kuen. Yet the moment Mei-Kuen walked out of the Canada Customs room carrying two suitcases with the easy determination of a Hong Kong street vendor, Sau-Ping felt her spirit snap to attention. This was real! Mei-Kuen immediately spotted her daughter and friend and exclaimed, "I have always wanted to see Gold Mountain. Now my dream has come true!"

"How do you like it so far?" laughed Sau-Ping, happy to see that her friend's heart had not aged in twenty-five years.

"Well, there is no gold, but the mountains here certainly look more magnificent than the mountains I've lived in! Has anybody ever been to the top?"

Lai-Sheung touched her mother's hair. "Grey hair! Old woman! We'll make you climb to the top."

"Hmm, I'm stronger than you are, I would bet. Who is this silent man? How do I say his name?" Mei-Kuen laughed, turning to Jack easily as if he were a proper Toi-Shaanese man.

From that day, Sau-Ping's life changed. She had a steady friend, and Mei-Kuen's good humour brightened her home and Canada itself. The worried that preyed on her, notably about her Canadian-born children and their futures, receded when Mei-Kuen was near. Mei-Kuen arrived at the house regularly to play mahjongg with Sau-Ping and her neighbours, Mrs Ma and Mrs Chan. Their converstions ranged far and wide.

When she learned that her daughter, Pauline, was dating another Caucasian boy, Sau-ping was less shocked than she would have been before Mei-Kuen's arrival. Jeff, Pauline's new boyfriend, was a fourth-year student in the Asian Studies department at the University of British Columbia. Eager to learn about Chinese culture and the Chinese people, he volunteered for as many Chinatown activities as he could manage. He and Pauline had met one another during a student protest against white racism.

The first time Sau-Ping met Jeff, he bowed slightly and greeted her in Mandarin. "It is a pleasure to meet you," he said, exactly like an educated human being. Sau-Ping was stunned, but she maintained her composure. It was harder to hide her amazement when she discovered that Jeff could play mahjongg. From Mei-Kuen, Sau-Ping had learned a clever Hong Kong trick: when making a judgement on the temperament of a prospective son-in-law, one should observe how he handles himself when he wins or loses a full hand of mahjongg. Jeff passed the test. When he won, he was gracious and unassuming. When he lost, he cheerfully congratulated the winner. After several mahjongg sessions, Sau-Ping decided Jeff was a good man.

One day Jeff arrived at the door alone, dressed in his Western suit. He looked tall and official, like a Canadian judge, but Sau-Ping sensed he was nervous. Taking a seat in the front room, he scratched his ear, then straightened his jacket, then tugged at his trousers. Sau-Ping faced him calmly. As she had expected, he asked if he could marry Pauline. They talked for a while, but Sau-Ping explained she could make no decision without consulting her eldest son, the head of the family, Kin-Pong. That evening the Leung family sat down to a long conversation about white Canadians. Kin-Pong at first resisted Jeff's proposal to marry Pauline, but his own wife Katherine and younger brother Joe took Pauline's side. Finally Kin-Pong relented. At that moment, Sau-Ping happened to glance at her daughter-in-law. Katherine was beaming; caught by the light from the lamp, tears glinted in her eyes. She was happy her sister-in-law had found a kind man to marry.

Pauline herself graduated from UBC in 1981 with a degree in Social Work. She soon found a job as a counsellor for new immigrants, most of whom were from Asia. Joe Leung graduated in the same year but he took an engineering job far away, in Hamilton, Ontario, with the firm of Smith, Cartwright, and Chan. One fine day two years after Pauline's marriage to Jeff, Sau-Ping answered the telephone and heard Joe's voice. "I'm getting married, Mom," he said. Sau-Ping didn't answer for a moment, so Joe continued. "Her name is Jennifer, Mom. Jennifer Ip."

"Oh! Ip is a Chinese name, isn't it? Although not the way you say it."

"Jennifer is Chinese, Mom. Or should I say Chinese-Canadian. She's third-generation. She's a town planner."

Sau-Ping couldn't imagine what that meant ... town planner? "Does she speak Chinese?"

"Well ... actually ... no, she doesn't."

"You're going to marry a girl that doesn't speak Chinese?"

"Mom, what are you complaining about? You always wanted me to marry a Chinese. Come on, give me a break! She's Chinese."

Sau-Ping did not have the strength to travel to Hamilton to witness Joe's wedding, but Kin-Pong and Katherine attended and came back to report that Jennifer looked like a Chinese woman but did not act like one. She watched hockey on the television while Joe cooked! Sau-Ping tried to picture this alien scene, but all she could bring into view were two little women's feet propped up on a pillow. Still, she refused to worry about Joe's marriage. He had chosen.

More grandchildren were born. Fei-Yin had given birth to a son, David. Pauline gave birth to a daughter, Emily, who was taught to address Sau-Ping as *Ah Poh* (Maternal Grandma) in proper Toi-Shaanese from the time she could talk. Then Joe's wife Jennifer sent a letter announcing she was pregnant and asking her mother-in-law if she would kindly stay with the family in Hamilton to help during the birth. It was such a warm letter that Sau-Ping agreed to fly to Hamilton, though airplanes terrified her, and immediately began preparing for her role there. With the help of Mei-Kuen, she spent a whole week preparing a stew consisting of hard-boiled eggs, pork hocks, and ginger root cooked in a large pot of sweet black vinegar. After the contents had been soaked and simmered off and on for another two weeks, this delicacy was carefully dished into two large glass jars and sealed, ready for the new mother.

When Sau-Ping disembarked from the airplane, Joe and Jennifer were there to greet her. Joe teased her about her huge suitcases, not knowing how much nutritious food Sau-Ping had brought for Jennifer. When he spoke, his beautiful wife just smiled; she couldn't understand Chinese. Sau-Ping was driven to Joe's large house, where she quickly unpacked her bags, heart pounding, and descended from her bedroom to help in the kitchen. But Joe laughed when she offered, saying she probably didn't know much about cooking "lasagna." Sau-Ping soon discovered the cupboards of Joe's big house were stacked with alien foods purchased in small boxes and cans. But she had little time to worry about the food, for two days later the baby was born. A baby boy! Sau-Ping was overjoyed when she heard, for this patrilineal grandson ensured that the souls of Yik-

Man and her parents-in-law would find comfort in the afterworld – something that Kin-Pong's two daughters Josie and Winnie could not do, being female.

Sau-Ping's joy was shortlived. When Jennifer returned home with the baby, she refused to drink the rice wine cooked with chicken, black fungus, and ginger. She was appalled by the bowl of laboriously prepared stew, though it was thoroughly black, as it should have been, and deliciously flavoured by potent black Chinese vinegar. She bathed and washed her hair repeatedly, though Sau-Ping tried to warn her away from water. Worse still, she refused to let Sau-Ping hold the baby for more than a minute a day. And Joe allied himself with her. He would not let his mother go near the crib or even the nursery. Sau-Ping felt slighted, like a TB ghost.

Belted into the shivering airplane on the flight home, staring out over the tops of the clouds, Sau-Ping was haunted by visions of the Leung family spirits, hungry and abandoned, wailing as they slipped into a vast chaos. It was clear to her that baby Gordon Leung would not bother to tend the family's ancestral tablets or sweep the graves of his forbears in the Chinese Cemetery when he grew to be a man. Sau-Ping could almost hear the dry bones of Yik-Man, *Loye*, and Paternal Uncle yearning to return to Sai-Fok.

After her visit to Hamilton Sau-Ping was exhausted for days. She had no spirit; not even little Emily, her half-Chinese granddaughter, could cheer her up with Chinese nursery songs she'd learned from Pauline. But months passed, and Sau-Ping rallied. She returned to her regular mahjongg games, and at the mahjongg table she listened to her friends speak about the MacLean Park Senior Housing Project. Mrs Ma enjoyed it, they said. The rooms and buildings were clean, and there were many Chinese citizens of the right age living in the same complex, many Toi-Shaanese, not too many Hong Kong snobs, so a person could have a chat. What's more, the elected residents' committee planned and coordinated voluntary group activities, such as practising taichi at the top of Queen Elizabeth Park every morning, or going for long-distance outings. The committee members didn't come like Communists, knocking on the door to command participation. You could ignore them if you wished and watch Chinese television programs or listen to Chinese music or play mahjongg privately in your own apartment.

Sau-Ping never mentioned the MacLean Park Senior Housing Project to any member of her family, though in her heart she realized that the housing project appealed to her because it sounded like a quiet haven – like the maiden house. She might never have discovered that Kin-Pong and Katherine were also dreaming about a new place if she hadn't grown such large cabbages. One morning she grabbed some crumpled sheets of paper near the back door to wrap one of the huge, soiled vegetables. When she spread out the sheets in her garden, she saw before her neat, detailed drawings of two-storey Canadian houses, with every window and door outlined and tiny arrows pointing here and there. Sau-Ping rested on her knees, staring at the plans for the houses, two of which appeared to be as big as *yeung-lau* in Toi-Shaan. She had already guessed that her own report of Joe and Jennifer's substantial house in Ontario had nettled Kin-Pong, whose many years of dutiful work in the restaurant had made it impossible for him to attend university and fly off to work for Smith, Cartwright, and Chan. Now she guessed that Kin-Pong was dreaming of houses. This was no surprise. Houses had always been important to the Leung family!

When at dinner that evening Sau-ping pulled out the papers she had discovered, Katherine cried out and Kin-Pong looked sheepish. But moments later, he was describing the advantages of the North Vancouver suburbs, where the houses had plenty of "storage space" and a garage for cars, where the trees grew tall as pillars in the front yards. "And you would come with us, Ma," he said.

Sau-Ping replied, "To nice North Vancouver? Not me. I'm no nice North Vancouver lady. I belong in Chinatown. I cannot live in one more new world." Saying the words, she heard they were true.

Katherine and Kin-Pong argued with her, both declaring that they could never leave her alone, for she was the centre of their lives. Sau-Ping heard herself say, "I will not be alone. I will ask Mei-Kuen to move with me to the MacLean Park Senior Housing Project. We can get a double apartment. We will be like girls again." Her hand rose to cover her smile. Her son and Katherine sat dumbfounded. Looking at them, Sau-Ping laughed, and the laughter called up tears. A few drops of salt water slid down her face.

In truth, she was afraid that Mei-Kuen would refuse to go. Could a woman who had lived in the mountains with bandits now settle into the MacLean Park Senior Housing Project? But Mei-Kuen declared herself ready to move in with her childhood friend any hour, any day! Within a few months, Sau-Ping had sold the house purchased by Yik-Man in 1962 and used part of the proceeds to acquire a flat in the seniors' block at MacLean Park. Her new apartment was near Peach Garden Restaurant and located within walking distance of Chinatown's commercial hub. She could have plenty of visitors. And when the visitors left, she could live tranquilly with her first friend.

Sau-Ping and Mei-Kuen adapted to their new life happily, and Sau-Ping thought that at last her work was done and her adventures completed. But one month later she had a vivid dream. She was sitting in a brown, Canadian-style chair that had been carried to the shore of the pond in front of Sai-Fok's main ancestral hall. There under the old banyan tree, Yik-Man appeared in a white flowing robe. He whispered hoarsely, "Little Sister, could you show me how to get to my *yeung-lau*?"

"Here, walk this way."

Sau-Ping got up and suddenly noticed that there were no feet beneath the white flowing robe ... In a moment, Yik-Man's whole body began to dissolve in front of her.

It was months before Sau-Ping mustered the courage to announce her wish to fly to China. Kin-Pong was disapproving, Katherine uncertain, Jeff enthusiastic, and Pauline silent. Sau-Ping said, "I have asked Mei-Kuen to go with me, but she refuses to set foot in China again. She says let the Chinese rot. She would only go if the government promised she could feast on a Communist in Beijing."

In spite of himself, Kin-Pong laughed.

A voice spoke evenly. "I would go, Mom. I want to see your village."

Sau-Ping raised her eyes and met the gaze of her Canadian daughter, Pauline. "I have money from the sale of the house," Sau-Ping said.

Then Katherine spoke up. "I think you should tell your mother about the *yeung-lau*, husband."

"What is this?" Sau-Ping turned to her son. She thought her ears were playing tricks on her again in her old age.

Kin-Pong sighed. "I was going to announce this for your sixty-ninth birthday. I was ... well." He sat up straighter. "A friend at the Chinese Benevolent Association was collecting donations for community projects at home. So I donated five hundred Canadian dollars for the renovation of my Alma Mater, the Toi-Shaan Senior High School in Toi-Shaan City, and the money convinced the Chinese government that I was a 'patriotic Chinese.' I subsequently received a letter from the Toi-Shaan Overseas Chinese Affairs Office. Your *yeung-lau* has been returned to you. Wait, Ma ..." Kin-Pong reached out and held Sau-Ping's arm as she rose from her chair. "It will be a ruin. It will hurt you to see it, I'm sure. It will all be a ruin. That's why I don't want you to go."

"I have seen worse, son."

CHAPTER 22

A Long Way Home

6 AUGUST 1987

The foreign voice of one of the airplane maids came through the cabin. Sau-Ping noticed that all the passengers around her, including her Canadian-born daughter Pauline, began to buckle their seatbelts. "We're landing, Mom," Pauline said softly.

In the course of the flight Pauline had complained four or five times about how long it took to get to Hong Kong, yet for Sau-Ping the trip felt effortless, breathless, inconclusive. It had taken her eighteen days to reach Vancouver by boat in 1955; it took less than eighteen hours to return to Hong Kong by plane in 1987. That was not enough time for her to watch the clouds and daydream! She had not seen Hong Kong for thirty-two years and had not set foot in Toi-Shaan since 1952. Throughout the plane trip, sweet and bitter memories circulated in her mind. She was almost embarrassed, imagining that other passengers might hear the sound of her brain whirring – like the sound of a video cassette tape set at rewind.

She and Pauline manoeuvred patiently through the various checkpoints. They made their way through Immigration, collected their luggage, hoisted their suitcases onto a trolley, passed through Customs, and at last trundled through the automatic door into the large airport waiting-room.

"Auntie Sau-Ping, Auntie Sau-Ping!" It took a long time for Sau-Ping to recognize the caller from among the hundreds of people crowding around the ramp outside the automatic door at Kai-Tak. He was a sturdy man, tanned, with squint marks radiating from the corners of his eyes: one of her two eldest nephews who worked in construction.

"This must be ... Are you Tak-Kan or Tak-Keung?"

"Auntie, I am Tak-Kan, I am so glad you still remember our names. It's been a long time since you left for Canada."

"Yes. Many years."

"How are Fei-Yin and Yue Ming-Fai? I remember Fei-Yin was back for two weeks during Father's funeral. Such a long time ago! Are Kin-Pong and Katherine doing good business in Vancouver?"

To all these questions Sau-Ping gave ready answers. She reported recent news about Mei-Kuen and Lai-Sheung as well.

"Is this Cousin Pauline?" Tak-Kan glanced at Pauline for the first time. "She looks a lot like you. Does she understand Toi-Shaanese or Cantonese?"

Pauline returned the greeting in both Toi-Shaanese and Cantonese so as to impress her Hong Kong cousin.

"Where is your mother? And the rest of your brothers and sisters?" Sau-Ping asked.

"Ma is at home waiting for you in her apartment. She wanted to come to the airport, but I persuaded her not to. She is over seventy years old now, and I don't think she could fight the crowd at the airport." They were walking with the crowd as Tak-Kan spoke. "Tak-Keung and Tak-Wa are right now in Sham-Chun [Shenzhen]. They are negotiating with the Chinese side for a contract to build a hotel. You see, the three of us are now partners. We formed our own construction company to invest in China. Little Brother Tak-Wa is an economist, he knows everything about balance sheets, business contracts, and enterprise management. Tak-Keung and I know everything about construction. I came back yesterday for a break, and Ma said I should pick you up. But I'll probably have to be in Sham-Chun again tomorrow, I'm afraid. Please accept my apologies."

"You must be working very hard," said Pauline politely.

"Oh yes; but have no fear, we won't abandon you. My youngest sister, Tsoi-Lin, is staying with Ma and she can take you around. My other sister, Tsoi-Yuk, has gone to Beijing for a tour. Ever since her divorce six years ago, she has been travelling by herself quite a lot. She has money."

"Was her rich husband generous?" asked Sau-Ping.

Tak-Kan shrugged. "She hired a lawyer."

Tak-Kan was pushing the trolley with their luggage onto the elevator. The women followed him into a multistoreyed covered parking lot. He led them straight to a shining BMW, lifted their luggage into the trunk, and opened the door. They hopped in and found themselves heading out for a short car tour of Hong Kong. "This is for Cousin Pauline," said Tak-Kan. "Auntie, you know Hong Kong. But you probably won't recognize it now."

Sau-Ping gazed out at the massive city. "Yes, you're right," she said.

How clean and orderly Hong Kong had become! People lined up for buses and taxis, and they didn't dump their garbage everywhere. Only a very few streets had cooked foodstalls or fruit, vegetable, and meat pedlars. There were, however, a number of "women's streets" with vendors selling surplus or substandard clothing, custom jewellery, watches, belts, and other accessories.

Hong Kong was now a concrete jungle, full of highrises. Sau-Ping could not see any of the four- or five-storey tenement buildings that had lined the streets when she lived here in the 1950s. Since he'd been in the construction business for such a long time, Tak-Kan was able to answer Pauline's questions about city development and housing in detail. He explained to the two women that Hong Kong no longer had terrible problems with water shortages, since it had made a special arrangement to pump fresh water from the Pearl River across China's border.

They drove by Shek Kip Mei.

Sau-Ping gazed upwards, but couldn't see a single squatter hut. The bare mountain remained, but the huts seemed to have been wiped off its face. At the foot of the mountain a cluster of buildings had sprouted; Tak-Kan explained that they were low-price highrises for working people. The temporary relief camp set up for fire victims in 1954 had been now replaced by a small park. Looking at the children's playground equipment, Sau-Ping remembered the tents and parked emergency vehicles and recalled the bright colour of the blood she coughed into her palm.

"Has there been a flood of Chinese refugees into Hong Kong since the Cultural Revolution ended?" asked Sau-Ping.

"Well, there was. For a while. But once Deng Xiaoping's new economic policy was firmed up, very few people escaped from China. In fact, to tell you the truth, the traffic now often goes the other way around. Every day thousands of Hong Kong people cross the border to do business in China. Many go to tour the country. Many who escaped have returned to invest. You see, Auntie, land is so cheap and the wages are so low in the Mainland that Hong Kong manufacturers are closing their plants in Hong Kong. They simply locked the doors, laying off the workers without compensation, and shipped all the machines to their new factories across the border."

Sau-Ping nodded, not knowing quite what to say. She was glad this had not happened while Fei-Yin, Tsoi-Yuk, and Tsoi-Lin were factory girls in Hong Kong, or they would have been deprived of their basic livelihood. At the same time, she hoped that if conditions were improving at the border cities of southern China, there might also be improvements taking place in the villages. But she guessed that this nephew knew little about village life in Toi-Shaan County. After all, his mother had left the village before he was born.

Sau-Ha's apartment in North Point, on the eighteenth floor of a twenty-storey building, was as different from her cubicle on Pitt Street as day from night. The place was bright and spacious. Sau-Ha occupied one of the three bedrooms, Tsoi-Lin the second, and the third was left for ironing, playing mahjongg, storage, and the domestic shrine for ancestral tablets. Except for Tsoi-Lin, all Sau-Ha's children were married and living in other residences.

Sau-Ping greeted her sister with joy. Sau-Ha had worked so hard when her children were young, she deserved to live a more comfortable life in her old age.

The long-separated sisters talked and talked through the night until their throats were sore. In the morning, Tsoi-Lin took Cousin Pauline shopping through all the famous "women's streets" in Hong Kong and Kowloon. With the help of Mei-Kuen, Fei-Yin, and Katherine, Pauline had drawn up a long shopping list for herself and her relatives in Vancouver. Pauline bought so many clothes and accessories that she had to buy a big new suitcase to carry them in. Auntie Sau-Ha laughed when she saw it and offered to keep the huge suitcase in her spare room while Pauline and her mother travelled inland to Toi-Shaan. "I am glad this isn't India so you couldn't buy an elephant."

"I hope the Canada Customs officials don't give you any trouble!" Sau-Ping teased, as Pauline spread her purchases throughout the main room to show her aunt and mother. "If Mei-Kuen were here, she would tell you to take to the streets and sell most of them so you could make a little money. She would show you how!"

"Oh yes!" laughed Sau-Ha. "Mei-Kuen never let any customer in Hong Kong escape. She was a legend!"

"And soon I will see our village again," said Sau-Ping. "I will see the maiden house, if it is still standing."

Sau-Ha nodded thoughtfully, almost sadly, and did not speak.

After three days in Hong Kong, Sau-Ping and Pauline got their visas and were ready to take the six-hour ferry trip to Saam-Fau in Hoi-Ping County. From there they climbed into the back of a truck to travel to the Overseas Chinese Hotel in Toi-Shaan City.

Every mile astonished Pauline, who had brought her camera. Sau-Ping, who was quick to notice how things had changed, was also amazed. The moment they climbed out of the truck in front of the hotel and began to drag down their luggage, Pauline touched her mother's arm and pointed. There was a wedding banquet at the hotel. The bride and the groom had arrived in a van decorated with pom-poms. Sau-Ping found herself translating the sights for her foreign-born daughter. When an old lady opened up a red umbrella over the bride as she descended from the van, Sau-Ping whispered, "To shield the bride from wandering spirits." Then she stared. The bride was wearing a Western-style wedding gown – and it was pink! "I have never seen a pink wedding gown for a bride," Sau-Ping said quickly to her daughter.

"I guess it's a compromise. Not Western white, not Chinese red," said Pauline.

"No red veil over her face, no sedan chair, no wailing songs," whispered Sau-Ping.

"People invent new ways," her daughter replied.

After making sure that their luggage was properly delivered and their room prepared, Sau-Ping and Pauline descended to the dining-hall, where they sat in a corner that had been screened off from the wedding celebration. Fifty tables of guests filled the rest of the grand hall.

It was a noisy party, with loud traditional Cantonese music that alternated with strange hybrid sounds. "The kids of my clients from Hong Kong love that. It's called 'Canto-Pop,'" said Pauline. The waitress told Sau-Ping and Pauline that the groom was a very rich Gold Mountain guest from Los Angeles. He had paid the bride's family us$2,000 as a bride price!

Sau-Ping enjoyed talking to the waitress. She had not heard such a beautiful Toi-Shaanese accent in Vancouver since the early 1970s.

Dinner was good too. Sau-Ping thought it was better than anything she had eaten in Vancouver's Chinese restaurants. She loved the Toi-Shaan tea and the local dishes she had once heard village men describe when she was young. Here in her bowl, after so many years, were all the delicacies she'd never had the chance to taste before. In her day, no decent women would dine out in public, particularly in the company of men. Even though Sau-Ping had been rich enough to live in a *yeung-lau* in Sai-Fok village after her marriage, she had never once dined out in a restaurant.

Returning to their room after dinner, Sau-Ping and Pauline passed the open door of a large hotel suite and then found themselves walking alongside a queue of teenage girls who were waiting in the hallway. "What is this, a modelling contest?" Pauline whispered. All the girls were nicely dressed, and each held a package of seasonal fruits as a gift. "I don't know," Sau-Ping replied. The whole thing looked strange to her. "But I will ask."

What a pleasure it was to be able to speak effortlessly to clerks, maids, waitresses, and even people passing in the hall! When the maid arrived in their room to deliver two thermos bottles of hot water, Sau-Ping asked her what the young women were lining up for. The maid replied that it was the day for the interview.

"What interview?"

"A Gold Mountain guest came back from the United States to choose a Toi-Shaanese girl as his bride. His mother wrote her former acquaintances, and the word spread. These young women have all come to try their luck."

Pauline understood. "This is a bride contest!" she sputtered.

"They have come to try their luck," the maid repeated, "to marry the Gold Mountain guest. They have to look good, and their birth dates also have to match that of this Gold Mountain guest. His mother paid to have a Daoist priest in the room to look at the birth dates of those girls who are lucky enough to meet the approval of the man."

Pauline dropped into a chair and folded her hands in her lap. Sau-Ping guessed that she was waiting for the maid to leave the room so that she could exclaim over the injustice of the situation outside, where girls were displayed like vegetables for sale. But to her surprise Pauline kept quiet, even after the maid had gone. The two women rinsed their faces and hands and drank tea made from the hot water in the thermoses. Sau-Ping realized that her daughter was trying hard to perceive and understand China; she did not wish to make easy judgements.

The next morning, Sau-Ping and Pauline rented a van with a driver to take them from Toi-Shaan City to a guesthouse in Shaan-Tai Market. Surveying the market from the moving van, Sau-Ping barely recognized it. There were new shops, general stores, and small factories. The clothing pedlars were selling Hong Kong fashions and accessories of all descriptions and colours. At the edge of the market, across from a new four-lane highway, was a building with several wings. At the front of this complex was a huge track-and-field stadium surrounded by high walls. The driver told Sau-Ping and Pauline that this was the renovated Tuen-Fan Junior High School financed by donations from "patriotic Overseas Chinese" from North America and Hong Kong. Sau-Ping was filled with wonder. She asked a hundred questions, and the experienced driver patiently answered. When they arrived at the guesthouse, the driver waited outside while they checked into their room. Then they asked to be taken to Sai-Fok.

After travelling for ten minutes or so, Sau-Ping recognized the paddy-fields she and her mother-in-law used to work on. She cried for the driver to stop as she pulled open the great door of the van and stuck her head outside. Looking at the paddy land was like staring hard into the palm of her own hand. The familiar shapes and rows were virtually part of her body. Yet the land smelled different – there was no scent of manure. Back in the van she asked the driver about the manure, and he replied, "Oh, fertilizer comes in bags now, in powders."

In the next moment, the van was crossing near Sai-Fok River, where Sau-Ping spotted a new stone bridge that had replaced the wooden plank she used to cross when heading home after a hard day of farm chores.

The driver slowed down and parked. "This is Sai-Fok village. Should I wait for you here?"

"This is Sai-Fok?!"

Sau-Ping stared around, trying to get her bearings. She could not find the village path leading to the *tiu-lau*. Instead, the van had travelled on a broad paved road and parked right in front of the *tiu-lau*! An imposing village gate rose up before her.

Sau-Ping and Pauline descended from the van and stood in the shadow of the gate. Pauline murmured, "This is where you lived," and Sau-Ping nodded agreement, though she could almost imagine that the driver had played a joke on them and dropped her off at the wrong village. None of the houses inside the gate fit with the landscape she held in her memory. In place of the low-lying baked-mud homes there now stood tall buildings of three and four storeys whose outer walls were decorated in multicoloured ceramic tiles, with verandahs extending handsomely from the doors.

But this had to be the right place. The line of mountains had not changed. From her few years of language classes, Pauline could read the Chinese calligraphy boldly written at the village gate. A little dazed, Sau-Ping said, "We will walk in." They paid the van driver his return fare, as dictated by custom here, and turned to face Sai-Fok.

A man stood in the road before them. He did not move. Sau-Ping walked forward. Kin-Pong had written her brother-in-law, Yik-Mo, to tell him that she planned to visit, and in the letter three possible dates for her arrival had been mentioned. Could he have been waiting at the gate for hours each of those three days?

She held up her hand. The man nodded. He was much skinnier and more bent than she would have imagined, and his hips were set at an odd angle. His hair was white as lamb's fleece. Lightly she touched his arm. "How long have you been standing here?"

"Not long," he said. "I have time. I did not want you to be lost on your return."

The man limped towards Pauline, and Sau-Ping realized that his left leg was shorter than the right. She guessed he had been injured in the labour camp. She said, "Pauline, this is your father's younger brother. You should address him as Yik-Mo *Shuk Shuk.*"

"It is good to meet you, Uncle," said Pauline carefully in Toi-Shaanese.

"It is good to see you and to see your mother," said Yik-Mo. "I will lead you through our village. And then you will come to my home. There is one man who wishes to see you," he said, turning to Sau-Ping. "Uncle Siu Kong, the retired brigade party secretary."

Sau-Ping looked into the face of Yik-Mo, a face that had once been an intimate part of her life, but she discerned no shiver of distaste or hatred.

Yik-Mo returned her gaze directly.

"You speak to him now? You ...?"

"I think he was not a bad man."

"I'll meet with him then."

"He also wishes to show you around the village to tell you about the improvements. And he wishes to apologize as a representative of the Communist Party for persecuting Overseas Chinese families."

Sau-Ping nodded. She could never have explained to her daughter or even to Yik-Man himself how fully, in that moment, she felt the impenetrable wall of years that separated this day from the day she had gripped a little piece of field dirt in her hand and fled Sai-Fok with her children. The man before her was no longer an intimate. Their years of companionship were gone. She would honour this brother-in-law for his courage – a courage she recalled distinctly as she recalled the heft and scent of that dirt – but she would never be able to tell him anything much about the life she had lived and the lessons she had learned since her departure. And he would never truly describe his years in the labour camp and his equally hard life after his release. That story was done. He had lived in this village all his life.

Sau-Ping followed Yik-Mo around the side of the *tiu-lau*. They talked about details and architecture. Sau-Ping noticed that the tall iron gate was gone. Yik-Mo explained that space inside the *tiu-lau* was now used for storing miscellaneous items ranging from industrial waste to large farm tools to hay. Sau-Ping explained to her daughter that formerly each *tiu-lau* had acted as a defence tower. The villagers used to keep weapons stored there in case of attack by bandits or peasants from rival lineages. "No more bandits?" she asked her brother-in-law.

"No. We've had peace," he said plainly.

They walked towards the paddy-fields. Sau-Ping noticed that the bamboo grove surrounding the village had not grown back since the Communists had sheared it away, but other growth had healed the scars. It was harvest time. Under the blue sky the paddy-field looked like a sea of moving gold when the gentle breeze blew on the ripening rice. Sau-Ping noticed that her daughter hadn't complained at all about the hot, sultry weather in the countryside the way she had complained in Hong Kong. She was enthralled by the scenery.

Farm women cutting the rice shoots wore broad-brimmed sunhats, colourful tops, and rolled up pants.

"Are there always only women in the fields, or only in some seasons? When do the men help?" asked Pauline in Toi-Shaanese.

Sau-Ping said, "The women farm."

But Yik-Mo raised his hand and nearly smiled. His eyes brightened for a second. "Your mother doesn't know," he said. "During the period of the communes, men and women both did the farming. There were men's groups and women's groups, each with a separate farm chore. I have been in the paddies – with these feet!" His eyes truly sparkled, and for a moment Sau-Ping felt that they might become friends again. "But for six or seven years now, most of the farming has been done by mature women. Young girls are employed in village enterprises, or they might help their mothers runs a small business from the home. The men are no longer doing full-time farming, although they might help during harvest time. They move into off-farm employment outside the village. Some operate repair shops in Shaan-Tai Market. Others go to work in Toi-Shaan City. Still others are moving around in teams to do construction or transportation work. Since married women have to stay home to take care of the children and the men's parents, they naturally do most of the farming. The few men who stay permanently in the village work the buffalo or the hand-tractor. They do the ploughing for the village women for a fee."

The trio moved closer to the paddy-fields. Pauline was busily snapping pictures. She asked her mother discreetly, "Could I go in among them?"

"You cannot step on the rice."

"What's that thing?" Pauline pointed to a device that a woman was pushing between the rows of rice. It looked like a metal baby buggy.

Sau-Ping had noticed the contraption earlier – there were a number of them dotted throughout the fields. "I don't know. Brother-in-Law, what is that?"

"A husking machine. Driven with the legs. Now the women no longer strain their backs beating the rice bushes against a bamboo stand to remove the kernels from the husks. You step on the leg pedal like you would with a sewing machine and that turns the cutter."

Pauline moved along the edge of the field, zooming in for a close-up of the funny husking device. The women at work glanced at her, then returned to their labours. Sau-Ping felt as if she were standing at the edge of an enormous painted picture – it was odd not to move forward into the field with a cutting blade of her own. Her eyes swept from one detail to the next. She saw bicycles toppled in the grass near the fields, one of them already piled high with dry grass and rice stalks for fuel. So women no longer carried their burdens on long bamboo poles – they slipped along on wheeled machines! She also noticed a small group of farm women resting in the shade, enjoying soft drinks, popsicles, and ice-cream. Next to them, the frozen desserts pedlar leaned against his bicycle. Pauline had already spotted this group. She moved towards them cautiously, as if afraid they would rise and take flight like sparrows. As Sau-Ping watched, one woman's popsicle tumbled off the stick. Her friends laughed, and she laughed with them. She picked up the bit of coloured ice and tossed it behind her.

"Ah," said Yik-Mo. "Here is Uncle Siu Kong."

Sau-Ping turned to face the man whom years earlier she had feared more than any other man in her life. He also looked thin and grey but somehow not so weathered as her brother-in-law, Yik-Mo. Greetings were cordial. Siu Kong began immediately by apologizing for the persecution of Overseas Chinese families. Sau-Ping nodded, thanking him, though in the back of her mind she kept a little suspicion alive: what did the Chinese leaders want from the Overseas Chinese now that would prompt them to offer apologies?

Siu Kong pointed out all the modern innovations that Sau-Ping and Pauline had already noticed, then told Sau-Ping the women now had access to running water. It was no longer necessary for them to tote buckets of water on their shoulders. Realizing that here was a man who enjoyed speaking like a teacher, Pauline began asking questions about village life. In her childhood, she had heard about the maiden house and the wonderful festivals from her mother. Had any of those cultural traditions survived the Cultural Revolution? she asked.

Siu Kong served up information generously. Young women and men were no longer segregated into maiden houses and boys' houses; they could speak to one another and choose their partners, but in fact many were still shy. They relied on "introducers," he said.

Sau-Ping glanced at Yik-Mo. He stood easily, listening to his old tormenter, and when they began to walk towards the old ancestral halls, he followed.

Sau-Ping spoke up. "Do the village maidens nowadays sing to beg for embroidery and weaving skills from the Weaver Star?"

Yik-Mo said, "Ready-made clothes now. Not much need for home weaving or embroidery."

"Many of the old superstitions have not been revived," declared Siu Kong firmly. "Prayers to the Weaver Star, they are part of feudal superstition. The same is true of the Hungry Ghost Festival. Hanging old clothes on trees and placing bowls of rice outside the village to feed the hungry ghosts, that is superstition."

Sau-Ping nodded silently, recalling how Siu Kong had once knelt and offered his own bowls of rice to feed his hungry ancestors. He had prayed fervently for revenge against the Leung lineage. Somehow she doubted whether even now this retired brigade party secretary was as free from "superstitions" as he claimed.

Sau-Ping now stopped at the big banyan tree that shaded the main ancestral hall. For years she had thought of this tree when she was troubled by the dispersal of her family and used it to reassure herself that drooping branches would root again in new ground. Now she placed her hand on the strong trunk, saying to her daughter, "This is the place where your father kicked the door of my sedan chair when I was a new bride."

Pauline stared at the ancestral hall in the middle of the village. With her limited vocabulary she read the words, "Leung Lineage Main Ancestral Hall," and pointed them out to her mother. They had been newly repainted above the entrance to the building. Pauline asked if she could look inside.

Siu Kong opened the door to let the group in. A loud chugging noise and the overpowering smell of green plants greeted them. For a moment Sau-Ping felt frightened. When she lived in Sai-Fok, women had been strictly forbidden to enter this place. She remembered that in the olden days, before the Spring and Autumn Rites, Siu Kong was ordered by Uncle Leung Kwok-Yung, the lineage chief, to clean all the ancestral tablets in this hall. At the end of the ritual ceremony, Siu Kong was also told to chop up and distribute the ritual meat for the male members of the Leung lineage. And Siu Kong, the *sai-tsai* who lacked the necessary means to marry for himself, had been one of the men assigned to carry her own sedan chair when she arrived as a bride. His life had been scarred by humiliations. Eventually the body of the lineage chief, Leung Kwok-Yung, lay in the dust, smeared with blood, as payment for these humiliations ... among others. Eventually she herself had been forced to run towards the sea with her children as payment for these humiliations.

Sau-Ping tried to shake these thoughts out of her head. She wondered if her brother-in-law ever crouched over his terrible memories anymore and tried to make sense of them. Sau-Ping's eyes swept through the interior of the Leung ancestral hall. This male sanctuary had lost its traditional splendour. She had imagined an imposing altar and a heavy display of ancestral tablets; instead she saw great piles of sticks tied together and men working strange cutting machines. The ancestral hall had become a bamboo factory.

Pauline looked at the political slogans on the inside walls of the main ancestral hall, which were partially blurred by several layers of paint. Still, she could recognize the characters that said, "In Agriculture, Learn from Dazhai!" and "Never Forget Class Struggle!" She read them quietly to her mother, commenting that Jeff's books about Maoist China had listed these slogans.

Chop, chop, chop, Sau-Ping thought to herself, as she tried to remain cheerful and polite throughout the tour. Chop, chop chop, bamboo stems were cut to regulation size. Chop, chop, chop, men were cut to regulation size. Sau-Ping had noticed that her daughter was careful in selecting the questions she posed to the retired brigade party secretary. He was not truly frightening, but both women sensed that the wrong question might make him freeze, and this might pain their relative, Yik-Mo.

The group returned outdoors, shutting the sound and smell of the factory behind them. Sau-Ping noticed that the smaller ancestral hall in honour of the second branch of the Leung lineage was gone; it must have been torn down during the Cultural Revolution. Now the space was used to dry grain. Behind it stood a huge building with a playground in front. Siu Kong explained, "This new building was the old Sai-Fok school, previously funded by corporate property of the second branch of the Leung lineage. The new Sai-Fok school was completed three years ago. The money came from the Overseas Chinese. These donors insisted that a portrait of the founder of the second branch of the Leung lineage be installed in the school hall."

"Are there any ritual activities in the school then?" asked Sau-Ping directly. Siu Kong's little speech made it rather obvious why the Chinese government had decided to offer apologies and restitution to the Overseas Chinese. Money still flowed in the old directions.

He answered her without embarrassment. "Strictly speaking, ritual activities in honour of founding ancestors are considered feudal superstition and not allowed. But Overseas Chinese returning home for visits would be deeply disappointed if they could not pay homage to their lineage founders, so we do our best to accommodate their wishes. Since there is no corporate property to finance any ritual activities, the Overseas Chinese visitors pay for the ritual pork for ancestor worship during the Spring Festival."

"Is ritual pork still distributed to the village households after the ceremony? Do women have a share these days?" asked Sau-Ping.

"I am afraid old traditions cannot be easily changed." Siu Kong seemed reluctant to pursue the subject.

Pauline had intuited her mother's thoughts. She pointed to a building with a green-and-blue tiled roof that stood besides the Sai-Fok Primary School. Though built in the traditional style, it was obviously new. "Did the Overseas Chinese donate money for this building as well?"

"Yes," Siu Kong said. "This is a new community hall donated by the Overseas Chinese two years ago. It is used for occasional village feasts during the Spring Festival or Mid-Autumn Festival. Richer Overseas Chinese also hold parties here to celebrate weddings, sixty-ninth birthdays, births of sons, housewarmings, and so on."

Pauline noticed the hooks hanging from the ceiling and asked what they were for.

"They are for hanging colourful lanterns on the fifth day of the first lunar month."

"Uncle Siu Kong," asked Sau-Ping, "isn't this the same idea as the Lantern Festival? On the fifth day of every New Year holiday," she explained to Pauline, "whichever families had a son born, adopted, or purchased the previous year would hang lanterns from hooks on the ceiling of a makeshift hut, and the men would hold a village feast to celebrate the addition of new members to their lineage. When your brother Kin-Pong came into our family, we had a lantern. It was beautiful, with stars on it, I remember."

"But not for Big Sister Fei-Yin?" asked Pauline, knowing the answer.

Sau-Ping shook her head. Pauline's question reminded Sau-Ping that her own doubts about village customs would be more than matched by her Canadian daughter's. Though she had grown to appreciate her Chinese cultural heritage, Pauline was deeply disturbed by the traditional Chinese attitude towards women. Sau-Ping sighed. The world was a tangled place. She did not know the answers. She only knew that in Sai-Fok there had been life, and life continued. Celebrations, patience, vengeance, misery, joys, and torment were all known here.

"Here is the New Village section of Sai-Fok, as you remember," Siu Kong said.

What New Village? Sau-Ping could not tell where the Old Village ended and the New Village began, for in some cases the houses in the Old Village were much grander than the old *yeung-lau* in the New Village built by the Overseas Chinese in the late 1920s and early 1930s. She saw that a number of *yeung-lau* had been retrieved by their owners and beautifully renovated, but others were crumbling, stained, deserted. Many of the multicoloured glass windows were broken. The iron bars at the windows and the iron gates at the entrances to the private gardens were all gone.

Sau-Ping glanced at her brother-in-law. His face was expressionless. Perceiving an unspoken message in his silence, Sau-Ping guessed that all the iron decorating and protecting the *yeung-lau* of the New Village had been confiscated by the Communists and that some of the worst damage had been done by the Red Guards; their actions had been described to her years ago by Kin-Pong and Yik-Man, who heard such news from friends at the Chinese Benevolent Association.

Yik-Mo suddenly stopped. On her right Sau-Ping saw the outer wall of an old, battered *yeung-lau*. Slowly she realized that it was her old home, this ruin, the most beautiful home she had ever owned.

Siu Kong was saying, "I would like to apologize on behalf of the government for the damage done to your *yeung-lau*. It was a 'historical mistake!'"

Sau-Ping kept her mouth shut. She understood that this "historical mistake" would have to be repaired with more money from the Overseas Chinese. How much money over the years had her male relatives poured into this village, money stirred up out of hot woks and stained sinks, money grown from thousands of dirty dishes, money sent from Canada, where the work never ceased and a Chinese waiter swallowed white men's insults for lunch and dinner? Sweat and blood money.

"We are now returning this property to your family," said Siu Kong. "If nobody in your family is planning to retire here, the local government will guard your *yeung-lau* to prevent any future acts of vandalism. However, if you so desire, you can also ask Yik-Mo or his family members to take care of it for you."

Then he added, "Auntie Sau-Ping, I am very glad that in these few years many former villagers are returning to participate in the major festivals and to renovate their *yeung-lau*. Do you remember Mr Leung Yik-Kwong? He used to be your next-door neighbour in the New Village. He was one of the major donors behind the building of the new village community hall and the renovation of both the Sai-Fok Primary School and the Tuen-Fan Junior High School. Just last month, he, his wife Yi-Lin, and his daughter Chun-Fa came home to retrieve their *yeung-lau*. The work has begun."

Siu Kong swept his arm towards the *yeung-lau* that stood next to Sau-Ping's ruined house. Indeed, work had begun. Two of the walls looked cleanly washed and the broken tiles had been removed. Clean, square holes awaited new windows. Sau-Ping distinctly remembered those terrible nights when her family and Yik-Kwong's had feared speaking to one another lest they be accused of collusion or resistance.

Of course she remembered Leung Yik-Kwong's family! Fleeing terror, they had crowded together in the same boats that sailed from Kwong-Hoi to Hong Kong in May 1952. Yik-Kwong and his brother Yik-Nang had been so helpful to Sau-Ping's family during their three disastrous years in Shek Kip Mei. How could she not remember? Sau-Ping politely asked the retired brigade party secretary if he could give her Yik-Kwong's address in Hong Kong. He said he would be glad to help.

"Then there was Mr Leung Yik-Faat," Siu Kong continued "and his son, Kin-Tsoi. They both returned to visit Sai-Fok this January. Mr Leung Kin-Tsoi had lived in Vancouver for years. Did he look you up when he was there? He and his father are making big money in Hong Kong now. They are donating a lot to beautify the village. They plan to finance the building of a pavilion on the banks of Sai-Fok River in honour of their ancestor, the former lineage chief Mr Leung Kwok-Yung."

Sau-Ping froze. She thought about the woman, Sing-Fan, who had been beaten to death by Yik-Faat, and she thought of another woman, Ming, who had been battered by his son, Kin-Tsoi. But she said nothing. There was no use speaking about the crimes of the lineage chief Leung Kwok-Yung the swindler, his son Yik-Faat the snake, or Kin-Tsoi, Yik-Faat's tiger son. If Sai-Fok and the retired brigade party secretary, who had himself been repeatedly humiliated by the lineage chief's family, now wished to arrange a reconciliation in order to attract more Overseas Chinese riches, that was their business. It was a tainted business, though, and it almost made her question her own nostalgic wish to return to the village.

Sau-Ping glanced at her daughter. Pauline knew about Yik-Faat and Kin-Tsoi, and Sau-Ping could see the signs of rage in her trembling head and wide eyes.

There was silence.

"I have been very happy to show you our village, Auntie Sau-Ping and Miss Pauline," Siu Kong said. "I know you must wish to visit your relatives." He politely shook their hands and left.

The small, subdued family party headed towards Yik-Mo's house, the same house where Sau-Ping had lived as a bride. She was relieved to see that it was still a decent house. Yik-Mo introduced Sau-Ping and Pauline to his wife, Taai-Ngan, his daughter-in-law, Kam-Laan, his fifteen-year-old granddaughter, Ah Ying, and his nine-year-old grandson, Kei-Taan. He explained that his son, Kin-Chung, was at his meat store at Shaan-Tai Market and wouldn't be back until dark.

Sau-Ping gave a red packet to everyone in Yik-Mo's household. She produced several cans of salmon, packets of wheat crackers, short-bread, and Swiss candies for the family. She handed Yik-Mo a receipt for a colour television set with a proper stamp from the Chinese Customs at Saam-Fau Pier in Hoi-Ping County. Yik-Mo thanked her, obviously delighted with the gifts. He said he would send his son to Kwong-Chau as soon as possible to pick up the television set at the depot next door to the Overseas Chinese Hotel there. Sau-Ping laughed and spoke with her sister-in-law, whom she had never met. The woman was gracious and reserved. She had also lived through years of imprisonment in a labour camp, and there was a sadness in her eyes that never quite disappeared. The same was true for Yik-Mo. Sau-Ping hoped that her relatives would not think she had returned to the village to flaunt her wealth.

Pauline touched her mother's arm and pointed to the ancestral altar in the loft. The sight of the tablets comforted Sau-Ping. She saw that Yik-Mo's daughter-in-law had already prepared everything for the family worship. "Yik-Mo," she said. "I am glad that you have done this for us. I hope it does not endanger you."

"No, no. People in our village no longer have to be so secretive about worshipping their ancestors at home."

His wife spoke, surprising Sau-Ping with her torrent of words. "When Chairman Mao was in power, our neighbours would stop paying homage to their ancestors whenever a Work Team or a group of Red Guards were in the village conducting an anti-feudal campaign. The worst was during the Cultural Revolution, when several groups of Red Guards came around searching for ancestral tablets in every villager's home and destroying what they found. Many of our neighbours hid their ancestral tablets. As soon as the Red Guards were gone, my neighbours would put the tablets back in the loft and start to worship again. We watched. It was like playing hide and seek! But we didn't dare to play."

"Yes, we had great fun," said Yik-Mo sardonically.

Sau-Ping said, "But now the tablets can be prominently displayed at home?"

"Our county government allows it, yes. Old tablets have been repainted. New tablets have been made. Some use photographs of their ancestors. We ... we waited. We were among the last to dig up the tablets we had hidden. It was like harvest time."

Pauline spoke feelingly. "Why? Why were you the last, Yik-Mo *Shuk Shuk*?"

"I had all the tablets restored and the altar repainted in 1984. Since we were designated as landlord class, I had to be more careful." He then turned and spoke to Sau-Ping, "You'll find that the tablets for Father and Mother, Paternal Uncle Kwok-Ko, and Big Brother Yik-Man have been placed in the altar."

"You have done something that makes me feel I have not lost my home," Sau-Ping said. "Thank you." Unable to say anymore, she took the incense sticks handed to her by Yik-Mo's daughter-in-law. Pauline and Sau-Ping lit incense and kowtowed in front of the ancestral altar. They then poured wine in the small cups in front of the ancestral tablets and burned ritual money folded in the form of gold and silver ingots.

After the family ritual, everyone sat around the old eight-cornered table that had been miraculously retrieved after the Cultural Revolution. Though Sau-Ping tried her best to hide her thoughts, they dwelt on the last few times she had seen Yik-Mo before she fled to Hong Kong. In 1952 she had watched him kneeling on sharp stones on the stage at the struggle meeting. The Village Militia had slapped him repeatedly for daring to say that the Communist party had been unfair to the Overseas Chinese families. Sau-Ping had visited Yik-Mo in a makeshift jail before he was herded off to the hard labour camp. He had been young then.

But she lacked the courage to ask him about the years that had followed his arrest. She did not want to pry into the memories of this man who had lived for decades in a world so different from hers.

It was Pauline, the irrepressible Chinese-Canadian woman, who spoke. "Yik-Mo *Shuk Shuk*, my husband in Vancouver has studied the Chinese Revolution a little. You were in one of the hard-labour camps?"

"Yes."

"I would like to hear about it, if you do not find it too painful."

Sau-Ping glanced up carefully. She saw Yik-Mo take a breath and look at the ceiling. For a time he did not speak. His wife kept her eyes lowered.

Then: "It was difficult at the camp," he said. "I met Taai-Ngan there. She was also being punished because her father was labelled a counter-revolutionary. There was not enough food, and we were very cold in winter. It was difficult and if you became ill the guards just let you die. They liked a big cemetery. It was like a vegetable garden for them. We did not die. After five years of hard labour, we were sent back to Sai-Fok where we were to perform 'hard labour under supervision.' We were often given heavy assignments that made it impossible to sleep, our backs and arms ached so badly, and then we were told to donate our earnings to the production team. Every time there was some kind of political campaign, I and other 'bad types' in

Sai-Fok were dragged on stage to be beaten up. They made us wear wooden plaques and paraded us up and down the village paths. Fellow villagers would throw stones, pig shit, and cow dung at us. I was beaten so badly that my left leg was broken. I heard it crack, like a dry branch. It did not heal well, and now it is shorter than my right leg."

Sau-Ping could not watch her brother-in-law and listen to him simultaneously; the story was too painful to absorb through eyes and ears. She covered her eyes with her hands and listened.

"Then suddenly, one day in 1979, Uncle Siu Kong, who was then the Party secretary, called all the 'bad types' to his office. He poured tea for every one of us and apologized for the 'mistakes' of the Party. Then everything was to be forgiven."

Pauline cried out, "Just like that?"

"Little Niece, you don't know how it was. The world was turned upside down every four or five years. Even Uncle Siu Kong had his ups and downs. He had to go through criticism and self-criticism sessions every time the political wind changed. Now you know why he has become so polite."

Sau-Ping uncovered her face. "Yik-Mo, where is Wai-Fong, my bosom friend from Fung-Yeung village who married Leung Yik-Hung? Do you remember her?"

"Sister-in-law, of course I remember. Yik-Hung was the chair of the Peasants' Association when you escaped to Hong Kong."

"Yes," Sau-Ping responded, "and it was Wai-Fong who overheard the discussion at the Peasants' Association. She came to the *yeung-lau* to tell me of their decision to change our label to Overseas Chinese landlord class. I would like to see Wai-Fong again."

Yik-Mo shook his head. "They both died. I can show you where she is buried. Yik-Hung was beaten severely during the Cultural Revolution because they said he had Overseas Chinese connections."

"What? He was a poor man! Her house was like a pig's shelter."

"Yes, and our village is an Overseas Chinese homeland. You listened to Uncle Siu Kong, you must understand how the village continues to suck the blood of the Overseas Chinese. Most of us have some relatives abroad. Yik-Hung's father was a Malaysian Chinese, but he abandoned Yik-Hung and his mother when Yik-Hung was twelve. Yik-Hung was dirt poor even before 1949, you are right. That was why, in the early 1950s, he was chosen by the Work Team to chair the Peasants' Association in Sai-Fok. But during the 1968 campaign called 'Cleansing of Class Ranks' his political opponent started to dig for dirt. Yik-Hung was designated a foreign spy because of his father. He was beaten so badly that he soon died. Wai-Fong hanged herself."

Sau-Ping's tears began to fall. Sorrow surged in.

"There were so many tragedies during the Cultural Revolution, Sister-in-Law," Yik-Mo said. "Do you remember Leung Ting-Ting? She was the daughter-in-law of Auntie Leung Siu-Hing. You saw her wedding ceremony, when the groom was represented by the cock – remember? But Auntie Leung Siu-Hing's son abandoned his wife and never sent remittances. He never came back from the United States. I don't believe the bride laid eyes on her husband even once. I tell you, I remember the day the cock died, she was the one who chopped off its head. But she was accused of having Overseas Chinese connections because of her husband. She jumped into the Sai-Fok River."

Pauline cried out, "Why is it that when the powers change, women suffer much more than men? This woman Leung Ting-Ting didn't ask to be married to the Gold Mountain guest."

"But Little Niece," replied Yik-Mo calmly, "it is *good* to be married to a Gold Mountain guest. Look, your mother married my brother, a Gold Mountain guest, and now you people are living so well in Vancouver."

Sau-Ping noticed her sister-in-law touch Yik-Mo's hand. The two exchanged glances.

Yik-Mo sighed. He turned his attention from Pauline to Sau-Ping. Their eyes met. Yik-Mo said, "In fact, I would like you and your family to help me find a Gold Mountain guest to marry my granddaughter, Ah Ying. You have lived in Vancouver's Chinatown for such a long time, you must know some unattached Chinese man looking for a wife?"

Sau-Ping felt an enormous, shocked silence engulf Pauline. And she discovered that she herself had been caught off-guard by Yik-Mo's request. But it took only a moment for her to adjust and understand. Of course: for Sai-Fok villagers, the Gold Mountain remained a shining, much-coveted goal. She said, "Most of the unmarried young men I know are local-born Chinese, Yik-Mo. Few can understand the Toi-Shaanese language or culture."

"But we don't care as long as they are willing to marry Ah Ying. We don't even mind if Ah Ying marries a foreign devil. Pauline, you married a white guy, and see how blessed you are!"

Pauline nodded politely but could not speak. Sau-Ping understood that her daughter had grown fond of her uncle in a few short hours, and she had been moved by his tales of persecution. But his offer to barter off his granddaughter shocked her. The complications were too harsh for a Chinese-Canadian to swallow.

Yik-Mo continued. "What about new immigrants in Vancouver? Do you know any who might be interested?"

Sau-Ping replied, "Well, the rich Hong Kong immigrants probably won't be interested in marrying village girls in Toi-Shaan. Only those who cannot speak English and are employed in low-skill and low-status jobs might consider coming home to look for a wife. This is because their chances of marrying local Canadian women are very slim. But life for village girls in Vancouver isn't easy. They often don't have a community to help them. They can be lonesome."

"But there is a chance?" Yik-Mo demanded.

"We don't care how old the man is," added his wife.

"As long as he is willing," said Yik-Mo. "I know a villager who married his daughter to a sixty-four-year-old Gold Mountain guest. If you find any widower in Vancouver looking for a young second wife, you can also show him Ah Ying's photo."

Pauline's voice cut the air. "Ah Ying has just turned fifteen. How can you think of marrying her off to a sixty- or seventy-year-old man she doesn't know?"

"We want her to go to the Gold Mountain."

"Why?"

"Women have no future here at home doing farm chores."

"Can't they find jobs as shopkeepers or factory girls in Shaan-Tai Market or Toi-Shaan City?" asked Pauline. "Haven't some barriers to women been broken by the revolution and the reforms?"

"If they are lucky enough to find employment, they can. However, most village girls are not very well educated, so it is easier for them to marry a Gold Mountain guest."

Yik-Mo continued. "I missed my chance to go to the Gold Mountain because of the Communist revolution. I do not wish to see my descendants miss theirs. With the new immigration laws, if Ah Ying marries a Gold Mountain guest, she could sponsor her own parents to go to Canada to retire when they reach sixty-five. Then my son and his wife can sponsor Ah Ying's younger brother, Kei-Taan, as the last member of the family."

Sau-Ping felt weary. She wished to shield her daughter from too many more dangerous surprises. "We will do our best to help, Yik-Mo," she said. Soon after, Yik-Mo paid two fellow villagers who had motorcycles to take the women back to their guesthouse at Shaan-Tai Market for the night.

The following morning, Sau-Ping and Pauline went with Yik-Mo to sweep Leung Tsing-Haan's grave, which he had already cleared and tidied. In the evening, the two visitors hosted a dinner party at the *tang-liu* for the villagers. Sau-Ping and Pauline sat with the women, and Yik-Mo sat with the men. During the feast almost every woman, including Siu Kong's wife and daughter-in-law, advanced to make the same request of Sau-Ping and Pauline: Please find a husband in the Gold Mountain for the young woman in their home.

By the end of the party, Pauline and Sau-Ping had a whole pack of young women's photographs in their possession, so many that they had to carry them in a cardboard box so as not to drop any of them. The load of pictures – a confusion of pretty young faces all askew – reminded Sau-Ping of the forty young women's photographs she had received from Hong Kong when she had decided to help Kin-Pong find a wife. This method was not alien to her. But it continued to shock her daughter. Pauline spoke less and less over the next few days and took fewer pictures.

After two days of visits in Sai-Fok, Sau-Ping and Pauline were ready to set out for Sau-Ping's natal village of Fung-Yeung. Before they left, Sau-Ping told Yik-Mo that she would arrange to have the bones of Yik-Man, *Loye*, and Uncle Kwok-Ko transported back. He said he would see that they were properly buried. Pauline muttered, "Send live girls to Vancouver and dead bones to China. What an exchange." Sau-Ping quietly told her to hush.

Sau-Ping left money to pay for the renovation of the *yeung-lau*. Next time, she told Yik-Mo, visiting members of the Vancouver branch of the family might be able to enjoy the village house instead of staying in a guesthouse. She offered Yik-Mo's family the use of the renovated building.

Sau-Ping and Pauline spent their time in Fung-Yeung talking to Sau-Ping's younger brother, Tin-Shaang, and his family, to whom they also delivered a receipt for a colour television set. Tin-Shaang took Sau-Ping and Pauline to sweep the grave of the Wong ancestors. As they had in Sai-Fok, the two visitors gave a party for the villagers of Fung-Yeung and again came away with a cardboard box full of photographs of village girls.

Finally Pauline and Sau-Ping took the bus from Shaan-Tai Market to Toi-Shaan City, where they rented a van to take them to Saam-Fau Pier in Hoi-Ping County. They were ready to leave China.

For the first few hours of the six-hour boat trip from Saam-Fau to Hong Kong, Pauline said very little. Sitting in their assigned spot, the two women drank tea and ate soya sauce chicken with rice from lunchboxes. Rather than watch a Hong Kong film on the boat's TV screen, they went out on deck at the stern of the boat, where the men were smoking. They talked about Jeff and Emily and about the gifts they had bought for the family in Vancouver, gifts that were waiting in the huge suitcase in Sau-Ha's Hong Kong apartment. The boxes of girls' photographs were stuffed in their luggage on board ship.

A great bird flew over the deck. Pauline shaded her eyes to look at it. She said, "Is he trying to leave China too?"

Sau-Ping replied, "During the years when I lived in China and your father lived in Vancouver, I often imagined myself transforming into a bird."

Pauline sighed. "Mother, I'm puzzled. I am trying to be fair, I'm trying not to judge people whose lives have been so hard. But tell me this: why do people in Sai-Fok or Fung-Yeung still want to leave? From what I gathered, the government's policies have given the Toi-Shaan economy a big boost. People can worship their ancestors. They can choose their own occupations; even farming seems easier. Toi-Shaan City and Shan-Taai Market looked prosperous to me. The peasants in Sai-Fok and Fung-Yeung are getting rich – look at some of those houses! Judging from what you've told me about your past, their standard of living is probably much higher than it's ever been."

Sau-Ping listened silently to her daughter's argument. Pauline resumed. "There's political stability, it seems to me – no more bandit attacks or lineage feuds or warlords and soldiers roaming around, or cruel Japanese invaders, or Red Guards. The schools and other public buildings look wonderful thanks to all these donations from the Overseas Chinese. And every Overseas Chinese wants to visit home – just like you! So why do the Toi-Shaanese want to give it all up and leave their native communities to wash greasy dishes in Canada or the United States? The girls would have no outside contact because they can't speak English, and if they're married to strangers who are only looking for submissive women to serve them, they'll probably be abused. Cold climate. Second-class citizenship, even now. Language difficulties. Do they really think that North America is covered with gold?! Can't someone tell them it's not!"

Pauline's voice had risen in pitch as she argued against an invisible opponent. Sau-Ping said simply, "There is more money in Canada."

"And what about Ah Ying or other young women in Toi-Shaan? They must be better educated than you were, and according to Jeff, Chairman Mao at least preached in favour of women's equality and freedom of choice in marriage. Isn't that right? So don't they feel at all resentful that a member of the senior generation is openly arranging a blind marriage for them at the tender age of fifteen? How do they feel when they are being used as a means to obtain remittances or high-quality foreign goods for their parents and their brothers? How do they feel when they are used as a bridge to get the male members of their household to Gold Mountain?"

Pauline's face was drenched with tears, as if she'd been standing in the spray of the great ship. "Can you imagine putting yourself in Ah Ying's shoes, Mom?"

"Yes," said Sau-Ping.

Glossary of Terms

Ancestral altar – A sacred place at home for domestic worship of ancestors

Ancestral hall – An imposing building in a village that serves as a ritual focus for a lineage. Here, patrilineally related villagers pay homage to the founder of the lineage and all the subsequent illustrious ancestors.

Ancestral tablet – An object of ancestor worship. Each is a small rectangular wooden board with the names of an ancestor or ancestors written on it representing the soul(s) of the departed.

Bare sticks – Men too poor to marry, who therefore had no chance to produce male descendants to continue their family line.

Blood debt – Criminal acts causing the death of innocents.

Boys' house – A house used as segregated sleeping quarters for a group of young men (usually about nine or ten of them). In Toi-Shaan County, the purpose was to provide night-time privacy from the female members of their own households from the time they turned thirteen to the time of their marriage. These young men returned home in the daytime.

Canto-pop – Popular songs that originated in Hong Kong featuring a combination of Cantonese and English lyrics.

Catties, or *kan* (*jin*) – A unit of weight, about half a kilogram.

Chinese Immigration (Exclusion) Act – A Canadian government act passed on 1 July 1923, excluding all Chinese from entering Canada. It was not revoked until May 1947.

Ching-Ming (Qingming) – Grave-sweeping festival for honouring ancestors.

Chue-shi (zhushi) – Pig shit.

Corporate property – Land belonging to the ancestral hall. It is managed by lineage leaders on behalf of the male members.

Generation name – The same middle character in a name, used as a generation marker for all males from the same lineage in the same generation.

Gold Mountain guests (*kam-shaan haak* or *jinshanke*) – Overseas Chinese who sojourned at one point or another in either the United States or Canada. This term originally means an Overseas Chinese who came to California or British Columbia in the 1850s and 1860s to prospect for gold.

Grass widow – A married woman whose husband lives elsewhere permanently.

Kwai-mooi (guimei) – A young Caucasian woman, literally "foreign devil maiden."

Hat-Haau (Qiqiao) – A festival that takes place on the seventh day of the seventh lunar month, celebrating the legendary reunion of the Weaver and the Cowherd in the Milky Way.

Head tax – A tax that was collected from every Chinese entering Canada between 1885 and 1923. It increased from fifty dollars in 1885 to one hundred dollars in 1900, and then to five hundred dollars in 1903.

Heung (Xiang) – An administrative village.

Hungry ghosts – Spirits that had no male descendants to worship them after death. They wandered around looking for food, clothing, and other comforts to sustain their ghostly existence.

Koon-Yam (Guan Yin) – Goddess of Mercy.

Kung-hei faat-tsoi (*gongxi facai*) – A New Year's greeting. Literally: may you be prosperous.

Kwaan-Kung (Guan Gong) – God of Loyalty.

Lineage – A group of villagers with the same surname and related to one another along patrilineal lines, tracing their genealogical connections to the same focal male ancestor.

Loye (*laoye*) – Father-in-law in Toi-Shaanese dialect. Literally, master of the house.

Maiden house – A house used as segregated sleeping quarters for a group of young women (usually about nine or ten of them). In Toi-Shaan County, the purpose was to provide night-time privacy from the male members of their own households from the time they turned thirteen to the time of their marriage. These young women returned home to help with farm and domestic chores in the daytime. In silk production areas of South China such as Shun-Tak County, maiden houses sometimes became centres for marriage resistance.

Mau (*mu*) – A unit of area, 0.067 hectares.

Mid-autumn Festival – A festival that falls on the fifteenth day of the eight lunar month when the moon is at its roundest and brightest of the year. It is usually the time for family reunions.

New Village – The section of a village in which the houses are mostly *yeung-lau* (foreign-style mansions) financed by Overseas Chinese money.

Old Village – The section of the village made up of old-style one-storey buildings made of inferior building material.

On-yan (*anren*) – Referring to one's mother-in-law in Toi-Shaanese dialect. Literally, the comfortable one.

Overseas Chinese – An ethnic Chinese living outside of China.

Pa (*ba*) – Referring to one's father in Toi-Shaanese dialect.

Paper son – A male immigrant entering the country pretending to be the son of a citizen.

Po-cheung (baozhang) – A government-appointed village head whose function is to spy on villagers and to enforce government directives.

Po-kaap (baojia) – A system of village control in China.

Poh (po) – Referring to one's maternal grandmother in Toi-Shaanese dialect.

Red packet of lucky money – Money put into a small red envelope either to bribe someone, or as a gift during Chinese New Year or family celebrations.

Ritual pork – Roasted pork that had been placed on the ancestral altar during ancestral worship and was subsequently distributed to male lineage members.

Saam-Yap (Sanyi) – Three Counties: Naam-Hoi (Nanhai), Poon-Yue (Panyu), and Shun-Tak (Shunde) in Kwong-Tung (Guangdong) Province. These counties are the place of origin for a large number of North American Chinese.

Sai-tsai (xizai) – A bondservant for the lineage.

Shuk-Shuk (shushu) – The term for addressing father's younger brother in Toi-Shaanese dialect.

Snakehead – Someone who smuggles people out of the country.

Spring and Autumn Rites – Rituals performed during Spring and Autumn by lineage members in an ancestral hall.

Struggle meeting – A mass meeting conducted by Chinese Communist Party representatives in which offenders were often beaten in public and made to confess.

Sz-Yap (Siyi) – Four Counties: Toi-Shaan (Taishan), Yan-Ping (Enping), San-Wooi (Xinhui) and Hoi-Ping (Kaiping) in Kwong-Tung (Guangdong) Province. These counties are the place of origin for a majority of the North American Chinese.

Taam (*dan*) – A unit of weight, about fifty kilograms.

Tang-liu (*dengliao*) – A lantern hut used by villagers for the annual celebration of the arrival of male descendants (by birth or adoption) to the lineage.

Tea money – a bribe.

Three obediences – A woman was to obey her father when young, her husband after marriage, and her son when she is old.

Tiu-lau (*diaolou*) – Village fortress.

Tong-kwai (*danggui*) – A Chinese root crop with high nutritious value.

Tong-yuen (*tangyuan*) – Sweet dumpling.

TB ghost – a derogatory term used in Hong Kong to refer to a tuberculosis patient.

Wai-Heung (*Weixiang*) Day – This occurs on the thirtieth day of the sixth lunar month. On this day, the villagers hide at home because of the belief that the King of the Earth has left to make his mid-year report to the Jade Emperor, a chance the demons would use to create havoc on Earth.

Work Team – A small group of outsiders designated by the Communist government to live in the local community temporarily in order to promote a government policy or conduct a campaign.

Yeung-lau (*yanglou*) – Foreign-style mansions built in the villages, financed with Overseas Chinese remittances.

Yue-Laan (*Yulan*) – Hungry Ghost Festival, which occurs on the fourteenth day of the seventh lunar month. Ritual money, food, and clothing are presented to wandering spirits as a form of expiation.

Yuen-Siu (*Yuanxiao*) – Also known as the Lantern Festival, held on the fifteenth day of the first lunar month to celebrate the first full moon of the year. It marks the last day of the Chinese New Year festivities.

Bibliography

SOUTH CHINA

Ahern, Emily M. "The Power and Pollution of Chinese Women." In *Women in Chinese Society*, edited by Margery Wolf and Roxane Witke, 193–214. Stanford: Stanford University Press, 1975.

Ceng, Yangfu. *Guangdong Caizheng Jiyao* (*Essentials of Financial Administration in Guangdong*). Nanking: Government Publications, 1936.

Chan, Anita, Richard Madsen, and Jonathan Unger. *Chen Village under Mao and Deng*. Berkeley: University of California Press, 1992.

Chen Jitang Jinianji (*Commemorative Writings on Chen Jitang*). Taipei: Government Publications, 1957.

Ch'ien, T.S. *The Government and Politics of China, 1912–1949*. Cambridge, MA: Harvard University Press, 1950.

Chu, T.T. *Local Government in China under the Ching*. Cambridge, MA: Harvard University Press, 1962.

Freedman, Maurice. *Lineage Organization in Southeastern China*. London: Athlone Press, 1958.

– *Chinese Lineage and Society: Fukien and Kwangtung*. London: Athlone Press, 1966.

Hammond, Jonathan. "Ecological and Cultural Anatomy of Taishan Villages." *Modern Asian Studies* 29, no. 3 (1995): 555–72.

Hsiao, Kung-Chuan. *Rural China: Imperial Control in the Nineteenth Century*. Seattle: University of Washington Press, 1960.

Huang, Jianyun. *Guangdongsheng Taishanxian Diqing Tonglan* (*The Human Geography of Taishan County, Guangdong Province*). Guangzhoushi: Chinan University Press, 1990.

Kaiping Xianzhi (*The Gazetteer of Kaiping County*). Hong Kong: Chengwen Publishing House, 1933.

Liu Zhongmin, ed. *Guanghai Shihua Suoji* (*An Informal History of Trivial Matters in Guanghai*). Taishan City: Taishan Government Publishers, 1992.

Mei Yimin. *Duanfen Zhilue* (*A Brief Chronicle of Duanfen*). Taishan City: Taishan Fengling Wenxueshe, 1991.

Neinam's Flowers. Duanfen Zhen, Taishan County: Duanfenzhen Government Publications, 1983–91.

Peterson, Glen D. "Socialist China and the Huaqiao: The Transition to Socialism in the Overseas Chinese Areas of Rural Guangdong, 1949–1956." *Modern China* 14, no. 3 (1988): 309–35.

Potter, Jack M. "Wind, Water, Bones, and Souls: The Religious World of the Cantonese Peasant." *Journal of Oriental Studies* 71 (1970): 139–53.

Potter, Sulamith, and Jack M. Potter. *China's Peasants: The Anthropology of a Revolution*. New York: Cambridge University Press, 1990.

Siu, Helen F. *Agents and Victims in South China: Accomplices in Rural Revolution*. New Haven: Yale University Press, 1989.

Stockard, Janice E. *Daughters of the Canton Delta: Marriage Patterns and Economic Strategies in South China, 1860–1930*. Stanford: Stanford University Press, 1989.

Taishan Qiaowu Bangongshi, ed. *Taishanxian Huaqiao Zhi* (*A Chronicle of Overseas Chinese from Taishan County*). Taishan County: Overseas Chinese Affairs Office Publications, 1992.

Taishan Wenxi (*The Cultural History of Taishan County*). Taishan City: Taishan County Government Publications, 1983–87.

Vogel, Ezra F. *Canton under Communism: Programs and Politics in a Provincial Capital, 1949–1968*. Cambridge, MA: Harvard University Press, 1969.

Watson, James L. "Chattel Slavery in Chinese Peasant Society: A Comparative Analysis." *Ethnology* 15, no. 4 (1976): 361–75.

Wolf, Margery, and Roxane Witke, eds. *Women in Chinese Society*. Stanford: Stanford University Press, 1975.

Woon, Yuen-Fong. *Social Organization in South China 1911–1949: The Case of the Kuan Lineage in Kaiping County*. Ann Arbor: Centre for Chinese Studies, University of Michigan, 1984.

– "An Emigrant Community in the Ssu-Yi Area, Southeastern China, 1885–1949: A Study in Social Change." *Modern Asian Studies* 18, no. 2 (1984): 273–306.

Wu Xingci and Li Zhen. "Gum San Haak in the 1980s; A Study on Chinese Emigrants Who Return to Taishan County for Marriage." *Amerasia* 14, no. 2 (1988): 21–35.

Yang, C.K. *A Chinese Village in Early Communist Transition*. Boston, MA: MIT Press, 1959.

HONG KONG

Cheng, Tong Yung. *The Economy of Hong Kong.* Hong Kong: Far East Publications, 1979.

Dwyer, D.J., ed. *The City as a Centre of Change in Asia.* Hong Kong: Hong Kong University Press, 1971.

Hambro, Edvard. *The Problems of Chinese Refugees in Hong Kong.* Leiden: A.W. Sijthoff, 1955.

Ingrams, William Harold. *Hong Kong.* London: Her Majesty's Stationery Office, 1952.

Jarvie, Ian C. and Joseph Agassi, eds. *Hong Kong: A Society in Transition.* London: Routledge and Kegan Paul, 1969.

Johnson, S.K. "Hong Kong's Resettled Squatters: A Statistical Analysis." *Asian Survey* 6 (1966): 643–56.

Hong Kong Annual Report. Hong Kong: Government Printing Office, 1950–55.

Hopkins, Keith. *Hong Kong: The Industrial Colony.* Hong Kong: Oxford University Press, 1977.

Huang Nanxiang. *Xianggang Gujin (Hong Kong Past and Present).* Hong Kong: Benma Publishing Company, 1991.

Leeming, Frank. *Street Studies in Hong Kong.* Hong Kong: Oxford University Press, 1977.

Maunder, W.F. *Hong Kong Rents and Housing.* Hong Kong: Centre of Asian Studies, Hong Kong University, 1969.

McGee, Terry G. *Hawkers in Hong Kong: A Study of Planning and Policy in a Third World City.* Hong Kong: Centre of Asian Studies, Hong Kong University, 1973.

Salaff, Janet W. *Working Daughters of Hong Kong: Filial Piety or Power?* Cambridge: Cambridge University Press, 1981.

Savidge, Joyce. *This Is Hong Kong Temple.* Hong Kong: Government Publications, 1977.

Szczepanik, Edward. *The Economic Growth of Hong Kong.* London: Oxford University Press, 1958.

Tse, F.Y. *Street Trading in Hong Kong, Parts 1–3.* Hong Kong: Chinese University of Hong Kong, 1974.

Wu, Hao. *Xianggang Huiwang (Hong Kong: A Nostalgic Look).* Hong Kong: Chuang-Yi Publishing Company, 1990.

Yuan, Bang. *Xianggang Shilue (A Brief History of Hong Kong).* Hong Kong: Zhongliu Publishing Company, 1993.

VANCOUVER

Anderson, Kay. *Vancouver's Chinatown: Racial Discourse in Canada,
   1875–1990*. Montreal: McGill-Queen's University Press, 1991.
Chan, Anthony B. "Orientalism and Image Making: The Sojourner in Cana-
   dian History." *Journal of Ethnic Studies* 9, no. 3 (Fall 1981): 37–46.
– *Gold Mountain: The Chinese in the New World*. Vancouver: New Star Books,
   1983.
Chan, Kwok B. "Coping with Aging and Managing Self-Identity: The Social
   World of the Elderly Chinese Women." *Canadian Ethnic Studies* 15, no. 3
   (1983): 36–50.
Chong, Denise. *The Concubine's Children: Portrait of a Family Divided*. Toron-
   to: Viking Books, 1994.
Choy, Wayson. *The Jade Peony*. Vancouver: Douglas and McIntyre, 1995.
Hyung-Chan, Kim, and Nicholas Lai. "Chinese Community Resistance to
   Urban Renewal: The Case of Strathcona in Vancouver, Canada." *Journal of
   Ethnic Studies* 10, no.2 (1982): 67–82.
Johnson, Graham E. "Ethnic and Racial Communities in Canada and the
   Problems of Adaptation: Chinese Canadians in the Contemporary Peri-
   od." *Ethnic Groups* 9, no.3 (1992): 151–74.
Lai, David Chuenyan. *Chinatowns: Towns within Cities in Canada*. Vancouver:
   University of British Columbia Press, 1988.
Lee, Sky. *Disappearing Moon Café*. Vancouver: Douglas and McIntyre,
   1990.
Li, Peter S. "Immigration Law and Family Patterns: Some Demographic
   Changes among Chinese Families in Canada." *Canadian Ethnic Studies* 12,
   no. 1 (1980): 58–73.
– "The Use of Oral History in Studying Elderly Chinese-Canadians." *Cana-
   dian Ethnic Studies* 17, no. 1 (1985): 67–77.
– *The Chinese in Canada*. Toronto: Oxford University Press, 1988.
McEvoy, F.J. "A Symbol of Racial Discrimination: The Chinese Immigration
   Act and Canada's Relations with China 1942–47." *Canadian Ethnic Studies*
   12, no.3 (1980): 24–42.
Ng, Maria Noelle. "Travelling Women – Review of Jinguo: Voices of Chi-
   nese Canadian Women." *Canadian Literature* 140 (1994): 92–4.
Tan, Jin. "Chinese Labour and the Reconstituted Social Order of British
   Columbia." *Canadian Ethnic Studies* 19, no.3 (1987): 68–88.
Wickberg, Edgar, ed. *From China to Canada: A History of the Chinese Commu-
   nities in Canada*. Toronto: McClelland and Stewart, 1982.
Women's Book Committee, Chinese Canadian National Council. *Jin Guo:
   Voices of Chinese Canadian Women*. Toronto: Women's Press, 1992.
Woon, Yuen-fong. "Social Discontinuities in North American Chinese
   Communities: Case of the Kwaan in Vancouver and Victoria, 1880–

1949." *Canadian Review of Sociology and Anthropology* 14, no. 4 (1978): 443–51.

– "The Voluntary Sojourner among the Overseas Chinese: Myth or Reality?" *Pacific Affairs* 56, no.4 (1983–84): 673–90.

Yee, May. "Chinese Canadian Women: Our Common Struggle." *Canadian Ethnic Studies* 19, no.3 (1987): 174–84.

Yee, Paul. *Saltwater City: An Illustrated History of the Chinese in Vancouver.* Seattle: University of Washington Press, 1984.

– *Tales from Gold Mountain: Stories of the Chinese in the New World.* Vancouver: Douglas and McIntyre, 1989.

Yip, Yuen Chung. *The Tears of Chinese Immigrants.* Translated by Shang-Tai Chang. Dunvegan: Cormorant Books, 1990.

Yu, Miriam. "Human Rights, Discrimination, and Coping Behaviour of the Chinese in Canada." *Canadian Ethnic Studies* 19, no.3 (1987): 114–24.